PRAISE FOR CHARLES WILSON:

NIGHTWATCHER

"Splendid . . . A lean, tight, compelling story that was over much too fast. I wanted more." —John Grisham

"Wilson throws one curve after another while keeping up the suspense like an old pro; the whole book rushes over you like a jolt of adrenaline." —*Kirkus Reviews*

SILENT WITNESS

"Uncommonly well plotted." —*Los Angeles Times*

"Wilson spins an entertaining yarn; a straightforwardly written story of sexual obsession, guilt and cover-up." —*Chicago Tribune*

THE CASSANDRA PROPHECY

"Masterfully plotted, breathlessly paced . . . Sparkles off the page . . . Charles Wilson is a born storyteller." —*Clarion-Ledger,* Jackson, Mississippi

"The twists and turns never stop in this tale of murder, deceit, and treachery in the Deep South . . . Will keep you guessing until the very end." —*Mostly Murder*

WHEN FIRST WE DECEIVE

"Steadily accelerating suspense, deft plotting and a broad cast of likeable characters."
—*Publishers Weekly*

"Charles Wilson, who has made a solid name for himself with 'Nightwatcher' and 'Silent Witness,' continues his string of tightly plotted suspensers."
—*Chicago Tribune*

DIRECT
DESCENDANT

Charles Wilson

St. Martin's Paperbacks

To Linda,
the woman I knew I would never
be lucky enough to marry,
and did.

My special thanks to those without whose help this would have never been a novel:

To Dr. Richard Hay, Dept. of Geology, the University of Illinois at Urbana—his grasp of the ancient, and what could be possible with the ancient, is amazing. Any mistakes that might be in this novel are certainly not his.

To Dr. Craig Lobb, Dept. of Microbiology, University of Mississippi Medical Center, for his timeless patience in answering question after question, and for his suggestions of ideas of which I hadn't even dreamed. Again, any mistakes are mine.

To Brandie Roaten, who helped enormously with questions I had about people and places in Memphis.

To Kay Pittman Black of the Shelby County, Tennessee, Sheriff's Department, who went out of her way to help me with my questions regarding law enforcement procedures in Memphis and the surrounding area.

To Destin Wilson, a son who impressed me greatly with his innate feel for what wasn't working, and what was—and could explain why.

To Jennifer Enderlin, my editor at St. Martin's Press, who professes she couldn't be an author, and yet was able to explain in detail to me how a sequence I thought I couldn't write, should be written. Thank you again.

To Natasha Kern, my agent, who, after my having sold my first novel without an agent, and then having told audiences why agents weren't necessary, taught me why they were. She is superb.

And, once again, to Tommy Furby, who claims he is a practicing attorney, but actually is the most demanding critic on earth, and the one who continuously has given me the confidence to write.

CHAPTER 1

"**H**e was angry, Mother." The little girl, her blonde curls hanging in front of her face, stared down into the glass display case at the shriveled body of the Ancient Man. Around her, dozens of people milled about the big exhibit room, most of them perusing the prehistoric artifacts arranged in long lines against the walls. A few were looking at the equipment used on the expedition that made the discovery. An elderly couple stared at the large mounted placard next to the main entrance. On it was a photograph of Dr. Cameron Malone, the paleontologist who had led the expedition.

Cameron Malone himself, in his early thirties—and looking even younger with his thick, dark hair hanging nearly to the collar of his sport coat—stood back at the center of the room, on the opposite side of the case from the little girl. He had been amused at her remark, and now watched her stare at the Man's drawn face, where his mouth gaped wide and his lips pulled back from his blunt, cracked teeth. Then she moved her gaze to the great slashes across the stomach and the deep holes dug into the thighs, narrowed her eyes, and looked up over her shoulder at the heavy-set woman standing behind her. "He was angry, wasn't he, Mother?" she repeated. "He didn't like the people hurting him at all."

Now Cameron saw the woman look across the case at him. "What *did* cause his wounds?" she asked.

He shook his head slightly. "At this point we're not certain, except possibly the wounds to his thighs. Since each of them has an almost identical amount of flesh removed, we believe they occurred during some type of burial ritual."

The woman nodded, looked down through the glass for a moment more, then caught her daughter's hand and directed her toward the main exit. The child glanced back at the case and then up at her mother. "He *was* angry," she insisted. "He was *very* angry." ·

At that moment, Dr. Baringer came back from the water fountain with a paper cup in his hand. Middle-aged, slightly overweight, and wearing a plaid coat and red bow tie over white slacks, he looked much more the stereotyped image of a paleontologist than Cameron did, and most of the visitors with questions about the exhibit had directed them to him. Having overheard the child, he looked at her and her mother on their way across the floor, then dropped his gaze to the Ancient Man's gaped mouth.

"He does look a bit put out, doesn't he, Cameron? Reminds me a lot of my brother-in-law—always has his mouth flapped open complaining about something. The way the skin is starting to crack, that reminds me of my brother-in-law, too. Name's Fred. Drinking is what did it according to my sister. But I don't know. She married him over in the Middle East when she was a nurse there. I'm not so certain he didn't always look like that."

Cameron smiled, and looked toward the little girl and her mother stepping from the room out into the hall-way, then had his view of the pair blocked as a tall, thin man passing behind them stopped and stared toward the case. Dressed in a black suit that fit too tightly, he resembled something between a too-thin English butler and Ichabod Crane. Cameron nearly smiled again, then had his attention drawn to the announcement it was closing time being broadcast through the room.

Baringer glanced at his watch. "Well, that's it," he said. "I suppose I need to be on my way."

He held out his hand and Cameron grasped it and shook it firmly. "Have a good flight."

"And you a good meal," Baringer said, and then chuckled. "I'll bet it's chicken." The two walked to the room's main exit, paused to shake hands a last time, then went in opposite directions, Cameron moving up the hallway toward the front of the center while Dr. Baringer moved down it, toward his car parked at the rear of the building.

A hundred feet ahead of Baringer, Dr. Noel Anderson, tall and thin in his tight, black suit, hurried around a corner into an intersecting corridor, ceased his long strides and looked back over his shoulder. No one was in sight.

He strode quickly to a closed door a few feet away. The rectangular sign on it read: EMPLOYEES ONLY—STORAGE ROOM.

He opened the door, stepped inside the dark space and closed the door behind him.

A moment later, a uniform-clad night watchman came by the door, nodded at Dr. Baringer as they passed in the hall, and walked on toward the exhibit room where the Ancient Man was displayed.

Stepping outside the center into the humid air that had hung heavily over Memphis all day, Cameron glanced at a group of older patrons boarding a tour bus parked at the curb, then walked toward his car, a white Maxima sitting under the glow of a street lamp.

A few minutes later, he had driven the short distance to the Peabody Hotel. Once inside the Memphis landmark, he crossed a carpeted hallway into a sprawling lobby and lounge area, the plaza where guests could lounge and have a drink as they watched the famous

parades of the Peabody ducks on their way from the
elevators to the ornate water fountain at the plaza's center.

He entered the Chez Philippe through a doorway sit-
uated past the big bar in the plaza, and was shown by a
waiter to a table on the second level of the three-tier
restaurant.

A half dozen men came to their feet at his approach.
The pudgy, red-haired man who had been sitting at the
head of the table turned back to face the others. "May I
introduce Dr. Cameron Malone," he said.

Cameron held out his hand first. "Dr. Jensen."

The man shook it warmly. "Dr. Malone." Then Cameron reached across the table to shake each professor's
hand in turn. Dr. Jensen motioned for him to sit in the
chair next to his, then remained standing as the other
professors settled into their seats.

"And now, as dean of the science department and
host of this welcoming dinner," he said, "it falls to me
to give a brief background of our guest and new colleague." He pulled a sheet of paper from inside his coat
and unfolded it.

"Born on a farm outside of Greenwood, Mississippi,"
he started, then looked at Cameron.

Feeling a little awkward at so formal an introduction,
Cameron nodded.

"His family still lives there—the fourth generation, I
believe."

He looked again, and Cameron nodded again.

"Dr. Malone attended prep school in Missouri—Missouri Military Academy, known for its academics; went
on to the University of Missouri, obtained his doctorate
at Berkeley, then returned to Missouri where he lec-
tured at the university for three years. He relinquished
that position when he undertook the expedition to Italy. His contract at Memphis University is for this
year . . . " Jensen looked directly at him. " . . . and
we hope he enjoys his stay so well that he continues on
with us."

Someone near the end of the table clapped lightly and Cameron smiled politely in that direction. Dr. Jensen folded the paper and replaced it inside his coat.

"Now I suggest we order dinner. Then I am sure Dr. Malone will be happy to answer any questions you might have."

One person didn't wait. "Dr. Malone. There has been quite a raging controversy in regard to your discovery's age. Could you comment on that?"

Cameron realized from her voice that the speaker was a woman. With no make-up on her broad face, her short brown hair cut and combed like a man's, and dressed in a tailored, boxy pantsuit, he had completely missed that when shaking hands. He looked down the table at her.

"Professor—"

"Dr. Higgonbotham," the woman said.

He nodded. "Yes, doctor. While I don't know if you could quite term the controversy *raging*, there *has* been some initial skepticism. But I can assure you there is no way our original dating is going to be found faulty. Of course that's not to say there won't be some continuing dispute as to other aspects of his existence."

The woman's knowing nod and smug expression told him she could be counted among the skeptics, and Cameron felt a slight irritation. Damn, he thought, with all the intelligence supposedly concentrated among prehistorian scholars, one would think there would be some common sense present too. What did they think he and Baringer had done—faked the find, faked the dating? That thought made him even more irritated, for he knew such was in the minds of some scientists, and that possibility largely the reason he hadn't been offered funding for a subsequent expedition.

The storage room door slowly opened. Dr. Anderson, now wearing a black ski mask, peered down the wide, dimly lit hall. He moved quickly toward the room where the Ancient Man was displayed.

At its doorway he hesitated, staring at the glass case at the center of the room. He looked back across his shoulder down the hall. He felt his hand tremble. This was taking more out of him than he thought it would. He took a deep breath and walked toward the case.

Reaching it, he ran his eyes slowly around the rim, checking for wires, then dropped his gaze to the small refrigeration unit pumping frigid air into the foot of the case. He saw no sensor or alarm of any kind. But who would think somebody might steal a mummified man? What would they do with it?

The fools. They should have burned it and spread its ashes at sea. For now he would bring their arrogant religion down around their heads.

He stared directly at the shriveled face, drawn taut, the cheeks hollowed, the eye sockets distorted and sunk back in the head, and the nose, pulled flatter by the shrinkage of the skin than it would have been during life. And the way the mouth gaped open caused even the chin to seem less prominent, by allowing it to sag closer toward the neck. With a little imagination backward into so-called evolution—the way prehistorian scholars would be certain to guide the thinking —the face could end up being viewed as belonging to a creature not much more advanced than a hairless monkey. He could see the artists' renditions now. Even if a courageous independent tried to faithfully reconstruct the face, there would be misconceptions—there always had been before.

And finally the missing brain. He moved his eyes to the patch covering the top of the skull. If everything else failed them, they had that. At the very least they would use its absence to paint a portrait of something no more reasoning than a zombie. He wondered if the brain really had been missing when the body was discovered, as reported, or had it been removed afterward? They had had their way for so long.

But not anymore.

Feeling satisfaction in that thought, the barest of

smiles crossed his face under his mask, and he closed his eyes in bliss.

Then a barely perceptible sound traveled down the wide hallways and into the great room to his ears, and he tensed—until he realized it was only the air conditioner coming on.

But the next sound might not be so innocent.

Hurrying now, he removed a pair of surgical gloves from his coat pocket and slipped them on, then pulled a screwdriver from inside the coat. He worked quickly on the screws to the thin metal strip that held the glass panels in place.

In less than a minute he had eased a panel to the side, sunk to his knees, and slipped his narrow upper body through the opening into the frigid air over the man.

"I'd be interested in how you obtained your original funding for the expedition?" Dr. Higgonbotham asked. "Your young age, your lack of previous expedition experience—there were a number of paleontologists eminently more qualified for such an undertaking. If you don't mind my asking—"

Cameron didn't. That was a logical question on its face. Though the way the woman had phrased it caused the other professors to stare in her direction. He sipped from the Jordan cabernet sauvignon Dean Jensen had ordered, then placed his glass back on the table.

"My best friend at Berkeley came from a quite wealthy family. I approached his father with the proposal that his company fund the expedition—and I lucked out."

"I see," the woman said, and nodded knowingly.

Thinking it's not what but who you know, Cameron thought—and she would be right about that. If he hadn't had the personal connection to the family, he probably never would have gotten the man to listen to his idea; no one else would.

"It certainly wasn't all luck," Dean Jensen interjected. "I would remind you Dr. Malone graduated at the top of his class at the University of Missouri, studied under the renowned Dr. Baringer at Berkeley, and, in fact, as part of the package he put forth to obtain his financing, was able to offer Baringer's accompanying him on the expedition."

He had actually graduated third, thought Cameron. But the point was well taken—especially Baringer's agreeing to co-head the expedition. He returned to his steak.

But not for long.

"Excuse me." It was Dr. Higgonbotham again. "Doesn't the fact that his cranial capacity is equal to ours cause you to have some doubts?"

And this was a welcoming dinner? Cameron thought. He had been questioned less stringently at some of the news conferences. "You mean doubts about his being dated at five hundred thousand years?"

"Yes."

"As a point of fact, doctor, his cranial capacity is actually not the same as ours. At over fourteen hundred cubic centimeters it is slightly above the mean for Homo sapiens—modern man, if you will. But there is a precedent for that in the Heidelberg jaw, dated at over four hundred thousand years, and the occipital bone found in Vértesszölös, Hungary."

"Yes, Dr. Malone, but neither of those demonstrated the large cranial capacity in combination with a high forehead and prominent chin—as in your discovery's case."

"Maybe and maybe not. There was not enough evidence to interpolate with certainty that they didn't come from a human closely resembling us. It was only assumed they didn't."

He waited a moment, until the woman's mouth started to open again, then added, "And those who assume often make fools of themselves."

He caught a glimpse of white teeth across the table as one of the professors smiled. The other men dug into their plates. Dr. Higgonbotham stared for a moment, then returned to her salad.

Perspiring profusely beneath his mask, Dr. Anderson slid his thin body out of the display case.

Working hurriedly, he fitted the glass panel back against the side of the case, aligned the metal strip over the holes in the glass and tightened the screws into place. Pausing a few seconds, he looked around to see if there was anything he might have dropped. Satisfied he had left no traces, he turned and hurried toward the room's main exit.

"Don't move!" came a hoarse voice from behind him. "Don't you even twitch."

He didn't hesitate, dashing through the doorway and out into the hall. The night watchman pounded after him. A room to the right was completely darkened and he sprinted inside it. He saw the dim opening of another exit at the back of the room and ran toward it. Just before reaching the opening, he suddenly angled to the right and crouched behind a display case of ancient rocks.

The watchman dashed into the room and stopped. Gray-haired and breathing hard from the run, he held a big black revolver out before him as he slowly scanned each shadowy exhibit. His gaze moved to the light switches on a panel near a door at the rear of the room —and he started toward them.

As he passed the case of ancient rocks, he glanced at it then reached for the light switch.

Dr. Anderson wrapped his hands around a clay bust on the floor at the side of the case and stood. The watchman spun around—too late. The clay bust shattered as it smashed into his face and he fell backward to the floor. His heels kicked twice against the tile. Then he was still.

A minute later, a door at the rear of the center opened and Dr. Anderson strode from the building.

Brushing clay dust from his dark suit as he walked, he hurried through the night toward his car parked near the Mid America Mall. The bright lights of downtown Memphis illuminated his way.

CHAPTER 2

They all stood around the table now. The sound of a harp wafted gently through the restaurant. Dean Jensen laboriously filled out the credit card slip. Dr. Mildren, a squat man with a pleasant face and flecks of gray dotting his black hair, walked around the table to Cameron.

"Dr. Malone."

"Yes, sir."

"I don't mean to impose, but I, uh, wonder if you might do me a favor."

"Certainly."

"I have a son—sixteen—quite a good football player." Dr. Mildren looked sheepish, as if embarrassed that his statement might be taken as a father's bragging. "He's so into football, he's beginning to let his grades slide noticeably. And, quite frankly, he looks upon what I do as the most boring thing in the world. So it doesn't do me a lot of good to talk to him. At least it hasn't to date. If you could speak to him for me, show him it doesn't have to be one or the other, that he can do both, like you did."

"I'd be glad to. But I'm afraid I'm going to sound just as boring to him as you say you—"

"No, no. He heard Dean Jensen talking about you, and he was all ears. He wished he could have come here tonight to meet you."

"Certainly. I'll be glad to speak with him."

"Thank you, Dr. Malone. I'll be in your debt." He started to turn away, and then stopped. "By the way, Dr. Malone, why *didn't* you go on and play college ball? I'll have to admit that had I been given the chance . . . " He looked down at his round, soft stomach and smiled wistfully. "Dean Jensen says you *really were* quite a big name in high school; he said we certainly tried hard enough to sign you."

"Tell Dr. Jensen I said thanks for the compliment, but as a not-all-that-fast six-foot, hundred-and-seventy-pound back I wasn't exactly destined for a future in pro football. So I opted for the academic scholarship, and spent the time keeping my nose to the books—as the better part of valor." He had gotten a little cocky with his answering Dr. Higgonbotham, so why not show a little humility now?

"I see," Dr. Mildren said. "Well, do you mind keeping that to yourself when you talk to my son? I mean I know he's not going to forego playing college ball if he is afforded the chance—I don't wish for him to forego it. I just want as much effort put into the books."

Cameron never got the chance to reply, as a tall, dark-skinned man in a rumpled business suit stepped up beside him and spoke his name.

"Yes."

The man nodded his thanks at the waiter who had guided him to the table, and then looked back at Cameron.

"Dr. Malone, I'm Detective Powers. Lieutenant Warrington wants to see you down at the convention center."

"Excuse me?"

"Somebody broke into your exhibit. He wants you to tell us what they were after."

In a musky-smelling room in an old motel in the city, Mary Jenerette wiggled her hips as she pulled her pantyhose up her skinny legs. The short, graying man sitting on the edge of the bed leaned over to put on his shoes. His effort caused his stomach to bulge over the waistband of his slacks. When he finished, he straightened, took a deep breath and stood. He walked toward the dresser against the back wall.

Her purse sat there, and she watched him closely. When he reached for it, her eyes narrowed. His hand went on past the purse to his wallet. He opened it, took out a ten dollar bill and held it out toward her.

"A tip," he said, and grinned, his pale, fat cheeks rising with the effort.

Ten lousy dollars, she thought as she reached for it, but said, "Why, thank you, love," and leaned to buss his forehead with her bright red lips. She slipped the bill up under her skirt into the waistband of her pantyhose.

He smiled and reached for his coat laid across the table next to the room's window. Mary stepped to the door, peered through the peephole, and then looked to see if a shadow could be seen under the bottom of the door. But the door fit snugly against the metal threshold.

They always did, she thought, despite her seeing a detective in a movie look under a motel room door and notice a villain hiding below the peephole outside. But the movie *had* been of the made-for-TV type. She had read that they had smaller budgets—probably not enough to hire a writer who knew any better.

"What are you doing?" the man asked, his brow wrinkling.

She didn't bother explaining as she opened the door and started down the concrete landing in front of the units. He better be glad she looked at all. Once she hadn't, and the guy with her suffered a terrible beating from the kids waiting outside.

Punks, crackheads, just plain mean people, she thought as she walked down the steps toward the parking lot, they were everywhere now. She would give anything to be able to save up enough money to move to a small town. A little doughnut shop somewhere on the Gulf Coast would be just fine.

Yet no matter how many hours she worked, she never could get ahead. In fact she didn't even have a checking account at the moment. The little that had been in it had been cleaned out the week before to pay off a fine for soliciting.

Damn cops, and damn judges, and damn her choice of careers, she thought as she slipped behind the wheel of her faded, blue Mustang. She should have become a masseuse like her mother wanted her to be. At least if she had she wouldn't have to stand on the street to attract a man. Her mother had preached that to her time and time again. But who listened to their mothers when they were sixteen, sick of school, and already knew how they were going to make their fortune?

Her hand trembled as she reached for the ignition, and she shook her head. Sixteen, she thought again; fifteen years ago—and as stupid as any kid could get.

By the time she reached Louie's, in the basement of an old building not far away, her trembling had grown worse, and she quickly swallowed three of the tranquilizers out of the bottle he sold her.

Secure now in the tranquilizer's presence, she decided to call it a night and drove on to the old, rundown complex where she lived.

Feeling good now, even smiling as she walked down the landing toward her apartment, she suddenly stopped at the presence of the tall, dark shape a few feet from her door.

Her feet already twisting around, ready to run, she paused as the thin figure turned toward her and she saw in the dim light that it was Mr. Johnson.

At least that was what he had told her his name was. She had figured he was some kind of con man when she first met him. She had been even more sure of that when she opened his glove compartment one day and saw his car's registration made out not to the Mr. Roland Johnson he claimed to be, but to a Dr. Noel Anderson.

But he hadn't ever touched her; it had been no con when he said he wasn't interested in that, though she would have just as soon he had used her rather than making her submit to all the tests he had required. And over and over again, a urine sample, a blood test, one after the other, at least a half dozen times in the five months she had known him—*making certain you are compatible,* he had told her.

Compatible? Compatible to what? He scared her, there was no getting around it, he was weird. But he was also absolutely the wealthiest man she had ever met. He had given her fifty dollars for each test and said that when he was ready she would receive twenty thousand dollars. *Twenty thousand dollars*—she would have swung from a vine and jerked off a monkey for that kind of money.

"Mary," the figure called softly, "is that you, Mary?"

She walked on toward her door.

When she stopped before him he said, "I'm ready."

She knitted her eyes questioningly. "Ready?"

"Yes, Mary, ready."

"You mean now? Tonight? Like this minute?"

"Yes, Mary."

"But—" *She almost said Dr. Anderson.* She didn't need to blow this one. "But, Mr. Johnson, it's the middle of the night."

"I'm quite cognizant of the time, Mary."

"I have all my clothes to pack."

"Of course, Mary, I'm here to assist you."

"The landlord. I'll want to be coming back here when it's over. I have to give him notice that—"

"Mary, we'll mail your check in each month."

"Why keep—"

"Now Mary, don't let that concern you. I have decided it best that you don't stop your rent here. I'll come by once a month and pick up your mail. Of course I'll pay the rent—anything else that has to be paid."

"Well, seems like an awful waste of money to me."

"Mary—Mary, you have complied with your end of the bargain, haven't you?"

"Yes, I 've told you. I haven't been with a man since we met. And I'll tell you right now it's been hard getting by on two-fifty a week. But when I agree to something, that's how it is."

"Good, Mary." He nodded toward her door. "We need to hurry now. I have something in the trunk that can't sit for too very long."

Cameron followed the police detective down a wide hall inside the Cook Convention Center. As they neared the doorway to the Ancient Man exhibit, his nervousness grew worse. He hurried across the tiles to a side of the glass case and looked down into it.

The body looked untouched. Nothing seemed different from how he had last viewed it except for the smudges of black, fingerprint powder brushed at several spots around the rim of the glass. He released a breath he hadn't realized he had been holding. A stocky, middle-aged man in a dark suit stepped up beside him.

"I'm Lieutenant Warrington."

"What's happened?"

"The case was entered. That's all we know at this point."

The nervous sensation was back. But still there was nothing to see. What could . . .

"We were wondering if you would mind going inside the case and see if you notice anything."

Cameron nodded. He damn sure *was* going inside it.

The next words came from back toward the doorway and were softly spoken. "The workmen will be here soon."

Cameron looked around at the young female sergeant as she walked toward them. Slim and taut in her uniform, her dark hair pulled back in a tight French roll, she resembled a model more than a police officer. Despite his concern over the break-in, he had to make a small effort to look away from her and back at the lieutenant. "You said it was a man who entered the case."

"A tall, thin male, is all we know. The watchman only got a glimpse of him."

CHAPTER 3

The black Lincoln Town Car moved slowly across the old I-55 bridge spanning the Mississippi River at Memphis. Mary looked across the front seat at Dr. Anderson, alias Mr. Roland Johnson, who stared down the pavement ahead of them. As always, he had been exceedingly polite, carrying her suitcase to the car, holding the passenger door open for her, and asking if she needed to stop to buy any toiletries before they crossed into Arkansas. Yet for some reason she felt nervous, nervous to the point of wondering if she should have ever gotten into the car with him in the first place—and going God only knew where.

She glanced back over her shoulder at the lights of Memphis slowly falling behind them. She grasped her purse tighter. The tranquilizers were inside it and she could take one without water. She had many times before. Yet she didn't dare try it in front of him. That was one of his main rules—absolutely no drugs of any kind.

She felt her hand tremble. She tried to fill her mind by thinking about all the movie stars she admired. The old ones. She couldn't care less about the new ones, unless John Wayne counted as a new one. He was the most recent star among the ones she loved. And James Dean, he would have been a relatively new one if he had lived—at least not too awful old now, and she liked him, too.

Humphrey Bogart, James Cagney, Greta Garbo. . . . *It wasn't doing any good.*

Jesus! she thought.

And they continued on down the pavement into the dark.

Cameron had waited for what seemed like forever for a pair of workmen in brown overalls to arrive at the Convention Center. Now, as they came across the floor, he had to make an effort not to stare in irritation at them. Lieutenant Warrington instructed them that the outside of the display case had already been dusted for fingerprints, but that they were to be careful not to touch the inside of the glass. "Especially careful," he added.

It took only a minute for them to remove one of the side panels, and Cameron stepped forward.

"You, too, Dr. Malone," Lieutenant Warrington said. "Real careful about touching anything."

Cameron knelt and slipped his upper body through the opening into the cold air over the Man.

Holding his hands back against his chest, he looked at the brown and shriveled face, but saw nothing unusual there. The opening in the skull where the brain had been removed was still covered by the patch attached in Italy. It didn't look touched.

He ran his gaze down the brown upper shell. There were the spots where the flesh had cracked, but those had always been there.

The great slashes across the stomach also seemed untouched.

Then he started back over the body again, this time leaning closer and carefully focusing on each square inch of skin. Once again, he could see nothing unusual, not on the face, the chest, the stomach. . . . And then he noticed the slight, almost imperceptible depression at the juncture of the inner thighs—as if something had been wedged against the skin. He leaned closer still.

In the side of the scrotum, in flesh that looked more like pressed wood than tissue, a scalpel or other thin, sharp instrument had created a tiny incision. *What in the hell for?*

His eyes narrowed with his next thought and he felt inside his coat for his pencil. It was a metal type filled with a lead core. He screwed the core out and broke off the lead, then leaned toward the body. Gently, he inserted the lead into the incision and moved it slowly down until he felt resistance.

"Dr. Malone," the lieutenant said.

Cameron ignored him. He carefully pulled the lead back out and looked at how far it had penetrated. A half inch, maybe. He looked back at the incision for a moment then slid outside of the case and looked at the lieutenant. "There's an incision in the side of the scrotum."

The lieutenant didn't have to ask what it would be for, his questioning expression did that for him.

"I'd just be guessing what it means," Cameron said. What he wondered most about was a sperm sample— and the incision *was* deep enough.

The female sergeant spoke now. "You couldn't really clone a man, could you?" she asked. "I mean using sperm from a body that old."

Cameron was impressed that she grasped so quickly the possibility of what had been removed. But not so impressed at why she thought the sample might have been taken. He shook his head. "No, you can't clone anything as complex as a man, from sperm or anything else. You can't clone anything in fact—not in the sense you're suggesting."

"But you hear cloning discussed all the time."

"Miss . . ."

"Sergeant Adrian Cummings."

"Sergeant, what you hear is conjecture about a process that will undoubtedly take place some day. But, with present day technology, it isn't possible."

"Maybe I used the wrong word, doctor. What about using the sperm for artificial insemination?"

"If you were talking about sperm being frozen from

inception—as in a sperm bank—that of course is an everyday occurrence. But not his.''

Her expression showed she still wasn't satisfied. ''Doctor, he's in a refrigerated case. I read in the paper that the rock slide where you found him had been created by a receding glacier. Wasn't he frozen?''

''Yes, but take my word on it, it doesn't matter. His sperm would be useless for what you suggest.''

Dr. Anderson drove his Lincoln into the yard of an old farmhouse, stark and at the same time shadowy in the dim moonlight.

As Mary stepped from the car she stared past the knee-high weeds to the sagging roof over the small porch. Whatever color the wooden siding had once been, it had turned dark. This couldn't be where they were going to live. It couldn't be.

Dr. Anderson lifted her bag from the back seat and came around the rear of the car.

''It's quite nice inside,'' he said, and started toward the porch.

Suddenly her eyes focused on his thin back. His black coat was so tight it looked wrapped around him—like a cape. She was reminded of Dracula. She felt a surge of anxiety and glanced back up the dark road. Why in hell hadn't she told someone where she was going? She couldn't. She hadn't known herself. She closed her eyes a moment, then started forward.

The steps creaked as she went up them, then the boards as she walked across the porch, each noise causing her to become a little tighter. She felt like she was going to faint like women in those old Civil War movies.

Then Anderson opened the door, and she felt a little better seeing the living room furniture—a couch, with end tables, lamps on each of them, a small coffee table in front of the couch, and an easy chair facing back toward the table.

It wasn't that the furniture was all that great. But it

was real furniture, not a chopping block or a table with leather straps and buckles.

She was especially pleased to see there was a carpet. It was faded from dark blue to gray and soiled in several places, but it was something to walk barefoot on in any case. She loved to walk around without shoes and couldn't picture being there for nine months and not ever being able to walk without getting splinters in her feet. She had thought about that when she saw the outside of the house.

As Dr. Anderson turned on one of the table lamps, she looked back to her right. At the entrance into the small kitchen there was a card table, two chairs pulled up against it. That was the same thing she ate off of in her apartment, so *it* wasn't bad, at least.

Yes it was. Everything was horrible. She had expected much more considering all the money he had. He couldn't possibly really live here. She clutched her purse tighter as she felt the start of another anxiety attack.

"Follow me," Dr. Anderson said. He carried her suitcase toward the hallway off to the left of the living room and diappeared down it.

At the hall's entrance she veered wide out toward its far side, slowed and leaned her head forward to peek down it before going any further.

Dr. Anderson already had walked from sight. Through a doorway partially open to the right of the passageway she could see the dim illumination of a small lamp. She took a deep breath and slowly walked toward it.

She stopped at the door, hesitated a moment, then carefully pushed it the rest of the way open.

Instead of a bent, lanky creature wearing a black wig and holding up the knife he had used to stab Janet Leigh—what she had feared she might see—only Dr. Anderson stood in the room. He had a soft smile on his face. She released her breath audibly.

He indicated the room with a sweep of his hand. "How do you like it?" he asked.

Compared to what she had been faced with from outside the house, even in the living room, it was like she had stepped into a palace.

The bed was a new one, with a solid, wooden headboard. A brass lamp sat on a shiny bedside table. The cover on the end of the bed was a thick, soft one, and the sheets, the top one turned back a foot, were a pale gray satin—real satin. The walls had even been freshly painted a soft pink, though whoever had done the work had gotten a little on the ceiling. The only thing old was the dark green carpet.

"I love it," she said. She really did.

She noticed for the first time the white material in his hand. He held it out toward her. It was a hospital gown.

"Get into this," he said.

CHAPTER 4

It was past midnight by the time the officers had finished with their work in the exhibit room, trying to lift fingerprints from the glass on the inside of the case, collecting the bits of the shattered bust, and making rough notes for their later typed reports. Cameron waited all this time, made sure the glass was once again securely screwed to the side of the case, then walked to his car, drove out of the center, and turned left onto Riverside Drive.

He looked through his passenger window to the wide Mississippi to his right. A dimly lit tug in the channel at the center of the river pushed a line of barges south toward New Orleans.

Nearer the bank and separated from it by a narrow stretch of dark water was the long shape of Mud Island, a tourist center and amusement park at one end, a cluster of apartments at the other. He was familiar with the area.

As an eighteen-year-old, he and several of his friends had come up from the Delta to a rock concert held on a barge moored in the narrow strip of water, their way of celebrating their pending entrance into college. Becoming rowdy, a beer too many maybe, but mostly due to their high spirits, they had been escorted off the barge by concert security guards.

Stripping naked, and balancing their clothes above

their heads, they let themselves down into the cold water and swam back to the far end of the barge.

Climbing up onto the stern of the steel structure, they had found they were in the entertainers' dressing area, and been greeted warmly by the amused band members.

He looked now at the spot they had traversed, and saw in the moonlight a dark, swirling whirlpool created by the river's swift current.

He shook his head in amusement. Those had been good times. Chancy maybe, there had been other incidents, too, that would have turned his parents prematurely gray if they had known, but good times nevertheless.

Then the good times had continued. Blessed with an ability to mentally assimilate material quicker than most, he hadn't had that much trouble with his studies, leaving plenty of time for other things. Then, after only three years of lecturing at MU, he landed the funding for the expedition—most people spent years in the classroom before even going on an expedition, much less heading one. And then the discovery of the nearly perfectly preserved prehistoric man—one thing after another, always going right.

His mother had said that was partly because of his personality—an optimist, one of those glass half-full rather than half-empty types. "You tend to only remember the good things," she had said, "and that makes you all the more confident, and that leads to success." She had used as an example the time when over a span of the first three-quarters of a football game, he had carried eleven times for no gain or a loss, then saw that crease between guard and tackle, juked a too-hard charging linebacker, and sprinted seventy-one yards for the touchdown that won the state championship.

"But I knew the hole would eventually be there," he had told her. "My line was too good for that not to happen."

"See what I mean?" she had answered.

He smiled, but then it quickly dissipated. Now he was faced with something different. The final acceptance of the Ancient Man for what he was, the ending of the skepticism, depended not on his own quick mind or athletic ability, not on him in any way, but on the opinions of others—some of them not all that ready to accept what he needed because it went against their own long-held theory. But it would happen, he knew; he *was* that much of an optimist. What other choice did they have? And then he thought of the intruder again, and what reason the man could have possibly had for entering the case.

That still had him upset when he arrived back at his apartment. But then as he stepped inside the door, his basset hound, long and low to the floor, walked slowly from the hallway into the living room and stared hard at him, allowing a little amusement to replace the irritation in his mind.

He looked down at the white, whiskered face and sagging jaws. "So I didn't get back when I said I would, Napoleon, and you've been waiting to go outside. Well, I couldn't help it. Some nut broke into the exhibit. What do you *think* about that?"

At Cameron's emphasis of the word *think,* the dog's eyes stared up at him.

"I said what do you *think* about that, Napoleon?"

The dog raised his long face toward the ceiling and gave a short howl.

Cameron nodded. "My sentiments exactly, Napoleon." He opened the door again, and stood to the side.

The dog walked slowly toward the doorway, but stopped short of stepping outside and looked to the left and right with his wrinkled head.

"Still remember the cat that got you, huh? Well, it was your own fault. Now go on. I have to call Dr. Baringer."

The dog moved slowly forward, crossing the concrete landing onto the grass in front of the apartment.

"Don't get too far away or the dogcatcher will get you, Napoleon."

The animal looked back toward the door.

"Yeah, Napoleon; what do you *think* about dogcatchers?"

The dog raised his head and gave another short howl.

Cameron grinned and walked to the couch, sat on its far side and reached for the telephone on the adjacent end table. In a few moments Dr. Baringer's sleepy voice came back over the line.

He came wide awake at the explanation of what had happened, then listened intently as Cameron described all he knew about the break-in. Despite the seriousness of the events, Baringer chuckled at the female sergeant's suggestion of cloning. But Cameron had thought further about that as he had driven to his apartment. "I'd like to be around when it does happen," he said. "There's a zillion groups out there working on genetics, from big corporations to characters in their garages, all of them looking for a breakthrough that could mean billions. It'll happen. Someday we'll look up and somebody will be asking for permission to use DNA from Abe Lincoln's mother and father to bring him back."

"Not while you and I are still alive."

The room looked as shabby as the rest of the old house in the lowlands across the Mississippi River from Memphis. The flowered wallpaper was faded gray, streaked and peeling in places where rain water had come through the roof and seeped down the walls. The carpet, once a dark blue, was now more a dirty brown and soiled in spots, and a cobweb hung from the ceiling, connecting two walls at a corner of the room. The odor of mildew was strong.

Yet all the equipment in the room was sparkling new —the high-intensity lamp straight out of its crate and shining down on the sheet; the operating instruments, wrapped in sterile gauze and lying on shiny steel trays, glinting the lights' reflection. Mary lay under the sheet pulled up over her face, her hospital gown soaked with her sweat, her skinny legs held wide up in the stirrups of the cushioned examining table, her arms strapped to the sides of the table.

She tried to clear her head of the sedative Dr. Anderson had given her, tried to feel what he was doing—and was frightened to the point of trembling. "Is it going to hurt?" she asked for the tenth time.

He pulled the sheet from her face, startling her. He had been at the other end of the table—she thought he had, anyway.

She stared at his surgical gown and gloves. She didn't remember him putting them on.

"I have already finished," he said, smiling softly down at her.

Already finished? No more? That's all? *I would have swung on a vine and . . .*

Still thinking about the twenty thousand dollars, she drifted off to sleep again.

Dr. Anderson stared at Mary for a few seconds, waiting for her breathing to become deep and rhythmic.

When it had, he lifted a clear plastic mask from the bottles of anesthetic and oxygen strapped to the head of the table. He laid it over her nose and mouth, then reached back to the tanks and partially opened their valves.

Continuing to hold the mask firmly in place and staring at his watch, he reached with his other hand to her wrist and monitored her pulse.

After a couple of minutes he placed her arm across her unconscious form, removed the mask, hung it back on the tanks and turned and walked from the table.

In the small room he had selected for his bedroom, he changed into a pair of comfortable cotton pajamas. A small cassette tape recorder lay on the bedside table. He took it into his hand, sat on the bed, and turned and laid back against the headboard.

"Day one," he started.

CHAPTER 5

Cameron came awake shortly before noon. *A sample?* was the first thought he had. His second thought was about the man who had climbed inside the case, and he ached to know who the bastard was—who he represented. He had to represent somebody. His next thought had to do with how much he was still so bothered by the incident after a night of sleep, feeling worse rather than better. He certainly felt more anger at what had been done.

It was only a tiny, almost unnoticeable sample, most people would say, why are you upset? Be glad there was no serious damage done. No serious damage, he thought. Hell, you could cut the man up into a million similar-sized pieces and each one would represent something serious—hours and days and weeks and months and years of education, the sacrifices his family had made in sending him to prep school, the begging he had done to raise funds for the expedition.

Still playing irritating thoughts back and forth in his mind, he let Napoleon outside, lifted the newspaper thrown on the landing in front of the apartment, and walked into the kitchen and opened the refrigerator. He had forgotten to stop by the grocery store again. He found a tin of tuna fish in one of the cabinets, added a blob of mayonnaise to it, a dab of Tabasco sauce, some more Tabasco sauce, and juice from a jar of sweet pickle relish. He forked the mixture between two pieces of toast, then poured himself a glass of orange juice and walked into the living room to watch the news as he ate.

The night watchman had come through surgery in stable condition, the announcer said.

Cameron stopped the sandwich halfway to his mouth. He hadn't been told there had been a confrontation. The lieutenant had said the watchman had only gotten a "glimpse" of the man. Hell, what were they doing holding that back? It was *his* exhibit. He reached for the telephone on the coffee table.

In a few seconds he had obtained the number of the Criminal Justice Center from information and punched it in.

The officer answering the telephone said Lieutenant Warrington was not presently in the building, but asked him to leave a number.

"It was my exhibit that was broken into last night. I was wondering if the watchman got a description? The TV said he was in a fight with the man." *Who, I might add, you bastards didn't mention,* was what he really wanted to say.

"Yes sir, I believe that's correct," the polite voice came back. "But you'll have to speak with Lieutenant Warrington for any details on that case. If you'll leave your number I'm sure he'll call you when he has the time."

"Is Sergeant Cummings in?"

"Adrian or Gerald?"

Adrian or Gerald? She was married? Or had a brother who worked on the force? Maybe just the same name and not any kin. He found himself surprised that he was wondering. "Adrian Cummings," he said.

"No sir, but I'll be glad to leave word for her too. What's your number?"

He gave it to the officer, reminded him of his name, then replaced the receiver in its cradle. He finished the last couple of bites of his sandwich as he walked toward the bathroom.

An hour later, shaved, showered, and dressed in a short sleeve pullover, khakis, and black Chuck Taylors, they still hadn't called. Had the intruder been black or white, tall or short? Was he someone already known to the police? And why, again, had they held back from him that the watchman got more than a glimpse? That still rankled him.

He looked across his living room at the television. The watchman's name was John Clack, a widower with no immediate family in the area, the newscast had said. It had also given the name of the hospital where the surgery took place. He grabbed his car keys off the counter and, stepping around Napoleon asleep in the middle of the floor, strode toward the door.

Thirty minutes later he met with more frustration. The middle-aged woman at the hospital's information counter looked down in front of her for Mr. John Clack's room number, and a strange look crossed her face.

When she raised her face to speak again, her voice was suddenly monotone. "I find no patient by that name listed."

Maybe not John Clack, but her tone indicated she had seen *something*. Maybe a John Doe with a note out beside the name saying the room number shouldn't be given out to anyone.

He stared at her, and she stared back at him—her stare nervous and unsure, his annoyed. It wasn't her fault. She had only told him what the instructions allowed her to say. He was letting his irritation get out of hand. He forced a pleasant smile to his face, turned, and walked away from the counter.

Back along the wide, first floor corridor he found the bank of pay telephones he had passed when entering the building.

He located the hospital's main number in the telephone directory and punched it in. He waited for the operator to answer, then tightened his voice and spoke in a brusque tone.

"This is Lieutenant Warrington, Memphis Police Department. I need to speak with the officer on duty in Mr. John Clack's room."

The ensuing silence lasted so long he began to wonder if he had been cut off. Then the woman's voice came back across the line.

"I'm sorry, I can't seem to find anyone by—"

"This is official police business, ma'am. Would you please ask someone who knows? Tell them Lieutenant Warrington needs to be connected to that floor immediately."

A longer silence followed. Too long. He looked over his shoulders toward the bank of elevator doors a hundred feet down the floor. What would he do if an officer ran out of one of the doors and sprinted in his direction.

"Union East, Nurse Langston speaking."

The response directly from the floor caught him off guard, and he had to think quickly. "Is Dr. Thompson at your station?"

"Excuse me?"

"This is Dr. Wilson; is Dr. Thompson at your station?"

"No, sir."

"Well, I need to speak to him right away. Have you seen him on the floor?"

"I don't believe I know a Dr. Thompson, sir. I can ask one of the other nurses."

"What floor is this?"

"Seven."

The section of the seventh floor on that side of the hospital contained scores of rooms. Cameron walked slowly along the hallways, peering into the rooms with open doors and looking at name tags on those that were closed. The sound of his footsteps on the tile floor caused a white-uniformed woman in one of the nursing stations to look up. She didn't say anything and he continued on down the corridor. A pair of nurses, one unusually attractive with long auburn hair, passed by him on their way to the nursing station. He looked back over his shoulder at them, holding the auburn-haired one's tight figure in his gaze for a long moment, glad that he could focus on something else, his irritation starting to fade back to within normal limits now.

Then, facing forward, he had to step quickly to the side to avoid colliding with an orderly directly in his path. Before Cameron could say "excuse me," the man, bent on his hurried task, had passed by and strode rapidly on down the hallway.

Cameron kept his eyes studiously to the front now. He came to an intersection of corridors. Stopping, he looked to his right and saw a uniformed police officer standing to the side of a closed door fifty feet down the hall.

When he approached the officer, the man looked hard at him.

"Excuse me. Is this Mr. Clack's room?"

The officer didn't respond.

"I'm Dr. Malone. It was my exhibit that—"

He didn't finish as Lieutenant Warrington stepped from the room and closed the door behind him.

"Dr. Malone?"

"Lieutenant. I heard about the watchman this morning. Was he able to give you a description of the man?"

Warrington didn't speak for a moment. When he did there was an obvious note of irritation in his voice. "How did you know he was on this floor?"

"I overheard a couple of nurses talking in the lobby."

"I don't suppose you caught their name tags?"

"No."

The door to the room opened again. Sergeant Adrian Cummings stood there, still doing wonders for her uniform. Past her on the bed the watchman, his face swathed in bandages with one eye peering through, lay propped up on some pillows.

Cameron looked back at Warrington. "Did you get a description?"

"He was attacked out of the dark. All he remembers is the guy running away—in a black suit and hood. Tall and skinny is about all we have beyond that."

The sergeant added in: "He said that when he saw him leaning over the glass, it reminded him of a giant black widow at the edge of the case," she said.

A black, skinny, long-limbed spider passed through Cameron's mind. Skinny. Black suit. *Ichabod Crane. Or a too-skinny English butler.*

Warrington noticed his expression. "What?"

"There was a man in the exhibit room yesterday. He was thin—unusually so. He was looking back toward the case when I noticed him but I can't remember his face; my attention was drawn to how tight his suit was. It was black." He tried to recall further but he couldn't. "I don't see any features, just a face looking back toward the case. He was white—pale looking."

Warrington nodded. "Yeah, well, as many people been through this exhibit, I'm sure there was a bunch slim and in a dark suit. Even if the face does come to you, I don't see it helping much. How would we put a name to it?"

The sergeant's brow wrinkled in thought? "Dr. Malone, I, uh—" Then she shook her head. "Never mind, it's not important." She looked at her watch and back at the lieutenant. "I've got to be running," she added. "I've only got about an hour until I have to be at a deposition." He nodded, and she started down the corridor. Cameron stared after her.

"Doctor," Warrington said, calling his attention back to him. "I tell you what, If the face does come to you, go ahead and give us a call. Maybe we can put a composite together. I guess we could run it in the paper and see if anybody did recognize it."

Cameron nodded. "I'll be certain to. By the same token, I would appreciate it if you would let me know if you find out anything else.''

"Sure," the lieutenant said, and turned back to speak with the officer who had been guarding the door.

Cameron hurried his steps in the direction the sergeant had gone. In a moment he turned a corner in the corridor to see one of the elevators fifty feet away closing behind her.

He hurried on to the second elevator door and jabbed his finger against the call button.

CHAPTER 6

The trip down from the seventh floor of the hospital seemed to take forever, the elevator door opening at every floor, and Cameron was surprised Sergeant Cummings was still in view when he reached the ground floor. She was turning into the cafeteria.

He stopped at its door, watched her as she got a hamburger and glass of tea from the serving line, paid the cashier, and walked to one of the many empty tables in the room. Then he walked toward the table.

She raised her face at his approach. "You miss lunch, too?" she asked.

"You started to say something upstairs."

"It was nothing."

"Like it was nothing that the watchman got close enough to whoever broke in last night that there was a fight—though you all told me he only got a *glimpse* of whoever it was? And upstairs a minute ago, your lieutenant seemed more interested in finding out who told me where the watchman's room was rather than anything I had to say about seeing somebody who might fit the description of whoever it was. You'll excuse me if I wonder if there's something else you're not telling me."

She stared at him for a moment. "What makes you think we owe you any answers?"

"It's my exhibit."

"It's our investigation, doctor. And the less we say

about the particulars to the subjects, the more likely we are to hear something ourselves that might ring a bell."

"To the subjects? I'm supposed to be one of the suspects? Hell, I was the one who found the body. If I wanted to do something I've had a million chances when I was alone with it. And why would I?"

"We didn't know who the insurance was made out to, for one, doctor. And we assumed it would be highly insured. How did we know that whoever the intruder was wasn't there to do some destruction?"

"The insurance is made out to the Italian government."

"We know that now."

Christ, he thought, they *had* wondered.

"It was about frozen elephants," she said.

"Excuse me?"

"What I started to ask you about upstairs. But you blew me off pretty good last night. So I decided I didn't want to put up with that again."

"I'm sorry, but I don't understand what you're—"

"Last night I suggested the sperm—if that's what the intruder did take—might be intended for artificial insemination. You told me to forget it, it couldn't have happened. I didn't like the way you put it—take my word on it, are the words you used—so I went to the library today to see for myself about the effects of freezing." She reached for her tea glass.

He pulled a chair back and set down across from her. "Sergeant, I . . . do you mind if I call you Adrian?"

He wouldn't have been surprised at that point if she said she did mind, but she didn't, nodding her permission.

"Adrian, I didn't mean to blow you off. I apologize if you took it that way. But it's just not possible for—"

"Doctor, there have been dozens of ancient elephants—mammoths—found that were frozen. There was one found in Siberia that was over ten thousand years old and his flesh was so fresh people could still eat it. In fact, people did eat some of it—a bunch of Russian scientists held a banquet."

He nodded.

"You knew that, didn't you?"

"Yes."

"Well, why couldn't a man end up the same way?"

Before he could answer, a waitress carrying a tea pitcher stepped up to the table and nodded at Adrian's half-empty glass. Adrian smiled politely up at the woman. "No, thank you. I'm fine."

As the woman said something about the "excellent chocolate dessert" they had, Adrian continued to look up from the table, giving him a studied look at her profile, her nose, prominent, but not too big, her high cheekbones and her eyes that were big too, and round and deep brown, and, above them, eyebrows thick and dark enough to never need the aid of an eyebrow pencil. Were her coloring a slight bit darker he could be staring at an Indian princess—and despite his irritation at her lecturing him, he found himself now thinking how her looks intrigued him more than any woman's he had ever seen. And then she was looking back at him.

"Well?" she said, and he had to scramble to remember her last question—*why couldn't a man end up the same way. Permanently frozen.*

"We're not talking about ten thousand years, Adrian, but five hundred thousand. Glaciers came and went over all those years. He could have thawed out and frozen a dozen times."

She shook her head in disagreement. "The mammoth had buttercups in its mouth. Buttercups only grow in the summer, it said. So how did it die with buttercups in its mouth and not rot before the weather turned cold enough to freeze him? Well, the article said that he must have fallen through the top of an underground cave where there was still permafrost; permanently frozen ground—you know what that is too. It would be like falling into a freezer. After he was frozen I don't see how it would make any difference whether ten thousand years had passed or five hundred thousand, so long as the permafrost stayed frozen. And the article said there is permafrost that has never thawed. There was some even found on a Pacific island by a drilling crew. A tropical climate and yet, under the ground, there was still permanently frozen soil. Did you know that? Of course you do. And you also know mountaineers fall into crevasses in glaciers every year. They're frozen when they die. How can you know that didn't happen to your discovery?"

"For one thing, we think he went through a burial ritual. The flesh taken from his thighs and the removal of his brain indicate that."

"Indicate, maybe, doctor, but how can you be sure that wasn't done to him while he was being killed? Then they threw his body into a crevasse?"

"Okay, we can't know for certain. But even if something along those lines occurred, it wouldn't change things. For the sperm to be frozen is not enough in itself—not for what you suggest. It has to be held at extremely cold temperatures to remain stable. If not, it would be what we call self-digested—broken down, similar to what meat does as it ages in a freezer."

She stared back across the table at him. "Why is he so well preserved? The newspapers are full of that being the reason there has been so much controversy as to his true age. He should be—at the most—bone fragments. Isn't that right?"

"That's been true in the past."

"Uh, huh," she said. "In the past. But not now, right? And I read something else this morning, too. I always thought dinosaurs were gray, at least dark colored. I saw where none of you really have any idea what color they were. Gray's just an artist's perception. And the article said that more than once a museum skeleton of some prehistoric animal has had to be dissasembled after a new find showed that it was actually a compilation of parts of a couple of different animals found in the same pit. So not everything in your profession is so pat, is it?" She sipped from her tea, then looked at her watch and stood.

"So now you know what I started to say last night," she said, looking down at him, and then smiled. "And now I'm even with you for blowing me off."

Then, still smiling, she turned away from the table and walked toward the cafeteria exit, and he watched her go, as did a couple of other young male nurses in white pants and shirts at a table a few feet away. As she disappeared through the doorway, one of the men looked at him, smiled, and shrugged.

He returned the smile and looked toward the empty doorway, and imagined her still standing there, not only the most striking woman he had ever seen, but with a quick mind, too, what with her thinking about a possible use for the sperm the very moment he emerged from the case. And she was not just quick, she then had gone to a library to research her thoughts when she wasn't satisfied with his answer. Soft spoken the night before, the easy genuine smile she had given the waitress even in the midst of lecturing him—she could fit ladylike into any situation, but also was strong enough to face the things a cop must. Or to give a lecture to someone who had blown her away, he thought, and smiled. He leaned back in his chair and stroked his chin, all these thoughts going through his mind, and her face in his sleep the night before.

Dr. Anderson stepped inside the old farmhouse and, carrying a small cotton sack filled with something heavy from his car, walked past Mary to his bedroom. He closed the door behind him.

Mary stared after him. The old black metal box he had brought in the night before still sat outside his room. An occasional wisp of smoke rose from the front of the box where one of its locks didn't hold the lid completely tight. He *was* weird.

She turned and pulling back the sheet nailed over the

window beside her, stared through the dusty panes at the willow trees and thick clumps of tall johnsongrass dotting the muddy ground across the gravel road. Down the road to her left was more of the same. And to her right, the same again. *Just nothing.* And certainly no people—except for the old crazy woman a half hour before. Walking slowly past the house, she had worn work boots no less, and what looked like a flower sack for a dress, and carried a garbage bag full of something over her shoulder. Who but some old crazed person would come down this road, unless they were lost; who would ever come down to such a desolate spot? How in the world could she stand to be in such a place for nine months, without ever going anywhere else? That had been Dr. Anderson's deal. But nine months? She looked at the old television at the far side of the living room. It picked up only one channel, fuzzy at that, no movies to speak of, and none of her favorite soaps. *Jesus, nine months.*

Inside his room, Dr. Anderson raised his recorder to his mouth. "Two-thirty P.M., experiment day one," he started. "I am only hours into the experiment and it is already apparent that I am going to have difficulties with subject. She is restless, openly expressing her resentment of both my confining her to the house and my limiting her physical activity. But what other choice do I have? Since so much of this experiment is outside the realm of what is now scientifically accepted I have to be cautious at every step. . . ." He pushed the recorder's stop button.

Especially cautious. Not only with her health but with documenting every step of the experiment in detail. He couldn't allow the prehistorians a chance to contradict what he was about to prove, as they had so often before evaded acknowledging the obvious.

He sat quietly a few seconds, nodded, and raised the recorder back to his lips.

"When Neanderthal Man was discovered and had a

brain as large as ours, the evolutionists joyfully proclaimed that he was the step directly before our kind. Since we no longer possessed his sloping forehead and overhanging brow, his discovery was also *proof* of how we had evolved.

"So what happens then? Finds at Steinheim, Germany, and Swanscombe, England, unearthed men with features already very similar to ours, men who lived as long as two hundred fifty thousand years ago, over three times as far back in time as the Neanderthal Man.

"What did the evolutionists say then? How did they escape the corner into which they had painted themselves? They glossed over the fact by simply saying that, on further study, Neanderthal Man was simply an aberrant variant of *Homo sapiens* that did not survive. So it didn't matter that he appeared to be a step backward in evolution when compared to other men even earlier in time.

"And what about the long-held belief that the apelike Australopithecines of five million years ago evolved into our kind through a series of progressions? That theory was also shown to be wrong when the so-called more evolved 1470 man, looking very little different from mankind today, was found in association with Australopithecines in the same layers of sediment at Lake Rudolf in Kenya. Quite obviously that meant that 1470 man had not evolved from Australopithecus but rather existed at the same time. In fact 1470 man had been making a meal of these creatures, as evidenced by the charred bones found at the site.

"So do the evolutionists now admit they were wrong about Australopithecines, too? No, they couldn't, without casting serious doubt on evolution itself. They instead contend they remain correct in their original theory—that the unevolved Australopithecus found with 1470 man was simply a wayward, side branch off the main trunk of evolution. So it was of no consequence that certain of them stayed the same over a period of five million years—while, of course, the ones that were our *true* ancestors were evolving all the time.

"But they are wrong. They are completely wrong. By the time this tape is heard by the scientific community, all will know how wrong they have been. And a leap back five hundred thousand years will leave an inescapable conclusion even for the simplest of minds. There never has been a difference—there never has been an evolution of man."

He lowered the recorder. There has never been. He knew if he were to meet the very first man and woman there ever were, he wouldn't be looking at anything different than what he saw on the street every day. Of course there would have been other kinds of mankind around back then, too, the so-called links and offshoots, some of them probably still unknown, some of them no doubt terrible to behold. But however terrible they had been, man had somehow survived and kept procreating and was the only order left today, no different from how he had always been.

And that included man's innate intelligence, his ability to assimilate facts and act on them. Not a prehistoric man with a somehow diminished intellectual ability despite a cranial capacity as large as modern man's. But he knew that would be the next thing claimed, since the Ancient Man had his brain removed—there had already been an article published suggesting such a possibility. Anything for an excuse. Anything to claim that the Man was different in at least some way. But he wasn't—and he intended to prove that where there would no longer be any kind of disparagement. His lips tightened. *They had even laughed.*

Maybe not to his face, but that was worse. Like his mother had done when as a teenager he had brought Rachel over to the house to introduce her. Poor, and from the other side of the tracks, but yet so beautiful, the queen of the local Watermelon Festival, and he had been so proud she had accepted his offer of a date.

Surprisingly, despite all the lectures his mother had

given him about staying to his own kind, she had been exceedingly nice—or so he thought. Then he had returned home after taking Rachel back to her house, and his mother was cleaning the back of the couch with a rag. He was young then, he hadn't noticed how theatrically she was working at her task—to pull his attention to it.

He had asked, and his mother had remarked about the grease Rachel's thick, long hair had left there. Nothing more, just the grease in her hair.

And he had never dated her again.

His lips drew tighter still. Just like the prehistorians, his mother, all those so-called experts in archaeology and paleontology, all using ridicule to try and force him into saying his theory couldn't be correct. But it hadn't worked. As cruel as had been his mother's game it had also prewarned him, steeled him from future such attacks, and he had never wavered. And now, the truth that would vault him ahead of any prehistorian who had ever lived, made theory, and lied, was at hand. His hand.

He took a deep breath, nodded to himself, and then, slowly began to smile. Still smiling, he reached to the table beside his chair, laid the recorder on it, and turned on the police-band scanner there. A moment later he reached to the radio next to the scanner and added the sound of a news talk show host with that of the officers talking back and forth. He lifted a gynecology text off the stack on the floor next to his bed and began to read, and listen—carefully.

It was nearly five when Cameron made up his mind to call Adrian at the Criminal Justice Center. If he was going to ask her out, that's where he was going to have to call. She wasn't listed in the telephone directory. The officer answering sounded like the one who had answered earlier that day, and asked the same question he had before when Cameron asked for Sergeant Cummings: "Adrian or Gerald?"

"Adrian," Cameron said.

"Just a moment and I'll ring her."

A nagging thought passed through Cameron's mind again. "Excuse me, officer."

"Sir?"

"They wouldn't be related, would they?"

"Sir?"

"The sergeants."

There was a moment of silence, then, "Mr. and Mrs., the last time I heard."

Cameron stared a moment at the wall.

"Hello."

It was her voice.

He moved the receiver around in front of him and looked at it.

"Hello?"

He placed the phone back onto its cradle.

CHAPTER 7

Memphis University commenced classes the next week, and Cameron gave his first test two weeks after that, then graded the papers and returned them to the groans and smiles of the students the following Monday. When the bell rang, he rose and walked out into the hall.

Dean Jensen came down it, and stopped in front of him. "Cameron," he said.

"Dr. Jensen."

"You still haven't heard any more from the police?"

He shook his head. "I doubt very seriously they gave it much of a shot. I can't see a break-in and assault being their highest priority with everything else that goes on."

"The tissue that was taken—could there be somebody out there so demented as to collect something like that? Some rich nut wanting a piece of the world's oldest body? I mean it makes you wonder, doesn't it?" Then Jensen glanced at his watch, nodded his good-bye, and continued down the hall.

Wonder? Cameron thought as he watched Jensen walk away. He almost laughed considering the wondering he had been doing himself. He had even gone to the library to research what he could. The temperatures within a glacier certainly weren't cold enough to preserve the chromosomal structure in sperm, it would have broken down—his reading only reaffirmed that.

But out of the millions of sperm would they all have ruptured, each and every one spilling their contents into an impossible soup?

That was what he kept wondering about. Could even one of the sperm have kept its contents intact, broken down alright, but still contained, like water in a sagging balloon?

There had been animal research where much younger, broken down structure within a sperm's body *had* been dumped into an egg. Most of these experiments had led to either nothing at all happening, or a fertilization taking place resulting in a gross deformity. But there had been rare cases when normal fertilization had been achieved, and a normal birth followed.

Of course no such experimentation had been done on a human egg—that would be beyond ethical boundaries. But had there been any such unannounced work done?

But then he was fantasizing, wasn't he? Dreaming.

And then he smiled a little. So what was so new about dreaming for him? He looked at Dean Jensen now nearing the far end of the hall. He was certainly a reasoned man, prominent in his field, the epitome of an academician. But Cameron had known that wasn't for him ever since he had been a little boy in the Delta, excited at the find of prehistoric sharks teeth in the cotton fields, realizing that the whole area had once been a deep ocean—and that a different kind of people had lived there. And what other exciting things were there left to find out? What exciting things left to discover—maybe things almost imaginable. His life, he had realized at that point, was to be one of adventure, discovery. Had he been born a century earlier he would have been among the first to strike out West, excited, looking forward to what was to be found—not leaning against a blackboard in a classroom, lecturing, slowly beginning to watch more and more TV.

And so what was wrong with dreaming the impossible, being excited, being driven by it? And not too very long in the future, he would have to be on another expedition—looking again for things to discover. It bothered him greatly that he wasn't already.

But patience, let all the controversy calm down, let the Ancient Man prove whatever he was called on to prove, and he would be on his way again.

Yet, *Christ*, what more was there to prove? The sediment in which the man had been found corresponded perfectly to the period in question. The thermoluminescence test backed that up. Maybe no corresponding animal fossils had been found, or no tools that would lend credence to the dating, but how much was needed to convince the skeptics? Dozens of finds had been confirmed with much less. Hell, Davidson Black announced Peking Man with little more than two isolated teeth.

Then, willing his mind to slow, he thought patience again. When the Italian government made the details of the tests public there would be no more skepticism except from the most dogmatic of those against moving the origination of modern man back that far in time. It was just his nervous mind going back and forth. Was that what paranoia was? It was only that it meant so much to him.

And then a good thought going through his mind; what if the sperm *was* somehow viable? That would only add to the discovery—make the Ancient Man even more significant.

Then he frowned. That somebody else might already know the answer to that, the intruder, or whoever the intruder was in the employ of, made him livid.

Now he shook his head in irritation with himself. His mind had flip-flopped for too long, angry at times, nervous at times, not confident as near as often as he would like. And he wasn't used to that. He looked down the hall to a pay telephone on the wall, then walked toward it.

A moment later he had reached the Criminal Justice

Center. Neither Lieutenant Warrington nor Adrian were in, and the officer who had answered didn't know whether there had been any progress on the case—for that matter anything about the case. It certainly didn't have the center buzzing.

At the old house in the lowlands outside of West Memphis, Dr. Anderson stood in the living room and watched Mary at the window to the side of the front door. The dim sunlight coming in through the sheet hung inside the panes passed through her nearly transparent gown, exposing her body almost as clearly as if she wore nothing.

She did it on purpose, he knew. She had been trying to entice him the entire time they had been there. She was not only a prostitute, she was a whore. And though he felt sorry for her because of that, he had also worried about it when he had first approached her, worried that the genes that led her to her kind of life would be half of the child's chromosomes.

In fact, knowing the type individual he was going to be faced with in procuring someone to carry a child under the circumstances he demanded, he had gone to the black market and obtained an egg for two thousand dollars. For five thousand more he had been given the name and address of the woman who sold the egg. Other than her being greedy enough to be involved with the unscrupulous doctor who had obtained the egg for him, she seemed relatively normal—a wife of a small-town pharmacist with two apparently normal children of her own.

So now he had the best of both worlds, an egg with acceptable genes and a woman of Mary's class and lack of feeling who would bear the child and not hesitate an instant in giving it up and going on about her business, never thinking of anything again but the money she received. He had done all that was within his power and now all he could do was wait and . . . his thoughts suddenly ceased at what he saw.

Mary had turned from the window, giving him a side view of her body—and revealing the barely perceptible, curving bulge.

"Mary!"

She looked at him as he suddenly strode toward her. "What?"

He stopped in front of her and reached his hand toward her abdomen.

She stepped back. "What?"

"Stand still, Mary, please." He felt the bulge.

She stared down at the spot, and her eyes widened. "I'm not pregnant," she said quickly. "I mean I wasn't already. I swear. I couldn't have been." She forced a smile to her face. "I swell up sometimes—a little bit. You know, water."

He didn't answer.

"Remember, I just had my period a week before I came here."

"It's okay, Mary." He felt the bulge again. He noticed her hand tremble. "It's okay, Mary."

"I haven't entertained a trick in months; since you started paying me not to. I swear."

He knew she was lying. But he had checked her carefully both for disease and to make sure she wasn't pregnant before he inserted the egg. Yet, now she appeared at least three months pregnant, maybe four. He shook his head in confusion.

"What?" she asked.

He tried to think.

"I swear to God, Dr. Anderson. I—" She threw the back of her hand to her mouth.

He raised his eyes to hers. "You know who I am."

She shook her head. "I won't ever say whose child it is. Your secret will be safe. I swear it. What would I gain to say anything about you?"

He laid his hand gently on her shoulder. "It doesn't matter. I was afraid some day you might decide you wanted the child back. I—"

"No, I'd never do that. Not ever."

"Mary, I told you, it doesn't make any difference." He forced himself not to stare down at her abdomen again, turned and walked slowly back across the living room floor, his mind swirling with thoughts.

She couldn't be three or four months pregnant.

But she was.

He raised his thin fingers to his chin and stroked it nervously.

He suddenly thought of the trees in the room he kept locked, the only place in the house without sheets nailed over the windows. He walked toward the hall.

CHAPTER 8

After Dr. Anderson stepped inside the room, he closed and relocked the door behind him, then turned to stare at the two small trees sitting before separate windows, each tree short, their trunks bare and topped with a cluster of pinnately compound leaves, their bases planted in a washtub filled with rich loam. He walked to the nearest tree and stopped.

Their seeds had come from Egypt out of a vase buried in a pyramid many centuries before. There had been quite a large number of the seeds, nearly a hundred in all. The company where he had been employed had been contracted to germinate ten of them, and he and a colleague had been assigned the task.

Six of the ten had sprouted into date palms—what they were said to be before they had been delivered to the labs. He had been ecstatic to see a direct descendant of something so long ago be no different from the kind of palm present now in tropical Africa and Asia.

That the palms from the seeds weren't different from their modern relatives didn't, of course, prove anything about evolution. In the first place, most any college freshman could tell you that a few centuries was not a long enough span of time for any kind of evolution to have taken place, whether you were talking about plants or animals. Secondly, plants, to his way of think-ing, did not evolve so much as they mutated, an entirely different concept from so-called human evolution. Still, he enjoyed the trees, reveled in them as a visual symbol of his overall beliefs.

Then he had read of the discovery of the 500,000-year-old man, and how well it was preserved. How the body prior to its discovery had been buried in rock deep beneath a receding glacier and how it was being kept in a refrigerated display case to prevent deterioration, much as a salvager of a sunken Spanish galleon kept its timbers in salt water to prevent their drying and falling apart.

His interest pricked, he went to a library and found a photograph of the man in a copy of *The New York Times*.

His pulse had surged at what he saw.

There was some injury to the stomach and the thighs, that was obviously how he met his death. There were some cracks in the hard brown shell, but that damage could have easily been done within the rock slide. It couldn't be deterioration, for there was none other evident, right down to the testes being in perfect condition.

Seeds, he had thought. Sperm was the seed of human life. The sperm would be dry but would still have its DNA present. If only the corpse had been quick frozen at its death and remained that way all the time it had been buried. And what else could have happened but that, considering how well the body had stayed preserved for so long?

He had made his plans at that moment, planning on flying to California or New York. What did he have to lose if he was assuming too much? Then *The Commercial Appeal* had announced the exhibit was being diverted to Memphis for a six-week stay. So he bided his time and waited for the exhibit to reach the Cook Convention Center, with whose layout and procedures he was already familiar.

He looked back at the tree, basking in the warm September sunlight coming through the window. He hadn't been able to resist having something for his own that was so close to his philosophy. It had been easy. Two of the seedlings had simply died—that's what he told the owner of the company.

He reached out and gently touched the dark green leaves. He had chosen well when he decided which of the seedlings were the healthiest. The two in the room with him had in fact steadily outgrown those in the lab. Not by much, maybe ten to fifteen percent, but a difference nevertheless. Their growth was probably due to the care he gave them. No child had ever been fed and watered and caressed more carefully.

But there was one other possibility.

There were two reports of similar unusual growth in palms from the seeds contracted to other labs. Could it possibly be where the seeds originally came from that made the difference? There was no way of knowing if they had all been collected at the same time and place. What if some had come from an area where it was difficult for them to survive. Would the ones that did survive be the ones that grew and produced seeds the fastest?

What then about mankind five hundred thousand years ago? Were humans such a hunted creature, so prone to death and extinction, that their reproductive rate, even the rate of growth of the child in the woman's womb, was much faster than it was now— maybe only two to three months to birth rather than nine months? Was that possible?

He pondered longer, tried to think of a precedent that would seem to allow that possibility. But he couldn't. It was a known fact that when animals with normally high reproductive rates became overabundant in an area, they often quit having a large number of young until their numbers thinned. By the reverse of that, when these animals' numbers became scarce again, they often started having multiple young.

But there wasn't any difference in the animal's length of gestation, only in the mother's fertility.

Then another thought occurred to him. He should have thought of it right off, but he wasn't a gynecologist and it was hard to remember everything, even if he had studied on his own for so long. It was the mother's system that determined the length of gestation. The sperm made no difference in that, so the five-hundred-thousand-year-old sperm couldn't have possibly made any difference.

Then, slowly, a smile came to his face. It grew broader, broke through, and he chuckled. He clenched and unclenched his hands in excitement. His scientific mind, his logical way of thinking, had sent him directly into wondering how Mary could have reached the stage she had. But, really, what difference did it make? The important thing was that she *had* reached a stage of pregnancy at all. He could have made a mistake when he thought he separated a single sperm to use. So many other places for a mistake. In fact he hadn't counted on the process working the first time—that's why he had so much of the sample still frozen. There would be other prostitutes to use again, he knew, and try he would, again and again, until it had worked or his life ran out of time. But for it to work the first time!

His smile broadened. He had even studiously forced himself to avoid testing her since he had inserted the egg. He hadn't been able to bring himself to face the prospect of having failed the first time—likely though that was. *Then* for it to work *the first time*.

He *had* succeeded.

Suddenly his thoughts swept back to Mary, and he became solemn again.

With her already restless, what would now happen with her stomach showing an unmistakable sign? For the present she would think she was pregnant before she arrived at the house and hadn't realized it—that she had fooled him by talking about her tendency to swell. She was probably planning on staying around for at least another couple of weeks. At least that long, trying to find where he had the money hidden before she ran.

But what then? She would be alert to her rate of growth now, would grow more worried day by day. In a week or two she would come to the realization of what was really happening to her. She would become hysterical, out of her mind with terror. Maybe he wouldn't be able to handle her at all then, maybe it was better now.

With that thought, he looked at the cotton bag sitting on the floor against the far wall. The shape of the chains coiled inside it looked like long, curled snakes, but much more friendly in nature, much more useful—as was the small box whose outline was apparent atop the coils. He unlocked the door before he turned back to the bag.

CHAPTER 9

Thirty minutes after Dr. Anderson had entered the room with the ancient date palms, he emerged and walked into the living room. Mary stood against the window next to the front door.

"Mary."

She looked toward him, then dropped her gaze to the floor.

"It's okay, Mary, I told you I wasn't angry." He forced a pleasant smile to his face. "What is it you've desired for so long?"

She wrinkled her brow questioningly.

"To eat, Mary. What is it you have been wanting to eat?"

She still looked confused. "A steak?"

"Yes, Mary, a steak. How many times have you asked me for one of the steaks in the refrigerator? I've always told you they were for a special occasion. *The* special occasion—after the baby was born. Well, I've decided that I've been too strict."

Her face beamed.

Then her forehead suddenly wrinkled again. *He had been so adamant in the past about her having to wait.* He had bought the steaks only because she had insisted. He was some kind of crazy vegetarian. He had tried to brainwash her about animal fats and all that kind of crap. But he had just said . . . "You mean I can have one now? For real, Dr. Anderson?"

"Yes, Mary—for real." Poor girl, he thought, to subject her child to that. What she ate the child had to endure. But it wasn't her fault; her education was so totally lacking. "But first you have to go get into bed while I prepare it."

"In bed? It's not even dark yet."

"But you haven't had your nap today."

"You just said you were being too strict."

He nodded. "Other things—like my not allowing you to eat meat, Mary. But you do have to continue with your rest." He walked toward the kitchen.

At the sink, he filled a glass half full of water, then walked back to her and held it out. "And your vitamins," he said, and reached inside his pocket for them.

She frowned, but took them from his palm.

He watched her as she swallowed the pills and chased them down with the water. "Go on, now," he said softly.

She stood still a moment. It was so early.

"Go on," he repeated. "Be a good girl for me."

A steak, she guessed, was worth almost anything—any kind of *real* food other than the damn vegetables—raw, canned, in soups—the whole damn kitchen was stuffed with them. She turned and started for her room.

Jesus, she thought as she stepped inside it and shut the door behind her. When she finally got away from this place she hoped she never saw another vegetable in her life. Or vitamins.

She looked back over her shoulder at the door, then looked down at the slight bulge.

Three or four months pregnant? The reason she had been able to fool Dr. Anderson was partly because she couldn't believe it herself at first. She did use condoms —always. Yet sometimes things happened, condom or no condom.

And there was her irregular cycle; she could have been pregnant for months and not known it. She couldn't remember the last time she did have a period. In fact, before she knew how much money was at stake in carrying his child she had told him about how irregular she was. But he had said it didn't matter, that he was providing both the egg and the sperm.

And the money, too. He was providing that too. He swore he had it and more at the house, though she had tried and tried to find it without success. *The prick,* she thought for the hundredth time, *it better be here.*

She looked at her stomach again. It wouldn't be long until it really began to grow. Another couple of weeks, in a month for sure, and she would be big enough there would be no fooling him anymore. He might not be an Einstein, but he wasn't a total idiot.

A couple of weeks, she thought again, a month maybe. She could find anything in that length of time. She would just have to be quiet and look while he slept at night.

Satisfied with her plan, she nodded, walked to the bed and slipped under its covers. The old tabloid Dr. Anderson had brought for her lay to her side and she picked it up and turned to the story she had been reading earlier, the one about the *real* man who had been seen on the moon. She had known all along that was going to happen—it had been just a matter of time. And she bet there were people on Mars, too—those canals and all, just wait and see.

As she started to turn back to the story and read it again, a new thought entered her mind. She moved her hand to the bulge in her abdomen.

She *was* thirty-one. How many more years did she have left to bear children of her own? Not only the part about how long her fertility would last, but how old she could be before she was too old to play with her children as they grew up?

But then that was why she was here. She had planned on using the twenty thousand dollars to open her doughnut shop, a place of work where her children would respect her. She didn't want them to know what

she did for a living now, like her mother had let her
know. She couldn't put them through that, not after the
way it had bothered her.

She closed her eyes. She hated what she was thinking. Not just the part about not letting her kids know,
but also her knowing in her mind that what she did was
wrong. It had to be wrong, didn't it, if she didn't want
her children to know about it?

She shook her head. She didn't want to think about it
that way. She stared up at the dirty, rain-stained ceiling.
That was her life—*dirty. Stained. Forever.*

Her lip trembled, and for the first time in a long time
she felt tears well in her eyes. *Damn life, damn it all to
hell and back.*

A sound outside her door caught her attention, and
she looked in that direction. What had it been—a metallic sound? She wasn't positive but it almost sounded
like a bag of bolts being set on the floor.

She heard the sound again. She turned on the bed
and stared at the door. What in the hell was Anderson
doing? Not much telling, the weird bastard.

She heard the sound still again, a continuous sound
this time, like . . . she couldn't place it even though
she recalled hearing the same sound in the past. When?
What?

An anchor chain!

It had been during a World War II movie. The battle-
ship had weighed anchor and the chain coming back
aboard the big vessel had made a sound like that when
it passed across the deck.

She sat up in bed. *An anchor chain?*

Her door opened. Her blood chilled. Dr. Anderson
stood there, his tall, thin body framed in light from the
hallway. He held a long chain in each hand. At the ends
of them hung handcuffs.

"My God!" She came up off the bed and jumped to
the back wall of the room. The sudden effort caused
her head to spin so rapidly she had to steady herself
against the wall.

"Mary," Anderson said softly, stepping into the room. "I have something I have to explain to you."

Her eyes were glued to the chains. Past them, she saw a cloth bag lying crumpled on the floor in the hallway.

"Mary, the egg I implanted was not only for a new child but was also for a little experiment of mine. I want you to be the first to know that it has worked."

Experiment. Her eyes widened, and she looked down at her flimsy nightgown. She moved her hand to her belly and felt the bulge.

"Mary, I have developed a uh—" He knew he had to be careful with the technical words or she would never be able to understand what was happening—what he wanted her to think, anyway. He couldn't tell her everything—that it was happening without his knowing why. He was afraid her mind couldn't take it.

"Mary, I have developed a process whereby a gene I alter in the fertilized egg enables the fetus to grow much faster than is normal."

"My God, please!" she suddenly wailed at the top of her lungs. "Pleeease!"

"Now, now, now, Mary, don't be upset. There's no need. In fact, quite to the contrary. You are part of a great new benefit to womankind. From now on they won't have to carry children for nine months. All the discomfort will be gone in a matter of only eight or nine weeks."

She shook her head back and forth. "I want out of here," she gasped, "right now!"

He smiled gently. "Now, Mary, think, have you suffered any discomfort?" He knew from observing her she hadn't.

She looked toward the sheet covered window at the side of the room.

Dr. Anderson quickly stepped toward it, the long chains dragging noisily across the floor behind him.

"No, Mary, don't try to run. You might hurt my baby."

He was also concerned about when she would pass out from the drug he had given her, and stepped closer, ready to grab her when she fell.

But she never did. Instead, only a few seconds later, still looking toward the window, she slipped slowly down the wall to the floor and collapsed gently over onto her side.

CHAPTER 10

Cameron stood next to the pay telephone in the hall outside his classroom. *Knowledge was the sum total of what had been learned in the past,* he thought. When something new came along, that became knowledge, replacing the old.

He smiled a little at his thought—directed again toward the possibility of the Ancient Man's sperm somehow being usable. Then he felt a little foolish at the thought. And that was what his mind had been doing for weeks, back and forth, and then back and forth again. *And he had had enough of that.* There was one way to find out for certain, though he hated to subject himself to what he was going to have to go through to know. Nevertheless, he reached for the telephone receiver.

It took the secretary nearly ten minutes to get Dr. Baringer out of class and to the telephone.

"Cameron?"

"Yes."

"Some news on the man who entered the case?"

"No."

"Don't tell me it's more bad news, Cameron."

"No."

"Damn, Cameron, if I have to keep guessing, I expect a prize if I hit on it."

"I'm still thinking about why he would have taken a sperm sample."

"So what's new? You've been doing that ever since the break-in. And you called me away from a lecture to remind me? You do still have my home number, don't you?"

"I—"

"It's you young guys, is what it is. Every generation more spoiled than the one before it. If you want something you want it right now, no waiting at all. You especially. On top of being impatient you are impetuous. In fact, probably the most impetuous student I ever taught. Well, what is it now? I mean in particular. Surely there is something *in particular* for you to get me out of class."

"I want you to contact the Italian authorities and get permission to take a sample of the Ancient Man's sperm."

There was a moment of silence, then Baringer's exploding voice: "My God, you have lost your mind. You want to destroy my reputation."

"You handled all the negotiations. You have a better rapport with them than I do."

"Based on respect for my credentials, Cameron. I ask for something like that and they're not only going to want the body sent back immediately, they're going to be calling the State Department and telling them to send somebody down here with a net."

"That will be one of the eventual tests anyway. There will be samples taken from several places on the body. I just want one taken from the testicles, the DNA analyzed—now."

"I thought my condescending manner would bring you back to your senses. You really are serious, aren't you?"

"I wouldn't have called if I weren't serious."

"No, I don't mean serious about the sample being taken. I mean you really believe the sperm could be viable—what do you think it was made of back then, stainless steel?"

"We'll know for certain after testing."

"Cameron, presently some highly regarded people in our field are wondering if we are somehow perpetrating a hoax. Until this moment that bothered me. Now, I'm not certain I don't prefer that over being ridiculed."

"I—"

"Say no more. We are partners. I'll contact them. But I'm damn sure going to phrase the request differently than you have. Maybe I can convince them we need to test the area where the intruder worked to see if any bacteria might have accidentally been implanted when the incision was made. I've worried about that. We can take a look at the DNA then. But it's going to take a couple of weeks at the least to get all the paperwork out of the way—assuming they go along with the request. Maybe longer. I'm certain they will want to send a representative over when the sample is taken. I'm wondering if you can last that long without going completely crazy."

Cameron smiled as he replaced the receiver.

But after two weeks had passed and the Italians hadn't yet even officially responded to Baringer's request, and it was now time for the exhibit to move on to New York, he became even more exasperated. He didn't know if his constant wondering could be considered intellectual curiosity, obsession, or madness—like Baringer said. He shook his head in irritation, looked back at his desk to make certain he wasn't forgetting anything, and walked from the classroom.

Mary's eyes were wide as she stared down at her abdomen, distended into a large mound. Her vision swirled. She lay her head back onto the pillow. Moving her legs to try and get more comfortable she felt the sharp pain from the handcuffs locked around her ankles, heard the sound of the chains rubbing against the foot of the bed frame. *God, help me.*

Still moving slowly so the awful dizziness wouldn't increase, she turned her head to the side and looked at Dr. Anderson sitting in the easy chair he had pulled into her bedroom.

"Please," she said. "I'm so sick."

He raised his face from a paperback novel and smiled softly. "You're going to be fine," he said. "Trust me." He looked toward the television he had placed on the card table for her. The fuzzy image of a horse and rider in a cowboy hat galloped through the clutter of poor reception. There was no sound.

"Want me to turn the volume so you can hear it?" he asked.

She slowly turned her head back to stare up at the ceiling. As she did, she felt a cramp in her stomach. Her throat tightened. Several minutes passed, then several more. She began to relax—and felt it again. *God!* She closed her eyes. She was so scared. She looked back to the doorway.

"Please, Dr. Anderson, please. Please let me go to the hospital. I'm starting to have the baby."

Cameron arrived at the Convention Center about forty-five minutes after he left the university. The overall-clad workmen had already removed everything from the exhibit room except for the display case containing the Man. Now they hoisted it slowly on to a long, flat gurney.

As well trained and careful as they were, Cameron almost cringed. One slip, smashing the glass panels, and it would be like several guillotines slicing through the body. Dr. Baringer had said their best chance for attracting independent funding outside of the foundations would come out of the city-to-city tour. Maybe some philanthropist interested in paleontology would take pity on them. He had written a special funding plea in the pamphlets that were made available to each person who came to view the man. *Well, a slip with the glass and they could have several tours at the same time.* Cameron smiled, more because the men now had the case securely in place on the gurney than at his attempt at humor.

The man in charge of security at the Center walked up to him. "Another exhibit safely on its way," the man said. "I am sorry about the break-in. We have started keeping the surveillance cameras on at night since then. If they had been running at the time, we'd already have the bastard who hit poor Edgar. You know he lost partial vision in one eye."

Cameron looked at the wall to his left and back to his right. The man pointed toward a ventilation grill near the top of a far wall. "There's one in every exhibit room. They're all concealed."

Cameron felt his pulse quicken. "Do you keep the tapes?"

"Until an exhibit has been checked out as leaving here in good condition—nothing missing or damaged. That's what they're for, really, for insurance purposes. If something is damaged by one of the patrons, or stolen, we have them on video."

"I want to see the one from the day of the break-in."

"We didn't have it on at night then, I told you."

"No, not the man who hit the night watchman. A man who was here that afternoon—before I left."

Dr. Anderson stood at the foot of the bed watching Mary squirm. He had only one concern remaining.

Could the irradiated living sperm he used to elicit fertilization have worked while the full complement of the Ancient Man's DNA *hadn't* achieved transfection? Could the child in fact now only have the benefit of the one full set of chromosomes from the egg?

If not enough of the male chromosomes had been transferred, she would have aborted immediately, at least by the time the bastula had started forming and found itself missing much of its building blocks.

But what was enough? What if there were sufficient DNA transferred to effect the formation of the fetus and cause a birth, but not enough for the child to be normal? There had been births where a child lacked one chromosome. He had read the theory that the lack of a key gene could lead to deviant behavior. What about the lack of several genes? What if the child were born mad? What if its features were distorted? He could not have that for proof.

Mary groaned loudly, yanking him from his thoughts. The chains dragged across the bed as she moved her legs in agony. She looked up at him. Suddenly her eyes widened and she screamed loudly as she raised as far as the straps across her chest would allow her.

Cameron stood in the small security viewing room and stared at the grainy image from the video tape running on a small screen in front of him. He saw the man stop behind the woman and her child.

"Stop it there!"

As the image froze, the security guard operating the video recorder looked up at him. "Which one are you looking at?"

"The tall man in the black suit."

"That's Dr. Anderson."

Cameron stared at the guard. "You know him?"

"He's by here all the time. Always wearing that same suit. A cheapskate like you wouldn't believe. He told me he used to sit through a movie two or three times to get his money's worth. But he said he found he could get more enjoyment here at the center. He could see everything then go back and look at just what he wanted to rather than having to sit through a whole movie waiting to get to the part he was interested in. Every time I saw him after that I thought about buying him a bag of popcorn and a Coke."

Cameron had tried to keep his excitement from showing as the man talked. Now he made sure his voice was level. "What's his first name?"

"I don't have any idea. He introduced himself as Dr. Anderson."

* * *

Dr. Anderson looked down at the child in his arms. It was a boy, a normal child in every respect, except the bright blond hair was much thicker than he would have thought a newborn's to be.

Mary suddenly bucked and screamed, startling him, nearly causing him to drop the boy.

She screamed again.

His eyes widened at the sight of the second child.

At a pay telephone near the Convention Center's entrance, Cameron turned quickly to the yellow pages, looking for medical professions.

"Dr. Malone." It was the security guard who had operated the video machine. "I remember him saying he was a history teacher," the guard said. "If that helps you any."

Cameron closed his eyes in irritation. Not a medical doctor, not someone in the medical field, but a Ph.D. There would be dozens of ordinary Andersons in the directory. *Shit!* he thought, and then as quickly wondered why he cared so much. He had the name. The video tape showed the face clearly. The cops could do the rest.

But on the other hand, Lieutenant Warrington had ignored him to the point of never calling him back, even after saying he would. How much stock would the lieutenant now put in a call telling him the name of the man who had been at the Convention Center the afternoon preceding the break-in?

In fact, how much stock could he himself put in that? A thin man simply stopped for a moment in the exhibit room just before a thin man broke into the exhibit? But there was also the tight dark suit in both instances. It could be.

Then again, why the sudden surge in excitement he felt? Because the man who had broken into the exhibit had personally affronted him by the break-in? The excitement of the chase?

He smiled. Maybe again like Baringer had said—crazy.

And then a sudden thought among the wonder. There would be dozens of different Andersons in the phone directory, but, maybe . . . a long shot at best, but it would take only a moment to check. He opened the directory to the residential listings.

There was one Dr. Anderson listed without either the designation physician or DDS following his name—a chiropractor or a Ph.D. A Dr. Noel Anderson—listed as living in Whitehaven.

Dr. Anderson, his forehead covered with a light sheen of perspiration, his eyebrows knitted in confusion, placed the second baby into the crib next to the first child and stared down at them. Both boys—but not identical. The second child had the same bright blond hair as the first, the same slightly protruding chin. But the chin didn't protrude quite as much. And there was a difference in size, the first child was slightly longer and stockier than the second. *But it couldn't be.* He had fertilized only one egg. Twins from one egg *had* to be identical.

Cameron turned down a narrow residential street in Whitehaven, an older area of Memphis pressed tightly against the Mississippi state line to the south. As he drove by the address provided in the telephone directory for Dr. Noel Anderson, he saw there was no car in the garage of the small, redbrick house. The grass inside a short, cyclone wire fence encircling the house stood several inches tall, wilted and brown. A sign on the fence had KEEP OUT printed in big block letters with a magic marker, but the gate to the yard was open, tilted over at an angle with weeds growing up through it. Dr. Anderson could very well be in class right now but, all in all, it looked as if the house hadn't been occupied in some time.

He drove by the house again, then a third time, then pulled to the curb and parked.

He sat there for several minutes, staring at the house, thinking, interspersing that with idle glances at the heavy, dark clouds moving in east over the Mississippi River toward the city.

The cloud bank began to occlude the sun, the area growing darker. A gust of wind came down the street, rustling the yellowing leaves of the occasional big oaks along the pavement. The weeds sticking up through the tilted gate in front of Anderson's weaved. An amusing scenario went through his mind.

Adrian was right, Anderson had stolen a sperm sample to use in an attempt to bring back a half prehistoric man, half human. He had dumped the sperm contents into an egg; a gross deformity had ensued, a long-tailed monster with sharp teeth had sprung from the incubator, seizing Anderson by the throat. The gate now tilted and weeds grew in the yard because there was no longer anyone alive to keep the place up; the creature now prowled the rooms, looking out the windows for who would come inside next.

He smiled. There really had been a new strain of cow found recently in Vietnam's jungles, a calf that appeared for all the world to be a throw back to prehistoric times.

An armored, prehistoric fish, thought extinct for a million years, had been caught only a few years before off the Philippines.

Both of these instances were fact, not fantasy. What had Adrian said? *"So not everything in your profession is so pat, is it?"*

Something could be known that wasn't everyday knowledge—a large percentage of the commercial discoveries over the years had been made by people working out of their homes. Couldn't there also be a scientific discovery made in that fashion?

But he was putting the cart before the horse. Was the Dr. Anderson who lived in the house he was staring at a thin man who owned a black suit, or a short, stocky man who taught PE at a local high school?

It wouldn't take the police long to find out. *If they didn't have a hundred more important things to check on.*

He was already there. He would instantly recognize the face if it was the same one that appeared on the tape. It would be easy enough to explain to whoever opened the door that he was a private detective looking through the neighborhood for a man behind in his child support. If, in fact, anybody did still live there. He opened his door.

At the house, no one answered his ring of the door bell. He pushed the button again. After his third attempt without any response, he glanced at the house next door. One of the neighbors would know where Anderson taught—and if he were skinny or fat.

But before he stepped away from the door, on impulse he tried the doorknob. It turned.

He hesitated a moment, then cracked the door open. A small living room area greeted him, empty, without even a stick of furniture.

His eyes narrowed, he edged the door open farther. He saw the entrance to a breakfast room and kitchen. There was no table, nothing on the counters.

He glanced over his shoulder up and down the darkening street, then slowly pushed the door the rest of the way open.

"Anybody home!" he shouted, then stepped quickly inside and shut the door behind him.

A moment later, inside the dark interior of the house, the electricity not working, he found that one of the bedrooms did have a bed frame and bare mattress, but there were no clothes in its closets and no toiletries in the bathroom.

He walked into the kitchen and looked at the layer of dust covering the counter tops and the dusty space where the refrigerator had been. He moved to a garbage can at an end of the counter.

Peering down into its dark interior, he saw it was half full of trash. A stench came from it. He reached his hand down inside the can and lifted out a small, rigid paper packet, its lid curled back.

It was the kind of fast meal container one placed into the microwave to cook its contents—a vegetarian meal, in this case. The remnants of vegetables sticking to the inside of the container were dried hard and black. He laid the packet on the counter and brushed his hands together.

Next, he went into the utility room at the end of the kitchen. There, in a corner illuminated by what little light was coming through the room's sole window, he saw a small, white card lying in a corner.

He picked it up and turned it over. The black, block lettering at its center read:

> DR. NOEL C. ANDERSON. PH.D.
> ASSISTANT CHIEF OF RESEARCH
> GENETICS DEVELOPMENT, INC.

"I want to hold my babies," Mary said weakly from the bed. It was the fourth or fifth time she had said the same thing, each time interrupting his thoughts. He stared back at her face, as pale gray as her pillow case.

"Please, Dr. Anderson," she begged. He heard the choking sound in her voice, and that did bother him.

His eyes briefly closing in irritation, he lifted the larger child from the crib and carried it to her.

"I want to hold my other baby, too," Mary said as she folded the child to her breast.

He went back to the crib and lifted the second boy into his arms. Identical twins, yet not identical, he thought for the hundredth time. The rapid gestation—he had thought about that a million times. His mind swirled in confusion. Then he saw the look on Mary's face. "What?" he asked.

"His head!" she said.

He saw nothing unusual, no mark of any kind. "What do you mean?"

At his words, the child at her breast rotated his head toward him, completely in control of his neck muscles.

"See!" Mary exclaimed.

The child in his arms moved and Anderson looked down at him. The baby stared back at him with deep dark eyes—focused eyes.

"What have you done?" Mary sobbed.

The child at her breast made a strange guttural sound. The one in his arms followed with a more normal sound of a baby.

He suddenly realized he didn't want to take the child to Mary. He didn't want her to be holding the one she held, either. She was weak. She could drop him, hurt him. He turned and moved back toward the crib, lay the child on the small mattress and walked back to Mary and reached for the one in her arms.

She shook her head.

"It's best, Mary," he said softly. He pulled the baby from her despite her trying to hang onto him. "You need your rest."

He studied the face of the child all the way to the crib. After he placed him on the mattress, he walked back to Mary's bed. She looked up at him with eyes that appeared clouded. "Dr. Anderson, I want to hold my other baby for a minute, too. Please."

He smiled softly down at her. "I think it would be best if you tried to go to sleep now, Mary. I'll watch your babies for you."

She shook her head. But the movement was very weak. Her color was absolutely gone. The lower half of the satin sheet had turned dark with her slow hemorrhaging. Her mouth opened, but she didn't say anything. He smiled and patted her hand, then returned to the far wall and began to slide the crib from her room.

Mary said something, but he didn't pay any attention, engrossed as he was in not shaking the children too hard as he moved the crib out of the room.

When he shut her door behind him, he heard her call out weakly, then heard a loud thud as she fell from her bed. As he pushed the crib down the hall toward his room, he could hear the chains yanking against the foot of Mary's bed. By the time he had reached his door, all sound from her room had ceased.

CHAPTER 11

By the time Cameron drove from Anderson's house to east Memphis and out highway 78 to the sprawling, concrete block structure housing the offices of Genetic Development, Inc., it was well after 5 P.M. But the owner, a middle-aged, affable man with a thick beard, hadn't left yet.

"This was Anderson's office," he said as he swung back the door to a tiny room furnished with only a small desk, a straight-back chair, and a line of old wooden shelves beside the desk.

"Like I said, he turned in his resignation a couple of months ago and left for a research job at a small university in the northeast. I knew that was going to happen if he ever got an offer. There's no doubt about how brilliant he is. And that's all he ever talked about when he could be drawn into a conversation—doing research for some university. But I wasn't really sure he would ever get an offer. Not if they held an interview and got a good look at him first—and saw how he thought. Are you with the police?"

Up to that point, he hadn't asked why information was being sought about Dr. Anderson. Cameron looked back at him, sizing him up for the kind of story he would want to hear before disclosing anything further. But the man had seemed nice enough and confident in his manner. There was no need to lie, he decided.

"No, I'm not with the police, only interested in what happened to him. I'm a scientist, too."

When the man didn't immediately respond, Cameron added, "But I am in contact with the police," *A little leverage couldn't hurt.* "You said 'how he thought'?"

The man still didn't speak. Finally, he said, "I just told you he took a job with a university in the northeast. What do you mean, what happened to him?"

"He didn't show up at that job."

"Didn't show up?"

"No. You were saying—'how he thought'?"

"He didn't think conventionally—about a lot of things. When he told me he hadn't been out with a woman since he was in college—that's the first time I looked up. He owned only two suits. Told me he didn't see any need for more, only needed one to wear while the other was being cleaned. I paid him a good salary, and yet he brought his lunch in a brown paper bag every day—said he couldn't afford to go out to the buffet like the rest of us. And one for the books, considering his field—he didn't believe in evolution either. In fact that was his big thing, said that all the other geneticists were in on some kind of conspiracy. And I don't mean he was some kind of Christian fundamentalist, either. He said they were both just theories—creation and evolution. I often wanted to ask him where it all did start then—in the very beginning. But thought better of getting into that kind of conversation with him. Once he started on that subject, you almost couldn't shut him up. Squirrely, all right, but I guess he covered up at whatever interview he had to take." His forehead suddenly wrinkled. "You're a private detective, aren't you? The family has you looking for him."

Cameron put on a sheepish look and nodded slowly. "Yes, but they didn't want the word to get out that he had disappeared. Not at least until they know a little more."

The man nodded his understanding. "I can see that. Knowing Anderson he might have just decided to do nothing for a couple of months. That happened once here, believe it or not, at least for three days—and right in the middle of our busy season. When he finally showed back up for work he said he had just decided to take off for a while. He later told one of the men here that what really happened was he got lost and couldn't find his way back here. You know, like lost it mentally for three days. Man he told said he figured Anderson slipped him that because he wanted it to get back to me. Was afraid I was going to fire him, and thought it'd make me sympathetic if I thought he had mental problems. You believe which ever story you care to. Like I said, he's strange, all right.''

Cameron moved into the tiny office. Shelves against the wall held papers and folders of every size, many of them dusty. A stack of magazines were piled high on the very top of the shelves. He walked to the shelves and lifted the top magazine from the stack. It was a several-months-old issue of *Progressive Farmer.*

''We co-op advertise in it with some of the big seed companies,'' the man said from the doorway. ''Don't know what real good it does for us. We don't deal with farmers directly. But like I said, it's co-op, and the companies pay near a hundred percent of the cost, so I don't see that it hurts any, either.''

Cameron looked back at the man. ''You deal only in plant genetics?''

''Only seed crops—mostly. Every now and then we'll do research on a grass. Once worked with a company into trees.''

''No animal experimentation then?''

The man shook his head. ''That's big company stuff.''

Cameron lifted another magazine from the stack and fanned through it. Again it had to do with farming.

''Did Anderson's father hire you?'' the man asked.

''Yes.''

''Then you know what Anderson's like.''

When Cameron looked back at the man, he explained. ''His father called here once, reversed the charges from Blytheville, Arkansas. Just like his son, expecting me to pay for it."

The telephone rang in the man's office, but he ignored it. "Talked to me a bit when he found out his son wasn't in. Now wouldn't you be embarrassed if I caught you reversing the charges? But not him. That's like Anderson, too; nothing perturbed him. Like when he showed back up for work, walked in here like he'd just stepped out a minute for a leak."

The telephone rang again. "Noel, senior, and Noel, junior—two peas out of the same pod."

As Cameron lifted another magazine from the stack, the telephone rang for the third time. The man looked across his shoulder. "Excuse me," he said, "let me catch that. Might be some kind of order."

As the man disappeared back into the hallway, Cameron glanced through the magazine, then laid it back on top of the stack and walked around to the rear of Anderson's desk where he opened its center drawer.

The inside was stuffed full of pens and pencils, paper clips and staples and what looked like a half box worth of wadded Kleenexs.

The big top drawer on the right of the desk contained a dead plant in a plastic pot.

He opened the bottom drawer. A lone, glossy magazine lay at its bottom. It was another genetics magazine, no different from several of the ones lying in the stack on top of the shelves. He lifted it from the drawer. It opened to a spot where it had been opened many times before.

A page had been torn out.

Dr. Anderson sat on the edge of the bed and stared into the crib at the two blonds. *Only hours old,* he thought, and their degree of muscular control beyond comprehension—turning their heads and focusing their eyes immediately upon birth, able to crawl within minutes. What would be next? he wondered, and was immediately answered as the larger child rolled to his stomach and, pushing his hands against the mattress, lifted his upper body, pulled a knee under him, and slowly came to his feet. He tottered, steadied, and walked to the crib's wooden rail.

Anderson, his hand unsteady, raised his tape recorder to his mouth:

"The larger child seems to be the one to first take each succeeding step in their development—taking his bottle, rolling to his stomach, sitting up in the crib. Then his brother always immediately—"

He stopped speaking as the second blond struggled to his feet at the center of the pen and, holding his bottle tightly in both hands, walked tottering toward his brother at the rail.

"Then his brother always immediately follows. The smaller child has at this moment risen to his feet and walked across the crib to his brother, who only a moment before did the same. Still, I am not yet ready to concede the larger child as the more advanced of the two. For one thing his progression toward speaking seems to be less advanced than his brother, as he has yet to voice anything but a guttural sound, a noise somewhat similar to the harsh low growl of a dog. I hope there is not a physical problem associated with his speaking ability!"

The library closest to Cameron's apartment didn't have a copy of the same issue of the genetic magazine he found in Anderson's desk drawer. He finally found the correct issue early the next morning at the University of Tennessee Medical School, and turned quickly to the page that had been torn from Anderson's copy.

On one side of the page was the continuation of an article about seedling corn. The other side contained a much shorter article, one discussing the merits of using an electro-gene pulser as opposed to chemical shock—*when moving DNA through an egg membrane.*

CHAPTER 12

After Cameron left the library and drove to the university, he took a few minutes before his first class to telephone the Criminal Justice Center. Neither Lieutenant Warrington's nor Sergeant Adrian Cumming's whereabouts were known. After asking to speak to any officer interested in the Convention Center break-in he was put on hold for a full two minutes, then a female officer answered, a Sergeant Joni Henderson. He told her about Dr. Noel Anderson being the man he had seen at the Convention Center, about the page torn out of the genetic magazine, and that the owner of Genetics Development had said Anderson had left for a position at a northeastern university.

Sergeant Henderson was silent for a moment.

"Let me talk to the lieutenant about this," she finally said. "I'll get back to you."

Of course she didn't, and after his last class he started toward Blytheville, Arkansas, driving along the miles of flat farmland stretching as far as the eye could see. Within an hour he had stopped at a service station off I-55 inside the town's city limits. He walked to a telephone booth where he opened the directory and found the proper address.

A few minutes later, not far from the old strategic air command base to the north of town, he stared at a small, white, wooden frame house—Mr. Noel C. Anderson, Sr.'s residence. Large oaks rose from the shallow front yard, and a concrete walk led up to the door.

He rang the doorbell and waited for a few seconds. Somebody was home since both a several-years-old blue Chrysler and a beige Taurus were parked in the driveway. As he started to push the doorbell a second time, the door opened and a slim, white-haired woman in a print dress smiled pleasantly at him.

"Mrs. Anderson?"

"Yes."

"I'm Cameron Malone—from Memphis."

Her smile broadened. "One of little Noel's friends?"

"No, ma'am, I'm with a magazine doing a story on genetics. I was in the area and thought I'd see if he might have come here over the weekend, or where he might be. No one answered at his home in Memphis."

"I have no idea how to get in touch with the boy. That's what I was just telling the police officer."

She had said *just*. "They called you today?"

"No," a voice said from behind the woman. "I came by."

It was Adrian. Before he could speak, she quickly added, "I told Mrs. Anderson how the department needed an expert on genetics to answer some questions on one of our cases."

The woman beamed proudly. Adrian smiled at his questioning expression. "Won't you come on in," the woman said.

He stepped inside the small living room, which was comfortably furnished with an old fabric couch, a coffee table, and a pair of leather recliner chairs. Adrian moved to the couch and sat on one end. She reached to the table for a glass of iced tea set on a napkin.

"Would you like a glass of tea?" Mrs. Anderson asked. "It's sun tea."

"It's good," Adrian said and nodded at him.

"Yes, please."

"Sweet or unsweet?"

"A little sugar would be fine."

The woman walked slowly toward a doorway off to the side of the room. Adrian waited until she was out of sight, then looked at him. "I didn't want her to know why we're looking for him, in case he does call here."

"Frankly, I'm surprised you're here."

"Why?"

"A break-in and assault, after this length of time. I just don't see it being in a high priority category."

"I could lie to you and tell you how dedicated we are. But the fact is, if the mayor hadn't been embarrassed because of it making the national news, I wouldn't be here. That and the fact you called and told Joni about the article in the genetics magazine. You got the captain a little curious. Still, you notice they didn't send one of the detectives to interview the woman. You still don't think it's possible to bring back something from sperm that old?"

"One in a million. A billion. If every condition is just right—and I can't see how that's possible."

"Oh, I see," she said in a theatrically serious voice. "You can't see, but no longer quite so pat, huh?"

He ignored the sarcasm. "I'm here, aren't I?"

"As a magazine reporter."

"I wanted to be able to ask questions without having to answer too many myself. What does your department think now?"

"What is there to think? Anderson was at the Center, but along with God knows how many others that day. Of course the other visitors didn't all tear out an article like that. But he is a geneticist. From the looks of his lab he obviously was into some animal research on his own. So I don't—"

He had silenced her by holding up his finger. "Wait a minute. Slow down. His lab?"

"He had a laboratory in his attic. There were test tubes filled with God only knows what. Marks where other equipment had sat. Captain brought a member of the UT medical staff over to Anderson's house. He said

Anderson was conducting tissue experiments." She smiled. "Modern tissues."

"I didn't think about an attic."

"You were at his house?"

"That's how I found out where he had worked. From a business card I found."

Adrian frowned. "Going into someone's house is pushing it a little. If you come up with anything else maybe you better call us first."

"That would be fine if anybody would ever call me back—you included."

Mrs. Anderson's coming back into the room kept Adrian from responding. The woman handed him a glass full of dark iced tea. "Might be a little strong," she said, "I use more tea bags than most."

He sipped from the glass. Strong was an understatement. And it was sugared so heavily it tasted almost syrupy.

"Good, isn't it?" Adrian said, and smiled.

"Perfect," he said.

The woman smiled and moved to an easy chair across from the couch. She took on a wistful look as she settled into it. "Little Noel will be so disappointed. Two honors like this in the same week—the police needing his opinion, and a magazine here to do a story on him. And he so yearns for honors."

"I would have thought a man of his preeminence would be used to this," Adrian said.

"That's sweet of you to say, miss, and he does deserve honors. He's so brilliant. But I'm afraid that's the one thing his life is lacking—praise." Her face suddenly twisted into a worried expression, and she looked back at him. "You wouldn't mention my saying that in your article, would you? I mean it sounds so negative."

"No, ma'am, I won't write a word about it. You were saying the one thing his life is lacking . . . "

"Praise. He was always so brilliant, did everything the teachers asked of him from the first grade on. A straight-A student, and of perfect deportment, too. But instead of praise, that created jealousy. The children. They taunted him. Even some of the parents—he was so far ahead of them mentally.

"But I told him not to pay any attention to that, his day would come. With his mind, it had to. And, to him, that meant research at one of the Ivy League schools when he finished with his doctorate. But he was never able to obtain employment at one of them. Not and do the kind of research in which he was most interested. He would go up for an interview, we would think it was promising, and then he would come back without an offer.

"He said it was always the research—they just wouldn't let him do it. That's why he finally ended up taking the job with Genetic Development. Temporarily, he said at the time, but he's been there for years. It's so much less than what he deserved."

"Well, then you must be happy for him now," Adrian said, "with his finally getting to do work at a university."

The woman tilted her head questioningly. "I'm afraid I don't understand what you mean."

"The owner at Genetic Development said your son told him he was taking a research job at a university in the northeast."

The woman nodded. "I'm sure little Noel did say something like that. His pride, you know—especially after the kids around here teased him, and now are grown up and would know what he did. The job he took was one on an egg farm in Texas. The owner needed him to help develop a superior breed of layers. Raised his salary considerably and, next to wanting to do research at a college, that's always what little Noel has thought about most, making money, saving it, really. With big Noel on mental disability like he is, little Noel has always worried that he might find himself in some kind of situation like that and starve if he didn't have enough savings. It's hard to believe how conservative he is with his money. About the only thing he's ever splurged on is a car. He owns a Lincoln, a beautiful solid black one, says little cars are too dangerous. Never would think of calling us long-distance. A real waste of money, he always said.''

''You don't happen to know the name of the farm or the town where he's employed now?'' Adrian asked.

''I don't recall the name if he ever mentioned it. That doesn't sound like a very caring parent, does it? But so long as we get our letters, we know he's okay. That's how its always been.''

Cameron beat Adrian to the punch. ''You've received letters from him?''

''Oh, every quarter. With only Noel senior's disability check coming in, we couldn't keep our heads above water if it wasn't for little Noel's helping out. Tight as he is with his money, we are his family.''

He nodded. ''When did you receive your last letter.''

''A few weeks ago.''

''Three weeks,'' came a barely perceptible voice from within the hallway. ''Eighteen days, to be specific.'' A thin, stooped man with long white hair appeared at the hall's entrance. He wore a pair of yellow pajamas emblazoned with wildly colored cartoon characters and was barefoot, his feet long and skinny.

The woman smiled apologetically. ''Big Noel is a late riser,'' she said. ''He usually works all night.''

''Doing things,'' the man said.

Cameron glanced at Adrian.

''It was eighteen days ago,'' the man repeated. ''Had our two thousand dollars in it,'' he added.

The woman nodded. ''In cash. Little Noel always sends cash. I'm so worried it's going to be stolen some day.''

''Do you still have the envelope the money came in?'' Adrian asked.

''Got every one of them, from the first he ever sent. Keep them in his scrapbook.''

''From West Memphis,'' the man said. ''The envelope was postmarked in West Memphis.''

The woman looked up at her husband. "Why did you say that, Noel?"

"That's what they're wanting to know," he said, "or they wouldn't have asked."

"I don't understand what you mean," the woman said.

"Probabilities," the man came back. "You don't see that?"

When the woman didn't respond, he said, "You have my coffee ready?"

"No, Noel, these people came—"

Her husband had gestured back over his shoulder with his eyes.

She rose from her chair, smiled apologetically at them again, and said, "Excuse me." She walked in the direction of the kitchen.

The man looked at them. "Trouble with Noel, he has a gap."

"Excuse me?" Cameron said.

"A gap," the man repeated. "When he starts thinking in one direction, he ignores what doesn't fit with his thinking. How could any university want him to be doing research when they know he's going to ignore any result that doesn't mesh with his way of thinking? In other words, he sees only what he wants to be there." The man's eyes narrowed. "Do you understand what I mean?"

Cameron nodded. "Yes."

"If you don't, you weren't listening," the man said, and continued to stare at them. After a moment Adrian said, "We do understand." But that made no difference in the man's look. And then Mrs. Anderson was hurrying into the room with his cup of coffee.

When she gave it to him, he looked back at them for a moment then disappeared down the hallway.

Cameron came to his feet. "You wouldn't happen to have a photograph you could spare, do you—for the magazine?"

"Oh, surely," Mrs. Anderson said, and got him two from a drawer under a table lamp.

As they walked from the house and the woman closed the door behind them, Adrian looked back over her shoulder.

"Damn," she said. "A gap? There's more than that missing in that man's case."

Cameron handed her one of the photographs, keeping the other for himself.

CHAPTER 13

Dr. Anderson stood beside the crib and tried to get the larger infant to take his bottle. He had named him Cain, as he had named the smaller child Abel. What could be more fitting than bestowing on them the same names as the first children of the earth—both sets would have looked identical in every way important. All children from all time would. Smiling, nodding at his thought, he again pushed the bottle toward the child's mouth, and again Cain turned his head.

Anderson stepped back and looked down at the boy. This was a matter of deep concern to him: While Abel had taken immediately to a bottle, and in fact had one now, Cain had refused all but his first few offerings of formula, had refused to take any more over the last twenty-four hours. That couldn't continue. Could there be a stomach problem? What was he to do? Force-feed him?

Cain's lips suddenly tightened, and his eyes narrowed.

On the way back to Memphis, Adrian's beige Taurus followed close behind Cameron's Maxima. Through his rearview mirror he could see her constantly using the cellular phone he had handed her. When they stopped at a service station close to the West Memphis, Arkansas, exit, they met between the two cars.

Adrian shook her head. "The Crittenden County Sheriff's Department checked for his name at the water department, the electric and gas companies, and the post office. There is no Noel Anderson living in the county—at least not under his real name. I told the sheriff about the photograph. He said if we brought it to him he would have it circulated among his deputies. I guess that's about all we can do right now."

He was silent for a moment, his thoughts already on another subject. "He would have needed some equipment—some pretty expensive equipment. His bank would have copies of who he wrote checks to."

"Not a single check for any kind of equipment," Adrian said. "Lieutenant Warrington had his records checked. There was one interesting thing. He cleaned out his account a little over a week before the break-in. Two hundred thousand—all cash."

"Two hundred—"

"Uh huh. And what does a geneticist make? That kind of money, withdrawn in cash, caused Lieutenant Warrington to start thinking about dope dealing. He sent drug dogs over to Anderson's house, but they found no sign. We heard his mother talking about how tight he is. He could have legitimately had that kind of savings." She shook her head. "When you get down to it, we're back to nothing again—nothing that can't be explained away. He lied to his boss about what kind of job he was taking, but his mother said that was pride. And the letter, postmarked in West Memphis, the obvious direction he would have been driving leaving Memphis for Texas—that would be right at least. I guess next the department will try to confirm where he is in Texas and have somebody out there speak to him. The mayor's pressure should get at least that much done. I wonder how many chicken farms there are in Texas?"

Cameron shook his head, then glanced at his watch. "You hungry?" he asked.

"Uh huh, I am."

* * *

Cain grunted his guttural sound and pulled on the play-pen's rail. He began shaking it, raised his shoulders in a strained effort—as if he were trying to escape the confining quarters.

Anderson, trying to comprehend, set the bottle aside and reached for the boy, and the child immediately quieted.

Anderson lifted him from the pen and put him down on the floor. Now Abel made a sound, and Anderson reached back inside the pen and lifted him from it. Cain was already out in the hall, and Abel followed after him.

Anderson stepped into the hall and watched them move like surefooted elves down the corridor, past the back of the couch in the living room and on into the kitchen. In a moment they were shuffling back down the hall again, and went on past him. Reaching its end, they turned and started back again. They were exploring. Anderson smiled.

Now they were in the kitchen once more. They stopped in front of the refrigerator. Cain stepped close to it. Now Abel did. Their heads began moving back and forth. Cain stepped closer. Abel stepped closer. Cain's face leaned so close to the refrigerator his nose almost touched the door. He tilted his head to the side. Listening? Smelling? *Sensing?*

The two turned to face him. "More!" Cain suddenly said, the first word he had spoken.

Anderson walked slowly up the hall to the kitchen. As he neared the refrigerator the twins stepped to the side and turned to face it.

When he stopped and looked down at them, their faces tightened, and they looked up toward the freezer compartment.

Unsure, he raised his hand and opened the compartment.

They immediately pointed toward Mary's butcher paper-wrapped steaks.

"More!" they said in unison.

* * *

Adrian sipped from her tea, then looked at the glass. "This tastes like water after what Mrs. Anderson served us." She lifted her sandwich from her plate, but hesitated before moving it to her mouth. "Why do you just call him Ancient Man? Every other discovery I read about was given a name."

"That's the name we gave him. Rather Baringer did. He said that a discovery that far back in time couldn't be called anything else, that he had to be the quintessential ancient man, the benchmark for all time. So he remains both in fact and name, *the* Ancient Man."

She smiled, her soft smile—and her big eyes, all of her attracting him in a way he had never thought possible. He had a strong rule when it came to married women. A hard, fast rule—stay away. Yet if there was ever a woman born who could get him to go against all he believed in . . . Christ, he thought, and stood.

She stared up at him.

He forced an apologetic smile. "Sorry, but I'm going to have to run. I have an appointment . . . with a student."

The wind blew gently across the damp, flat fields behind the old farmhouse, the tall weeds that dotted the fields weaving slowly in the dim light of the halfmoon. Dr. Anderson, his arms spread under the bloody, sheet-wrapped body of Mary, came around a rear corner of the house. He stopped halfway to the front of the house, just under the only window to that side.

Behind the window panes, two pale foreheads appeared above the sill, two sets of dark eyes stared down as Anderson laid Mary's body on the ground and picked up the shovel he had earlier used to dig a shallow trench there.

CHAPTER 14

Cameron stood at the pay telephone down the hallway from his classroom. "Lieutenant Warrington, please."

"Sorry, sir, but he's not in."

Christ, did the man never work? He struggled a moment. "What about Sergeant Cummings—Adrian Cummings?"

In a few seconds her voice came across the line. "This is Sergeant Cummings."

"Adrian. I was—"

"Oh, hey, Cameron. I was just thinking about you. We received a fax from the FBI a few minutes ago. There's no Dr. Anderson working at any chicken farm of any description in Texas, at any kind of farm—at least not under that name."

And that took until the end of November to find out —two damn months since they were in Blytheville? There would be withholding taxes held from Anderson's paycheck, his driver's license, a lot of other ways for the government computers to find all the Noel C. Andersons in Texas in a matter of minutes. Then the elimination process wouldn't have taken that long. Not if they really wanted to find somebody. No wonder criminals thought they had a free rein. But, even worse, there would probably have been no report at all except for Dr. Baringer. "What I was calling to tell you, Adrian, was that Baringer said he had called Washington last week, got a couple of senators to promise they would see what they could do for us. I guess they just did.''

His last words came out in a tone more sarcastic than he meant for them to. But what the hell.

"I understand your frustration, Cameron, but we've got more crime in Memphis than we can really get to adequately. A simple breaking and entering—"

"I know. Well, anyway, you know now he lied about where he went. What's next? Or is there anything next?"

"It's like I told you, we only have so many officers in the department. It won't be forgotten, though."

And then she added, "I'm sorry, Cameron, I really am." His irritation at the Memphis police doing nothing, lost out to the softness of her voice in his ear now, in his mind a dozen times since he had met her. And then her next words:

"How about our getting together for a free lunch on the police department—meaning me. Sort of my apology to you."

He knew better than to even contemplate that, especially with how he already felt, and yet a "yes" was on the tip of his tongue when she spoke again. "You're not married, are you?"

He stood there confused.

"Cameron?"

"Yeah. I . . . no, I mean, no, I'm not." Her asking him if he were married? Why, unless . . .

"I knew you weren't," she went on. "I didn't see anything in your file about a wife. But with what I've just gone through I'm going to be sure. Even for lunch."

"You're not married?"

"Thought I was, for six years. Turned out I wasn't, though, just the particular one he went home to at night. I'm divorced now."

"Adrian, I thought . . . " What had he thought? He had been told—but who the hell cared. "Lunch is a deal." He looked at his watch. He had a class at one-thirty. The hell with it too. "You are talking about to-day, aren't you?"

He heard her light chuckle. "Cameron, you are wacky. I think you're getting ready to tell me you had other plans when you didn't answer, and now your voice suddenly sounds like you can't wait. Men—you especially. No, I didn't mean today. It's twelve-thirty already, I've already eaten. I meant *one* day."

"What about dinner then, tonight—on me."

Eight hours later, she repeated how "wacky" he was after he told her why he thought she had been married. "Maybe you should have asked me," she said.

"Adrian, how was I supposed to know the officer would say something like that if it wasn't true?"

"One of Gerald's buddies. Or any of them, I guess. They stick together, and he's big into this is just tempo-rary between us. Besides the divorce was just final a couple of weeks ago. When you called, the guy was technically right—I guess I still was Mrs. Cummings. But he knew better."

He thought about the time he had wasted. He looked across the table at her. She had her hair down, the first time he had seen her that way, its ends resting gently on the shoulders of a white blouse. As beautiful as she had been with it up, she was even more so with her face framed by its thick, dark fullness. She had to have done something special to her eyes for the night; they were not merely captivating now, but drawing him into them.

As she finished her wine, he lifted the bottle and leaned toward her to refill her glass.

"You trying to get me where you can take advan-tage?" she asked and smiled.

"I was counting on my charm to handle that."

"There really is something to that, Cameron—alco-hol, not your charm. I read where it causes an increase in the estrogen flow in a woman's body."

"That sounds clinical enough to take the romance out of it."

"The bottom line's the same," she said. "But I warn you, I'm a strong woman."

He smiled. "Now that sounds a lot better—bumps, bruises. Maybe we're getting someplace."

She frowned a little. "I meant I'm not easily influenced—by charm or alcohol." Then she shook her head. "You know I say that, and yet here I am kidding around like this. An hour ago I wouldn't have—before the wine. And just so you don't get any wrong ideas, I am only kidding around."

"Not a single wrong idea anywhere in my mind," he said, then smiled again. "You think we need one more bottle?"

"Cameron."

And that was how the rest of the dinner went, bantering back and forth, saying absolutely nothing of any substance, almost like they were a couple of silly teenagers on a date. But, somehow, he recognized that was what she wanted, maybe because of the stress of her job. He could imagine what a cop, any cop, had to face each day on the street. A little silliness was probably what a doctor would have ordered for her.

A little after midnight, he escorted her up the stairs and down her apartment landing to her door. She turned to face him and draped her arms over his shoulders. "It was a lot of fun, Cameron. Thank you." She kissed him gently, and then didn't move her face back but a couple of inches, her eyes staring into his. He kissed her, then harder, and her lips parted wider, and he pulled her against him, feeling the tight outline of her body against his. She broke the kiss before he did, and placed her hands against his chest.

"Thank you, again. It really was a great night."

He nodded, leaned forward to peck her lips gently, then stepped back from her.

But she still made no attempt to turn toward her

door, making it apparent she wasn't going to until he was on his way.

Then a mischievous smile crossed her face and she turned sideways and theatrically placed her hands over the lock and knob of the door, and looked back at him.

"Strong," she said. "I told you."

He smiled and shook his head in amusement. "Goodnight, Adrian."

As he moved down the landing toward the steps to the parking lot, he heard her opening her door, and then she called after him.

"Really did enjoy it."

Dr. Anderson laid awake in his bed, occasionally hearing the twins pass by his door. How did they go so long without sleep? They never looked tired. And their size now, growing from the day they had been born as if each minute had been an hour—already the size of preteens. The fish crawled out of the sea and eventually became mankind, according to the evolutionists. Was there something to that after all? Fish, many of them, had their babies after only weeks of gestation, the young often growing to full term in only months. If there were evolvement into monkeys and birds and all else, then was that any less strange than different types of humans evolving into creatures with different gestation periods, different growth rates?

And then he shook his head in disgust with himself. Here he was looking to evolution for an answer, the very theory he had proved wrong. Look at their faces, their bodies, no different from any others now. And just because he still had some questions, here he was mentally taking the same path the prehistorians took, change over centuries, evolution—the easy way out. No, not him, yet there was so much to learn about them. But so tired. So tired from trying to keep up with them, recording everything he could on his tape recorder or video camera.

And then, his bed soft, the twins now silent, without meaning to, he fell asleep.

A moment later there was movement outside his room, and then his door slowly cracked open, remained that way for a moment, then slowly shut again.

A few seconds later, the back door to the house closed silently.

In seconds, Cain and Abel, short and stocky with thick blond hair, stood among the weeds in the field behind the house. Their heads rotated slowly back and forth. Suddenly they froze, both staring in the same direction. They began to move in that direction, slowly at first, then gaining speed. In a moment they were trotting.

The gray white of a rabbit's fur dashed out from behind a clump of tall grass—and they were after it.

Cameron, his head propped in his hands on his pillow, looked at the first ray of light coming through his bedroom window. His first thoughts after lying down were of his date with Adrian, but that had passed quickly, and ever since he had thought of Anderson—was he the one? And why in hell do I care so much if he is? Obsessed with it—the sample, who took it, why? Was he that upset because someone had violated his discovery? Or was he thinking more along the lines that some use could be made of the sample that would upstage the discovery itself—*his* discovery? Was it just disgust that the Memphis police seemed not to care all that much? Why else would he have jumped in his car and made the trip to Blytheville, and then, ever since, felt a compelling urge to do more?

But, though he was sure everything passing through his mind was part of his compelling urge to act, no one thought brought a definitive yes. Nothing seemed to be the single overriding factor in his compulsion. Maybe it was simply what brought him into paleontology in the first place—the mystery of things unknown. The excitement. His wonder at what really was out there to be discovered. A challenge.

If he could just figure out how to go forward with the game.

CHAPTER 15

Cameron stepped from his car. He looked out over the weed-filled fields to that side of the river. He felt foolish and excited at the same time. He walked toward the front of the old wooden store.

He passed the Coke machine setting on the porch jutting out from the building and stepped inside. A thin, gray-haired man in a pair of overalls leaned jackknifed over a worn, wooden counter, his narrow, whisker-stubbled face in his hands.

"Howdy," he said, straightening and flashing a toothless grin. "What does that there Maxima get a gallon?"

"Twenty something miles on the highway."

"Figured that. I mean I figured it got more'n mine. On its last legs, I been tellin' Edna. Old Buick's been a good one, but it's just over the hill now. But she won't hear of our buyin' anuther one; says we need to save the money for our burial, not have to be worrying about burdening the kids with somethin' like that after we're gone. Me, I say after I'm gone, how am I gonna be worryin' about any burden I left behind." The toothless smile flashed again. "So what can I do you for?"

Cameron held out the photograph of Dr. Anderson. "You haven't seen him before, have you?"

"What's he wanted for?"

"Nothing really. It's a family matter."

"I see," the man said, and scratched the stubble at his

chin. "Nothin' really, huh? No, haven't. Least not in person."

"Excuse me?"

"Sheriff's deputy was by with that same picture there a few weeks back. Family matter, huh?" His eyes ran up and down Cameron's sport coat and slacks. "FBI?"

"No."

"Not gonna say, huh? Well that's all right too. Ain't none of my business no how. You want to leave your number? That's what the deputy did."

"I can leave the photo here if you don't mind. My name and number is on the back."

"Don't mind none," the man said, holding out his hand for the photograph.

Once back outside on the wooden porch, Cameron stared down the gravel road and then the paved one intersecting with it. He looked at his watch, up at the bright sun, then walked toward his car.

That night, coming back from eating dinner, Adrian hesitated at her apartment door, then surprised him by opening it and stepping inside in front of him. As he shut the door behind them, she walked toward the small kitchen off to one side of the living room.

"I bought a bottle of wine," she said back over her shoulder.

He stood where he was for a moment, then walked to the small coffee table at the back of the room, went around it, and lowered himself to the couch there. In a few seconds, Adrian walked toward him with two half-filled plastic wine glasses.

"Not the ultimate in drinking utensils," she said as she handed him one. "But cheap. And on a cop's salary . . . " She touched her glass to his, then settled down a couple of feet away from him.

"And how was your day?" she asked.

"I had fifty copies made of Anderson's photograph."

She wrinkled her forehead questioningly.

"I wrote my name and number on them and gave them out in West Memphis today."

"Cameron."

"My father always said if you wanted something done right you needed to do it yourself." He smiled. "Seriously, its been over two months since you gave the Crittenden County sheriff his photograph. You said yourself what kind of priority your department was giving to finding him. What kind of priority do you think Anderson is to law enforcement in Arkansas? He's probably in Texas mating chickens to ducks or something, but I thought I'd use a little of my spare time to find out if somebody had seen him come into a grocery store, a service station, something. If he's over there he wouldn't be hiding even if he is the one who broke into the case. He wore a hood and gloves. He wouldn't think anybody would know it was him."

"Cameron, if he is the one—he's nuts. He has to be. How do you know what a nut might do? A clay bust was used on the watchman. A gun might be used on you."

"Adrian, whoever took the sample did so for a specific reason. Genetic experimentation is growing like wildfire, with no real rules set out yet—everybody basically just doing whatever they want to. Could the real nut have been a man or a company that knows something they haven't released yet? Anderson's boss and his mother said that his dream was to work in research. He is bound to have contacted companies as well as universities. What if he ran into a company that did know something we don't? Was working on something?"

"Like what?"

"If I knew that, I wouldn't be thinking about it all the time. But in any case, I didn't see how it would hurt to take a few photos over there and see if somebody might have seen him. I've already run some of the rural roads and driven through about every neighborhood I can find. You know I don't have to actually see *him*. I might spot his Lincoln."

"What's its license number?"

"I don't have the slightest idea."

"I'll make you a deal, Cameron. I'll get the number and take off tomorrow afternoon and go over there with you. One time. We do all the rest of the looking you want, then that's the end of it. At least nothing else without telling me first."

Dr. Anderson, relaxed now after several hours sleep, listened to the twins moving past his door. He smiled softly. His twins. His mother had told him of the joy of childbirth, but he would have never guessed in a million years if he hadn't experienced it himself. Still smiling, he reached to turn on his favorite relaxation. Soon the sound of voices over the police-band scanner and the newscaster's high-pitched tone as he announced the next day's weather over the AM radio swelled from his room.

Suddenly the sound of the newscaster ceased.

All that could be heard was two sheriff's deputies talking back and forth through the night.

The first one said, "This Dr. Malone character said he saw him at the Convention Center right before the break-in."

"So what?"

"So we got a pointy head intellectual type saying something that don't mean nothing even if it is true. Then Memphis hands it over here to us to check out—like they got some lead that Anderson moved over here. You know what it really is, don't you? Memphis didn't want to mess with it in the first place. But some high muckety-muck didn't want to take a chance on making some bigger shot mad, so they find some reason to shovel it over here. Like here it is only Tuesday afternoon and I've already been handed more to do this week than I can shake a stick at."

"Work don't bother me that much. Otherwise I'd just be home with Ethel. What does bother me is his butting into our business. How would he like it if I was over there telling him how to run his—whatever'n hell he does?''

"Damn straight. You said he was over here yesterday asking around?''

"Hit stores all through town, giving out pictures of Anderson. Sheriff had a woman call in this morning and said he'd been by her house—out in the country—asking if she had seen Anderson or a black Lincoln. Scared hell out of her, is what he did.''

"Gets a load of buckshot in his butt he'll go back to what it is he does and leave us alone. Dr. Malone—that's going to be one name I'm going to put on my list to remember to dislike.''

"Dr. Malone,'' the other deputy repeated.

The sound of the police scanner suddenly ceased in Dr. Anderson's room.

Cain and Abel stood outside in the hall.

They had listened too.

The wine bottle sat empty on the coffee table. Adrian set close to him now, her fingers trailing across his forearm. As the TV show faded to a commercial, he slipped his arms around her shoulders and gently pulled her face toward his.

Her lips were soft as she kissed him back. He kissed her more deeply, and she responded. In a moment they were kissing passionately. He pressed her backward on the couch—and felt her body stiffen.

He drew back from her.

She closed her eyes briefly, then looked directly at him. "It's been years since I've been out with anybody but Gerald. I started dating him while I was still in high school. It's been so long, I keep feeling like I'm on my first date. I can't help it. I'm sorry.'' She stopped, and shook her head. "No, that's not true.''

At his questioning expression, she said, "Cameron, the first boy I ever went out with I fell hard for, thought I had anyway. We're talking junior high, and he was the big stud in school, a sophomore, football star and all that bit, damn good-looking. I was sure I was going to marry him until he dropped me for the homecoming queen. I didn't really date again until high school." She took a deep breath.

"And that was Gerald. I was a sophomore then. It was right after Daddy was killed in a car accident. I've looked back on it and maybe I was looking for someone to protect me, take Daddy's place. In any case, I fell head over heels for him, even tried to make a go of it after I found out he was stepping out on me. You don't know how hard I tried. Now I'm starting to like you— the next guy I go out with, and it scares me. What if it would've been somebody else I met—would I have started liking them, too? Whoever I meet? You see how I fe—" He placed his fingers against her lips.

"Shhh," he whispered, "Neither one of us are psychiatrists, and it really doesn't matter anyway. Let's just hang loose and see what happens." He leaned and kissed her on the forehead. "No problem."

But there was. On the way to his car he looked back at her standing in her doorway. She was dumped by the first boy she cared about, then married an asshole. Was that the whole of it? Or had the first guy dumped her and then her husband running around because there was nothing for him at home—nothing from her?

He shook his head in disgust with himself. So a girl didn't jump in bed with him within the first couple of dates, and he was wondering what was wrong with her. What was wrong with him? He knew he was thinking the way he was only because for the first time he was really falling himself, what if he got dumped?

Then another thought: how much *had* she loved her husband? She had said, "You don't know how hard I tried."

His jaw tightened at that. Was he only someone to help her get over her broken marriage? If that was the case, he didn't think he would mind her telling him nearly as much as his having to put up with the wondering.

Then he almost smiled as he remembered back to when he had acted so dumb over a junior high cheerleader—the first girl he thought he was in love with. But even the way he acted then hadn't been this bad; he wouldn't have acted this bad in the first grade.

CHAPTER 16

Cameron slapped his hand disgustedly at the top of his steering wheel as he braked at a stop light at an edge of the town. He looked at the few photographs he had left on the passenger seat. And didn't anybody own a damn black Lincoln in West Memphis—Anderson or otherwise? It seemed nobody had ever seen one driving the streets or parked in front of a house or apartment complex. And nearly everyone had said a sheriff's deputy had already asked the same questions.

The light turned green and he started ahead. A mile down the pavement the street intersected with a blacktop running out toward the Mississippi River lowlands. He turned onto it and looked into the distance ahead.

"This is getting old," Adrian said, and yawned.

Much closer to the river, a frail looking old woman in work boots and a hand-sewn dress trudged along a seldom traveled gravel road running through the lowlands. A few minutes before she had twisted her ankle in a rut and the pain was only now beginning to subside. She carried a garbage bag over her shoulder. In another bag inside that one were over thirty pounds of catfish steaks wrapped in brown butcher paper. Anyone who would have seen her thin frame would have bet she couldn't carry that much weight from her little shack on stilts

next to the river—two miles down the road behind her
—to the gravel road's intersection with a paved road
five miles ahead. But she made the trip at least twice a
month, taking the fish to trade for flour, salt, sugar, and
other necessities. Occasionally she ended up having to
walk two miles farther to the small country grocery
store where she shopped. But everybody in the area
knew her and she usually was able to get a lift after
reaching the more traveled paved road.

She looked ahead of her off to the left, at the two
blond-headed youngsters playing in front of the old Phillips farmhouse. The farm had been deserted for several
years, ever since old man Casey Phillips died and his
children refused to come back from St. Louis to run the
place, what there was of it—a couple hundred acres of
wet lowland. Then the man in the new black Lincoln
Town Car had moved into the house a little over three
months before.

She had wondered why a man who could afford such
a car would live there—*probably hiding from somebody or something.* She knew she wouldn't have the
house, not with all the leaks in its roof.

She looked back at the children as something flashed
in one of their hands. Another flash beamed from the
second child's hand. She narrowed her eyes.

As they continued their game and she drew closer to
the house she saw what caused the flashing. They each
held a small piece of broken mirror in their hands and
were catching the sun's rays.

One child would catch a ray and beam it toward the
other who would catch it with his piece of mirror and
beam it back. They were jumping and darting from side
to side. Occasionally, one fell like he was shot and lay
on the damp ground in his nice new jeans and shirt,
and the game would stop for a few seconds until he
rose again.

It was almost like they were playing cops and robbers
or cowboys and Indians, she decided, with the pieces
of mirror as their weapons, the flashes of light, bullets.

She had never seen anything like it before, and a smile crossed her face, something that seldom happened.

Suddenly the children stopped their playing and looked up the road toward her. She noticed how bright their blond hair was. Coming up the road a couple of weeks before, she had seen them standing in front of one of the sheets nailed over the house windows. She had noticed how bright their hair was then, but had laid it to the way the light reflected through the window panes. But it really was bright, almost as if it were about to glow.

They were older than she thought, too, eleven or twelve years old with square jaws and nearly as tall as she was, rather than the three- to four-year-olds she had thought they were when they had stared from the window.

As she came closer to where they stood across the roadside ditch from her, she looked straight ahead; she always minded her own business. But as she passed them they started moving along the other side of the ditch in pace with her, staring at her.

At first it annoyed her. But they *were* only children, and she probably did look strange in her ankle length, hand-sewn dress, work boots and shawl—and they had to be wondering what she had in her sack. She flashed a toothless grin in their direction.

Their faces remained expressionless. The larger of the two started mimicking her short halting steps. She looked straight ahead.

"Come," the larger one suddenly whispered in a voice she barely heard.

Her brow wrinkled, but she kept her face straight down the road.

"Come," he said again, a little louder this time.

She wasn't positive whether he was directing the word at her or at his smaller brother. She looked out of the corner of her eyes across the ditch and caught a glimpse of his dark eyes staring back into hers. For a moment she felt a weird sensation of being drawn to him. She forced her gaze forward again and quickened her pace.

"Boys!" came a sharp voice from the porch. "Boys! You come back into the house this minute."

She looked at the tall, thin man at the front door. His pants were too short, exposing his dark socks, and his long wrists showed past his shirt sleeves. The children ignored him, continuing to keep pace with her. The taller one's eyes were burning into hers again. She snapped her head back down the road.

"Boys!" the man repeated. "Come into the house this minute!"

The larger child quickened his pace, drawing slightly ahead of her. She could feel his gaze though she wasn't looking. He thrust his square chin out toward her over the ditch and spoke in a low voice. "You come into the house."

The smaller one was suddenly moving ahead of her down his side of the ditch. She couldn't help but see him as he looked back at her. He pointed off in a direction to the rear of the house and she glanced that way.

Fifty feet behind the house, an old shed with a sagging tin roof was framed in the dwindling sunlight. The shed's door was set ajar, partially open. She could see only a dark void past it. The boy continued to point in that direction. "You come into *that* house this minute," he said.

"Boys!"

The two stopped and looked back toward the tall man walking hurriedly from the house toward them. When he stopped he glared down at them then raised his face to her, staring with his cold, bloodshot eyes— as if he blamed her for the children's actions. Moving even faster now, she glanced at the old shed.

You come into the house, rang in her ears, almost as if she were still hearing them say it. *You come into that house this minute.* And she felt the strangest urge to turn back and go toward the shed—no matter that she was now as scared of the two boys as she would have been were they the spawn of the devil himself.

CHAPTER 17

Anderson heard the door shut. Already angry that while he had gone to hide the Lincoln, Cain and Abel had slipped outside and been seen by the old woman, his face twisted into a scowl. He came out of his chair, walked into the hall and stared down it.

In the dim last rays of the setting sun cast through the kitchen's sheet-covered window he saw the two of them working with something on the card table. He strode toward them.

He stopped in shock when he saw the rabbit's bloody body lying between them.

"No! You can't do . . . " His eyes widened when he saw the blood dropping from Abel's hand.

"What have you done to yourself!"

He rushed to the boy and grabbed his hand.

A cut ran diagonally across his palm. But it wasn't bad enough to need suturing. Anderson looked at the long butcher knife lying on the table. He looked at Cain and saw the smear of blood on his thigh at the edge of his underwear. Blood dripped from his hand, too.

"Both of you!" Anderson shouted, "Have you gone crazy?" He stepped to Cain and grabbed his hand, turning it over so he could see the cut.

Only the thumb was injured, again not deeply enough for stitches, but bleeding freely. He looked back at the remains of the rabbit.

"More," Cain said.

Anderson glared. "No more!" he exclaimed. He pointed toward the bedroom. "Get in there this minute!"

Cain made a guttural noise in his throat. "More," he repeated, low this time.

Abel said, "More."

Anderson's lips drew into a tight line. As they did, Cain's eyes narrowed and he uttered his guttural sound.

"And I'm sick of that noise, too, Cain. You can talk. Say what it is you mean." He pointed a long finger toward the hallway. He could feel his blood pressure rising. "Get into the bedroom—*now.*"

Abel suddenly turned and walked in that direction. Cain remained where he was and darted his eyes toward the back of Abel's head.

Abel stopped and turned back around.

Anderson's eyes tightened. The disrespect. It was Cain's fault. It was always the same, Abel trying to do as he was told, his older brother interfering.

"Dammit, Cain! Don't defy me."

Anderson stepped forward and raised his hand, ready to strike the boy if he didn't move.

Cain *roared* his guttural noise.

Anderson, startled, froze with his arm above his head.

He suddenly realized how he was acting. And acting that way to the miracle of the ages. His miracle. He lowered his hand.

He forced his voice to a level tone. "I'm sorry. I'm sorry, Cain. Please go to your room. Please."

The boy stared for a moment, then started toward the living room. Abel fell in behind him as he went past and the two continued on toward the hallway.

Anderson watched them until they were out of sight then leaned back against the refrigerator until his racing pulse begin to slow. How was he supposed to control such stress? He walked toward the hall bathroom.

With the time it took to get what he needed from the

medicine cabinet above the toilet, he felt much better as he stepped back out of the bathroom. He went to the bedroom where he dried the blood from Abel's hand, applied Neosporin to the cut and wrapped his palm in gauze.

Cain's stocky young shape lay sprawled on his bed. He looked at the ceiling and didn't move when Anderson knelt on the side of the mattress and took the injured hand into his own. He never looked as his thumb was bandaged.

"Now, both of you, please, I don't want you to get out of bed again. Please."

Cain didn't respond. Abel looked at his brother for a moment then stepped up onto the mattress, across Cain, where he settled down onto the bed and slipped under the covers.

Anderson moved out into the hallway and shut the door behind him. In the living room he lifted his tape recorder off the end table and settled onto the couch.

"Evolution experiment, day one hundred and one; random notes to myself regarding characteristics of the children born of the Ancient Man. First, with them being born after only six weeks, it is undeniable that a gene ascribed to the spermatozoa was generally dominant in the birth process of five hundred thousand years ago. Considering that the so-called power packs of an embryo's growth are known to be completely contained in the egg in the modern birthing process, I remain at a loss here. This new phenomena will have to be studied at greater length, as will Cain and Abel's subsequent—"

The tape had quit turning.

He opened the recorder.

Only a short segment of the tape had been used but it had twisted and jammed. How many was that now? he thought angrily. He had tried to save money by buying an off-brand, and at least a half dozen of them had already malfunctioned, some with crucial observations, now hopelessly locked where they would neither go

forward nor backward. He closed his eyes, tried to keep
his pulse from mounting.

After a few seconds, he pulled the jammed tape from
the recorder and slipped it into his pants pocket. One
more breath to steady himself, then he reached to an
end table, opened its drawer, lifted out a tape, and inserted it into the recorder.

"Evolution experiment, day one hundred and one;
random notes to myself . . . " And he had to stop. The
stress. Where had he been in his thoughts? He shook
his head. He was so tired. He leaned his head back
against the couch.

He remembered he was starting to speak about the
twins physical phenomena and then record what was to
him the most mystifying of all that had occurred. He
pushed the record button again:

"It has been only slightly over eight weeks since Cain
and Abel were born, yet their level of physical maturity
would indicate children of eleven to twelve years of
age, their rate of physical growth at first approximating
a year for each week, then rapidly accelerating—much
like the pregnancy did.

"Yet, as uncomprehensible as this is, I feel that their
mental advancement has been more astounding. For
while physical growth is genetically determined, and
much of their physical activity can be ascribed to instinct—the need to exercise, the need to seek food, and
so on—that is not the case with their mental prowess.

"And once again I wish to stress I am not talking
about an intelligence quotient here, not speaking
merely of their ability to learn, but rather the knowledge that they already possess—evidently have possessed since they were born.

"For instance, though in my immediate presence I
have heard them speak only monosyllable words they
could have learned from me and from what they have
heard on television, I overheard Abel speak in a language that could not have been learned in any such
manner. And *it was* a language, though I am not at all

certain it is still present on earth. It was a high, rapidly-spoken group of monosyllable words spoken in a rhythmic manner—definitely structured. It was uttered by Abel when Cain was out of sight. And Cain did respond, coming to Abel only moments afterward. A language is not instinct, but can only be learned.

"Further, when a big storm swept over the farm two weeks ago, neither of them were frightened by the lightning and thunder. In fact, they were not even curious enough to look away from the television set. To me that can only mean they were already aware of lightning and thunder. And that can only mean they had heard it and seen it *before*."

He switched off the recorder and sat in silence. He was going far in his hypothesis, extremely far. But there were the other signs he had seen, too, all of them pointing to the same conclusion.

He raised the recorder back to his lips.

"It is now my belief that at least some of what Cain and Abel's forebearers learned *had* to have been stored genetically and passed on to them—there is no other way for them to be possessed of the knowledge they have. And, if I am correct in my hypothesis, then mankind since their time has somehow lost the greatest gift ever bestowed. To have children born with part or all of the knowledge their parents possessed is staggering in its implications. It could mean—according to the extent this prior knowledge was passed on—that a child at birth could be aware of as little as merely his surroundings and his parents' language, or, at the other extreme, a mathematician's newborn son could conceivably already know how to calculate problems, a neurosurgeon's son born already equipped with the ability to perform brain surgery.

"And what of such a child's grandparents, their parents, and their parents? Is there a limit to what was passed on, or was it cumulative? If it was cumulative, all inclusive, then all the knowledge ever possessed by the sum total of the child's forebearers would be his to pass on to his children. If this were still true, then there would be no time wasted on education as we understand it now, but only research, pushing the levels of knowledge to a point where man would be . . . would be . . . *a god*—knowing everything.''

He lowered the recorder. What had happened to this gift? How had it been lost, lost as was also lost the rapid rate of gestation and the quick growth after birth—but this gift a million times more important than a mere physical propensity.

Or maybe the gift hadn't been lost, he thought, not in the sense that it had been bred out of mankind. He narrowed his eyes as he pondered the thought. He had sought to bring a representative of an Ancient Man back to show they were as advanced as man today—that there had been no evolution. He wanted to show that while all the various stages of man had existed, they had coexisted together, not one evolving into another, the weaker races killed off—only modern man surviving. But what if there had been even another form of man back then, one unknown to date and one also killed off, but a man much more advanced than those who had survived?

Was that possible? That wouldn't be survival of the fittest. Or did something else play into their extinction? There was their rapid gestation rate—perhaps it was a form of the increased fertility that animals near extinction show. Maybe there hadn't been very many of these advanced people, and even though they were much more fit than other kinds of man, perhaps they lost out to the sheer numbers of the other races during some kind of struggle between them. That was possible, a much more intelligent form of man existing back then, but one overwhelmed like the barbarians had overwhelmed Rome—the race's genius lost forever.

He stared blankly at the ceiling. He thought back through history where from time to time there had arisen a man above all others. And a new thought came from that.

Had not all of this race been wiped from the face of the earth, but a few survived to mate with lesser man and from time to time produced offspring of gigantic intelligence and ability? There was the total taking over of the egg's function by the implanted sperm. He had witnessed that in his experiment. But what if those people who had survived from this long-ago race only been women? Would their eggs, used to being dominated by the genetic makeup of the sperm, rise to dominance itself when fertilized with the sperm of an ordinary human being and replicate another super being?

Would it happen only every so often, not every time? There were genetic characteristics and ability passed on now, hair color, physical size, eye color, intelligence—a number of things. Frequently a generation is skipped, and then the second or third generation shows the dominance.

Could such a thing have happened from time to time through history, this great genetic trait lying mostly dormant then expressing itself in kings who became legends, great generals who could not be beaten, men of science who seemed to be well beyond their time, even those people who seemed to have genuine psychic ability? Nostradamus?

He heard a metallic sound down the hall, and his brow wrinkled. He heard the sound again. *They were playing with the chains.* His eyes closed. Not in bed as he had told them, not getting their rest. When would it all end? When would they learn what he said was law? He rose and walked toward the bedroom door.

Inside the nearly dark room, Abel stood in the middle of their mattress. Cain stood on the floor. They had one of the chains between them and were pulling on it in a game of tug of war, expressionlessly. Anderson's anger dissipated. Other than once when he had observed them playing with mirrors, this was the only time he had seen any kind of activity suggesting play. Rather than say anything, even reach to turn on the ceiling light, he began to make mental notes of the activity.

Then he noticed the gauze bandage lying on the floor. He looked back at them. They had removed their wrappings. Without stopping pulling on the chain, both of them stared at him.

He shook his head. "You took your bandages off. You'll get an infection!"

They kept pulling, staring.

He looked at Abel's hand, wrapped tightly around the chain. With the pressure the boy applied against the hard steel links, the wound should have been bleeding again. He flicked on the ceiling light and walked to the mattress. Abel released the chain, and it fell to the floor with a loud noise. Cain gathered the links toward him.

Anderson reached for Abel, not much shorter than he was due to the added elevation of the mattress. "Let me see your hand."

Abel looked at his brother.

Anderson caught the boy's hand and turned his palm up. His eyes widened. The gash was now no more than a slight red line. He turned and grabbed Cain's hand and looked at his thumb. He couldn't even see where it had been injured.

Couldn't even see where it had been injured. He thought back to a few minutes before, when he had thought of the possibility of some of those members of a vastly advanced race surviving—how much greater than mere man their offspring could have been. He stared at Cain's thumb, at the place where the cut had been. Healed itself. *Healed itself. Miraculously!*

His eyes widened with his thought. Jesus Christ had risen from the dead, according to the Christians. The Bible had been quite explicit on that point. Healed himself—even after he was dead. Could *He* have been one of them?

Anderson felt his hand shake with excitement. Then with his bringing them back through fertilizing the egg he would be the same as . . . the same as—*God Himself.* His spine tingled with the wonder of it all.

Still holding Cain's hand, he looked deeply into his eyes. *His son.* He created him. He.

Cain yanked his hand away with startling power and took a step backward. Anderson continued to stare at him, then back to Abel. They had to be aware of the great power they possessed. They could tell him.

He reached and caught Abel's arm, looked hard into the boy's eyes, the one most likely to tell him what he asked.

"You know why your hand has healed, don't you? You knew it would heal when you cut it, didn't you? How? Tell me, Abel, how could you know? Tell me. You can speak more than one-syllable words. I know you can. You can speak as well as I can, can't you, even in your own language, maybe in any language? How, dammit? How can you two do all you do?"

A chain whipped through the air behind Anderson and slammed hard into the back of his head, stunning him and knocking him a step forward. Turning around he was caught full in the face with another sweeping blow of the chain wheeled by Cain. Anderson's teeth crumpled and a wide gash opened across his face. His vision blurred and his knees weakened under him. He raised his hand as Cain drew back and swung the section of chain again.

With the enormous force of the swing behind it, the chain broke both bones in Anderson's forearm and whipped on around to slam into the side of his head. His knees buckled, he stumbled backward, his heels catching the edge of the mattress, tripping him, and he fell to the side, slamming into the wall so hard he jolted a board loose to jut out from the other planks. He slid down the wall onto his side on the mattress, groaned and rolled to his back, held up his arm, his hand and wrist dangling helplessly at an awkward angle.

Cain jumped to the mattress's edge, and with both hands propelling the section of chain, swung it down hard into Anderson's face. Abel yanked the section of chain that had been left on the mattress from under

Anderson and, with one motion, whipped it high into the air and down across the doctor's chest.

Anderson, reeling into unconsciousness, barely felt the skin of his chest burst in a spray of blood. He slowly moved his hands to the spot, felt the warm wetness seeping through his shirt, and raised his hand to stare at the blurred, bright red stain.

Abel swung again. Cain brought his section down hard again and again. Abel started whimpering, and as he did he whipped the chain down hard and jerked it back up again—faster and faster each time.

He kept flailing the bloody mass even after Cain walked toward the door.

CHAPTER 18

The Maxima's headlights shined down the road into the dark.

"Cameron, it's getting too late to be doing this. I don't imagine rural people are all that used to strangers coming up to their door in the middle of the night."

"I only have two photographs left."

"Then let's just stick them in mailboxes and be done with it."

He stared off to the right at the old farmhouse they approached. By the looks of the sagging roof over the porch and weeds in front of the house it appeared unoccupied. But the glow from his headlights had shown something covering the inside of the windows.

He slowed the Maxima.

Adrian looked at the house. "A kids' hangout," she said. "Those are sheets, not curtains hanging inside the windows."

He stopped the car.

"Maybe," he said. "But it's the first house we've seen on this road. There can't be many more; we're almost to the river. If anybody does live there they'll probably know every other family in this area."

Adrian shook her head in amusement. "You don't have to con me, Cameron. Go slide your photograph under the door."

He looked across the seat and smiled a little. "Looks

creepy. You want to go with me? You might get frightened."

"And jump into your arms?"

"Something like that."

"Real romantic in the middle of a . . . " She looked around them. " . . . almost a swamp. I'm the cop, Cameron, somebody in there ends up sticking a shotgun out the door, I'd probably be the one having to hold you."

"We could try it and see."

She faced the windshield and rolled her eyes. He smiled, lifted a photograph from the seat, opened his door, and walked back along the gravel to the place where an iron culvert buried in the roadside ditch allowed him to cross into the yard without having to jump across the stream of water coming down the ditch.

There was no car at the side of the house, but there *were* rutted tire marks in the dirt driveway, several sets. *And again the sheets.* Somebody. Kids, or occupants without much in life. He walked through the weeds, stepped up under the sagging roof and knocked on the door.

After a moment with no response, he knocked again, but still heard no sound of anyone in the house. He leaned back and looked at the windows, completely darkened, with only the dim illumination of the half moon showing the sheets hung inside the panes.

He knocked once again, this time loudly. After waiting a few more seconds he reached to the doorknob and tried it.

It was locked. *Somebody did live here.*

He knelt and slipped a photograph under the door.

Moving back to the culvert under the drive, he noticed the tire tracks again. There were several sets, or the same set coming and going several times. He looked toward the rear of the house. *Wouldn't it be hell if Anderson's Lincoln sat behind the house and he didn't even look?*

He looked at the nearest sheet covered window. *And wouldn't it be hell if some recluse who didn't want to be bothered was standing behind the sheet with a shotgun, watching a stranger contemplating walking around toward the rear of his house?*

He silently laughed that off. He had pounded hard on the door. Nobody was home.

He started toward the rear of the house.

At that moment a cloud moved across the moon, creating a dark shadow that raced quickly over the wide field behind the house, and enveloped him—and a cold chill ran up his back.

Damn, he thought, and would have turned around right then, except he was already at the side of the house. He glanced at the single window to that side, started past it—and his foot sank into the ground.

Startled, he yanked back on it, and stumbled forward —and both legs sank to his ankles. He tried to lift his foot, but only succeeded in burying his other foot farther. He grabbed at the dirt around his ankle and caught something in his hand. *Something cold and stiff and the size of a wrist.*

He nearly ripped his thigh muscles apart he lunged upward with such force, and was jerked back to the ground by the sucking dirt, landing on all fours—his face hanging over five, curled, thin black fingers.

Somehow he steeled himself.

He pulled on one foot until it slipped free of the dirt, then pulled his other foot loose and scooted back to hard ground. He stood. He looked back at the hand, then at the window nearest him.

He heard the quiet closing of the back door.

His face jerked to the rear corner of the house. He backed away, didn't take his eyes off the corner of the house until he was nearly to the roadside ditch. He jumped the water and went around to his door of the Maxima.

Adrian stared at the dirt on his shirt and hands.

"What in the world?"

Glancing back at the house, he lifted his cellular phone from the seat. "There's a body next to the house."

Adrian's hand grabbed inside her purse. He quickly punched nine-one-one into his phone.

"This is Cameron Malone. There's a body buried out here." At the shocked questioning response on the other end of the line he said, "Yes, a body. A dead person—buried in a shallow grave." He gave the road he was on and how far out it he was, then lowered the phone to the seat and looked back at the house. *There had been the sound of the door closing.*

Had there been a sound of a door closing?

"Adrian, I heard a door close at the back—I think." He looked at his hands and wiped the dirt on his pants.

Her automatic held up to the window now, Adrian stared toward the house. Then she opened the door.

He grabbed her arm. "What are you doing?"

"They could be running across the field behind the house."

"Shut the door."

As she did, he dropped the Maxima into gear, then backed it in a short turn, guided it toward the culvert, and gunned it forward into the yard. He swung far enough out to avoid the soft spot and the coiled fingers, and sped into the tall weeds behind the house.

He cut his headlights in a wide circle out over the empty field, then circled back in a tight turn and shined his lights out over the field again. He saw nothing but waist-high weeds and clumps of johnsongrass.

"The back door's open," Adrian said.

He spun the wheel once more and guided the front of the car toward the door.

The lights shined into the house.

He could see what looked like the edge of a card table, but nothing else. He looked at the windows along the rear of the house.

"If we have to be here, I'd feel better standing up close to the door than sitting out here for somebody to be looking at us." He glanced toward the field. "From either direction."

Adrian opened her door. He came out his side and they hurried to the house. He peered around the door facing as Adrian did the same thing.

The illumination from the Maxima's headlights cast shadows of their heads against the far side of a living room. A couch sat off to their right. The card table and the entrance to a kitchen were closer to their left. He looked back to the right and saw the dim outline of a hall entrance. He heard the sound of a siren coming from up the road. At the same time he caught the stench, light as it came out the door, but the same as he had smelled as a child when his father had butchered a hog—the sharp, light smell of bile.

A car braked hard on the gravel road in front of the house. Adrian glanced at him. A few seconds later a fist pounded on the front door. Adrian took a deep breath and, her automatic held out rigidly in front of her, stepped slowly into the house, and he went in beside her. The stench became stronger.

A fist slammed again against the door.

"Sheriff's Department!"

He glanced toward the hallway entrance back to their right. "I'll get it," he said and she nodded. She kept her automatic pointed in the hallway's direction.

He started toward the front door—and felt stickiness under his feet. When he stopped, Adrian stared at him. He knelt, but he already knew. He pressed his fingers to the wood flooring and pulled them back. He saw the red stain reflected in the glow of the Maxima's head-lights.

He came back to his feet. Trying not to think about what he was walking in, he stepped tentatively across the stickiness and around the couch to the door.

"It's me," he said through the door before he opened it. "Cameron Malone. I was the one who called. There is a police officer in here with me."

The two deputies had their automatics pointed when

he opened the door. The older of the two swung his flashlight toward Adrian.

Cameron looked at her. She held out her ID case; her badge glinted the flashlight's beam.

The deputies lowered their automatics.

"There's a body buried at the side of the house," Cameron said. He looked back at his footprints, outlined in red in the flashlight's glow.

The older deputy stared too. Leading the younger one, they moved into the house, toward Adrian.

Their flashlights now caught the smeared red line coming out from behind the couch in two directions—.one leading toward the kitchen, showing the mark of Cameron's shoes, the other running toward the hall-way.

They all moved toward the hallway, and the stench grew.

As Adrian pointed her weapon, the older deputy stood to the side of the first door on the right and pushed it open, then shined his light inside a room vacant except for an empty bedframe and dresser.

But the smear led to the second door on the left.

As the deputies walked toward it, Cameron saw the glow of dim moonlight under the door. The older deputy pushed the door back.

"Jesus Christ!" he said.

Adrian's eyes widened.

The younger deputy closed his eyes.

Cameron stepped forward. Blood was everywhere, splashed on the bed to their right and on the mattress against the far wall. But that was not what drew their eyes. They stared at where the stench came from, a fetid pile of shiny intestines forming a sloping, wide mound in the center of the room. And he now saw Dr. Anderson's face in person for the first time since that day at the Convention Center, the whole head lying on its side at the base of the mound, the mouth gaped wide, a short bloody stub for a neck, the skull cracked open and the scalp peeled forward, exposing an empty cavity.

The younger deputy's face paled. He turned and hurried up the hallway toward the living room. He barely had time to make it out onto the porch when they heard him vomit loudly.

Cameron didn't feel so good, either. But now that he had seen this much, he wanted to look for one more thing. It wasn't in this bedroom, nothing was but the bed, the mattress on the floor, a dresser, and the . . . he turned toward the next nearest doorway across the hall.

"Don't, Cameron!" Adrian said as he reached for the door knob. The older deputy stared at him.

He felt in his pocket but didn't have a handkerchief. He slipped his shirttail from his pants and used it to cover his hand, then opened the door.

It was completely empty, with part of the sheetrock ceiling hanging down and looking water-stained.

The next door on that side was where the deputy had first shined his light. The last room was the one they had passed.

It was locked. Cameron tried the doorknob harder, then walked toward the living room.

Adrian watched him as he circled around the wide smear of blood and glanced into the kitchen.

Nothing, no equipment of any kind.

Sergeant Gerald Cummings, blocky with thick arms, his long hair hanging down against his shoulders, spun the frightened teenager around and slammed him against the side of his sports car, then quickly handcuffed him.

A few feet ahead of the sports car, Cummings' partner, a much smaller, skinnier man, listened to the traffic coming across the radio in their unmarked car. He leaned out the open door and angled his narrow face back toward the sports car.

"Hey, buddy," he said. "You ought to listen to this.

Your ex and some doctor ran up on a body buried in a yard."

Cummings pitched the baggie of marijuana to his partner, threw open the rear door of their unmarked car and roughly pushed the teenager toward the back seat. The boy bumped his forehead hard on the top of the door frame, groaned in pain, and drew his head back.

"You little bastard!" Cummings roared, and whipped his forearm into the boy's side, doubling him over and knocking him sideways onto the seat.

"Easy, buddy," his partner said.

Cummings stared for a moment at the boy bent over and squirming on the seat, then slammed the door.

"Cameron Malone," he said. "Some fancy prick doctor with a little money. What do you expect from a whore."

"Thought you weren't going to put up with her doing that," his partner said and laughed.

His laughter trailed off at the cold stare he received.

"Just pickin', Gerald. Come on now, man."

CHAPTER 19

An Arkansas Highway Patrol cruiser, its rotating lights flashing a brilliant blue across the front of the old farmhouse, sat blocking the entrance leading into the yard. Three darkened sheriff's department cars lined the roadside ditch. A crime lab van backed slowly toward the front door. An ambulance had already left with the woman's body exhumed from the shallow grave at the side of the house.

Cameron stood near the front porch, asked to wait outside a half hour before by the Crittenden County sheriff who was now inside the house.

"Whoever did it had to have been who you heard coming out the back door," Adrian said. "But there are no footprints but ours."

Cameron didn't reply. He still couldn't believe he had driven around into the back yard like he had—before the deputies had arrived. Baringer was right—he was crazy.

An older deputy a few feet away slapped at a mosquito on his neck. "Here they come," he said.

At first Cameron thought the man was talking about mosquitos, then he looked in the direction the deputy stared. A TV van sped up the road toward the house.

"Never far behind us," the deputy said. "They've beat us to a scene once or twice."

The van slid to a stop a few feet short of the highway

patrol cruiser parked across the dirt drive. A young brunette with a wild, puffed hairdo looked toward them as she stepped from the vehicle.

A white-suited lab technician came out the front door of the house. He strained to hold a heavily loaded plastic garbage bag in his gloved hands as he walked to the rear of the crime lab van.

The sheriff stepped from the house. A tall, heavily-built man with a high forehead topped by closely cropped brown hair, he appeared to be in his early fifties and wore a dark suit.

He walked up to them. "Dr. Malone," he said, "Did you get a look at the symbols on the wall in the bedroom?"

Cameron shook his head. "I didn't even notice any."

"You're an archaeologist, right?"

"A paleontologist."

"Are there symbols involved with your profession? Symbols that mean things. Like maybe math symbols would mean something to a mathematician."

"Well, there are some things in the profession that are abbreviated."

"Dr. Malone, do you have any idea why Anderson would write your name while he was dying?"

Cameron knew he had heard wrong.

"What are you talking about?" Adrian asked sharply.

"It could be your name, anyway," the sheriff went on, still looking at him. "In his own blood on the floor."

Cameron, still stunned, shook his head. "What do you mean, 'it could be' my name?"

The sheriff glanced back at the house. "You've already been inside," he said, "seen about everything there is to see. I'd like for you to have a look at the symbols and see if maybe they'll jog something in your mind."

Adrian's tone was even sharper now. "What do you mean, his name?"

"You'll see," the sheriff said without changing expression. He turned toward the house. "Don't touch anything, Dr. Malone, anything at all. I don't think it's a very good idea for your prints to be inside the house."

Cameron glanced at Adrian. Once back inside the house and across the living room, he hung to the outside of the hallway to avoid stepping on the wide smear of red stain.

"Oh, yeah," the sheriff said back across his shoulder. "There was nothing in the locked room but a couple of potted plants. No machinery or equipment of any kind. Test tubes, nothing."

"Sheriff," Adrian said, "how do you know it was cannibalism and not some cult ritual?"

The sheriff stopped before he entered the room where Anderson had been found. He looked back up the hall toward the kitchen. "We got a pile of vomit up there where a deputy looked in the refrigerator. You're welcome to look yourself if you want to. But I don't think you do." He stepped on into the room.

The first time Cameron had been inside it he hadn't noticed how little illumination the dim overhead bulb gave. But it was apparent now as, back at the left of the room, a deputy held the beam of a flashlight on a dresser top to help another deputy see as he lifted fingerprints off the wood. They both had handkerchiefs tied around their faces. A dark green body bag had been draped over the mound in the center of the floor. The coverings of the bed against the wall and the ones from the mattress on the floor had been stripped. The mattress was soaked in a dark, almost black red.

"He evidently was first attacked on the mattress," the sheriff said. He nodded toward the floor at a pair of bloody chains. "That's what they used." He nodded to a wide pool of drying blood on the floor between the mattress and the bed.

"Looks like after a while he rolled off of it to the floor." Now he raised his face toward the symbols on the wall above the bed.

"Those jog anything in your mind?" he asked.

There were a couple of circles, an upside-down *L* and

an upside-down *V,* close together, and a star. Nothing even remotely resembling notations used in any science of which he was aware. He shook his head. "No."

The sheriff moved around the bed, squatted and pointed under it.

"He wrote *born C Malons,* here. Used his finger in his own blood."

Born? In the dim light under the bed, Cameron had to lean to see the writing clearly.

"See this?" The sheriff pointed to the right of the *s* at the end of *Malons.*

It looked like Dr. Anderson had started an *I* or an *L* and never stopped his downward stroke, the long line continuing out from under the bed and disappearing into the dark puddle.

The sheriff straightened. "He was trying to finish whatever it was he was writing when he was pulled back toward the center of the room. That line was the mark his finger left as it trailed out from under the bed."

The sheriff looked back at the writing. "If it *was* your name he was trying to spell out, he missed the *e* and put in the *s*—*Malons*—and what does *born* imply, in the context it's in?"

Adrian answered. "Born—something to do with the sample, Cameron?"

Before he could reply she added, "Born C—for Cameron. Malons—for Malone's. . . . " She looked at him. "If he was starting to make an *A* with his downward stroke, it could mean born Dr. Malone's Ancient Man."

She bit her lip as she thought. "Whether or not you say it's possible to transfer DNA—if it had been nine months since the sample was stolen."

Cameron was caught up in his own thoughts. He had seen Anderson at the center that day. The description the watchman gave, and Anderson's build—it was the same. Anderson referred to the Ancient Man even as he died. He had to be the one who had committed the break-in. And was whoever he was involved with responsible for this?

Adrian looked back toward the writing. "What did he mean? What was he trying to say? Something he was doing with an experiment—with the sample. Maybe something someone stole from him. Maybe the same someone who did this to him."

She ceased her words when one of the deputies lifting fingerprints off the dresser suddenly hurried toward the hall. His face was noticeably pale.

The sheriff turned and followed him, and Cameron and Adrian came along behind him.

Lieutenant Warrington waited at the front door. The sheriff stepped to him and shook his hand. Adrian smiled politely.

The lieutenant glanced at Cameron a moment then looked back at the sheriff. "You told him?" he asked.

The sheriff shook his head. "I was waiting for you to arrive."

The lieutenant didn't mince any words. "Dr. Malone, I don't guess you'd mind submitting to a polygraph, would you? You don't have to, of course."

Cameron was taken aback for a moment. Then he felt angry. Maybe they should check his canine teeth at the same time.

"Certainly," he said, not caring that his sharp tone betrayed his feelings. "Whenever you'd like."

"He did scratch something that could fit your name under the bed," the lieutenant came back. "You obviously have been hot and heavy after whoever broke into your exhibit. I think that it's—"

"I said whenever you'd like."

The lieutenant was silent for a moment, then nodded. "Okay, then. How about tomorrow morning? Say around ten-thirty or eleven?"

"Fine."

Cameron felt Adrian catch his arm, and they moved on out of the house into a brilliant TV light.

The deputy who had spoken to them before met them at the foot of the porch. He had a wad of chewing tobacco in his mouth now and rolled it to his cheek before he spoke.

"They were asking who you two might be," he said, and glanced toward the gravel road. "I told them I hadn't the slightest."

A flash bulb went off on the road.

Cameron looked out at the man with the camera. He wore a rumpled brown suit without a tie and a khaki-colored hat with a card stuck at the front of its brim. His appearance reminded Cameron of the photographers he had seen in old movies made in the forties.

The man raised his camera and the bulb flashed again.

"Don't know who that character's with," the deputy said. "He just come up."

"Let's go," Adrian said.

As they started for her car, a blocky figure walked toward them from the road.

Adrian's eyes tightened. It was her former husband. He came up to them and stopped. He wore civilian clothes, a pair of faded khakis and a sweat shirt; his long hair rested around his thick shoulders.

"What are you doing here, Gerald?" Adrian asked sharply.

Cameron caught the name. The man looked at him, then back at Adrian and smiled a little. "Don't flatter yourself, baby. Simple curiosity."

Cameron saw the man's eyes slide back in his direction.

"How many times you get to visit a murder scene where you know the killer hated the victim that bad, doc? Bad enough to eat him after he murdered him." He smiled again. "We never know how we might end up in this old world, do we, doc? You might think about that, doc."

A flashbulb exploded from the road. Gerald walked on past them toward Lieutenant Warrington.

Another bright flash came from the road.

Cameron felt Adrian tug at his elbow. "Come on," she said.

He thought a moment, then slipped his arm around her shoulders, kept it there despite the sudden tightening of her body, and started her forward toward his car.

When he opened her door, he looked back at Gerald staring their way, held eye contact as long as the blocky man did.

When they slipped inside the car, Adrian shook her head. "I'm not kidding around, Cameron, he's mean. You shouldn't push him. I mean it."

He put the Maxima in gear.

"Dammit, Cameron, for me, okay?"

He still didn't respond.

As they drove back along the gravel road toward West Memphis, Cameron's anger mounted rather than lessened. Her husband was stocky and broad-shouldered, but there was as much fat evident as muscle. No different from many of the types who hung around high school parking lots long after they graduated, then ended up bouncers in some beer joint—dim-witted, chunky thugs, bigger than everybody else since they were born, thinking that made them tough. But none of them were as quick as he was. Not even close. He had yet to meet anybody who was.

They used their arms more than their fists; wide, round house swings instead of tight directed blows. He had left a lot of those types lying on the pavement in Greenwood. Too many. His mother and father had become concerned, his father, especially. He was the one who, when worried that his son was going to be too small and lacking in confidence because of it, had taken him to the local boxing club. Then when what had been a smaller than usual boy in grade school became a muscled six-footer in high school, it was too late. The aggressiveness had always been there, the skills were then there too; while Cameron knew he had never been anything close to what could be described as a bully, neither had he walked the other way when trouble brewed.

Maturity had cured his problem, and let his mother and father forget the fears that he might someday look into a gun in a bar fight—it had been years since his last fight. But he was a long way from being defenseless.

How like a damn fool kid he was acting. He hadn't had such thoughts pass through his mind since he was in high school. And yet they were so strong now they almost had blotted out all thought of the horror he had just witnessed. He looked across the seat at Adrian.

She was the reason. Not her fault, but the reason nevertheless. Here he was, a paleontologist, supposedly studied and reasoned, now thinking like the cave men he studied. Baringer would be aghast. Not at the angry thoughts. Not even if he had heard the words spoken aloud; he had seen them surface in Italy when a drunken porter had gotten out of line, but luckily backed down and went on his way. Baringer would become aghast now in realizing how his young partner now suddenly felt about a woman.

And then, of course, the continuing mystery. They had now found Anderson. So what did that tell them for sure? Not a damn thing, no matter how the circumstances looked, at least not with certainty—at least not why the sample had been taken. *Born C malons;* it could only mean . . . no. There had to be something else.

Now Adrian looked across the seat at him. "I take back what I said about you jumping into my arms."

He smiled at her, and she slid across the seat to him, and rested her forearm on his shoulder.

"Really, not everybody would have driven around to the back of the house like you did."

"You were going anyway."

"I know," she said, and smiled softly. "Thanks for the company."

Then she looked back toward the windshield. *"Born,"* she said, "and then maybe your name—it is something to do with the sample, isn't it? From your man. He had to be the one. He was trying to clone—whatever you call it—trying to do something with the sample, wasn't he?''

''If he was, had he gone crazy or actually had a process he thought would work?''

And the worse part of it all—there was no more trail. Whatever Anderson had planned had died with him, and there were no more suspects to try and find, if anyone had been involved with him.

''Maybe the deputies will find some notes there, or something, Cameron—something that will give us an idea. One thing is for sure. If he is the one, and he was going to do anything with it, you know he already has.''

Cain wore jeans, a blue, open-neck pullover, and gloves —all clothes Dr. Anderson had bought him. Looking like any other young teenager with unusually bright blond hair and a slightly protruding jaw, he crouched in the darkness behind a hedge at the front of a yard off a narrow street. Abel, slightly smaller than his brother but with the same bright blond hair and dressed similarly, crouched a few feet down the hedge to the right. They watched the slim black teenager in jeans and a sweatshirt hurry along the sidewalk toward them. They crouched lower. She walked past Cain and he looked at Abel. Abel stepped out onto the sidewalk.

She was street-smart and didn't hesitate, spinning on her feet and already running the way she had come before Abel even came to a complete stop. She ran into Cain's arms.

She screamed. He covered her mouth. Abel grabbed her from behind, pinning her arms to her sides. She tried to struggle but it was as if she was in the grasp of two granite statues. She thought she was going to pass out.

In a minute they had carried her fifty feet down the street where it intersected with another one and stepped around the corner of the hedge to a van parked a few feet away.

Abel moved to the front of the van as Cain held the teenager, his arm around her shoulders and his hand cupping her mouth as he opened the back door of the van. He lifted her easily and stepped up into the rear of the vehicle. Abel started the motor, turned on the headlights, and pulled away from the curb.

Cain pushed the girl down onto her back on the hard metal floor of the van and ripped open the front of her jeans. Her eyes, wide, darted from side to side. He pulled her jeans down her legs. She screamed and lashed out at his face with her nails.

He backhanded her, knocking her unconscious.

A mile farther along the narrow tree-lined street, Abel saw the flashing blue lights. A little closer and he saw the police cruiser, its lights flashing, parked over at the curb. Two uniformed officers stood beside the vehicle. He slowed the van and stopped when one of the officers stepped out into the street and held up his hand.

The officer walked to the van. "Your license, please."

Abel stared at him.

A scream came from the back of the van. The officer grabbed for his revolver. Abel floored the accelerator. The tires screeched as the van lunged ahead, barely missing the second officer standing at the end of the patrol car. That officer pulled his revolver.

"No, they have a girl in the back!" the other one shouted.

They jumped into the patrol car, hit the siren and lights and, tires squealing, lunged after the van.

The officer driving gave his location and that they were in pursuit of a vehicle with a possible hostage.

The van's lights disappeared to the right. They slid around the corner. In a minute they were only a few feet behind the van.

The officer driving held his revolver in his hand. The

one in the passenger seat lifted a 12-gauge shotgun from its rack.

A block ahead of them, another marked patrol car, lights flashing at its top, slid to a rocking stop in the middle of a darkened intersection.

The van never slowed, veering to the left, crossing the opposite lane, and bumping on across the sidewalk and into a yard. Ahead of the van lay a narrow space between two small brick houses.

The van's sides scraped the corners of the homes as it passed between them with a sound of screeching steel and a shower of blue sparks.

The officer driving the patrol car braked cautiously as he approached the gap.

"Come on, dammit!" the other officer shouted. "They're getting away!"

The van slammed headlong into a thick brick post along a redwood privacy fence at the back of the yard, knocking the post down and riding up on top of it, where it hung, its front wheels in the air, its back wheels, still spinning, smoking against the grass. The driver's door flew open, and a blond teenager dressed in a pullover and jeans hopped out.

The patrol car skidded to a stop and the officers jumped from it.

"Stop!"

The blond grabbed the top of the tilted eight-foot fence and swung his leg over it. He sat at the fence's top for a brief instant looking back at the van, then disappeared to the other side.

The officers were almost to the rear door of the van when it flew open. A second blond jumped out, uttered a loud, guttural sound, and darted towards the fence.

The officers saw the dark-skinned girl, her face in her hands, the form of her bare body and her clothes lying on the van floor.

The officer with the shotgun dashed out to the side of the vehicle as the second blond started over the fence.

"Stop!"

The blond leaped from the top of the fence toward the next yard as the officer pulled the trigger of the shotgun, lowered it, and fired again. The two loads of double-ought buckshot alternately blasted fragments of wood from the top of the fence and riddled its center with holes.

The officer ran to the barrier, grabbed its splintered top, and pulled his body up to look over into the next yard.

He let himself back to the ground, a confused expression on his face. The other officer rushed up to the fence. "You got him?" he asked.

"No, I didn't." He shook his head in disbelief and looked at the shotgun.

"No, I didn't."

CHAPTER 20

After they stepped inside the apartment, Adrian turned and draped her arms over his shoulders. "Ease up," she said, staring directly into his eyes. "They didn't really have any choice but to ask you to take a polygraph—or else come downtown for an awful lot of questions. It *could* be your name under the bed. We found him—you and me. You had been looking for him without me."

"I'm not even thinking about that. It just caught me by surprise."

She dropped her arms from his shoulders and started toward her kitchen. "Want a glass of wine?"

"Be fine." He walked around the coffee table and lowered himself to the couch. In a moment Adrian was carrying two of the plastic glasses toward him.

"Born Dr. Malone's Ancient Man," she said as she handed him one. "After seeing that, if it had been nine months I would say the impossible happened. Or what did you say—a slight chance."

"Adrian, maybe he wasn't referring to born in a literal sense. It could be a descriptive word—the new day born of the sun, an action born of some steps that he was taking. What steps was he taking? Hell, all I wanted to do was find him so I'd quit thinking about it. Now I'm more confused than I was."

* * *

Missey grasped the stainless steel pole at the middle of the stage, hooked her calf around it and, keeping her full breasts arched high for the customers, spun backwards. She went around the pole once, twice, then the third time, each time sinking lower toward the stage's wooden floor.

With perfect timing, she finished her routine lying flat on her back, one knee bent and her other leg straight, her toes pointed, as the jukebox quit blaring. The men at the tables around the stage roared and clapped.

Except for the two blonds. They had stared at her expressionless the entire time she stripped, and still sat the same way, without moving. It wasn't that they hadn't enjoyed her routine. Their dark eyes had stared at every part of her body. Something about them intrigued her.

As she gathered her clothes off the stage and slipped them on she glanced back at them. The larger of the two raised his hand and beckoned.

She came off the stage and walked through the smoke-filled atmosphere of the club to their table.

"Boys."

Then her eyes narrowed. They really were *boys,* not more than thirteen or fourteen and looking it, with their smooth faces and dressed in too-tight pullovers and jeans. Whoever was on the gate had gone crazy letting them in. She shook her head and turned away from the table.

"Come here," one of them said, and she looked back over her shoulder.

"Listen, boys, you've had your look. Now you better get out of here before the boss sees you and has you thrown out."

The smaller of the two, though not smiling, had a pleasant look on his face, but the larger one's face, though he was expressionless, too, somehow looked hard, his square jaw jutting farther out than the other boy's. He stared up and down her figure.

His dark eyes locked on hers. "I want you to go with us," he said.

"Yeah, honey, you and about ninety-nine point nine percent of the rest of the hornos in here."

"Are you a prostitute?"

"Listen, little buddy, I—" She stopped in mid-sentence when the boy dumped a large wad of bills in the middle of the table.

She glanced nervously across each shoulder. There weren't any uniformed officers in the club, but there seldom were. Any of the men could be from the vice squad, but they usually sat at one of the far walls staring out of the corner of their eyes like they weren't really looking. Nobody had been doing that.

She looked back at the enormous wad of money unfolded on the table. The bills she could make out were hundred dollar bills. There had to be three or four thousand dollars lying there. She smiled at the boy. "Give me a minute to get my things together. I'll meet you out front. Wait at my car—a white Buick near the street." She walked away from the table.

At the bar she leaned over the counter and called for the bartender, a squat man in a wide, white apron.

When he walked up to her, she said, "I've got something that's been hanging on all week. Don't know what it is but it's really getting me down. I was wondering—"

"Some guy wants you to shack up with him," the bartender said.

She shook her head. "I told you I was feeling sick."

"You know the rules." He held out his hand.

"I tell you, Clarence, I'm feeling bad."

"Don't make no difference whether you're feeling bad or going to get screwed, Missey—the rule stands. You leave here before your shift's over, you owe fifty bucks and don't get paid for any of the night. You don't like that, take an Alka Seltzer and get back out on the tables."

"I got a break coming. I'll be back in a minute."

She turned and walked toward the door. If the kids didn't fork up enough money to cover the overhead she could come back in. She damn sure wasn't going to hand over fifty bucks, then find out the little bastards were just bluffing with money they had to slip back in daddy's pocket before the night was over.

Outside, the blonds were waiting near the rear of her car parked in the line close to the street.

"It's going to take two hundred bucks," she said, "and fifty. Two hundred fifty."

She looked at the smaller one. "And if this is going to be a three-way party it's going to be three-fifty—and that's only for an hour, too."

The larger blond turned toward her car and opened the rear door.

"You ain't got no car of your own?"

He nodded for her to climb inside.

She shook her head. "Nobody's driving my car. And the money's up front."

The taller blond looked at the smaller one.

She noticed the questioning look. "What?"

"We need the same thing," the bigger one said, reaching into his pocket for his wad of bills. He handed the whole wad to her.

"Uh, yeah," she said and started counting out her three hundred fifty.

The smaller blond held out his hand.

She looked at the money, so much money, and his hand held out for her keys. If she played her cards just right maybe she could end up with a lot more than three-fifty. Keep the bastards happy, she thought, and reached into her purse. "Yeah, okay, but be careful." She handed the keys to him, then looked back at the money. She couldn't believe he had thrust such a wad into her hand. She knew girls in the club who could cut an extra three or four bills off without ever being noticed.

The larger one pushed her toward the open door. She started inside the car. He pushed her again.

"Not so damn fast," she said. "We got all night."

The blond shut the door and turned toward her as the one in the front seat began backing her car from its space.

The one next to her grasped her arm and pushed her backward, trying to force her down onto the seat. Jesus, he was strong. She caught his hand. "Hey, the hour doesn't start until we get there, baby. You can take your time." She glanced at her arm. Damn if she didn't think it might end up bruised. They still hadn't taken back their money. She held it out to him.

He caught her thigh and yanked it around toward him, forcing her backward on the seat.

"Hey! I said easy."

He grabbed the top of her blouse.

"Dammit, will you slow down a minute?" He suddenly ripped her blouse down the front.

"Why, you crazy bastard . . ." Dark eyes peered down at her. "I want out of here." She tried to push him away from her and sit back up. "Now!" she said loudly. "I mean now, dammit! I want out of here now."

The car bounced out of the club's parking lot onto the street. She suddenly screamed for help as loud as she could. The blond in the front seat stared over the backrest. The one on top of her jabbed the heel of his hand into her jaw, knocking her unconscious. Her hand fell limp against the floorboard, quivered once, and opened, spilling the bills.

They drove to I-240 and crossed over to I-55 towards downtown Memphis. Missey came awake there, looked down to her skirt, still pulled up, and the blond now sitting beside her in the seat staring straight ahead—coldly, his face totally devoid of expression. She suddenly knew she was going to die.

She grabbed for her door handle. The blond reacted quicker than a striking snake, grabbing her hair and yanking her back, and driving the heel of his hand into her face again.

Her eyes rolled back in her head. He let go of her hair and she crumpled forward to the floorboard. They continued on toward the old Memphis-Arkansas bridge.

Taking the exit off I-55 toward West Memphis, they drove several miles then turned onto a gravel road.

Twenty minutes later, as they drew closer to the Mississippi River, Missey squeezed her eyes against her pounding headache and stirred. Shaking her head back and forth, she slowly pushed up off of the floorboard. She raised her head and stared up at the blond. The back of her hand came to her mouth. As he continued to stare back at her, tears began to run from the sides of her eyes.

She shook her head slowly in desperation. "Please, pleeease."

Abel turned off the gravel road onto a narrow, one-lane entry into a field, stopped the car, and stepped from it. In a moment he opened an old gate emblazoned with a NO TRESPASSING sign and came back to the car.

A half mile farther, Missey could see they were approaching a stand of towering oaks. Not far off to the left she saw a line of willows and, through them, the glistening of the moon off the dark water of the river.

She looked ahead of the car and saw nestled in the big trees ahead a faint, dark outline of a tall, two-story house.

When they stopped, Cain stepped outside and walked toward the house, which was festooned with decayed and splitting columns at its front. Abel stood in the car's open door. He held his hand out towards her.

She closed her eyes, trembling, slowly reached out for his hand.

His grip was strong too, but gentle. He was expressionless, but somehow there was a pleasant look about his face.

She looked in the direction the larger blond had gone and then back to the first. "Please, I beg you. Please let me go. Pleeease."

He pulled her slowly toward him, and she stepped out onto the ground.

They didn't go toward the front of the house, but around toward its rear. Near the back corner on that side and flush with the ground, a door stood open. It wasn't the rear entrance into the house. She could see that door a few feet away at the back of a wide, screened porch.

The blond nodded toward the open doorway. In the dim light she could see a descending staircase.

She drew rigid. "No!"

He grasped her arm, firmly.

"Please, I don't want to," she begged. She stared him directly in the eyes and shook her head back and forth.

He started her towards the doorway with no more effort than a man pushing a toddler along.

She stumbled at the top of the staircase and thought she was going to fall. Her foot pedaled against empty air. But she was held by his unmoving hands as if she hung from a steel hook suspended from a large crane.

She found a wooden step under her feet and they moved down the stairs. The dirt-floored area below them had no lights but was illuminated in dim shadows by the glow coming through a half-open doorway a few feet from the bottom of the stairs. Stepping through that doorway, she found they were in a room brightly lit by a single bulb hanging from a bare wire. She looked at the next doorway he pushed her toward. It was dark beyond that.

When they entered that black room he moved her a few feet and stopped. Her eyes quickly adjusted to a shape in front of her—the larger blond. She heard the unmistakable sound of a chain rattle to her left. Her stomach twisted in pain.

Oh my God, she thought and gasped. Her knees grew suddenly so weak she would have fallen but for the smaller blond holding her arm.

"Pleeease."

It wasn't her voice.

It came from the same direction as the rattling chain. She forced herself to look and saw the shapeless shadow next to the wall.

Her eyes went suddenly back to the larger blond moving toward her with a length of chain in his hand.

She tried to step back, but couldn't. It was as if her arm was locked in unyielding concrete.

The larger blond pulled her hands together and clamped a set of iron manacles across her wrists. He pulled on the chain, yanking her toward the wall.

"Pleeease," the shadow moaned again.

The voice was deeper than she had first thought—a man's.

She was turned around and felt her arms pulled above her, then heard the chain being looped over something above her head. Her arms were suddenly jerked higher.

The blonds moved down the wall, then there was the sound of a chain being moved again. She heard the man say "no" and whimper.

Then the three of them stepped from the wall and walked toward the light shining through the open doorway at the far side of the room.

"No, *señor*," the man protested, struggling against their grip.

The larger blond's hand struck quickly, and the Hispanic went limp. The two dragged him through the doorway with no more effort than if they had been pulling a trailing rope. Missey could hear his feet drag, *thump, thump, thump,* up the stairs.

Outside the cellar, the man's limp form dragging between them, the blonds closed the door and moved across the grounds toward the old, dilapidated barn, a couple hundred feet behind the house. A wisp of greasy, gray smoke came out of the loft and curled up in the dim moonlight.

When they opened the barn door and dragged the man inside, he began to come awake. His eyes widened. There was a smoldering fire at the center of the barn. Curling up from it was a dense, gray cloud of heavy smoke. Suspended upside down in it by a chain hanging from a rafter was the charred, blackened bottom half of a man, his legs and buttocks. The Mexican passed out.

CHAPTER 21

The next morning Cameron sat at his desk as his students turned in their test papers one by one, a couple of them shaking their heads in an obvious sign of how they had done. The last student to approach his desk was Lee Ann Pearson, *the student* as far as the males in the class were concerned, thanks to the tight jeans and blouses she always wore over her ample figure.

That was what she had on now—jeans and a red silk blouse, its material straining to contain her heavy breasts. She smiled down at him, her big eyes bright and captivating. He always had been a sucker for eyes.

He returned her smile. "Yes?"

"Dr. Malone, I was wondering if you ever tutored?"

"I've never been asked."

Her smile broadened. "Would you then? I could meet you wherever you want—at your convenience."

He smiled a little at that. "I've stuck pretty close to the text, Lee Ann."

"I know, but I'm just . . . after this test I know I'm really going to be behind. You see, I was sick and didn't get to study as I should have."

He had a large class and didn't remember the scores each student made on his other tests, but he seemed to recall she had done well. Maybe she was telling the truth. "How much lower did you do than you feel you would have normally done?"

"I don't know—pretty bad."

"Ten, fifteen points below your normal? What do you think?"

Her eyes narrowed questioningly. "I haven't thought of it that way. I don't know, maybe fifteen or twenty points, I guess."

"Okay, Lee Ann. I'll tell you what I'll do. Whatever you make on your score, I'll give you an additional fifteen points. That way you won't have to pull up on the next test to keep your average." He raised his forefinger to add emphasis to his next statement.

"But only this one time, Lee Ann. It's up to you from now on out."

She stared down at him for a moment, then suddenly nodded. "That's a deal. Thank you so much."

He watched her walk from the class room. *Tutoring,* she had said. *I could meet you wherever you want—at your convenience.*

She was unusually attractive. But that might be as much against her as in her favor. She was using her looks as a crutch.

The fifteen points he had given her didn't matter, whether she was lying or not. If she was telling the truth and really sick, she deserved the break. If she was lying and hoping to rely on her looks, the points would be quickly used up in her not being prepared time and time again. He glanced at his watch, walked to the door and pinned a note on it to cancel his afternoon classes, then drove downtown to the Criminal Justice Center.

Adrian waited for him inside the building's Poplar Street entrance. She wore a beige linen dress that fit her perfectly, and had her hair down, once again giving her the appearance of a model on assignment. She rode up in the elevator with him then led him to the room where the examination was to take place.

He felt a slight nervousness he hadn't expected and

wondered how that might affect the test, but relaxed somewhat when the examiner assured him it would have no bearing on the results.

All the questions were gone over in detail before the examination began. "So you don't get any surprises," the examiner explained. "The test isn't designed to catch you off guard."

Then it started, the examiner asking the obvious, if preposterous—was he the killer, had he been aware before the body was discovered that Dr. Anderson lived in the old farmhouse, had he known Dr. Anderson in the past?

After the session had concluded, the examiner looked up at Lieutenant Warrington and shook his head, then removed the blood pressure cup from Cameron's arm and started slipping the other attachments loose.

Though the examiner did as he said he would with the questioning, and though Cameron knew every answer he gave was the truth, perspiration had gathered on his forehead.

The lieutenant noticed. "Sorry to have put you through this, Dr. Malone, but the victim did scrawl your name under his bed, unless there *is* a Malons. Did you think anymore what it might have meant—born C Malons or Malone?"

"You can be damn sure I've been thinking about it. But other than what Adrian said last night—*born Dr. Malone's Ancient Man*—I don't have the slightest idea. And you're going to have to tell *me* what that means."

A pensive expression on his face, the lieutenant nodded. Then he shrugged. "Well, thank you again, Dr. Malone. If something does pop into your mind, let us know."

Cameron didn't even bother to tell the lieutenant to call him if he came up with anything that might more surely point to Anderson as the one who broke into the case. Why waste his breath?

"You ready to eat?" Adrian asked. "I know a great place for soups and sandwiches."

As they stepped out of the building into the bright sunlight, a long-haired brunette in jeans, T-shirt, and a windbreaker approached them.

When she stopped in front of them, Adrian said, "Cameron, this is Joni—my best friend. You spoke with her the day you called about it being Anderson at the center."

He smiled politely and the brunette smiled back at him.

"We're going to catch a sandwich," Adrian said. "Want to come along?"

"Too busy, Adrian."

"What are you doing here, anyway?"

"On my day off, isn't that the pits? Catching up on paper work."

A line of black men and women coming down the sidewalk caught their attention. The man in the lead, a tall, broad-shouldered, middle-aged man in a dark suit with a stiff white collar above the neck, carried a placard with JUSTICE FOR ALL emblazoned on it. The blacks glared as they went past and stopped at the front door leading into the station.

"The Reverend Balls," Joni said.

"Bolls," Adrian corrected.

"Bolls, balls," she countered, "one thing's for sure. He's slung with a couple, willing to lay his ass on the line for others, or else he has an eye for a good controversy and knows it'll put his name in the limelight— however you want to look at it."

Cameron looked back at the small group of people now starting to parade up and down in front of the station.

"He's Reverend Jonathan Bolls," Adrian explained. "A black teenager was raped by two blond teenagers last night. There were two other rapes—both committed by black assailants. One of them raped a black woman and was caught a couple of hours later. The other one raped a white woman and was shot to death running away from an officer who came up on the attack. But the blonds are still only God knows where. And on top of that there were no fingerprints left in the van—they wore gloves, evidently—and the officers say they didn't get a good enough look at them to even give an accurate description—other than they were blond teenagers. Add all of that up and you see what has the reverend upset—how it looks."

Joni nodded. "Every day that passes without the blonds being caught, the reverend will get more and more upset. Want to really have a lot of fun, let the blonds stick it to a couple more black women and get away with it. The department would start issuing extra bullet proof vests if that happens."

Cameron read a second placard now being held aloft:

A PISTOL AT A HUNDRED FEET
BUT NOT A SHOTGUN AT TWENTY FEET.
NO MORE LIES.

"What does that mean?" He nodded toward the placard.

Joni shook her head in irritation. "I personally know the officer who shot at the blond," she said. "He's telling the truth, but I wish he hadn't mentioned it. The black who was shot was running down a dark street, a hundred feet or better away from the officer who killed him—with a single pistol shot. The officer who took a shot at the blond was less than twenty feet away—just a little farther than the length of the stolen van the teenagers were driving, and he used a shotgun." She shrugged, admitting the unlikelihood of the officer having missed from so close a range. "Well, I have to be going. Catch you two later."

The soup and sandwiches at the little downtown spot *were* good. Partly, Cameron realized, because he had been unable to eat breakfast after rising with the scent of blood in the old house in Arkansas still in his nose— and the thought of Anderson's empty skull.

Adrian poked the last bite of her tuna sandwich into her mouth, then wiped her slim fingers on a paper napkin.

Cameron sipped his tea. It was good, but his thoughts weren't; he never had liked fanatics of any stripe—left, right, or in between, whatever their cause. "What does that guy think? Just because they were a couple of blonds, you should know who they were?"

"What?"

"The character leading the bunch with the signs."

Adrian shook her head. "He doesn't bother me. What does bother me is the credibility the press gives them when they say we don't care. People seeing that are going to believe it. I wouldn't want to be that poor young girl they're talking about, raped, and thinking nobody cares, that nobody is really trying to help her. I know how she has to feel—violated, used, like she was a piece of garbage. She's even feeling guilty, I guarantee it—I see it in rape victims all the time. Why didn't she listen to somebody, she's thinking? Why was she dumb enough to be in the particular place she was in? How come she wasn't alert enough to avoid it?"

She shook her head as she paused, but her thought now wasn't about the girl. "The captain didn't like me being out there with you last night."

"What do you mean?"

"You were looking for Anderson—police business. And there I was going along with you. I was on my own time, so there's not a lot he can do about it, we didn't do anything illegal. But I do have to get along with him."

She looked past his shoulder. "Joni must have changed her mind."

Cameron turned to see her friend approaching their

table. When she stopped beside them, she looked at Adrian.

"The chief wants to see you, Adrian, and Dr. Malone, too. He said *now*."

CHAPTER 22

Chief Young was a handsome brown-skinned black man with wide shoulders and greying hair. He met them in the front of his office right after his secretary had announced their arrival. He held a newspaper in his hand. He unfolded it and held it out to them.

It was a grocery store tabloid—*The Whole Truth*. Near the top of the front page, Cameron saw his own face staring back at him as he and Adrian stood in front of Dr. Anderson's house. In a photo next to his, Adrian's ex-husband and Lieutenant Warrington looked toward the camera. The headline over the photographs was dramatic:

PALEONTOLOGIST KEY TO APPREHENDING CANNIBALS
RUMORS OF A DEADLY PRESENCE BROUGHT FROM AN
EGYPTIAN TOMB

Cameron took the paper into his hands. "I've never been to an Egyptian tomb." He smiled.

Chief Young didn't. "It's the usual garbage you get in something like this, but it's also serious. It says you know who the cannibals are and it just hasn't come to you yet—some crap in your subconscious mind, the spiritual stuff that comes to you from time to time since you were in the Egyptian tomb they made up. Anybody crazy enough to do what those sickeys did to the doctor, they might be crazy enough to believe something like that."

Cameron had been about ready to laugh at the article. It now took on a different perspective. He looked from his photograph back to the Chief. "How did they get this out so quick?"

"It's a new tabloid that decided to headquarter here. Memphis has everything now. They used a wrap-around cover over the issue they already had printed. Must have rewrapped it only hours ago."

Cameron noticed the print under his photograph—and saw the mistake. He looked at the line under the other photograph. "They were in such a hurry they got the names under the photos wrong. Under my picture they say Adrian's standing next to Gerald Cummings—police sergeant."

Adrian reached for the paper. "Christ, I can't get away from him even in print. They've got your name under his and Lieutenant Warrington's picture. Maybe it wouldn't be so bad if the killers did take offense." She looked at the byline above the article—Ben Utterback. "Utterly wrong, Utterback old boy."

"Somebody serious enough, they'd get the right names with the right pictures," Young said. He reached for the paper, folded it and stuck it under his arm. "I did want you to be aware of it, Dr. Malone. You never can tell."

The car sat a hundred feet from a heavily wooded bank of an old slough running another hundred feet to the Mississippi River. Cain sat silently in the passenger seat, staring straight ahead. Abel opened the trunk and lifted two heavy black plastic garbage bags from it. He started down to the edge of the river—where the current ran strong.

A hundred yards out in the river, a small, green aluminum boat drifted silently on the brown water. The heavy-set game warden at the stern scanned the bank with his binoculars. He saw the stocky blond come down to the river's edge, lift a heavy-looking dark bag out over the water and shake it. His eyes widened behind the binoculars when the white flash of bones and the oily color of intestines splashed into the water. He grabbed for his motor, yanked the ignition cord, cut the boat in a sharp turn as it jumped forward, and flew throttle wide open toward the shore.

When the aluminum boat was fifty yards from shore the blond looked up, but made no effort to grab the other bag of evidence and run.

The warden didn't cut the throttle until he was only a few feet from the shore. The boat came on hard to the bank, banged up onto it and slid to a jolting stop. He slowly stood. "What you got there, boy? Deer out of season? More than likely headlighting them too."

The blond's expression didn't change. Out of the corner of his eye, the warden saw the other blond walking toward them. He slipped the safety strap back off his automatic and smiled.

"You and your buddy both gonna take the rap, or is it one or the other's turn?" He stepped from the boat into the soft mud, and walked toward the garbage bag in front of the blond. The second blond stopped next to the first.

"Twins, huh? Double good-lookin'." He laughed. He leaned toward the bag, unwrapped its top, then kicked it over onto the bank sloping down toward the water.

At the glistening intestines oozing out onto the mud, he didn't show any reaction. Nor did he when the arm and leg bones came out of the bag. At the sight of the ribs, his eyes narrowed.

The skull rolled out.

He grabbed for his automatic. Cain moved in a near blur, grabbed the man by his thick neck and lifted him bodily from the ground. Abel held the man's wrist and took the automatic from his hand. He threw it out to splash in the river. The man gurgled.

Cain squeezed his hands tighter, shook the man in a

rapid back and forth motion. There was a snap. The man went limp, his hands falling to his sides. Cain slipped the body under his arm and started back toward the car.

Abel began to clean up the mess, and was a few minutes in returning to the car. Cain sat patiently in the front passenger seat. The green aluminum boat revolved on the swirling of a whirlpool not far from the bank, broke loose from the suction, bobbed, and slowly drifted sideways down the river toward New Orleans.

After leaving Chief Young's office, Cameron drove his Maxima back to Adrian's apartment complex and parked in front of the swimming pool. When her beige Taurus drove in and parked under her covered space he walked to it and met her as she stepped outside the car.

The expression on her face told him she had something on her mind.

"I didn't get a chance to tell you downtown, but I found out some more about Anderson this morning," she said, "when the captain was getting on to me. Since your photograph was on the front page of that piece of junk, I think you should know. Nothing to do with the possibility Anderson stole the sample. The chief's not even thinking about that right now. There were two children there."

At his sudden wrinkling of his brow she said, "They weren't killed. An old woman who lived down the road said they were there, though, as late as yesterday afternoon—a pair of eleven- or twelve-year-old twins. Also, the woman buried at the side of the house—ME's preliminary report is she bled to death a few weeks ago while giving birth. Still another child unaccounted for. She had ID on her—a Mary Jenerette. We have a rap sheet on her. She was a local prostitute. She wasn't Dr. Anderson's girlfriend, either, at least not staying at the house of her own accord. She had a chain attached to her leg. You remember the room up the hall from where they found Anderson? Captain said the foot rail of the bed in there had scratch marks on it.''

They started up the stairs leading to her apartment.

"Her being local is one of the things that worries me, Cameron. Dr. Anderson was local. Was whoever killed him local too? Probably I'm off in left field, but I didn't want you to be opening your door to any strangers.''

He smiled a little. "You didn't have to worry about that.''

"It might be a cult. It might be anything. But the chief's beginning to wonder if the murder could have something to do with pornography, maybe child pornography. There was all the cash that Anderson had that's missing now, the prostitute chained to the bed, and the kids. In addition the Arkansas officers found a bunch of video tapes burned in the fireplace, and there were pieces of a crib that had been burned, too.''

She stopped in front of her door and pulled her key from her purse. "They're still looking for graves around the house, but right now we have to assume that whoever killed Anderson took the children—whatever the reason they were there in the first place.''

As they stepped inside the apartment she said, "I'm going to change into something a little more comfortable. It'll only take me a minute. I bought another bottle of wine this morning, if you'd like something to drink.''

He turned on the television. An announcer's voice played behind a scene of the house where they found Anderson's body. That same scene had been on about every half hour now, and the *Commercial Appeal* had headlined the cannibal story. The city was fairly buzzing at the horror. Cameron had seen and heard all he wanted to about it.

The naked body of the game warden pressed flat against an inside wall of the barn, a wire around his neck supporting his weight. Abel peeled a wide strip of skin down the stocky man's back. He used his fingernails, sharp and rigid as steel, to separate the skin from the grayish white connective tissue. He used a butcher knife, though, to saw the section of skin loose just above the buttocks, and pitched it aside. He also used the knife as he began scalping the man. A pair of large rats, sensing they had nothing to fear, ran from a pile of decayed straw and pounced on the slippery skin; they began dragging it back toward the straw.

"Did you find the wine?" Adrian called from the bedroom as he stepped from the balcony back inside the apartment.

"Haven't looked."

"It's in the cabinet next to the refrigerator. Would you mind bringing me a glass? They're in there, too, the plastic beauties."

He found the bottle and poured one of the small glasses half full of the clear liquid, then carried it down the hallway to her door.

She stood before her dresser mirror. She had slipped on a pair of tan slacks and a white blouse, but the blouse hung unbuttoned outside her slacks. He could see part of the thin line of her bra and the soft mounds rising above it. She caught the blouse and pulled it together then began buttoning it at the top.

He set the glasses on the dresser, caught her shoulders, and turned her toward him. She slipped her hands around his back.

He pulled her to him and kissed her, gently at first, and then harder, then moved his hand to her top button.

She caught his hand with hers, stopping it.

He didn't try to continue, but neither did he move his hand away.

She looked into his eyes for a long moment, then her hand slid away from his and up his forearm.

He moved his fingers again. The button came loose, and he leaned forward and kissed a side of her neck.

When he lifted his face, she stared back at him, then closed her eyes as he moved his fingers to her bare skin at the top of her bra, running them gently over the swell there, and then down lower, cupping her breast from the side.

Then he caught her bra strap and pushed it from her shoulder, and she came forward with her lips, kissing him as her arm slipped out of the blouse and the strap.

He caught her around her back and under her legs and lifted her. She kept kissing him, her hands moving up to the back of his head.

Even when he reached the bed and raised his knee onto the mattress, leaning forward to gently deposit her onto the cover, she didn't quit kissing him, hanging onto the back of his head and pulling him down with her, on top of her.

Now she worked with the buttons of his shirt, and he reached to those of her slacks.

In a moment she had pulled his shirt back from his shoulders and raised her hips and tugged her slacks down her legs.

As he came down against her and into her, he was careful, as careful as he had ever been, strong in his movements yet gentle.

Then as she rose on a wave that caused her to gasp her passion, he was swept away too, lost in her sweetness and her strength, all she was, and this too—more than he had ever felt before.

The two blonds sat across from each other at a table in the Memphis Public Library on Peabody. A stack of books sat between them—*Principals of Physics, South American Horizons, The Last Two Million Years, Strange and Interesting Facts,* as well as several advanced chemistry textbooks and other mixed titles, all of them either works on South America or technical, scientific manuals.

Abel read a work by Albert Einstein. Cain read from a trade electronics publication. Cain closed his book and Abel promptly followed suit. Cain stood. Abel stood. They walked toward the entrance of the library.

A thin, unshaven, older black man sat at a table along the way. He held before him a copy of a grocery store tabloid delivered to the library that day.

Cain stopped at the edge of the table when he saw the headline on the front page. He reached out his hand and pulled the paper from the man's grasp.

The man's eyes widened and his mouth gaped. Then he became angry. But when he saw Abel's dark eyes staring at him he didn't say what he had started to.

Cain stared at the photographs on the front page and quickly scanned the rest of the story.

The old man looked back over his shoulder toward the long counter and the librarians working there. Cain dropped the paper on the table, and the two walked on toward the door.

The old man looked back to the table at the paper and the photograph of Adrian and Dr. Cameron Malone side by side with the one of Lieutenant Warrington and Gerald Cummings. He looked back over his shoulder to the two blonds nearing the front door of the library. When they opened the door, the bright sunlight outside fairly glinted off their hair, and then they were gone.

The old man felt his hand tremble and clasped it with his other one. After a moment, he rose and walked to a pay telephone on a wall near the entrance to the building. He had enjoyed the warm day and the bright sunlight as he had walked from his home not more than a mile away. But for some reason now, he couldn't bear the idea of walking back there alone again. He asked for a taxi to be sent to the library, then walked to the door and waited inside the building until it arrived.

CHAPTER 23

Adrian's blouse and slacks lay on her bedroom floor. Cameron, a sheen of perspiration across his forehead, lay with the sheet pulled up to his waist, exposing his chest, tight with lean muscles. She rested her head on his shoulder and curled her body close to his. He played with her thick hair and smiled down at her.

"Chameleon," he mumbled.

She glanced up at him. "What?"

"Has anybody ever told you you're hard to figure?"

She looked away from his eyes again. She had been like that since they finished.

Men, she had said. *Women,* he now thought. What was it with her? And then another thought. Had she given herself to the sophomore football star, and then was dropped? Then she gave everything to Gerald, and how had that been repaid? Should he tell her that she didn't have anything to worry about, that he would be hers for as long as she . . .

And what else but that had Gerald and maybe the high school boy told her.

He took a deep breath. "Would you like a glass of wine?"

She nodded without looking at him. He came up off the bed, slipped his pants on, and walked toward the kitchen, past their still full wine glasses on the dresser.

He would give her some time. That was all he knew to do.

They stood crammed close together inside the telephone booth. Abel looked into the directory, and then raised his face to Cain. Cain lifted the receiver and punched in the number.

"Memphis University." It was a young woman's voice.

"Is Dr. Cameron Malone present?" Anyone who had heard Dr. Anderson speak would have recognized the tone.

"Just a minute, sir, and I'll ring his office."

They waited a full minute. Then the young woman came back on the line: "I'm sorry. Dr. Malone's not in at the moment. Would you like to leave a message?"

"I would like his address."

"I'm sorry, we couldn't give out something like that." The young voice lowered. "I'm sure you can find it in the directory."

"No. There is no listing for a Dr. Malone."

"Oh, I see. Well, he did move here just this fall. I don't guess it's had time to be listed yet. Sorry, sir."

Cain replaced the receiver. He looked at Abel. They both held in their minds the headline that had been on the front page of the tabloid in the library.

"He has reason to know," Cain said.

The telephone rang. Adrian, now back in her tan slacks and white blouse, reached to the kitchen counter and lifted the receiver.

"Hello. Oh, hey, Joni. What? That's none of your business." She looked at him. "No, that doesn't mean he's here. It just meant that it was none of your business."

She laughed softly at the next thing Joni said, then she listened seriously for a few seconds. "You didn't. You trying to get me up on a morals charge? Okay? Uh huh. Just kidding. Okay, bye." She replaced the receiver.

Cameron smiled. "The defender of truth and honesty."

"Jail's too full to worry about misdemeanors anymore."

He glanced down her body. "What about rape?"

She didn't respond. Suddenly she actually looked sad.

He shook his head. "Sorry, bad joke."

"No," she said. "That's not it. You made me think about the teenager who was raped. She was on TV again last night, a tape from the time right after she was raped. She was almost numb when they were talking to her."

"I didn't think they showed the victim."

"It was her idea. Or whoever talked her into it. If what they wanted to do was show how traumatic rape is, they picked the right victim. She looked like she was in a trance. Every time she started to talk, she burst out crying. She's just a little girl, maybe fifteen or sixteen. I hope to God she doesn't believe those characters who say we don't care."

She took a deep breath and shook her head. "Damn," she said. "Being a cop isn't all it's cut out to be. You know, I worked as a candy striper for a long time. I was thinking more along the lines of being a nurse someday, but then I married Gerald. We didn't have the money on hand for me to go on to nursing school, and he wouldn't co-sign a note. He talked me into joining the force. I've grown to like it. As much as anybody else likes their job, I guess. You like yours?"

"I like anything right now," he said, and stepped close to her, slipping his arms around her and pulling her close to him. He kissed her forehead. "You wanna cook some steaks?"

She pulled her head back. "I almost forgot. Joni said some professor called downtown looking for you. About a meeting you needed to know about."

"Who?"

"She didn't say. She told him you might be with me."

"Nobody knew I was taking a polygraph. I didn't think."

"You were on TV last night. Maybe you were today. Something was probably said about you taking the test."

"That'll be great. I'll have some students thinking I'm a cannibal."

She smiled, one of the few times she had since they had made love. "You want to call and see what it's about?"

"I could care less."

She set up off his shoulder. "Steaks sound pretty good. If you'll do the cooking, I'll supply the material. They're in the freezer."

The red Jeep Wagoneer turned into the complex and parked a couple of hundred feet beyond Adrian's apartment block.

"He has reason to know," Cain repeated. Abel repeated the same thing in his mind. They were at the height of their emotions now, their faces expressionless.

A car slowly driving past Adrian's apartment caught their eyes. A moment later the car went on by. Abel reached to the ignition key.

"The steak was great," Adrian said, laying her fork back on her plate.

"What did you expect; coming from me?"

"You know what I was thinking while I was eating it? That its DNA was broken down."

"I do enough of that kind of thinking for both of us." He looked at his watch. "Duty calls. Sleep anyway if I'm not going to have to cancel classes again tomorrow."

She nodded. "Yeah, me too."

"I don't normally volunteer to do dishes. But I guess your sleep is as important as mine."

"I'll catch them in the morning."

"You sure?"

She nodded again. "Yeah. I really am tired."

They walked toward the door, where he kissed her, then moved along the walkway to the stairs, down them, and across the pavement toward his car parked in front of the swimming pool. He didn't see the form crouched in the dark beside the car next to his.

Adrian pushed the curtain back and looked out the window at him. Then she saw the shadowy shape moving down the side of the car next to the Maxima. She grabbed the bottom of the window and yanked it up.

"Cameron—behind you!"

Cameron, opening his car door, whirled at Adrian's loud shout. The figure was already on him. A section of steel pipe came down hard. He dodged backward onto the car seat, kicked out hard with both feet, catching the burly, hooded figure in the chest and bouncing him backward against the next car.

Cameron jumped immediately back to his feet and struck out hard at the unseen face, grabbed the arm with the steel pipe and struck rapidly twice more with his fist. The figure was jolted back into the car. He tore his arm loose from Cameron's grip and swung in a round house with the pipe.

Cameron dodged beneath the arc of the pipe and struck out left, right, left with his fists.

The pipe came on a backswing, thudding into his ribs and bending him sideway. Gasping with pain, he threw his fist up hard, catching the figure on his jaw under his mask, jolting him. The man stumbled back a step. Cameron, immediately on him, hit him twice more, then twice again, his fists a blur; the man staggered out behind the cars and toppled backward to the pavement. Cameron came after him, but the figure kicked out hard, his feet catching Cameron in the chest and knocking him backward to the pavement.

A loud shot split the air. The figure jerked his hooded face toward the stairs leading from Adrian's apartment. Gun in hand she flew down the steps.

The man scrambled to his feet and ran toward the next apartment block.

Cameron sprang to his feet as Adrian dashed by him, and they both chased after the man, now darting between two sets of apartments.

They ran harder, between the apartments and into the darkness behind them.

He was gone.

The blocky, hooded figure hurdled through the trees. A branch slapped him in the face, and he cursed silently. He slowed his pace to a jog—in the nearly pitch-dark under the overhanging limbs they couldn't have followed him; no one could without eyes that could see in the dark.

He slowed still more.

He began angling toward the edge of the trees, in the direction he had left his car—and saw movement. His pounding heart caught. He started to dash to his left.

But he saw nothing more. *Had he only thought he had seen movement?* It had been near the edge of the trees, where the thinner growth overhead allowed partial moonlight through the branches to create a half-light half-dark. He had been almost sure. A siren erased his thoughts. Somebody in the apartment had called. He had to get to his car before they arrived. He started hard to his right—and again he glimpsed the motion. Sure now. A swift shape, just at the edge of the trees. The siren was closer. He had to get around them to his car. He sprinted forward. A branch slapped him again and he threw it back with his arm. They had been along the outside of the trees, keeping pace with him. *Bastards!* He hurdled hard through overhanging limbs and through a patch of briars pulling at his pants. His breathing increased. The siren pulled into the apartment complex. He stopped.

He turned slowly, silently, listening; were they coming in after him? He would hear them. He would circle back the way he had come. He squinted hard, looking in the direction of the movement. But he was far enough away from the edge of the trees now that he couldn't glimpse the half-light half-dark—only an occasional spot where a funneled beam of light came down through a break in the overhead.

He saw the brief flash—a narrow ray of moonlight blotted from view for a millisecond. It was a hundred feet away. He wasn't even sure. He edged backward. Suddenly a thin ray of moonlight twenty feet away blackened—a flash of blond hair.

And they were on him.

"Damn!" Adrian cursed under her breath. "Are you hurt?" She walked back to him. Cameron shook his head. She glanced on into the dark. They heard a sudden sharp groan—loud. Another groan. Then what sounded like the noise of football players thudding hard into tackling dummies amidst the trees. They darted forward as fast as they could go.

Fifty feet, sixty feet, seventy feet, they slowed their pace to go around a patch of briars.

No more groans had come their way. Adrian threw an overhanging branch back out of her way and increased her pace.

A hundred feet farther they came to a stop. Still no sound. She glanced over at him. Looking back past her, he glimpsed two shadowy figures near the edge of the trees.

"There," he said softly.

But not softly enough. The figures turned in his direction. He saw the long bulky form on one's shoulder. At that second Adrian surged toward them.

The figures looked at her. The bulky shape dropped to the ground. They dashed back into the dark trees off to their left.

Adrian ran harder. Cameron passed her. He came first to the form on the ground.

It was the man who attacked him. Adrian went a few steps farther. But there was no noise of the fleeing figures crashing through the undergrowth; not the slightest sound.

Cameron stared at the form. It was the man who attacked him, all right, but different. There were still the wide shoulders, but they slumped flat on the ground. The entire body spread out almost like a balloon full of water. One of the forearms bent awkwardly back at the wrong angle from his elbow. Cameron knew what he was going to find, but he knelt anyway and felt for a pulse on a thick wrist.

There was none.

Adrian walked back to the spot and looked down at the broken form. "Is he dead?"

Cameron nodded. He reached out his hand to the bottom of the hood and pulled it up past the man's face. His throat tightened.

Adrian brought her hands to her face. *"Oh, my God,"* she said in a low voice. "No."

The blood continued to widen from beneath her former·husband's head.

CHAPTER 24

Police Sergeant Gerald Cummings' graveside service took place three days later on a muggy Saturday morning. His next of kin—his mother, a distant uncle, and two cousins—added to the several police officers and a couple of friends to form an adequate group of mourners.

As the crowd dispersed after the preacher's final amen, Gerald's mother looked out across the tombstones to the street and Cameron parked there. He had wanted to walk to the grave with Adrian. But she told him it wouldn't be right. He knew the woman couldn't recognize him from such a distance, but her look made him feel guilty anyway. He was glad he hadn't accompanied Adrian.

In a couple of minutes, Adrian, in a dark, knee-length dress, and Joni, in uniform, came out of the cemetery and walked across the street to the car.

Adrian paused at the passenger door and looked at her friend. "Joni, could it have been whoever killed Anderson?"

Joni didn't answer for a moment. When she did her voice was low and gentle, but her words uncompromising. "Somebody who was scared he knew something about Anderson's murder would have just killed him, not beat him to a pulp like that. How many thugs had Gerald brought in after he worked them over—worked them over bad? The real thugs, they don't go to court to get even.''

"Uh huh, I know," Adrian said slowly. "He followed us, and they were following him, and he never knew it. When he ran, he must have run right into them. Two of them is all we know. Cameron and I didn't even get a good enough look to see if they were black or white. They had to have used lead pipes. Every bone in his . . . '' She shook her head.

Joni stared at her for a moment. "Adrian, he was a mean bastard. He didn't hurt only thugs, he was getting ready to hurt Cameron, maybe kill him. This one belongs to homicide now. That's where you need to leave it.''

The two women hugged each other. A moment later, Joni walked down the sidewalk toward her car. Adrian opened the passenger door.

"His mother didn't say a word to me," she said as she slid inside onto the seat. "If it had been my son I probably wouldn't have either.''

Cameron started the Maxima and guided it out into the street. "I still think you should take off a few days," he said, "like the chief suggested.''

She shook her head. "I need something to keep my mind occupied.'' She looked back across her shoulder to Gerald's mother, dressed in a long black dress and now closer to the grave, standing with her head bowed.

Her lip trembled. "Damn, if it could have been in a car accident or something, even if he had been shot. But to be beaten where half his bones . . . ''

He laid his hand gently on her shoulder. "Adrian, Joni gave you some good advice. We've talked about it and talked about it. It's not going to get any better.''

She nodded, was silent for a moment, then suddenly said, "I want to go to the Johnson girl's house.''

He looked at her.

"The Johnson girl," she repeated. "Cassandra Johnson—the teenager who was raped.''

He continued to look at her without speaking.

"Cameron, if she's thinking nobody cares, she's got to be dying inside. I want her to know I care."

Cain sat on a couch in the living room of the old columned house; the flickering light from the television set cast dancing shadows across his otherwise expressionless face. The screen showed the funeral scene—the burial of Sergeant Gerald Cummings.

Cain's eyes narrowed slightly. Abel, coming in the back door with a heavily loaded black garbage bag, stopped where he was. *Cameron Malone?* they both thought. Cain came off the couch. Abel left the garbage bag lying next to the back door.

A few seconds later the red Jeep Wagoneer moved out from behind the tall, columned house and toward the entrance road.

Cassandra Johnson lived in a racially mixed, upper-middle-class section of town, most of the houses in the eighteen hundred to twenty-five hundred square foot range.

Her address was that of a small, redbrick two story. There was a new white Cadillac and a several-year-old red BMW parked in front of the garage.

Adrian adjusted her dress and rang the doorbell. Somebody pulled the curtain back at the side of the door before they heard the lock turn.

The black woman facing them was about Adrian's height, maybe five-six or a little bit taller. She had straight black hair.

"Yes?"

Adrian produced her badge from her purse and smiled softly. "This is the home of Cassandra Johnson?"

"Yes, it is."

"This isn't official, ma'am," Adrian said. "I'm just coming by on my own to see how she is doing."

The woman didn't say anything for several seconds. Her eyes narrowed a bit. "How do you think you'd be doing, officer, after being raped and nobody cared about it? Now, if that's all you need, I'm busy."

Cameron had to bite his tongue not to speak. Listen, he wanted to say, *care*, what do you mean care? How much more could a person care than to come straight from burying . . .

But he got no farther with his thought. She was a mother suffering terribly for her daughter.

The woman continued to stare. Cameron laid his hand on Adrian's shoulder to turn her back toward the car.

"What is this?" a large, dark-skinned black man said as he stepped up behind the woman.

He wore a red sweater, a pair of black slacks, and soft leather house slippers. His graying hair was clipped close to his head.

"You two go on," the woman said. The inflection in her voice had changed, almost like she was urging, not demanding anymore.

"What's going on?" the man asked.

The woman dropped her gaze.

Adrian looked at her a moment then turned back to the husband. "I'm Sergeant Adrian Cummings. I came by to see how your daughter was doing. Nothing official."

"Doing?" the black man asked, raising his voice. "Would you like for her to tell you?"

"No, Charles," the woman said, "I told you—"

"I don't give a damn what you told me." He looked back over his shoulder and called loudly toward the living room.

"Cassandra! Come here a minute."

The woman stared up at the man then turned and moved back into the house.

The girl came slowly down the hall. She was a thin, light-skinned child, with straight hair like her mother's, about five-seven—attractive, in a loose, white sweatshirt and faded jeans.

"My wife says we hide it," the man said, still talking

too loud. "Hide it, how? She's gonna have the child, not no abortion, and evidently—" He looked back at the girl who stopped just behind him. She dropped her eyes at his stare.

"Evidently," the man continued in his same loud voice, "she thinks keeping quiet about who the bastard was who got her pregnant is something to be proud of."

Cameron looked at Adrian. She had a questioning look, too. "She became pregnant after the rape?" she asked.

"Afterwards, hell," the man almost shouted. "We took her in to the doctor yesterday because we were worried the rape could have transmitted a disease. No disease at all the doctor said, only she's nearly two damn months pregnant. Now she won't tell us who the boy was. Well, she can raise the kid without any help from him and can get a job, too; the hell with going to college if she don't care anymore than to keep lying to me—right to my face."

Cameron felt a pang of helplessness. He had never had a day when he felt so sorry for so many people at the same time. Adrian handled it much better than he could have. She held her hand out toward the girl and smiled. "I'm Sergeant Adrian Cummings, Cassandra."

The girl stepped to her father's side and reached out and grasped Adrian's hand.

Adrian, continuing to smile, shook the girl's hand gently. "I know we haven't been able to catch the ones who raped you, but I wanted you to know we're still trying. We won't give up."

The girl glanced sideways at her father, then nodded at Adrian.

"I raised her as good as I could." The father still spoke loudly. "She gets raped and I go all to pieces feeling sorry for her. My little baby—my little virgin baby, I tell everybody, spoiled, ruined by a pair of white bastards. Then this comes up; she wasn't a virgin. She's still lying. I *was* a virgin, Daddy, she keeps saying." He shook his head in disgust. "Being pregnant don't take away from what those white boys did. But what they did don't give her no excuse for what she had been doing before that, either. Wrong's wrong."

Cameron wanted to knock the man clear into the living room. He tightened his fists at his sides, ached to do something. He looked at Adrian. "Let's go," he said, his voice nearly breaking with anger.

Adrian reached into her purse and pulled out a card and ballpoint pen. She wrote her name and telephone number on the card as the father stared down at her. She handed it past him to the girl.

"If there's anything you need, anything you're wondering and want to ask about, call me at that number. I have an answering machine. If I'm not there, I'll call as soon as I get back in and get your message. I'm sorry for what you're having to go through." Adrian glanced at the girl's father. "All of what you're going through."

As Adrian turned away from the door and Cameron started to follow her back toward the car, the girl spoke for the first time. They turned back for a moment.

"I *was* a virgin," she said. Her lip trembled.

Her father stepped in front of her and slammed the door.

When Cameron reached Adrian's car, he slid in under the steering wheel and slammed his door in disgust.

"A bastard like that doesn't need to have children."

Adrian glanced back at the house as they pulled away from the curb.

"If we catch the ones who did it," she said, "they'll never be convicted after the defense attorney puts her on the stand—not if she's still swearing she was a virgin before the rape. She's in shock. She needs help, and she's not going to get it from her parents."

She looked across the seat at him. "I want to go by Lieutenant Warrington's house."

The red Jeep Wagoneer drove along a street next to the university campus. Dozens of people walked everywhere, though it was Saturday. Cain faced forward. Abel turned the Wagoneer back in the direction it had come. Their minds, always at top efficiency, wasted no time, flicking forward to the last item they needed.

CHAPTER 25

Lieutenant Warrington came outside to talk to them on the covered stoop of his home. He was still in the uniform he wore to the funeral.

"I don't see how we can do anything about it," he said after Adrian explained what happened. "It's up to her family to get her psychiatric help."

"We have to do something," Adrian said. "Even if we catch the two boys, they'll walk with the condition she's in. What jury's going to give any credence to testimony by a girl who was obviously pregnant when she was raped and swears under oath that she wasn't. Her medical records will be conclusive. Even if we weren't talking about losing a conviction, she needs help anyway. No telling how much deeper she's going to retreat into her world—especially with parents like she has. I came to you because I know how close you are to the chief. He can go to the mayor. Somebody can do something."

The lieutenant cast his eyes down to the ground and shook his head again. "If I go to him, and he agrees, if everybody wants to help—it's still up to her parents."

"Maybe Reverend Bolls will talk to them."

"Who's going to Bolls and ask him?"

"I will."

"Adrian, you have pressure enough on you as it is

right now. You need to go home and take a couple days
off, or you're the one who's going to be needing help.''

"Will you go by and see the chief—and Bolls, too?''

"I'll make a deal with you, Adrian. Promise me you'll
go home and not put anything else on your mind for
awhile, and I'll go by and see the chief—first thing Monday. It'll be up to him if I speak to the reverend.''

"Thank you.''

"Honey,'' came a soft voice from inside the house.
"You have a telephone call.''

"Thanks, lieutenant,'' Adrian said again.

The building supply store in West Memphis not only
catered to walk-in customers, but had a large collection
of materials used by contractors.

Cain stepped inside the store, looked around for a
moment, then started across the floor toward the rear
of the building. Abel followed.

A heavy-set, middle-aged salesman in brown coveralls
stepped from behind a counter and, a polite smile on
his face, hurried to meet them. Service was the watch
word of the store. But as he stopped before them, they
ignored him, passing by him and continuing on across
the floor.

At the rear of the building, Cain stopped and stared at
the rolls of heavy-duty electrical wire wrapped around
big spools. Seeing the size he needed, he moved to the
spool and immediately began unreeling the wire.

The salesman hurried up to the two.

"If you'll tell me how much you need, I'll measure it
off for you.''

Cain continued to unroll the wire, looping it into a
coil as it came off the spool. The salesman stared but
didn't say any more; he didn't know who Mr. Rodgers'
best customers were, and the kid evidently was satisfied
with an estimated quantity.

In a minute, Cain stopped unrolling the wire, hooked
it into the notched cutter on the side of the spool, and
severed it at exactly seventy-eight feet.

He handed the coil to the salesman, then reached into his pocket, pulled forth a large wad of bills and held them out.

"Just a moment," the man said and hurried back to the counter where he began measuring the wire with a yard stick. The two blonds followed him there and silently stared.

The man smiled politely and hurried.

"Seventy-eight feet," he finally said, and quickly ran the price up on his calculator.

Cain laid the wad of money on the counter. The man stared at the bills for a moment, then picked out two twenties.

"Thirty-nine fifty," he said, "including tax."

Cain gathered the rest of the money back into his hand and reached across the counter to take the roll of wire from the salesman before he could drop it into a bag.

"Uh, thank you for your business," the man said as the two walked toward the door. He held the fifty cents change in his hand.

Outside the store, Cain and Abel didn't walk to the red Jeep Wagoneer in which they had arrived, but to an old Ford that an older couple had parked in the strip center a minute before.

Cain slid in on the passenger side while Abel walked around to the driver's door.

In a moment the old car roared to life, backfired once, and slowly backed from its parking spot.

At the far side of the parking lot, a lanky man in bib overalls sat in his pickup and stared at the blonds driving the old Ford away.

"Did you see that?" he said.

The man on the other side of the seat spit a stream of tobacco juice out his window and nodded. "Yep, sure did. Stole it as sure as shootin'."

The first man looked at his 30-30 in a rack across the rear window of the cab. "Let's git 'em."

The man in the passenger seat grabbed the dashboard and yelled, "Go!"

The pickup burned rubber as it jumped forward toward the exit from the parking lot.

The pickup screeched to a halt at an intersection. Beer bottles on the floor board crashed together with such force that one broke.

The narrow faced man driving looked to his left and back to his right.

"Where in hell did they git to?"

"There, Henry!" the man in the passenger seat exclaimed. He pointed out the window down the road to his right. The Ford was just turning off onto a narrow paved road running toward the lowlands near the Mississippi River. The pickup's engine roared, its wheels squealed, and the man on the right grabbed the dash again.

A mile along the road leading toward the river, Cain looked over at Abel. Abel tightened his hands on the steering wheel. They knew the pickup was coming, though neither had looked behind them.

A minute later the pickup neared their rear, then whipped out to the left and drew alongside them. A blocky, middle-aged face stared at them down the barrel of a 30-30.

"Pull the damn thing over!" the man roared. "You're caught!"

In the Ford, Abel slowly lifted his foot from the accelerator at Cain's unspoken command.

"Pull 'er over or I'm fixin' to shoot!' the man leaning out the window roared. Then he got a better look at the two in the car. His brow wrinkled and he looked back over his shoulder to Henry. "It's a couple damn kids!" he exclaimed. "I ain't gonna shoot no kids."

Henry kept his eyes on the road. "You don't have to shoot 'em. Shoot the car."

"How in hell's that gonna help the owners, Henry? Wait a sec. They're pullin' over."

"Keep a bead on 'em. Lot of little peckers nowadays got guns."

The man with the rifle nodded and peered down the barrel again.

In a minute, the two vehicles sat side by side on the narrow blacktop.

"What now?" the man with the rifle said.

"Get in with 'em. In the back seat where's you can guard 'em. I'll follow behind you back to town just in case."

"Just in case what?"

"Hell, man, you're the one totin' the rifle. Shouldn't be no *just in case* unless'n you fall asleep."

The man with the rifle opened the door and stepped outside. The teenagers stared straight ahead through the windshield of the old Ford. The man leaned foward and peered past the blond driving the car to the other blond on the far side.

"Now, I'ms gittin' in with ya, and we're headin' back to town. You got that?"

When neither boy did anything but continue to stare straight ahead, the man stepped closer to the car.

Abel's hand suddenly shot out the window and grabbed the end of the 30-30's barrel.

"Henry!"

Henry saw the broken beer bottle on the floorboard and grabbed its jagged half, threw open his door and jumped out to the pavement.

He ran around the front of the pickup, then suddenly stopped as Abel wrenched the rifle from the man standing by the car. *Uh, oh*, Henry thought.

The blond laid the weapon in the seat beside him and opened the car door. He stepped outside.

Henry peered forward through the car's window to see what the other boy did. That one, too, opened his door and stepped outside, then started around the front of the car.

Henry sneered, hefted the half of the broken beer bottle in his hand, and stepped rapidly toward the boy facing his partner.

"Git the hell way from that car, boy," Henry roared, meaning to step up to it and reach inside the window for the rifle.

The boy suddenly reached out a hand and caught the man in front of him by the throat.

"Hey!" Henry roared and stepped forward. Cain stepped in front of him. Henry looked at the dark eyes glaring at him. The kid was facing a beer bottle and staring like that. *He had to be on dope.*

"You little bastard," Henry roared and lunged forward with the bottle.

Cain caught his wrist and twisted it, instantly snapping the bones. Henry screamed. Cain caught his throat and, extending his hand upward stiffly in the fashion of a Nazi salute, lifted him bodily, kicking, from the pavement.

A minute later, the old Ford started down the narrow blacktop again, the 30-30 lying in the seat between Cain and Abel, the two men's lifeless bodies stacked on top of each other in the rear floorboard.

In twenty minutes they passed through the old, wooden gate with the no trespassing sign and stopped. Abel stepped outside, pulled it shut, and hurried back to the car. It backfired and started forward again.

At the big columned house, Cain stepped outside the car and Abel drove on to a thick, tree-shaded clump of shrubs off to the far side of the house.

A few seconds later he carried the two bodies, one under each arm, toward the barn.

When he came back outside, he went to the car, opened the trunk and lifted out the roll of wire, then moved into the house and up into the attic.

Once there, he began running the wire from the section they had already installed inside the wall, laying the new strip across the floor to the two-way radio, now modified to the standard they envisioned.

After he finished with the last connection, he turned and looked at his brother.

Two levels below, Missey, her arms stretched above her head by the chains bolted high up the wall, shivered as she sat in the cold darkness on the cellar's dirt floor. She closed her eyes and began sobbing again.

"Missey," came the soft voice from a few feet down the wall to her left. "That doesn't do any good."

It was Lee Ann speaking. She had not cried once since she had been carried down into the cellar three nights before, her skirt and blouse ripped, the blonds obviously having already mated with her.

"Okay, Missey?"

Missey shook her head and started sobbing once more.

"No, Missey, you have to keep strong. We have to be alert. They're not going to kill us. You've seen that. We have to be ready if a break comes our way."

What, Missey thought, *what could we do if we got the chance against two crazed men as strong as granite statues?* She started crying again.

"Please, Missey, you're making it hard on me, too."

Missey raised her face and looked in the direction of Lee Ann's voice. "There's nothing we can do," she choked.

"There might be something," Lee Ann said. "We have to be ready if . . . " Then her voice broke, and she started crying, too.

In a moment they were both sobbing loudly, hopelessly. Their wailing filled the cellar and escaped through the narrow window at ground level, floating up through the cold, dark night to the attic of the old house.

There, Cain raised his head and listened for a moment, then looked back down at Abel, sitting on the dusty floor arranging transistor tubes and blank circuit panels into an arched, electrical circular pattern in front of him. The two-way radio, capable of reaching halfway around the world, sat off to the side. Cain gave a silent command, and Abel reached for the radio and slid it over in front of him.

Cameron and Adrian had barely arrived back at her apartment when the telephone rang. It was Lieutenant Warrington.

"It's too late for the case now," he said. "The Johnson girl went down to her church and begged the Lord to help her. She was so hysterical the reverend called 911 for help. The media monitored the call and beat everyone down there. Her condition will be all over the air now."

And it was, on all the TV stations, and repeatedly, presented in a way meant to invoke sympathy for the girl, but nevertheless destroying her ability to be a credible witness if those who raped her were ever caught.

Adrian's lip trembled as she watched the screen. Cameron felt deeply for her, and awkward too, finally slipping his arm around her shoulders. "God, Cameron I'm such a wimp!" she exclaimed, then broke out sobbing. He pulled her close, wrapping both arms around her, and held her that way until she stopped.

Lee Ann sobbed, but more in anger as she pulled hard on the chain looped above her head. She began sawing it again, pulling down with first her left hand and then her right. The sound of the chain moving back and forth against whatever secured it to the wall caused a dull sound, not a metallic one, maybe something that would saw in two. She pulled harder. The raw circles around her wrist began to bleed freely.

She sawed harder. Warm blood trickled down her arms and dripped onto her shoulders. She sawed harder.

Missey kept whimpering softly, every few seconds

making a loud, short, high-pitched wail. Yeep. Yeep. Yeep.

Lee Ann closed her eyes and tried not to hear it. It was like a fire alarm with low batteries. Yeep. Yeep. Yeep.

It was maddening, like the dripping of a water torture. Lee Ann sawed harder.

She was bathed in a rectangle of bright light.

Abel stood in the doorway to the room with the single light bulb.

Lee Ann quit sawing.

Abel walked directly toward her.

When he stopped, he stared with his dark eyes directly into hers, then looked up at the chain stretching above her head.

He knew.

He reached above her head and caught the links, pulled on them to test them, then turned and started back toward the lighted doorway.

His foot brushed the water bucket he had left for her the day before, and she looked at it. She had turned it over in her jerking, trying to break the chains loose. Her mouth was so dry her lips cracked. She would have given anything for a drink. But she would die before she asked him.

He stopped and looked back at her. His eyes went to the bucket. He moved to it, lifted it from the dirt floor, turned back toward the doorway, and walked through it and out of sight.

Lee Ann, her forehead wrinkled in thought, stared at the doorway, still open. They had never left it open before.

The wrinkles in her brow grew deeper. She looked up at the chain. She had made no noise, the sawing motion impossible to hear from more than a few feet away. Yet he had come and checked.

Suddenly he came back through the door. She almost hoped the bucket he brought back with him had no water. But it did.

Her lip trembled, and it took all she could do to keep from screaming her hopelessness.

My God in heaven, they can read minds, too.

He stared at her. Heard her thought. He loosened her chains. She sank slowly down the wall to the dirt; her tears began to flow again. She looked at the bucket of water as he set it on the floor beside her. Suddenly she ducked her face forward into the bucket, splashing the water out to the sides of the container and gulping her fill, almost strangling, wishing she could drown herself.

The wrecker's crane slowly lifted the front of the pickup from the pavement.

Off to the side of the blacktop, a Crittenden County deputy used a stub of a pencil to jot notes onto his pad.

"Belongs to Henry who, now?" he asked the old man who had called in the abandoned vehicle.

"Henry Carpenter. Called his wife. She said that he went into town to shoot a little pool with his cousin. I called there, too. Didn't get no answer."

The deputy printed the information onto the pad. "We have a game warden left his pickup setting on the road too. Didn't come back to the office." The deputy scratched his head. "Hope there's not something strange starting around here." Then he shook his head. "With all the drugs and stuff out there, not much telling anymore what some coked up bastard might be up to."

CHAPTER 26

Sunday they attended mass together, though Cameron was a Baptist. Monday, he was back at the university again, though his mind was more on Adrian's depression than his class. He thought of Cassandra and how her father had reacted. There should be some kind of law against a man like that having children. Your child was your child, whatever they did wrong—even the lowest members of the animal kingdom recognized that. Let the whole world desert a kid, that was fine, but his family was still supposed to be there.

His parents would be. He could be a serial killer and they would. Someway, somehow, they would still love him and stand by him—they were supposed to.

He shook his anger from his mind and looked out over his class. His students were looking over the tests they had taken a few days before. Most of the seats were empty, only a few students not yet finished with their review. That meant most of them were going to score well, again. He did have an excellent class.

His gaze fell on Lee Ann Pearson's empty chair, and that made him feel a little bad again. She had skipped classes ever since he had given her a break by adding fifteen points to her test. Though her original score had been a lot better than he expected.

To have it all, he thought, *looks and obviously more brains than he had given her credit for, then for her to have misread his gesture and relied on her looks. The fifteen points wouldn't last very long.*

Then he had a second thought. Maybe she really had been sick, and it overtook her again.

He smiled at himself. *Who was lacking brains?* But he had always been a sucker for eyes.

The bell ending his class rang, interrupting his thoughts. The students still remaining in their seats hurried toward the door. One of the boys said, "Whew," as he went by the desk. Cameron smiled again, finally starting to get out of his down mood.

"Excuse me," came a tiny voice from off to his left.

He turned in that direction. Even with him seated the gray-haired woman who had walked in the door wasn't much taller than he. She might have been five feet—maybe. She was a little dumpy and wearing a white dress that hung loosely on her. Both her build and the way the dress fit made her appear even shorter than she really was.

He rose from his chair. "Yes, ma'am?"

She looked at the last student going by the desk and waited for him to pass her on the way to the door. Then she looked back toward the desk again.

"I'm Lee Ann's mother, Mrs. Rosemary Pearson."

There was some resemblance there, even in the round face. "Glad to meet you. I'm Cameron Malone."

"I know. Have the police been by to see you yet?"

When he narrowed his eyes questioningly, the woman nodded and said, "Figured that. They think she's just run off with some boy. I know better than that."

"Lee Ann's missing?"

"Yes sir, Dr. Malone. And I can't hardly take it. She wouldn't have run off with nobody, no kind of way. Not my Lee Ann."

He didn't know what to say. "I'm sorry. Maybe she had somewhere she had to—"

He stopped at the woman shaking her head solemnly.

"No kind of way, Dr. Malone. She calls every Saturday without fail. This week she didn't."

He pondered for a moment. She needed to know. "She missed my class, Wednesday and Friday."

The woman shook her head. "She doesn't miss class, either."

"Yes, ma'am." In the name of helping her he had now added an extra three days to her worry.

She looked back up at him. "I thought maybe she might have said something to you if she was having a problem with anyone—you know, a jealous boyfriend or something." She shook her head. "No, I knew she wouldn't. I don't know what I was hoping—just was. But I've said my prayers, and I'm prepared for the worst, if it comes down to it."

"She'll turn up soon, Mrs. Pearson, and have some reason she hasn't called."

"Thank you for saying that, Dr. Malone, but I know that's not going to happen. She was right about you, though. She said you were a good man. She thought a lot of you, you turning her down about coming over to your place and all. She respected that."

He was taken aback. "You must be awful close for her to have confided something like that."

"We are, Dr. Malone—very close. But don't get the idea she was going to do anything like you're thinking if she came—that's just Lee Ann's way. She messed up and forgot when one of your tests was and blew it, and she wanted to butter you up so she could get you to drop the grade. She's on scholarship, you know, and has to keep her grades up."

"No, I didn't know that."

"Like I said, Dr. Malone, that's just Lee Ann's way. Back in Piggott—that's Piggott, Arkansas, a piece north of here, she had every man teacher in the school in her hand. She deserved to be valedictorian and would have gotten it anyway. But she didn't leave nothing to chance, neither, not nothing. That was just Lee Ann. She's always had a strong mind and always knew what she wanted to do—help abused children. She's intended ever since she was a little girl to make good grades, get a good job, then make enough money to be able to help children like that."

She glanced back to the door of the classroom. "Well, like I said, I figured the police didn't come by here. I was hoping maybe—somehow—you might know something. That one of you teachers might."

She looked to the door again. "Well, sorry to bother you, Dr. Malone. I'm gonna run on along and talk to her other teachers now."

"You didn't bother me at all." He wanted to say more. But what else was there to say?

As the woman shuffled from his classroom, he looked at Lee Ann's desk. The whole damn world seemed to be coming apart. At least his part.

As the woman walked out the doorway, a young, long-haired male student passed her coming into the room.

"Dr. Malone," he said, "you have two telephone calls in Dean Jensen's office. Both of them said to tell you it was important," he added matter of factly.

In the big, columned house in Crittenden County, Arkansas, Cain stood in the center of the attic, in the wide open area under where the rafters came together in a point.

He looked up at the transmitting antenna projecting through the hole they had cut in the roof. Abel waited in front of the two-way radio.

Cain lowered his gaze to his brother and nodded.

Abel depressed the switch to the recorder spliced to the radio, and the single attic bulb hanging from an exposed cord at the center of the attic dimmed. The message sped quickly up the antenna and radiated out into the bright, cloudless sky.

Cain waited a few seconds, mentally counting, then nodded again. Abel again depressed the switch.

A wisp of light smoke rose from the back of the radio

as the bulb dimmed once more then went out, leaving the attic in only the dim light from the hole in the roof as the message again sped up the antenna and flashed through the air with a vast surge of power.

In the cellar, when the light went out in the little room between the area where they were and the stairs leading up to the back of the house, Missey started crying again. Lee Ann fought back her tears by biting her lip.

When she felt she had her emotions in check, she looked over at Missey, squatting on the floor, leaned back against the wall with her hands held up in the air by the chains.

In the faint illumination that came through the narrow window at ground level, the silhouette of Missey's bulging stomach was apparent. Lee Ann looked down at her own stomach, still flat, and prayed.

Cameron's mother was on one of the lines in the Dean's office, and he took her call first. She had seen the article and his photograph in *The Whole Truth* and was worried about him.

"Mom, you can't believe anything you read in that rag."

"Somebody wasn't eaten by cannibals?"

"Possibly."

"That's what it said, didn't it? Your father and I don't like you mixed up in something like that. What do you know about ghosts from an Egyptian tomb, anyway? You've never been to Egypt—that I know."

"That's what I mean, Mom, the whole article was garbage. I knew the victim and went out to the murder scene. That's where they took that picture. I won't be having anything else to do with the case. So don't worry about it."

"That's what you said when you brought that box in your room with a water moccasin in it. Oh," she suddenly said, "thinking about that now makes me want to lift my feet off the floor. You know we never did find it."

"I promise, Mom."

"Okay, Cameron, if you say so. But be careful."

"I will, Mom."

"When are you coming down here to see us again? You know the last time was before school started."

"I'll try and run down there in a week or two."

"Good, we'll be looking for you. And bring that woman, too. What's her name?"

"Adrian."

"She was the one in the picture with you, wasn't she?"

"Yes."

"She's a pretty little lady. I'd like to get to meet her."

"I'll bring her with me when I come. Tell Daddy I love him, and you, too."

"He won't hear it until he's got the last of the soybeans in. I'll tell him then."

Dr. Baringer was on the other line.

"Where in hell did they have to go to find you? On the other side of the damn state? I've been holding for ten minutes."

"I was in class, and then my mother was holding on the other line."

"Well, I guess that's an acceptable excuse. How is she doing?"

"Fine."

"Good. Those damn Italian scientists, they not only won't give us permission to take a sperm sample, they're insisting now that we cut the tour short. They know some asshole in the State Department, too. I received a call from him saying maybe we should forget our contract and send the Ancient Man back to Italy now. America first, huh—bastard! But I'm not really concerned about that. Time it would take them to break the contract the tour would already be over. Why I actually called is to report some good news—possibly. I received a fax from a gentleman today inquiring as to how much it would cost to furnish us for another expedition.''

Cameron felt his pulse quicken.

''I have an appointment with him at his office in Chicago next week. He's never financed anything similar to this in the past, but seemed excited at the prospect when he was talking to me on the telephone. He was saying how a discovery like ours was going to put us in the history books—and maybe whoever became our financier, too. We're not talking about a patron of the sciences here. It's strictly an ego thing with him.''

''Who cares.''

''Precisely in line with my thinking, Cameron. And I will stress to him how important he could end up being when I meet with him. Well, guess I have to run. I knew you would want to know.''

Cameron thought about the man in Chicago as he replaced the receiver. Was luck going to strike twice? It certainly had the first time with his roommate's father. Then the estimates of the expedition's cost had turned out to be barely half of what they ended up spending. That had ended any chance of a second round of funding by the small company, no matter how great their discovery had been.

Then they had thought about getting funding from the foundations. That's who they had really been counting on for their subsequent funding anyway, especially after making the discovery they had. But the controversy had denied that. What if the Ancient Man did turn out to be from a period much closer than the first tests had indicated? The foundations didn't want their names attached to something that might eventually be labeled a fraud. They were obviously waiting for the scientific community to settle the matter once and for all.

Damn, he thought, how much longer was that going to take? How much longer until they could return to the spot? Somebody would. Somebody would scour the area like they wished to, trying to find another body, artifacts, something more that might be lying just below the ice—waiting.

He thought back to the telephone conversation. If anybody could talk the man in Chicago into going along with the financing, it would be Baringer. Maybe he could. He had an urge to cross his fingers, knock on wood—something. *Come on, Baringer, make him think he could end up being one famous son of a bitch.*

Then he thought about Lee Ann's mother and how worried she was, and about Cassandra, and how she had to feel now, and about Adrian, too. Whatever her bad times with Gerald, she had known him most of her life. And the way he died . . . and of course she was feeling badly about Cassandra, too.

Suddenly he couldn't help but feel guilty that he was so buoyed at the prospect of his possible good fortune. His guilt bothered him. He wanted to feel good. *Damn,* he told himself, *make up your mind.* He shook his head and moved out into the hall.

Damn, what a week.

"Gone," Clarence the bartender said.

The short, red-haired man who had inquired about Missey wrinkled his forehead questioningly.

"What do you mean gone?"

"Can't say it no plainer than that. Just gone. She's done it before, up and took off with some dude who had a few bucks on him—or she thought did. She'll be back when the money runs out. Always has come back."

CHAPTER 27

When Cameron arrived at Adrian's apartment, she opened the door for him, then quickly stepped back to watch the living room television. A pair of composite drawings depicting two blond children with square, protruding chins, completely filled the screen.

In the background an announcer's voice explained they were the children seen playing in front of the old farmhouse outside of West Memphis where Dr. Anderson had been murdered, and that they were missing now. The announcer said they were eleven to twelve years old and gave an eight hundred number for anyone who might have seen them to call. A thousand-dollar reward had been offered for information leading to their safe return.

"The chief was able to talk the old woman into coming in and undergoing hypnosis," Adrian explained. "Up until then she hadn't been able to describe them in enough detail. But under hypnosis they got enough out of her that they were able to form a drawing. Now if only somebody has just seen them and recognizes them from the composite."

She walked toward the kitchen. "Do you want a glass of tea?"

He shook his head.

She retrieved a glass from an overhead cabinet and filled it from the pitcher on the counter. As she lifted the glass to her mouth, he asked her if she was feeling any better.

"You want the truth?" she replied dryly.

The telephone on the counter rang, and she reached to answer it.

"Hello," she said, then immediately smiled. "Cassandra, how are you doing?" Cameron noticed the sudden tightening of her eyes. She shook her head at whatever the teenager had said.

"No, Cassandra, that couldn't be right. You need to—"

As she stopped with what she started to say, she looked at him. After a moment she spoke back into the receiver.

"Cassandra, I don't think you should tell anyone else that. I don't . . . no, I don't think you're crazy, but I think that if . . . okay, okay, go ahead. Uh huh, I'll listen." Adrian took a deep breath and looked very sad.

Cameron rose from the couch and walked to her. She reached out a hand and took his, squeezing it softly.

"Okay, Cassandra," she said softly. "I understand. Would you mind telling me where you are, so I can check on you from time to time?"

She paused a second then said, "No, I don't have to know . . . okay, but I need for you to keep it between us until I . . . " She struggled for what she wanted to say. "Until I can decide what will be the best way to bring it up. Okay?"

A moment later she nodded and said. "Good . . . uh huh. You be sure and call me back in a little while. I'll be thinking about it . . . you can trust me. You know you can." She replaced the receiver and looked into his eyes.

"Cameron, Cassandra's run away from home. She's going to call back here in a little while. You have to help me come up with some way of getting her to tell me where she is." She took a deep breath. "Her running away is not the worst of it. She says the two faces the TV showed are the two who raped her." She shook her head sadly. "Cameron, the old woman said the children were eleven to twelve years old."

"Is there a way you could get somebody to run a trace on your phone when she calls back?"

She nodded. "I feel so sorry for her. She not only said it was the same kids who were on TV. She said they were the devil, and she had proof of it now."

As she reached for the telephone it rang again.

She lifted the receiver to her ear and said, "Hello." Her eyes closed at the response.

"No, Cassandra," she said, "I haven't made up my mind yet; it's only been a minute. Cassandra, what you're saying, honey, is not going to do you any good if they ever catch the ones who raped you. If you tell everybody these two on the TV were the ones, then the defense attorneys will tear you apart if you ever have to ID the real ones. They—"

She nodded her head. "Yes, I said I believed you. I know you think that—"

She said no more, only listened. After a few seconds she replaced the receiver, turned and leaned back against the counter.

"She asked if I remembered how the ones who raped her had unusually bright blond hair. She said to look at the composites and listen to the description about the missing kids' hair." She looked toward the TV. A movie was now on the screen.

"Adrian, she's fixating on the hair. Anyone who has blond hair—bright blond hair—is going to be the one who raped her. You're going to have to get her out of—"

"Cameron, I wonder if there's any possibility? Any possibility at all?"

He waited a moment for her to continue with her thought. When she remained quiet, thinking, he said, "Give me a hint and maybe I can help you out."

She smiled a little, but it was quickly gone. "You know, Cameron, the woman who saw the kids was real old—ancient. Maybe her mind isn't all that good anymore; maybe her eyes might not have been all that good. I don't even know where the kids were when she saw them. They might have been out behind the house, maybe even inside it and she saw them through a window as she walked past it. Maybe they were older than she thought."

"You're thinking like around fifteen or sixteen instead of eleven or twelve? Come on. The woman would have had to be blind."

"Maybe she was, Cameron, as far as really seeing from any distance. I don't know. It's possible, according to how far away from her they were when she saw them. It certainly wouldn't be the first time an eyewitness was way off base in what she *thought* they saw."

"No, it wouldn't, and it wouldn't be impossible for you to be feeling so much for Cassandra you're letting your feelings override your logic."

"Cameron, what if the children out at Anderson's were members of the cult, or whatever they were? Instead of being kidnapped they were who did that to him—or helped do it?"

"Adrian, they weren't fifteen or sixteen. They were twelve at the oldest."

"Maybe. Let's go out there and see if we can find something that's been overlooked."

"Go out there?"

"Why not?"

"What would have been overlooked?"

"I don't know. There could be something. I wonder if they thought to look in the closet?"

"In the closet?"

"At their clothes. Eleven and twelve year olds don't wear the same things fifteen and sixteen year olds do. At least not in the same size; maybe not in the same styles."

"Call and ask what kind of clothes were found."

"There could be something else I haven't thought of, too. What will it hurt to go there and look?"

It was obvious in her tone she wasn't going to leave it alone. He stood. "Lead on," he said.

"Just a minute." She lifted the telephone and punched in a number.

After waiting for several seconds she hung up the phone. "I thought maybe the Johnsons would like to know Cassandra had called; that she was safe. But there's no answer. Maybe they're out looking for her."

Thirty minutes later they reached the old house. A sawhorse emblazoned with POLICE LINE—DO NOT CROSS still sat across the dirt drive into the lot. A yellow warning sign hung on the front door. Adrian moved up the steps and tried the door knob.

"Locked."

They walked around the near side of the house. Cameron stared into the open trench as they walked by it. He wondered how small the woman had been who had been buried there. There didn't look like there was much more space for a body than what would have been required for a child.

The rear door was locked too. Adrian walked back around the side of the house to the window close to the trench, and tried it. It opened a crack, then stuck.

He moved up beside her and pushed on the window frame, but had no luck. He looked around the area. An old, rusted shovel blade with part of a handle lay in a clump of brown weeds fifty feet away.

He retrieved it and came back to the window. Slipping the point of the blade into a crack at the bottom of the window, he pried against it, and it screeched open.

Adrian tucked her purse under her chin, put her hands on the ledge, bounced once and leaped her shoulders into the opening.

She squirmed, her tight slack-clad legs wiggling out behind her, and went over into the house, disappearing from view.

A moment later, she looked back through the opening and frowned. "If you think I'm going to wander

around in here without you, Cameron, you're crazy."
She glanced across her shoulder into the house's interior. "Come on."

He smiled, stepped to the window, and caught the
stench coming from inside. Not so strong now, but still
the same as he had smelled as a child on his family's
farm, still strong enough to cause him to picture Anderson's head.

Forcing the image from his mind, he stepped to the
window, lifted a leg over the sill, and slid inside.

He was in the kitchen. Though the sun was still high
in the western sky, the sheets nailed across the windows prevented much of the light from entering and
cast the living room in a dim twilight. All of the blood
that had been present before was still there, but had
turned a dusty black.

Adrian looked at a cabinet sitting at the far side of the
living room. "It won't hurt to look for photographs,
too," she said, and then walked to the cabinet and began opening its drawers. He started going through
those in the kitchen.

In a few seconds Adrian turned around to face him.
"Let's look in the bedroom closets."

He followed her down the hall. The first door on the
left was cracked slightly open—that was the one that
had been locked the first time they were there. There
was black fingerprint powder on the door knob, and
she avoided it, opening the door by pushing near its
center.

A pair of small trees, their branches drooping and
most of their leaves crumpled at the base of their
trunks, sat in big dirt-filled washtubs close to the room's
two windows. There were no closets.

The next door was across the hall. It had fingerprint
powder on its knob, too. It was the same room the
deputy had first looked into. There was a set of closets
beyond the empty bedframe. Adrian walked toward
them.

She stopped abruptly. *"Oh!"* she yelled, startling him.''

''What in the—'' He saw the rat run across the floor and jump up into the wall through a hole formed by a plank jutting out from the others.

He felt his sudden surge of pulse ease. ''Damn, Adrian, scare the hell out of me.''

''What do you think about me?'' She stepped slowly forward and raised her toe toward the angled plank. ''No,'' she said, shaking her head and lowering her foot. ''You do it.''

He stepped around her and kicked the plank back into place. He turned and stared at her.

''I'm sorry,'' she said.

She moved to the closet and opened it. It was bare. She walked to the dresser and glanced through its two drawers.

''There were closets in Anderson's room, too,'' she said.

At that doorway she glanced back at him, then stepped inside.

When he walked to the doorway she was looking into the two open closets on the far side of the room. They were both empty.

She turned around and stared down at the dried puddle of blood next to the bed. He ran his gaze around the room. One thing was there that hadn't been before: black fingerprint powder, on the chest of drawers—he remembered the officers working there—on the bed frame, and spotted up and down the straight-backed chair near the door.

He moved on into the room and around the side of the bed. He noticed the powder on the wall by the headboard. The officers had attempted to lift a blood-smeared, smudged palm print from a plank there. Though blood was nearly everywhere else in the room, that was the only place any was on the wall.

Adrian saw where he stared and came over to his side. She knelt and looked closer.

"He put his hand up here. Trying to stand—lift himself up? God, they used the chains on him and he was stil alive; he had to have been in such pain."

She leaned closer to the wall. Her eyes focused on a spot a couple of planks higher than the one smudged with the powder. "Is this edge a little farther out?"

He leaned forward. She pointed to the top of the board. Its edge did protrude slightly. A tiny smudge of dried blood was barely noticeable in the groove between the plank and the one above it.

She reached her hand close to the wall, extended a finger and used a fingernail to pick at the protruding edge. She suddenly drew her hand back to her chest and stood.

"What, Adrian?"

"What if it's another rat place?"

He reached out his hand and used his fingernail to pull at the plank, but it was rigid.

"I have something in my purse." In a moment she had produced a long, metal nail file.

He took it from her, pushed its point into the groove over the plank, and pried.

It swung back.

Curious, he moved his face close and looked down into the wall.

He saw the object.

It was small, rectangular, and black.

He looked closer. It was a tape, smeared with dried blood. He reached his hand down into the space.

"What are you doing—Cameron!"

He caught the tape with his fingers, lifted it from the opening and looked at the small letters printed in blue ballpoint ink on its side.

DR. NOEL ANDERSON—EVOLUTION EXPERIMENT DAY 101

CHAPTER 28

Cameron pushed the tape into the cassette player in his Maxima as soon as he shut the door.

He pushed the rewind button. He felt so anxious he almost couldn't keep from pushing the play button before the tape fully rewound.

Finally, it stopped turning. He quickly pushed play.

"Evolution experiment, day one hundred and one; random notes to myself regarding the children born of the Ancient Man. First, with—"

His turning off the tape caused Adrian to stare at him.

"Cameron, what are you doing?"

"He did use the sperm for . . . but the time frame isn't right. It was—"

"Cameron, will you play the rest of the tape? We can discuss it later."

He pushed the rewind switch, waited a moment, and pushed play.

"Evolution experiment, day one hundred and one, random notes to myself regarding the children born of the Ancient Man. First, with them being born after only six weeks—"

Cameron felt his mouth gape open.

"Don't stop the tape!" Adrian warned quickly.

"—it is obvious that a gene ascribed to the spermatozoa was generally dominant in the birth process of five hundred thousand years ago. Considering that the

*so-called power packs of an embryo's growth are
known to be completely contained in the egg in the
modern birthing process, I remain at a loss here. This
new phenomena will have to be studied at greater
length. As will Cain and Abel's subsequent—"*

At the ceasing of Anderson's voice a quick frown
came to Adrian's face. But the tape had stopped its forward motion on its own.

He backed it up and tried it again, but it wouldn't go
forward beyond the spot where it had originally
stopped.

"It's stuck."

They stopped in West Memphis where he bought a
small screwdriver and opened the case. In a few seconds he had fixed the recorder so the tape would continue on—but nothing more was recorded.

"He went mad, Adrian. Children born in six weeks."

"He sounded calm enough to me."

"Come on, Adrian."

She stared at him. "Cameron, at the very last of the
tape, Anderson is saying, 'Cain and Abel's *subsequent*—
was he going to say 'subsequent growth?' Maybe the
blonds *were* only eleven or twelve when the old
woman saw them, then as old as Cassandra said when
they attacked her. They're Cain and Abel."

"This is insane. I have to call Baringer. After I tell him
this he's going to worry about the ozone layer here."

"Cameron, Cassandra's pregnancy could be proceed-
ing that fast, too."

He stared at her. She lifted his cellular telephone
from the seat. In a minute she was in contact with an
officer at the justice center, who kidded her until he
understood she was serious. He had her wait on the
line for a few seconds.

Her next word was "chief," then she started explaining.

Cameron, lost in the swirling of his own thoughts,
dropped the Maxima into gear and drove out onto the

highway. When Adrian finished with her conversation, he looked toward her.

She took a deep breath. "For one, the chief thinks I'm a nut. So that makes him and you. For two, he reminded me I removed evidence from a murder scene. And you along with me again. He said I have a penchant for doing the wrong thing with you along. He's not too happy that the Arkansas officers hadn't already found the tape, either. I told him that the overhead light in Anderson's room was so dim I could understand them not noticing the plank wasn't tight against the others. Remember? The officers we saw in the room were using flashlights to help them see when they were lifting prints. When they were lifting the one on the wall, the flashlight's reflection would have made the area outside of its glow even darker."

Pausing, she shook her head in exasperation. "The chief said I better be thinking up excuses for what I did rather than thinking them up for the Arkansas officers."

She looked at the tape in his hand. "I really wonder how Anderson managed to sum up the energy to put it in the wall in the first place. And the house could have sat there another fifty years, fallen in on itself, and nobody would have ever seen what was in the wall. But what other choice did he have? The chief wants the tape brought downtown."

He shook his head. "Not this one. We'll make him a copy."

"It's evidence, Cameron. You don't have any choice."

"Then after I make *me* a copy."

Born of Dr. C Malone's Ancient Man, he thought. If he wasn't trying to say who killed him, then what could he have been trying to say? Born in six weeks. Then maybe saying they'd grown overnight to near teenagers. Jesus Christ, God Almighty, he *did* have to be crazy, didn't he?

Cassandra, tears seeping from her eyes, her body trembling and marked with a sheen of sweat, held the Bible from the motel room's bedside table as she stared up at the ceiling. She slowly moved her hand to her swollen stomach.

"God, please don't let it be the devil," she prayed, "please don't let it be." But she knew it was.

Her eyes moved to her stomach. The tests had said she was almost three months pregnant—and that couldn't be. She had left her house right after the officers had come by, Adrian Cummings and the man with her, the two who had left her the card.

She had planned on going to her best friend's house, but in the BMW on the way she had felt uncomfortable and lowered her hand to her stomach. It felt like the bulge had grown. Her blood had chilled in disbelief. She had turned and driven to a motel. Stripping, she had stared in the mirror.

It *was* bigger. She had immediately begun praying. In an hour the bulge was bigger—she could almost watch it grow. She had grabbed the telephone to call her parents, then laid the receiver back in its cradle. They would say it was her punishment. She didn't know what to do. She had stared and stared at the bulge, and it had grown.

By daylight, she thought of killing herself, but was too scared to try—and how? She looked as if she were at least six months pregnant now. *My God*, she screamed silently, *please help me*. It was the devil, she knew that. What had she done wrong?

A couple hours before, with little sleep since she had left her home, scared now into near shock, she had seen the composites on the room's television, was now absolutely certain that they were the devil. Sobbing, she had made up her mind what to do—what she had to do.

First, she had called Sergeant Adrian Cummings. They had to know what was out there—what had attacked her. She had called back a second time. They had to understand what she was saying. Now she knew they did, and everything would be okay, except for her.

She looked down at her stomach. She pulled the Bible closer to her chest and clutched the long shard of broken glass from the bathroom mirror in her other hand. She would kill him when he arrived. She would kill the devil's spawn and be rid of him. Then she would go back home and pray.

But she knew she was going to have to be brave; there would be the pain, then the moment when she musn't hesitate, musn't let it being a baby stop her. She knew that was going to be hard, but she was prepared. She hugged the Bible tighter to her bosom—and felt the first pain. God give her strength; please, God, be with her now.

CHAPTER 29

Old Jake Gaither, his thin body encased in long johns, suspenders, camouflage hunting shirt and pants, and wearing a pair of old rubber boots, took long lazy steps, sloshing along through the patches of water and mud covering the ground on the old Browning property. It was a shame for a farm once so prosperous and a family once so proud to have come to such an end. The government's meddling was what it was.

That's how it had been in this part of Arkansas and the rest of the Arkansas Delta. The Mississippi and Louisiana Delta, too, all fine farmland, growing cotton and beans and rice like no other place in the world. Then the government came along with their subsidies, giving a guarantee of profit on all that could be grown, and marginal acre after marginal acre was quickly converted to row crops, flooding the market with produce that could not be sold. Then the subsidies were reduced, and farmers who had invested all they could in new land were suddenly without a safety net and went broke.

The government, Jake thought bitterly. Let anything be going good and they would find a way to fix it. But not with him. They would never get him, not as long as he had his rifle and his eyes were still good. One day of hunting and he could bring in enough venison to last a month. What more was there to want?

And to hell with the so-called hunting seasons—more government meddling. Hunting seasons were for executives from the city who liked to hang a set of antlers over their mantle and brag about what a hard time they had had stalking their quarry. Crap! A near-blind idiot with a muzzle loader could shoot in any direction anywhere along the Mississippi River bottom and get all the game he took a mind to.

Especially on this farm. That was the only thing good came out of all the hell the place had suffered. The former cotton and bean fields now provided all kinds of wild growth the deer loved, and the bushes and thickets of young trees that had taken over the place gave them adequate cover from the weather.

But not from him, he thought, and smiled. He shifted his heavy 30-30 to his other hand, then suddenly stopped. He had seen movement on the top of the old plantation house that used to be the Browning home.

He saw it again—a man moving across the roof. Gaither quickly moved behind the cover of a tall, thick cedar, raised his rifle to his shoulder and peered through its telescopic sight.

It was a young blond. A thief would be a better way to put it. Thieves, plunderers, the creeps that swarmed to an abandoned dwelling like flies to a dead cow.

He had wondered why the house hadn't been looted earlier. But it *was* in the middle of five thousand acres of dormant land, a mile back from the road, with signs all over the place warning of armed guards.

Gaither smiled. The only armed man on the place in five years had been him. In fact, other than the couple times the bank had shown the land to prospective buyers, nobody had ever been there.

He adjusted the telescopic sight. Something about the man on the roof. Something. He continued to stare at the blond as he moved on across the shingles and stopped at a thin metal pole sticking up through a hole in the roof. The figure suddenly turned his way.

Gaither adjusted the sight again, focusing directly on

the man's face. He was maybe twenty, had a jutting chin and light hair so bright it seemed to glisten in the sunlight. The man kept staring. It looked like he stared directly back down the scope. But Gaither knew he couldn't be seen from his position behind the cedar.

Suddenly the man turned away and hurried up to the crest of the roof and over to its other side, disappearing from view.

Gaither lowered his rifle. There was something about the face. He knew the blond from somewhere, at least had seen him somewhere.

He would remember eventually. He never forgot a face after he once got a good look at it. He would remember where he saw the man, and when.

Meanwhile, there was nothing to do but turn around and slosh through the mud back to his jeep hidden in some bushes off the gravel road along the side of the farm that joined the River. Couldn't risk a shot at a deer with the man present. He could have been somebody the bank sent out to check over the place.

Gaither wondered what the pole sticking out of the roof was for. He had never noticed that before. If he hadn't noticed it, that meant it hadn't been there the last time he came by the house. He saw everything.

He thought and he thought as he trudged back toward his jeep. Finally he recalled the last time he had been by the house had been over a month before. He had been hunting on the farm twice since that, but never close to the house.

The blond's face appeared in his mind again. He still couldn't remember where he had seen him before, but he had.

When thirty minutes later he reached his jeep, he looked back toward the house, now hidden by the thick oaks between him and the place. The kid wasn't any relative or something close like that. He wasn't a member of any hunting club. Gaither couldn't think of any neighbors who had a kid who looked like that. In fact, there was only one family with a blond, and she was a girl.

Remembering where he had seen the blond had become a game now, an important one. He didn't mind the aches and pains his old body had begun to suffer at his age, but he would mind if his memory started going. He would remember. He opened the jeep's door and slid behind the steering wheel.

When he looked back in the direction of the house one last time, he caught movement out of the corner of his eyes.

It was a hundred yards back into the grounds and over to his right—something had flashed next to a thicket around an old pond that contained a lot of big bass and catfish. *Deer often drank there.*

Gaither reached back to the door handle, then paused. He was far enough away from the house now to take a shot, but it would be hard to walk up on a deer without the animal hearing him. Besides, his legs were beginning to ache from all the miles he had walked that day.

He reached to the glove compartment, opened it, and pulled out a nearly empty half pint of Jack Daniels. He unscrewed the lid and lifted the bottle to his lips, laid back in the seat to rest for a minute.

The figure flashed on around the pond, and came in a sprint through the bushes toward the jeep.

Cassandra tried to muffle her screams with her pillow when the baby started coming. She clutched the long shard of glass so tightly her hand was bleeding. She screamed again and pressed the pillow closer to her face.

The pain suddenly disappeared.

She lay tense, soaked with sweat, waiting. But the pain didn't come back. Suddenly she felt the slight movement on the bed.

She slowly raised her head and looked down at the blond child, squirming, his hands moving at his face.

She looked at the long, daggerlike piece of glass she held. Gritting her teeth against her pain she leaned forward and moved the pointed shard down over the child.

Another pain suddenly struck her, and she screamed before she could get the pillow back to her face.

The next contraction was the worst of all, convulsing her body, causing her to throw her head back in anguish and arch on her heels and shoulders.

She shuddered violently, screamed and passed out, her arm falling limply to a side of the bed and her hand opening, the shard of glass dropping to the thinly carpeted floor and shattering into pieces.

A fat, bald-headed man and a thin, stringy-haired woman, obviously drunk and looking like they had been partying for a week, turned their heads and looked at the door to Cassandra's room as they passed by on the sidewalk.

The scream they had heard was followed by a loud guttural sound.

The man chuckled drunkenly. "They're gettin' it, ain't they?"

The woman caught his buttock and squeezed. "Wait 'til I get you on that bed, baby, and you'll think gettin' it," she said.

Cain's face turned from the direction of Jake Gaither's jeep, and he stared back toward Memphis. Abel, a hundred yards off to the right where he was racing in a near blur, suddenly stopped and stared in the same direction.

Cain moved his head first to the right then back to the left, sensing. This went on for several seconds. Then he suddenly turned away from the bushes and started toward the big two-story house. Abel gave a last glance at the jeep, then turned and hurried back through the bushes to catch up with his brother. The jeep started forward, a bottle flew out the driver's side, and the old, battered vehicle moved slowly toward the gravel road.

After arriving at Adrian's apartment they copied the tape twice and were about to step back out the door when the telephone rang.

Adrian shook her head. "Probably the chief. I'm going to catch hell. I told him we were on our way nearly an hour ago."

After she lifted the receiver she said hello, waited a second then said in a soft, questioning voice, "Cassandra, is that you?"

She listened a few seconds. "Where?" she asked softly.

"Oh, no. It'll be okay, baby. We'll be there in a minute. Uh huh, I promise you, as quick as we can. You lay there and don't move."

She cut the phone off and quickly called 911, giving them the motel's address. Cameron came to his feet.

"What's happened?"

"She's given birth, Cameron—twins."

It took them nearly thirty minutes to get to the motel, an old, seedy one in a once residential but now industrialized part of town.

An ambulance, its red lights flashing, was parked in front of the motel entrance. Two attendants in white coats were talking to a man in suspenders and plaid pants.

"Down here, dammit!" Adrian shouted.

One of the attendants hurried around to the driver's door while the other ran her way.

Cassandra had said room 301, but she didn't answer Adrian's knock. Adrian knocked again, then reached for the doorknob.

It turned and she pushed the door open.

The teenager lay on the bed at the far side of the small room. Her face slowly turned their way, the color drained from it to the point where it looked like there was a white mask of death behind her light brown coloring.

Adrian rushed toward her, stopped and stared at the circle of blood on the bed. The attendant took one look from the doorway and hurried back toward the ambulance.

Cameron stepped to the side of the bed.

A guttural sound came from the bathroom door and he looked that way.

Adrian raised her hand to her mouth as a blond baby crawled into view.

Cassandra started crying. "I couldn't kill them," she said weakly in a pained voice so low it was almost a whisper. "I couldn't do it."

A second, slightly smaller blond crawled up behind the first.

CHAPTER 30

As the ambulance drove away from the motel, they all stared after it. Chief Young shook his head. "It's impossible," he said. "I'm standing right here as a witness before God—and it's impossible. If when you talked to her she'd been six or seven months pregnant—hell, if she'd even been five months—they could be premature, some kind of miscarriage—something. But how in the hell? The doctor did say she was just three months, didn't he?"

Without waiting for a response he said, "And crawling, already. Not much more than an hour old and crawling. Did you see their size?" He took a deep breath. "You have that tape?"

Cameron held it out.

Young nodded toward his patrol car.

They stayed inside the car as the chief played the tape. When, with an even more puzzled expression across his face, he started it over again, Cameron stepped out of the car into the fresh air.

Adrian joined him, and they both stared back at the room where Cassandra had been.

Finally Adrian turned to face him. "Only a few days for them to be born?" she questioned. "The ones at Anderson's took weeks at least."

He nodded. "I feel responsible."

"That doesn't make sense."

He looked at her. "You're saying something has to make sense now?"

She started to say something else, but didn't, and looked toward the car and Chief Young listening to the tape. A moment later, she faced him again.

"Cameron, what could Anderson really have proved that the Ancient Man himself won't eventually prove? After all the tests."

"Even with half the genes being from a woman of our time, a living, breathing human would certainly be more definitive, especially the brain, where intelligence and other facets of development could be studied, see how much lagging was in the hybrid—if any, if you want to think like Anderson was."

She started to speak again, but didn't as Chief Young stepped outside his car and stared their way.

"Damn!" was all he said.

Twenty minutes later in his sparsely appointed office, Young sank into the seat behind his desk. He shook his head for the hundredth time.

"We have to get somebody in here on this besides us." He reached for the telephone at a side of the desk. In a moment he was speaking to someone in the federal building.

"Don," he said, "I, uh—" He shook his head again. "Don, you're going to have to come on over here. I'm at a loss like you wouldn't believe, like you're not going to believe when you get here."

In less than fifteen minutes, Donald Edwards, special agent in charge of the local Memphis FBI office, had arrived. He was a short, stocky man, with graying hair clipped into a fifties crew cut. His suit was a drab brown and rumpled.

Adrian had said before he arrived that Edwards was normally a sullen-looking man, but he looked absolutely grim as he listened to the tape and the chief's story of all that had happened since then.

The only thing he asked when they were through was, "This isn't possible, is it?" Then he moved to the telephone on the chief's desk and punched in a long distance number.

When he made his connection, he spoke in a low enough voice that Cameron only caught a part of his conversation. But it was obvious that whoever was on the other end of the line was as incredulous as would be expected. Edwards ended the conversation with, "Yes, sir, I will," and replaced the receiver.

"Are you through with us?" Adrian asked Chief Young.

The chief looked at Edwards, and the agent nodded without saying anything.

"You can go," Young said.

The telephone on his desk rang, and he walked to it. "Young, here."

His forehead immediately wrinkled. "What?"

After a few seconds more, his forehead still wrinkled and his mouth open, he replaced the receiver and looked over at them. He didn't say I'm not believing this; his face said it for him.

"A man's just called his nephew who works on the force. Some old guy named Jake Gaither. He says he saw the spitting image of one of the missing kids we had on TV. The kid was on the roof of an old house at a fore-closed farm over on the Arkansas side of the river. But the guy who called in said it wasn't a kid, but a man—somewhere in his twenties."

Adrian looked at Cameron.

Edwards and Young were staring at each other, too.

Edwards finally broke the silence. "It has to be a mistake. You said it was an old guy who called in. Maybe he doesn't see so good. Maybe he only saw a man who resembled one of the kids."

Young didn't comment.

Adrian nodded. "Uh huh," she said wryly, "like the

old woman was mistaken, too—everybody's blind when it comes to these two.''

"But it's—'' Edwards started, then said no more. He walked to the desk and lifted Chief Young's telephone. He punched in a long distance number and turned his back to them when he spoke.

He gave a snappy, "yes, sir'' when he finished, then turned back to them.

He looked at Young. "Chief, we're taking this over. In Arkansas, too. Whatever we find over there, we don't need everyone and their brother knowing about it. I can control that better if no one but my people are along.''

He reached for the telephone again and looked back at Adrian.

"I'll get it started,'' he said, "but while my people are assembling and a search warrant is being drawn, I want to run over to the hospital and talk to that girl. I want you to go with me so there'll be someone there she knows while I'm questioning her.''

Fifteen minutes later they stopped in front of the hospital entrance, and in a few moments, walked down a wide hallway toward Cassandra's room.

Two hospital security guards stood outside her door. A slim, middle-aged black lady was leaning back against the wall crying hysterically.

"That's Mrs. Johnson,'' Adrian said.

Cameron heard Agent Edwards speak under his breath. "Don't let this be what I think it is.''

Led by the agent, they quickened their pace toward the woman.

One of the security guards, seeing Chief Young's uniform, hurried up the hall to meet them.

"There's been a kidnapping,'' the guard said breathlessly. "The two babies who came in with the teenager.''

Edwards closed his eyes. "When did it happen?''

"They couldn't have been taken more than five or ten

minutes ago. The nurse said she had just put them in the nursery and stepped away for a minute."

"Five or ten minutes!" Edwards exclaimed, suddenly coming alive. "Why you stupid son of a—" He turned and sprinted back toward the elevator, drawing his weapon as he ran.

"Damn, man," the chief exclaimed to the guard, then turned and sprinted after Edwards. Adrian ran after him. Cameron stood a moment, then turned and tried to catch them.

Mrs. Johnson's wail followed him down the hall.

When Cameron burst out through the front entrance of the hospital, it was just becoming twilight. Edwards had sprinted to his left. Young had gone to the right. Adrian was turning a far corner of the building and headed back to the other end. Cameron sprinted for the opposite side of the building.

Turning the corner, he saw a blond male in the white shirt and pants of a nurse's uniform sliding in behind the wheel of a Chevy in a parking lot to the left of the hospital. His throat tightened, and he dashed for the car. Jumping around its rear as it started to back from its space, he grabbed the driver's door handle.

The frightened nurse stared up at Cameron and tried to hit his lock. The door came open, and the wide-eyed man raised his hands and slid to the other side of the seat.

"Don't hurt me!" the man yelled. "You can have it." He opened the passenger door and jumped out, sprinting toward the safety of the hospital. He ran toward one of the security guards coming from the other direction.

Cameron heard the nurse yell, "Crazy son of a bitch is stealing my car!"

The Chevy continued to inch slowly across the lot toward a line of cars in the next parking lane. Cameron jumped inside, and threw it into park.

As he stepped from the car, he saw the nurse and the security guard slowly coming his way. The nurse nervously lit a cigarette. The guard had his hands extended out to his sides as he said something to the man, obviously trying to calm him and explain what had happened.

Adrian came dashing around the rear of the building, and Cameron trotted toward her.

She was breathing hard when he reached her. She shook her head.

"Nothing," she said.

A few minutes later they gave up the search. Agent Edwards, breathless from dashing through parking lots, leaned back against the front wall of the hospital and took a deep breath. He slid his automatic back into his shoulder holster and walked toward a bank of pay telephones near the entrance. Cameron moved beside Adrian and gently squeezed her shoulder.

She looked at him. He answered her question before she asked it. "It was the other blonds. They knew somehow. Somehow they knew the babies had been born." It had to be. He walked over to Chief Young and Agent Edwards, who was on the phone.

He stopped before Young. "I want to go over into Arkansas with you."

Young shook his head. "I'm not going; that's Arkansas, not Memphis, and this is federal business now."

Edwards finished his telephone conversation and replaced the receiver. Cameron looked at him. "There might be something over there I would pick up on immediately. There could be something there about Anderson's experiment—something you might not notice."

He *had* to go, to follow through on this as much as he was able. He waited anxiously for an answer.

"I guess you already know about all there is to know," Edwards finally said. "Okay, why not? You can ride with me."

CHAPTER 31

Forty-five minutes after leaving the hospital in Memphis, FBI Agent Donald Edwards' car led a darkened caravan of law enforcement vehicles past the gate and NO TRESPASSING sign at the entrance to the old Browning farm in Crittenden County. Before they were in sight of the house, several cars pulled to both sides of the road and agents carrying shotguns fanned out across the grassy fields. The rest of the vehicles stopped a hundred yards farther along the road and waited ten minutes to give the men on foot time to get into position.

Cameron, nervous with anticipation, looked toward the front seat to Edwards. "If they were the ones at the hospital, have they had time to get back here yet?"

"If not, we'll be waiting when they do. If these are the same ones, that is." He looked down at a copy of the composite drawing of the two.

When he raised his head he said to the driver, "Let's go on in."

The caravan inched forward again. Several of the cars had their doors open, agents hanging over them, ready to jump out at a second's notice.

Slowly the big, columned house came into view, towering and stark in the bright moonlight. There were no lights showing. Edwards lifted his hand toward the driver and he guided the car off to the left of the narrow way and stopped.

They stepped out onto the damp dirt. A half dozen shadowy shapes were climbing from the vehicles behind them. One big surveillance van a couple vehicles back in the line looked like a bulky tank in the dark.

Edwards pulled his automatic from inside his coat and started forward.

A hundred feet from the house, several of the men started trotting, angling toward both its sides.

Edwards stopped at the two concrete steps leading up onto the wide, wood-floored area under the columns. In the dim light the planks looked dark, with even darker areas showing where some of them had rotted and fallen in, leaving narrow gaps where a foot could fall through.

Edwards stepped to the front door, a wide, double one with a cracked, half-circle glass arch above it. The knob was frozen with age. Without anyone giving a command, two agents moved to the tall windows on each side of the door. A sharp, short screech sounded, and the window to the right raised.

The agent beside it stepped inside before Edwards could reach the window. He quickly ducked his head and disappeared into the house. Two other agents followed, then Adrian, her gun drawn and held in front of her, stepped through the window. Cameron followed her.

The agent who first entered the house stood silhouetted at a wide doorway back to the left. He stepped through it into the foyer and moved to the front door.

Edwards stood at a doorway twenty feet in front of them. When he disappeared through it, they followed. It led to a big, empty living room, dimly illuminated by the light of the moon coming through windows several feet tall at the room's far side. Small fixtures with broken glass surrounded the room. An exposed electrical cord hung where at one time there had been a chandelier suspended in the center of the room.

Several agents were in the room now, all alert and continually casting glances at the shadows. Back to the left, the entrance into the foyer and the edge of a wide flight of stairs could be seen.

Edwards switched on a flashlight Cameron hadn't noticed. In an instant the wide room was bright with the lights the other agents held.

An old couch sat at the far side of the room. Sitting on the floor in front of it was a TV set. Cameron looked at Adrian. She had her automatic in her hand.

"In groups of twos," Edwards whispered, "take this floor." Men immediately paired off and moved in different directions.

"Richard, Duease," Edwards said to two agents still standing in the shadows of the room they had first entered. "You two upstairs with me. "Sergeant Cummings, you, too—and, Dr. Malone, you stay right behind me."

A few minutes later they had quickly glanced through each of the upstairs rooms. Edwards looked up at the trapdoor leading into the attic.

The agent named Duease stepped forward, caught the string hanging from the door, and pulled on it. The door came down, revealing an oblong black hole above them.

Edwards shined the light through it as Duease folded the stairs down and started up them. Near the top, he raised his automatic and flashlight together, then suddenly lunged upward and looked quickly in every direction.

Cameron realized he had been holding his breath and released it as quietly as he could.

"Some kind of radio equipment up here," Duease said.

In a moment they stared at the two-way radio, its attached tape recorder, and several short cables running into its rear and attached to a larger electrical cable snaking across the floor to where it disappeared down a support wall. Edwards pulled a handkerchief from his rear pocket, folded it over his fingers and hit the recorder's eject button. He lifted the tape from the machine and slipped it into his pocket, then glanced at the agent nearest him.

"Get somebody up here to take prints." He turned and started for the trap door.

As they stepped out onto the house's screened back porch a light breeze blew past Cameron, and the unusual coolness on his forehead and neck told him he had been sweating. He looked at Adrian. She looked intent, too, her mind also obviously working overtime. She looked at him and smiled faintly.

Edwards opened the screen door and started down the steps to the backyard. Three men with flashlights stood several feet to the right, to each side of another door leading into the rear of the house at a lower level.

Edwards nodded in their direction, and they switched on their flashlights and jumped through the doorway.

One of them shouted they had found something.

Edwards hurried toward the door. It led to steps going down into a dank cellar with dirt floors and partitioned by wooden walls into different areas. Cameron caught the stench of body waste.

They passed through the first area toward a door standing open and the glow of flashlights beyond it.

One of the agents who had entered the cellar first, held the beam of his light on chains attached several feet up the wall and hanging down again to waist level.

Edwards stared at the chains and the dirt floor below them, then turned and started back toward the stairs, and Cameron and Adrian followed.

Back outside in the cool night air, Cameron took a deep breath. Where in hell were they?

"Out here!" a voice shouted from the barn, and he felt his pulse surge. They moved quickly toward the wide, bulky structure.

Inside the barn's big double doors they stopped and looked up in the direction the agent was shining his light. A pair of chains hung from the rafters. Directly under them were the sooty remains of a wide fire. The inside of the barn smelled like a smokehouse. Thinking that, Cameron looked up at the chains again and briefly shut his eyes.

Edwards knelt by the soot. He caught a small piece of charred wood in his hand, moved it to his nose and smelled of it, then suddenly threw it back into the soot where it kicked up a small cloud of black dust.

He stood. "We have to search this farm."

The agent next to him shook his head. "It's thousands of acres."

Edwards stood in silence for a moment, then turned and started for the barn door.

Adrian looked at the remains of the fire until Cameron touched her on the shoulder. She turned and they followed after Edwards.

Lee Ann's face was bent forward nearly to her chest by the steellike pressure of Abel's hand at the back of her head. A sharp pain was constant in her neck, and she feared if he pushed another inch it would break. His other hand over her mouth nearly suffocated her. Pressed back against the front of his hard body she felt like she was gripped in a vise.

She tried to look out of the corner of her eyes toward the side of the big house. But the bushes they stood behind were too thick. She rotated her eyes back to her other side to see Missey bent forward in the same painful position by Cain.

They had been unchained and hurried quickly from the cellar to the place they now hid. She hadn't heard the sound of any cars approaching, but out of the corner of her eyes she suddenly had seen the glow of several flashlights coming on nearly simultaneously inside the house.

Then she had seen through a gap in the bushes the first dark shapes come around the side of the house from its front. That had been several minutes before, when Abel had pulled her back hard against him and bent her forward at that very moment. The pain had been so bad she thought she was going to pass out. She was sure he was preparing to break her neck.

But he had only continued to hold her that way, as Cain had Missey. Then she had heard the shout from the rear of the house and, a few minutes later, the shout from the barn. A moment later a light had flashed across the bushes as if somebody walked that way with a flashlight, but no one had.

Cain uttered a low, rumbling guttural sound, and she rotated her eyes toward him as she felt Abel twist in that direction.

Cain looked at her. He had felt her stare. *Or heard her thoughts.* She remembered wanting a drink of water and Abel taking the bucket to refill it. She couldn't let him hear her now. She silently began singing in her mind.

Cain stared at her again. She felt Abel's grip tighten. They were wondering, she knew. Abel had only to add a slight more pressure and her neck would break. If he heard—

She sang harder, "Happy Birthday," as loud as she could in her mind. Don't think—sing, drown out her mind. She tried to add "God Bless America" to "Happy Birthday," trying to make both of them fill her mind at the same time. At every gap between every word she cursed violently, filling every void where a thought might escape.

Singing "Happy Birthday," "God Bless America," and cursing so loud it sounded like a scream in her mind, she slowly reached without bending for the branch lying on the ground before her. Louder and louder she sang, quicker with the words; she cursed over and over again. Her fingers were not quite able to catch the branch. She tested by slowly letting her knees give. Sing louder! She only moved an inch or two, but her fingers caught a twig coming up from the branch.

Louder, *ever louder,* screaming silently.

She caught the twig between two fingers and lifted it, moved her hand slowly and grasped the branch.

She felt Abel suddenly look toward Cain. A beam of light flashed across the bush. Someone was coming their way.

Oh God, sing louder.

She grasped the branch solidly now and rotated her eyes toward Cain. The beam of light flashed across his face. His dark eyes tightened again. His hand suddenly left the back of Missey's head and in the same motion came around hard to cuff the side of her jaw. Missey's knees buckled, and he lifted her off her feet and turned back into the bushes.

Lee Ann felt Abel's hand come off the back of her head and she ducked to the side and jammed the branch back over her shoulder as hard as she could.

Abel's hand poised to strike her jaw, the gnarled, brittle twigs of the branch jabbed hard into his eyes, snapping, gouging, and she slipped out of his grasp.

She screamed at the top of her lungs and hurdled through the bushes in front of her.

Edwards had his hand on his car door, opening it, when the scream caused his eyes to dart toward the thick bushes past the far side of the house.

"Stop!" came a shout from in that direction.

Edwards' hand went inside his coat and came back out with his automatic.

Cameron and Adrian stepped away from the rear doors and looked in the direction of the shout. Adrian reached inside her purse.

"Stop!" came another shout. "FBI! Stop or I'll shoot!"

The sound of a motor roaring to life came from the black darkness behind the thick brush. Then a shot. Two more shots, rapid, almost together.

Edwards dashed in the direction of the sounds. Flashlights pointed toward the area. Adrian started after Edwards. Cameron ran after her. All the officers were running toward the bushes now.

"Stop, dammit!" came another shout almost drowned out by the loud roar of the vehicle now sounding like it was moving rapidly toward them.

But it couldn't be seen.

Suddenly a shape sprang out of the bushes and rushed toward them. It was a woman, taking long, frantic strides, her ripped blouse fluttering out behind her.

Then an almost new blue Toyota burst through the bushes into the flashlight beams and roared after the running woman. Another shot rang out behind it.

Cameron's heart jumped to his throat. The car was going to hit the woman. But it flashed by her and came directly at them.

An agent appeared out of the bushes behind the car and raised his gun but didn't shoot because they were in his direct line of fire.

Edwards stopped. He faced the darkened car bearing down on him and raised his pistol in both hands, held it out in front of him, and waited. Adrian was raising her automatic. Cameron jumped to her, caught her arm and jerked her toward the safety of a tree off to the right.

"Dammit, Cameron, quit!" she shouted, trying to pull her arm free, but he dragged her on toward the tree.

When the car was almost on Edwards, he fired rapidly three times. At the last possible second, he dove to the side.

The Toyota roared past his rolling body, swerving between two of the parked cars and onto the entry road. Adrian fired after it.

Flashes came out of the darkness from both sides of the Toyota as shot after shot hit it, causing glass to fly into the air. Shards glinted in the moonlight.

Edwards sprang to his feet and dashed toward his car. Cameron and Adrian opened the rear doors and jumped inside as Edwards slid hurriedly behind the steering wheel.

CHAPTER 32

Edwards backed his car rapidly in a U turn. He floored the accelerator. Throwing a shower of damp dirt, the car lunged forward after the Toyota. Other agents were piling into their cars and whirling them around on the narrow road. In the moonlight, even with its lights off, the Toyota could be seen turning right as it reached the entrance to the farm. "Out of luck, bastards!" Edwards growled from behind the steering wheel. The road in that direction dead-ended at the bank of the river. Signs all the way along the road to the big columned house had given notice of that.

Edwards spun the wheel hard to the right; the car bounced out onto the road, threw a shower of gravel, and raced after the Toyota.

Cameron looked over his shoulder. As fast as Edwards was driving, the other cars were nevertheless catching up.

Looking forward through the windshield, Cameron saw the Toyota's brake lights flash red a hundred yards ahead of them, then veer crazily from side to side.

"Wreck the mother, bastards," Edwards growled loudly. He suddenly cheered and beat on the steering wheel when the lights cantered over on their sides and rolled over and over.

"Yeah!" Edwards screamed.

Now, Cameron thought, *get them!*

In only seconds, Edwards was nearly on the Toyota, over on its top to the left of the road, and he jammed on his brakes.

The car dipped its nose and slid sidewise. Cameron saw past the overturned car the two running figures, and Edwards hit his accelerator again. He lifted his automatic out the window. Adrian moved to a rear window on the same side and lowered it.

Another car suddenly whizzed past them on their right and, never having slowed, pulled rapidly ahead. A man with a shotgun raised up through a rear window.

The headlights of both cars highlighted the blonds as they left the road and sprinted toward the river bank.

The agent leaning from a rear window of the car ahead of them fired his shotgun, a bright flash leaping from its barrel. His car slid to a stop, and he fired again.

Edwards braked them to a stop and threw open his door. In the other car, a second figure raised out of the passenger window, leaned across the top of the car and held down on the trigger of an automatic weapon.

One of the blonds suddenly buckled forward, hit the ground with his shoulder and rolled. The other blond stopped.

Edwards leaped across the roadside ditch. The others followed him. "Hands over your head!" one of them yelled, "Now!"

The blond on the ground stirred, pushed his upper body up, struggled to his knees, and stared back at them. The car lights framed them both in brilliant detail, giving Cameron a clear view of their faces. They were very close in looks, but not identical, with the one on the ground also slightly smaller in build. Suddenly the one on his knees toppled over hard onto his face.

The second blond stared at his brother's smaller body, then looked back toward them. Cameron felt the dark eyes lock onto his. All the agents standing there with him, and the blond looked only at him, then glanced to his left at the river bank, twenty feet away.

"Don't try it!" Edwards shouted. "Put your hands above your head!"

The blond turned and lunged toward the water.

It took an instant to react to his sudden move.

Cameron saw it in the same way people who survive car wrecks sometimes register things so fast during the crash that everything seems to be in slow motion. Flashes came out of the dark off to the right, the *tat-tat-tat* of the automatic weapon, and the great flashes extending out the end of the shotgun. Edwards' automatic went *flash, flash, flash,* in a steady rhythm.

The blond took two great strides, a double short step, and, still ten feet from the water, left his feet, diving high out toward the river like a springboard diver rather than headfirst in a racing dive. Bullets tattooed his back, his shoulders arching back from their force; his head dropped forward, and he somersaulted head over heels to hit the brown water in a great splash.

Cameron started breathing again.

Edwards sprinted to the edge of the bank.

One of the men from off to the right reached the blond lying on his face, knelt beside him, leaned over and looked at his fixated eyes staring off to the side.

"He's dead as hell," he said.

"Son of a bitch ought to be," a second agent said. He looked down at the blond's vacant stare. "I was starting to wonder if I was shooting blanks."

The back of the blond's shirt was peppered with at least a dozen little round holes spreading blood. The right thigh of his jeans was riddled with shotgun pellets and his left calf showed a single small hole.

"PCP," the agent kneeling said as he came to his feet. "They get on that stuff you can cut 'em all to hell and they won't go down until you hit a vital organ."

Edwards stood silently at the edge of the river, looking into the water. Cameron stepped up beside him.

Edwards looked over at him and spoke. "These were the two who raped the girl, right?"

When Cameron didn't say anything, Edwards shook

his head questioningly and spoke again. "They have to be, right? Not the two the old woman saw. They couldn't be the same ones, could they?"

Several cars slid to a stop on the gravel road. In seconds at least a dozen more men came forward to the bank. Edwards told them what had happened and nodded them into the cold water.

"Hey, there's a woman in here!" came a shout from back at the overturned car.

In a moment the agent was pulling an unconscious woman out through one of the rear windows. They rolled her to her back. Adrian knelt beside her and stared at the dry, matted blood staining her lower clothes. An agent at one of the cars off to the right was calling for an ambulance.

Edwards looked back at the agents wading out into the river. It stayed shallow for four or five feet from the bank, then deepened rapidly. Soon the men were far enough out that the water came to their chests and they were feeling with their toes.

When a few minutes later they still hadn't found the body and one of the men called back that the current must have caught it, Edwards didn't answer, just gestured with a turn of his head for them to come on out of the water.

One of the agents, wet up to his waist, walked up to him. "What now," the man asked. "Get some boats out here to drag?"

"I'll call that in," Edwards said. "You go ahead and get everybody spread out up and down the bank, watching the water."

The agent, a stocky man who had been in the bureau nearly as long as Edwards had, wrinkled his brow. He looked out over the silty water, illuminated by the car's headlights for at least a hundred feet to each side and farther than that toward the middle of the river. There had been men watching the surface ever since the blond had splashed into the water. The agent looked back questioningly at Edwards.

"In case he's swimming under water," Edwards exclaimed.

The agent nodded. "I knew what you meant, Don. How long you figuring he can hold his breath?"

"Just do what the hell I told you!" Edwards was immediately sorry for his outburst. "I'm sorry; just do it, Fred, okay?"

As the agent walked off, Edwards ran his hand through his short, thinning hair and looked back at the river.

It was the stress of the job, he thought, that's what it had to be, working on his mind all the time, driving him half crazy, if not more than that. He thought of the tape, what the old woman had said, the babies being born after so short a time. Where were they now? His mind was spinning to the point he was almost dizzy. He looked back at the brown water flowing to his right on its way toward New Orleans, then turned and walked slowly toward the body lying twenty feet from the road.

Fred quickly passed on Edwards' orders. More than one of the men glanced back at Edwards' car as, flashlights shining before them, they spread out up and down the bank and began searching. But not a one of them had even the slightest thought they would see anything, and most of them holstered their weapons or carried them casually across their shoulders.

Adrian knelt at the side of the dead blond and stared at his face. After a moment she rose.

"It's them, Cameron; the eleven- or twelve-year-old kids at Andersons *and* the two teenagers who raped Cassandra. They are the same ones, aren't they? This one is for sure."

He nodded. It wasn't possible, but it was. The face staring blankly with fixed eyes toward the side of the road was the spitting image of the woman's composites of the two young children she had seen, except for a little more fullness to the cheeks and the stronger jutting of the chin.

The babies in the motel room had the same features,

almost identical countenances. Born in only a matter of days, from a father born in only weeks, from a father dead for five hundred thousand years, and all of them nearly identical. *What had Dr. Anderson brought back?* And, my God, from his discovery.

CHAPTER 33

Sitting in the rear seat of Edwards' car as they pulled into the yard at the old house, Cameron looked out his window and saw the young woman who had run from the bushes. A blanket wrapped around her, an agent was helping her to step up into the back of an ambulance that had just arrived.

As he stepped from the car, she glanced toward him —and then he recognized her. *Lee Ann!* She brushed through the hands of the agent and ran in his direction.

"Dr. Malone!" She threw herself against him. "They can read minds."

Edwards stared at her.

Cameron wrapped his arms around her back and patted her softly.

"They can, Dr. Malone. I saw them. They can read minds." She started sobbing hysterically.

In the car now on the way back into Memphis, Cameron was silent, lost in his somber thoughts. Lee Ann had finally recovered sufficiently to lift her face back off his shoulder and ask about Missey. Edwards told her the woman they had pulled from the rear seat of the overturned Toyota was fine.

Lee Ann had nodded, then asked if Missey's babies had been found—a pair of blond twins born that evening. Edwards had stared in shock, then looked toward the house and strode that way, calling several other agents along with him. But though they had then searched the house even more carefully than before, there were no babies to be found.

Adrian looked across the seat to him. "Cameron, what are they?"

He shook his head. What in God's name *had* Anderson brought back from the past?

Bob Golby stepped out of the terminal at the Memphis International Airport into the dark and looked for the sign pointing toward the short-term parking area. He didn't have the slightest idea where it was; Memphis was one place he had never been, a place he had never expected to be sent.

Spotting a wide sign mounted over the pavement, he started walking in the direction it pointed, taking long strides that matched his tall, lanky build. His light brown hair, often unruly, ruffled in the cool breeze from the south. But it was only cool, not freezing like it had been when he boarded his flight in Washington. He found the feeling rather pleasant. Halfway to the car he stopped, set his suitcase on the ground, lay his briefcase on top of it, then slipped off his suit coat and slung it over his shoulder.

At the car, a dark blue Buick with a Shelby County tag containing the sequence he had been given just before his flight, he sat his bag and briefcase down again, fished in his pocket for the keys he had been handed at the same time as the license number, and opened the back door, pitching his bag to the rear, but kept the briefcase with him.

Several minutes later he was on Riverside Drive. He looked out his window at the wide Mississippi to his left. Two bridges, the one back to his far left only dimly illuminated, and one ahead of him brightly lit, were both heavily loaded with traffic. He smiled. He knew a way to increase the traffic out of the city like it had never left before.

A few minutes later he had registered, asked for any messages for a Bob P. Golby, received a sealed envelope the clerk said had been delivered in the last few minutes, and walked to the elevators.

On his way up to his floor, he turned sideways to the young man and woman who had stepped into the elevator with him. He looked down at the envelope to make sure there was no special mark on it.

There wasn't. He had known there wouldn't be on this kind of job. But another job *could* have come up while he was flying south, could come up at any time, though it had been a good while since one had.

He glanced at the young man and woman now facing the elevator door. He knew they weren't married—no bands, no mark where they had been. The woman had seemed nervous with the quick smile she had given him, while the man stared at the flashing numbers marking the passing floors, impatient for them to reach their level. Even though obviously together, they acted almost as if they didn't know each other.

There were more reasons, too, why Golby knew they weren't married—little things, things he noticed or sensed, a gift he had that very few others did.

In his first federal job with the customs service in Miami, he could watch passengers coming down the long gangway, point one out to be searched and be right over ninety percent of the time.

He hadn't the slightest idea how he had acquired the gift, he just always had been able to read people—what kind they were, what they were capable of, and what they were doing. Any and everything about people; it was almost as if he could read their minds.

He thought of what he was about now, the reason he was in Memphis, and wondered if something came of it whether his gift would still work. That would be a bummer, wouldn't it, if it failed him at a moment that would have to be the biggest he had ever faced?

The elevator stopped at a floor below his, and the young man and woman stepped off into the arms of a gray-haired couple. As the door closed, the couple was saying how glad they were the younger ones were able to make it to the family reunion. The young woman mentioned she had just run into the man down in the lobby and found out he was her cousin.

Correct on not married, Golby thought, and as far as what he had expected they were going up to a room to do—he hadn't *tried* to notice anything about that, so that assumption didn't count.

He got off on the sixth floor, still without reading the note sealed within the envelope. He even took the time after laying his bag on the bed and taking out a toothbrush and comb to step into the bathroom, brush his teeth, and run the comb through his hair before he went back to the bed and sat on it to read the message.

He was surprised at what it said.

The blonds were dead.

They were his reason for being there in the first place. Half of his work already done before he arrived; that didn't happen very often, on any kind of job. He looked at the briefcase, opened it, and lifted out the papers inside. After spreading them out on the bed, he stared at each one in turn. There were the IRS reports detailing the lab equipment bought and paid for in cash by Dr. Anderson, the CIA reports on the damage to their spy satellite, and several other documents, all leading to his trip to Memphis.

And now all worthless. He leaned forward to the bedside table and punched the number he had been given in Washington into the telephone. He was surprised when the woman who answered said her husband wasn't in a gave him another number—a car phone. If her husband didn't answer it, she said, she didn't have any idea where he might be. *At this time of night?* Golby knew *his* wife would not put up with that, no matter what his so-called business was.

He left for days at a time, often couldn't call home even once, never could tell his wife where he had been or what he had been doing—and she never asked. But when he was in Washington, he had to be in on time every night—no excuses. It was her way of coping, trying to effect something resembling a normal married life, though he had warned her that was impossible before they had even become engaged. He smiled. She was a good woman.

When he rang the number of the car phone, FBI Agent Donald Edwards answered this time and said he would be by the Peabody to pick him up in fifteen minutes. The blonds were dead, the agent added. Golby said that he already knew that.

There was silence for a moment on the line. Golby thought of the agent wondering how he could have already known.

Then Edwards said, "And now we have four more."

Thirty minutes later, over his initial shock that the blonds in fact really had produced pregnancies that resulted in such short-term deliveries, that there were four new babies, and that the woman named Lee Ann was claiming they could read minds, Golby stared at the body of the blond lying on the gurney in the morgue.

He stuck his hands in his suit pockets. "Let's try to put what we know in perspective," he said, then he didn't even try. How could it be put in perspective?

After a moment, Edwards broke the silence. "I have the grounds of the farm being searched for the children. What we can do of that—it's thousands of acres." He stared directly into Golby's eyes. "What are they, Bob?"

Golby never turned his gaze from the blond on the gurney as he spoke. "I came to get the logical explanation for that, see where somebody had their story screwed up, get it all straightened out. That's what I do —and I'm not believing this. I don't know."

What was logical? The transmitter in the attic had the same fingerprints on it as were all over the house where Dr. Anderson's body was found. The doctor's prints were on the TV as well. One of the sets found in both houses belongs to this character on the gurney, though the size of his prints in the house were larger than the prints he left at Dr. Anderson's. That obviously was no longer some kind of mistake. There had been no prints left in the van; those blonds had worn gloves, the two officers had said. A set there would have at least taken away the possibility that there really weren't only four still left out there but maybe six.

Golby shook his head. "I've seen time after time when something looked one way; where you *knew* it was one way. There was always a logical explanation that came along. The one here couldn't be one of those the old woman saw, I'm telling myself; couldn't be— not logically or by any other way of thinking.

"But, then again, how could the ones at Anderson's have only taken weeks to be born, and now the ones to those women. . . . What're their names again?"

"Cassandra Johnson and Missey something. She was in such shock we couldn't get any more out of her."

Golby nodded. "Cassandra and Missey—and their babies born in only days. What are we supposed to assume, that the original sperm was so old it was like a battery about run down? And once the rate of gestation was speeded up, did that also follow through into how fast they're growing?"

Golby shook his head, numbed from his confused thoughts. "The tape out of the attic contained the same message on it the satellite picked up—so there's not any doubt that the blonds sent that. To whom? Maybe to the same person who has the babies now?"

A wry smile crossed his face. "Listen to me calling them persons. My mind won't let logic go. Persons— something explainable." He ran a hand around the back of his neck while he wondered how all he knew could be possible. Where in hell had they sent a message? *Who did they know?*

"Babies being born whose direct forebearer was a man who has been dead and rotted for five hundred thousand years," he said aloud, rolling the phrase slowly out of his mouth, like he was trying to taste it, trying to understand it. "Unless you want to believe that this character and his brother sent birthday greetings back in the past to an old relative, they sent a message to somewhere around here—here being the whole damn world, according to how strong the receiver is and where they sent it. But maybe pretty close to here. Maybe real close. Did the woman—Lee Ann— say any more than Missey's babies were born quickly, and that we're talking about mind readers here? As if that isn't enough said."

Edwards shook his head. "Nothing, other than she's giving us a hard time about staying in the hospital under wraps. She wanted to call her mother and is raising hell that we won't let her. What happens when she realizes we can't really tell her no, and she just steps down to the pay phone and calls?"

"We *can* tell her no," Golby said. "I can, anyway. She stays put until this is over. Both her and that other woman—Missey. By the way, how did you get that teenager to stay at the hospital—Cassandra?"

"I told her family what Washington told me to. That it was a genetic experiment gone bad. That the two kids who had volunteered for it had been affected adversely and gone crazy. I told them we weren't certain yet that both of them were dead and that if not, the one might come back for her and her family. If she did what we told her to, stayed put at the hospital until we found his body, then we'd testify for her in court as to what she suffered from the whole thing. Told her father there was no telling what it would be worth in monetary damages. He liked that. He understands he has to cooperate, too—until they're caught."

Golby nodded. "What's the paleontologist's name?"

"Cameron Malone."

Golby pondered for a moment, rolling his tongue around the inside of his cheek as he did. "I'm not so sure you shouldn't have quarantined him—and that female officer, too."

Edwards shook his head. "They wouldn't be so easily

talked into something like that. They know what's been going on from day one. We'd have to *make* them go somewhere if they went."

"I can get that done, if it comes down to it."

"There's another one who knows about this, too. A Sergeant Joni Henderson. Adrian's best friend."

Golby frowned. "Damn, how many more know?"

"I got the doctor and Adrian to swear to silence. I asked them to get Joni to do the same. Adrian said there would be no problem with that. I think we can trust them for a few days, anyway."

Golby nodded. "I believe I'd like to talk with them, especially the doctor. See if you can find out where they are. Get them together in one place so I don't have to waste my time. Tell them I'm retired, some kind of old FBI expert you've called back in to help you sort this out."

"What kind of expert would I be calling in?"

"That's none of their business," Golby said. "Tell them that if they ask."

The bright lights of downtown Memphis lit the sky in a wide glow, and only a couple miles up river the newer bridge was ablaze in lights, but it was shadowy dark at the bottom of the sloped concrete area leading from Riverside Drive down to the water. Homer Watkins was talking to himself as he picked up a long limb from the edge of the water. Homer Watkins had talked to himself ever since he had been beaten so badly by a couple of big black men. Before that he had talked to little boys of any color whenever he got the chance, and that was why he talked to himself now. The big black men, not trusting the justice system, had decided to mete out their own punishment for a child molester. They had meant to beat him to death. They had failed at that; nevertheless, he didn't remember what he liked doing before they had beaten him, and hadn't had any urges since, so, in truth, they had quite effectively rehabilitated him.

"Damn thing too wet to use. Get away from me, damn thing." He sent the limb sailing out to splash into the dark water.

"Damn one more dry one, and I'll make my damn fire. Damn right, I will." He shivered at the cold wind, and his face twitched. It had ever since the beating.

He moved farther down the bank, having to go slower than he had gone the year before because his eyes were worse; they kept getting worse. That was from the beating, too. But he was making it. Damn right, he was.

Especially his clothes, he thought, and looked down at them proudly. He had on a fine silk tuxedo coat and black wool slacks which, though rumpled, set him off quite well, except maybe for the old T-shirt he wore under the coat.

All the clothes, except for the T-shirt, which he had worn for a week, he had stolen from the back of a dry cleaning establishment when a man working there had foolishly left the door open after pushing a cart of clothes to the rear of the building.

Homer saw another stick at the edge of the river and reached for it. A hand shot out of the water and grabbed his wrist. A head came next, then a stocky body—all the while Homer froze with his eyes wide. In only seconds, what the black men had started was now finished.

But it was much more painless to Homer than had been his beating, just the quick snapping of his neck, and the seconds his eyes rotated wildly as he stared up at the blond standing over him.

CHAPTER 34

Adrian and Joni sat side by side on the couch in Adrian's apartment, Cameron a little way down from them. Bob Golby sat in an easy chair across the coffee table. Edwards stood next to the chair. Golby pushed an unruly lock of hair back off his forehead, then leaned forward and rested his arms on his knees.

"To get right to the point, Dr. Malone. With the prints from Dr. Anderson's house matching those off the TV and the transmitting equipment in the house where the blonds were, there is no doubt we are dealing with the child—the children, evidently—born of his experiment.

"Now, knowing that, and knowing where the blonds came from, are you aware of any evidence showing where any link of man had a different gestation period for its young? I mean all the way back to the monkeys. Is it possible that something like that could have changed during evolution?"

Cameron shook his head. "As far as evidence, no. But after what I've seen now, I can't categorically say it's not possible. In fact, it has to be."

Golby remained silent a moment, playing something through his mind.

Out of the corner of Cameron's eye, he saw Adrian's mouth start to open, as if she was going to say something. But it closed again. She began thumping her fingers on top of her thigh.

"Sergeant Cummings," Golby said.

"Yes, sir?"

"Do you have something you wanted to add?"

She hesitated a moment, then shook her head. "No, sir."

Golby spoke softly. "Go ahead, sergeant; we're all only speculating here."

Adrian caught her hair and pushed it back to the side of her face, fiddled with her hands a moment as she thought, then decided why not.

"Well, this probably sounds stupid, but if there *hasn't* been a link like that in the past, then . . . I mean . . . "

"Go ahead," Golby said.

"I saw how fast the babies were born, Cassandra's babies, and the two to that woman out at the house— Missey. I heard what Lee Ann said about their reading minds, and I saw the bullets hit them when they were running. I know they were hit several times before the one went down. A crazy idea passed through my mind about what they might be . . . like, uh . . . " She smiled feebly. "Like maybe aliens. Like the man Cameron brought back was an alien?"

Golby didn't show any change in expression. Cameron waited. The expression still didn't change.

"I'd probably think about the same thing, officer, if I didn't know better," Golby said. "Without a lot of explanation, I can only tell you it's not possible. There're all kinds of reasons it's not. Though my profession was law enforcement, believe it or not I have a degree in biology—a doctorate, in fact. Maybe I'm a bit rusty with what I learned, but no, I can assure you it's just not possible." He straightened and leaned back in his chair.

Adrian nodded. Cameron knew she was embarrassed by having asked in the first place and wasn't going to say anymore. But he also knew she wasn't satisfied with the question being shrugged off without any real explanation, that Golby expected her to believe what he said just because he said it.

Nevertheless, Golby *was* correct—that was one of the few things Cameron felt he could still be sure of. Despite the fascination aliens held in the general public's mind, they *were* impossible, at least impossible in the sense that even *if* on some distant planet there were such a thing, there was still no way they could look like humans. Or ever be able to travel to earth, either, no matter how advanced their civilization might be. He would explain why to Adrian after the others had left.

Golby yawned and looked at Edwards. "Well, unless you have something you want to say, I guess that's about it," he said.

Edwards shook his head. Golby looked back toward the couch. "I really only wanted to get to meet you three and tell you how much we appreciate you keeping all you've seen under your hats. It would start a hell of a panic if it leaked out. We do have something weird out there, aliens or not. We need a few quiet days to try and find the children without having to use manpower dealing with a public scared out of their wits."

He looked around the apartment. "I do need to make a phone call before I leave—if you don't mind. I have, uh—" he smiled "—an old friend in town who's waiting to hear from me. Would it be too rude to ask to—"

"Oh, certainly not." Adrian pointed toward the telephone on the counter.

Golby hesitated. "Now I'm going to be really rude," he said. "It's sort of an old *personal* friend. I—"

"Sure; there's a phone in the bedroom at the end of the hall."

Golby smiled politely, and started in that direction.

Ben Utterback, a short, stocky man with wiry red hair, had been a fairly good journalist on a prominent midwestern newspaper—until he got caught too many times spicing up a story so that his byline would be assured the front page. But he didn't care. The job he now had with *The Whole Truth* not only paid him much more than he made while working for the legitimate media, but allowed him to employ his artistic touch. In fact it was a prerequisite of the job.

He wore his rumpled suit and an old hat with a press card stuck in the brim, a little flair he thought went over well with women, expecially the mothering types.

It also made him look a little thick in the head, and that came in handy in putting his quarry off guard. Sort of the Columbo type.

As he neared the door leading into the morgue's vault area, he was already envisioning his headline:

BLOND CANNIBALS FROM AN EGYPTIAN TOMB

He already knew the dead one in the morgue was one of them—one of the two cult members responsible for Dr. Anderson's colorful death. He didn't drop a thousand a month in the right places not to be kept informed. He was glad the other blond had been lost in the river after being shot; that one's unfortunate demise would allow him to create a certain amount of fear in his story. *When was he coming back*—that was what he had yelled he was going to do when he outwitted the police and dove into the river, wasn't it? Utterback smiled, but it faded quickly. There would be a lot of boats out there dragging the river by first light. If some stupid asshole got lucky and snagged the corpse it would ruin his story.

But then that was unlikely. If they hadn't found the body at first, it meant the river's swift currents would have had time to get hold of it. The body could be miles downriver by daylight, maybe never found.

It would be great if the body got snagged on something, didn't rise to the surface and was never seen again. This story could be milked for a long time if a body didn't pop up.

Only thing he had to have was a photograph. A story just wasn't any good without a photograph. That's why he was here. A hundred bucks slipped to an orderly, maybe as little as fifty, and he bet he could take all the shots of the corpse he wanted.

A thought suddenly jumped through his mind. They were both blonds, weren't they? He could take several pictures of the dead one, use an air brush to rearrange the hair in one of the shots. He could end up with an article showing both the photograph of the dead one and an exclusive photo of the one still on the loose—the one who said he'd be back. He smiled again, stuck his cigar in a corner of his mouth, and reached for the morgue door.

As he did, something on its other side bumped it hard, and he had to jump back as it flew open. A gurney pushed by a male nurse in a scrub suit, mask, and cap came by.

The nurse paid absolutely no attention to him, as if he wasn't even there.

Smart ass, nearly run over my ass and act like you didn't notice it.

He stared for a moment at the sheet-covered body atop the gurney and decided to catch a shot of it rolling away. There might be some way he could incorporate that into the story. Nobody would know it wasn't the blond under the sheet.

He hurried after the nurse, stopping close behind him and raising the camera for a quick shot. When the flashbulb exploded, the nurse flinched and whirled around.

"Startle you, buddy?" Utterback asked, sort of glad he did after the man's rudeness.

As the nurse continued to stare, his jaw began to jut forward under his mask, as if he was so angry from being startled that he was thinking about doing something about it.

Well, come on, tough guy. You might get a little surprise. He had been an amateur boxer in his day and still stayed fit. He used his tongue to roll his cigar across to the other side of his mouth and stared back at the man.

The nurse suddenly turned and resumed pushing the gurney from the morgue.

"Chick, chick, chick," Utterback said under his breath, but he did keep it there. There *had* been something about the nurse's dark eyes, and he did have a rather stocky build. No need in picking a fight when he didn't have to—boxing skills or no.

He turned and started back to the door into the vault room.

Once inside it, he saw nothing but the lines of metal drawers surrounding the walls. There was always an orderly on duty, and often the medical examiner was present. He had known if the examiner was there that he would have to leave without getting a look—then come back when the doctor departed.

Where in the hell was everybody? Then he saw the white pants legs sticking out from behind a desk over to his right. The pants legs had dark shoes at their ends and they were turned toe down. His throat tightened.

Then he thought about the nurse who had pushed the gurney out the door, and his throat really tightened —mainly because he suddenly recalled the blond eyebrows.

Golby had been on the telephone in Adrian's bedroom for a good fifteen minutes when he suddenly strode up the hall, his brow narrowed in thought, a corner of his lip caught in his teeth.

"I need to speak to you outside," he said to Edwards. He walked on to the door without ever looking back at Cameron and Adrian and Joni. In a moment, the three were left alone in the living room.

"What now?" Adrian asked.

Joni shrugged. "Beats me."

Cameron stepped to the window, pulled back the curtain, and looked outside.

Edwards and Golby stood at the head of the stairs leading down to the complex's ground level. They were in agitated conversation, causing his curiosity to swell even more.

He released the curtain and walked toward the couch.

"Cameron," Adrian said. "Why didn't you ask him if they knew what that transmitting equipment in the attic was for?"

"Why didn't you ask?"

"Are you kidding? After I already sounded like a fool, I wasn't going to say anything else."

She stood and walked toward the kitchen. "Do you want a glass of wine?" she called back over her shoulder.

"No."

"You, Joni?"

She shook her head.

When Adrian came back out of the kitchen into the living room, she balanced three half-filled plastic glasses in her hands.

"Fixed you one, anyway," she said, handing Joni's to her, then one to him. She moved past him and sat on the couch, then looked over at him. "Was my question that dumb, Cameron?"

"How can any question be dumb now?"

"No, really."

"With the gestation rate they produced in the women, I thought about aliens myself, though I know better. An alien, if there is such a thing, wouldn't look like us. In fact they wouldn't look like anything you've ever seen. Because for them to do so they would have to have DNA itself as a genetic material, like we do. Then they would have to have a myriad number of base pairs arranged the same way we do, as other creatures who have evolved here do, and the DNA would have to be in an identical sequence on identical chromosomes. It isn't mathematically possible that they would have evolved in the exact same way as we have, as anything has on this planet."

Adrian's eyes questioned him. "Not possible?"

"One in a trillion chance, Adrian, a trillion trillion. No, it's not possible—not mathematically. If there is such a thing as an alien, then they're probably going to look a lot different than what we can imagine—however their DNA, or whatever they have in its place, lined up. They might not even be carbon-based, like we are—probably won't be. You're talking about something maybe breathing ammonia or something like that instead of oxygen. They might even look like some kind of appendaged rock, a big blob of silicon, anything."

"For the sake of argument, Cameron, let's say they hit on that one in a trillion chance—one in any number is not impossible. If they—"

"No," he said before she could go on. "Even if you want to assume what you say, it's still not possible."

"I don't understand—why?"

"Adrian, manned space travel, galactic travel at least, or intergalactic, isn't possible. Any life form from another place would have to be on a planet circling some far off star, planets we don't know about. At even the fastest speed that can be envisioned for a space craft of the future, it would take thousands of years to travel here from that far away. Being logical, can you imagine an alien mind—one that would have to be so much more advanced than ours to already have the means to travel through outer space—can you imagine such a society putting a crew on a ship for travel that would take untold generations of them dying and being born before they reached here?"

"Well, what are they then? They read minds, almost can't be killed, are born in weeks—days for the last ones. I don't remember reading about anybody like that belonging to the United Nations."

The telephone rang. She glanced at her watch, rose, walked to the counter, and lifted the receiver to her ear.

"Uh huh, Bob," she said. "No, he's not here. I haven't seen the chief in . . . what's that? . . . well, he didn't come by here. Maybe he called to get my address to give it to somebody else. We had a couple visitors he'd been talking to. They could have asked him for my address and then he called downtown to get it from you. But he hasn't been by-here. What are you trying to find him for?''

Almost instantly her eyes narrowed. There were several seconds of silence, then she said, ''Uh huh, if the chief calls I'll tell him.''

She replaced the receiver and looked back toward the couch. ''The blond's body has been stolen from the morgue.''

CHAPTER 35

When an officer held open the door to the morgue and Edwards and Golby stepped inside, a flashbulb erupted in their faces.

Edwards looked angrily at the uniformed sergeant who met them.

"What's he doing in here?" Edwards asked, nodding across his shoulder toward the photographer.

The photographer, a stocky, red-haired man wearing a rumpled coat and a hat with a press card stuck in its band, smiled back at them and stuck his cigar in a corner of his mouth.

"He's the one who discovered the body was missing," the sergeant said. "We're keeping him around for a statement."

"Well, get him the hell outside the area. Where's Chief Young?"

"We've been trying to find him. He's not at home." The sergeant walked to an officer standing a few feet away from the photographer and nodded toward him.

As the reporter was escorted from the building, a cloud of blue smoke trailing him, the sergeant walked back to them.

"You discovered anything else since we talked to you on the radio?" Edwards asked.

Before the sergeant could answer, Cameron, Joni, and Adrian stepped through the doorway. The officer who had just escorted the photographer outside walked to them and said something.

Golby stared toward the doorway. "Let them in," he said.

They came on across the tiled floor.

"How did you find out?" Golby asked.

"They called my apartment looking for Chief Young," Adrian answered. "He had called downtown earlier looking for my address."

Edwards nodded. "For me."

Cameron looked toward the door leading into the vault area. "What happened?"

Golby explained the simple facts they had already learned over the radio. Why shouldn't he explain? With a reporter being the one who found the body, everybody in Memphis would know soon enough.

A man in a male nurse's uniform had been seen pushing a gurney from the room when the reporter had arrived; the orderly was dead and lying behind a desk at the center of the vault room; the body of the blond who had been killed at the river was missing—maybe wheeled out on the gurney. The man pushing the gurney had a surgical cap over his head, but had blond eyebrows and a prominent square chin—the reporter's description. The male nurse from whom the killer obtained the scrub suit had just been found stuffed into a waste management container at the back of the morgue, his neck broken.

Adrian and Joni stared at each other

Dammit, this has got to stop, was the only thing Cameron could think. It has to stop.

Stepping outside of the morgue, Joni moved her hand to a side of her head and ran her fingertips along her hair.

"You know I was thinking about becoming a blond," she said. "You can forget that."

She glanced down the sidewalk to her unmarked car

parked along the curb. "Guess I better get on back to work. I'll see you all later."

As she walked toward her car, and he slid inside his, Adrian looked across the seat at him.

"You hungry?" she asked.

They stopped at an all-night restaurant. He ordered a veal cutlet and she chose spaghetti. She was strangely silent until her meal was served and the lanky waiter had walked away, then she looked across the table at him

"Do you think he's alive, Cameron? The one who we saw go into the river?"

"I'd believe anything."

"Why would somebody else steal his brother's body? And remember when I told you about the officer who shot at them that night they raped Cassandra—after they had wrecked their van? He *had* to have hit him yet he wasn't killed." Then she looked directly across the table at him. "You mind if I make an observation?" she asked.

He set his coffee cup back on the table as she continued. "I listened to Mr. Golby saying aliens weren't possible. Then I listened to you. You know what I think? I think you and him are like a couple of learned scholars sitting around a table in the tenth century, explaining why men can't fly—they don't have wings—then saying that even if man could develop wings, he still couldn't go across the ocean because he would get tired and have to come down—his muscles would give out. That's almost exactly like what you said, that even if there were aliens, then they still couldn't travel here because of the length of the journey, they'd grow old and die—like falling into the ocean."

She quickly sipped from her coffee, then reached for a Sweet & Low packet as she spoke again.

"I'm not saying you're not right, Cameron, but I am saying that you and Golby, like the scholars back then, are capable of thinking based only on what you already know. Maybe you and Golby can't conceive of what might be out there somewhere; something they have developed that you would never think of. *You* sure never thought the blond could grow that fast, even be born in the first place."

"Touché," he said. Her expression was so determined, he almost smiled despite how he felt.

"I'm not saying you're wrong, Cameron. I'm just saying how does anybody know what is possible if they're not even aware of what it would take to make it possible?" She paused. "Does that make any sense?"

"I got the general gist the first time."

"I just can't keep from thinking they really might be aliens." Her brow wrinkled again. "Did you hear me say *might be* instead of *were*, like they're not dead—at least maybe the one we saw fall into the water. Could he be alive?"

"We're back to where we started this conversation."

"Cameron, is there anything—I mean *anything*—that you've seen that would make you think there was even the slightest possibility there was such a thing as aliens? I mean back in the past, and not counting the reasons it's impossible."

"Well, I can add more fuel to your fire in the sense that there have always been legends. You've heard of the places in South America that look like what used to be huge landing strips when you look down on them from up high. There are geometric figures there, too— angles and triangles with the lines composing them running up to five miles long.

"In Egypt there are the pyramids whose bases calculate at exactly their heights times pi—built before that mathematical formula was even devised. Another thing not as widely known is that in many of the pyramids there is no evidence of soot. How did the Egyptians light their way in the tunnels if they didn't carry torches? And they didn't—no soot on the ceilings. And no soot in any of the chambers where they placed the coffins and arranged all kinds of displays—in perfect order. Again, this would have had to be done completely in the dark.

"And you can't count the number of ancient people who drew pictures on cave walls depicting objects that looked like some kind of flying machine, a saucer in some respects—some of them even depicting a fiery exhaust coming from the rear of the object. I've even seen reproductions of men in these machines sitting in what looks like a cockpit, wearing what Dr. Baringer has called a goldfish bowl turned upside down on their heads—a space helmet for all the world. I can go on and on with things like that which have been the subject of speculation for years."

Adrian nodded as she bit off a piece of garlic bread. "I read about the airstrips," she said. "Didn't some of the Indians in South America have a legend that they had been visited and ruled by gods in machines from the sky? Gods they expected to come back someday?"

"Uh huh, and not only in South America. That legend is common to many ancient people the world over."

Adrian shuddered. "I just thought again about what they did to Dr. Anderson." Then she narrowed her eyes at another thought. "If they're smart enough to have been able to get here, anyway—and the others coming from him, how would they look at us, like we were dumb cattle?"

So much had happened so fast that that had never passed through his mind. He didn't answer, just thought about it.

"Maybe that's what they were doing here in the first place, Cameron, harvesting, not just ruling. Those Indian tribes you were talking about . . . I remember reading about the Aztecs and the sacrifices they made to their gods. Human flesh. I read where one tribe once killed twenty thousand people in one day and carried their bodies into the forests for their gods. Where did they get the idea for that kind of sacrifice? Think about it. If you were going to give up something valuable to some deity you worshiped, it would be something really valuable, something you owned; not your next door neighbor, for God's sake. A dead body, what kind of offering was that to anybody that didn't make use of dead bodies?''

She looked at his plate. "And how do we make use of dead bodies, Cameron? We eat them. You're eating a baby cow.''

He looked down at what was left of his veal cutlet and laid his fork back on his plate.

"Damn, Adrian.''

"You are, Cameron, and you're not some kind of horrible cannibal. You're just doing what everybody's done since the world began. A cow is a beast beneath us in intelligence. Isn't that really the only reason we eat them? I mean if a cow's intelligence was close to ours, we wouldn't think of eating them. That *is* the only difference. Think about it. They're warm-blooded creatures just like we are, have babies, raise their young. . . . So if we are dealing with aliens and they're millions of years ahead of us in intelligence, they wouldn't see any more wrong in harvesting us than we do in slaughtering cows. They would be cannibals only by our definition; to them they're just meat eaters—eating things way beneath them in intelligence.''

Her forehead wrinkled in thought. "You know, on the other hand, somebody might think that since we look like they do, they would at least think twice about eating us—there *are* other kinds of meat. But I'm not so sure that would be the case. There were natives in Africa, Indians in South America, who looked alike, but that didn't stop them from eating each other. I bet you'd be surprised how many places there are where cannibalism still goes on today.''

She nodded at her own statement. "I'm just thinking out loud, Cameron. But it is something to think about, isn't it—I mean with what happened to Dr. Anderson.''

He laid his napkin over his plate. "Adrian, what you're doing now is not just guessing why they're cannibals. There is no doubt in your mind that they *are* aliens, is there? Okay, so let's play your game. If there were aliens here before—back five hundred thousand years ago—why did they leave? Why did they leave and give up a planet full of game, so to speak?"

"You tell me," she said, and lifted their bill from the table. She held it toward him. "Your turn."

He began to fill out the slip.

Adrian had a final thought. "In that article where I read about dinosaurs not necessarily being gray, there was something else, too. Didn't it take over a century for your profession to shift from the idea of them being cold-blooded, slow-footed creatures to warm-blooded, fast animals?"

"There is still some debate about that."

She frowned across the table. "Cameron, logic has its place, but when something hits you right in the face—"

At a booth in a far corner of the restaurant, Ben Utterback, his cheeseburger pushed aside, his cigar perched precariously on the edge of the table, scribbled furiously as he listened through the little plastic earpiece connected by a wire to the receiver in his pocket.

Now he looked out around his booth toward Cameron and Adrian as they rose and started toward the exit.

After they had walked from the building, he watched the lanky waiter who had been serving them walk to their table, pick up the credit card slip, then move to the ledge at the rear of their table and lift the napkin he had left folded there. He unfolded its edge and carried the little wireless mike back across the floor.

As the waiter returned the mike he held out his other hand for the missing half of a torn hundred dollar bill, and Utterback handed it over. Utterback took the credit card slip and read the name before handing it back.

The waiter glanced back in the direction Cameron and Adrian had gone. "Is it a woman stepping out on her husband? Or a man stepping out on his wife?"

"You'd never believe it," Utterback said as he stuffed his earpiece, into the pocket with the transmitter. He rose from the booth. "You'd never in a hundred years believe it, my man, but you will. Do you read *The Whole Truth?*"

"What's that?"

"Well, you would call it a grocery store tabloid, but it's not, it's a famous newspaper—going to be, anyway. Look for a special edition I can assure you will be out in a couple days. I promise you you'll get the biggest jolt you ever received—I double damn promise you that."

Utterback reached back into the booth for his cigar and his hat with the press card in the band, placed the hat jauntily to the side of his head, and walked toward the door.

A large private jet landed at the Memphis International Airport and taxied to the Air National Guard hanger at the north side of the facility. The plane was the eighth to land there in the last six hours. Over a hundred hastily summoned men and women were now in Memphis, representing nearly every one of America's top experts in their line of work.

Golby's immediate superior took up residence in a suite in the Peabody and called Golby's room. In a few minutes they and several other high-ranking officials were involved in deep conversation.

Elsewhere, the new arrivals were quickly moved to their quarters, most of the housing selected in such a manner as to allow the large number of personnel to come and go without causing undue notice. All of them were in one way or another connected with the hunt for the blond children and the two blond males, though nobody could be absolutely positive that any of them were still alive.

In the hope they weren't, that the body of the one who dove into the river would eventually float to the surface, over a dozen helicopters waited for dawn to take off and patrol the Mississippi downstream from the spot he had disappeared under the water. Coast Guard boats were already making their way up the river from New Orleans as fast as could be safely done. The first thing they discovered was the floating green aluminum boat.

CHAPTER 36

The front page of the following morning's *Commercial Appeal* highlighted the murders and the theft of the body from the morgue. The story was professionally done, with little speculation. But there *was* the theft of a body, the double murders, the fact—according to the FBI—that the body was that of one of the members of the cult who had murdered and cannibalized Dr. Anderson's body at his rented house outside West Memphis. The implication was obvious; the cult members might still be in the area. More than one gun was bought that day by families who had sworn they would never have one in their house, and three of the biggest hardware stores in the city were sold out of ammunition before noon.

Cameron finished reading the article, folded the paper, and laid it on his desk. He could really use something else on his mind. But even when he raised his gaze to his students, all busy at work, his mind was back to what was happening. All were busy but Lee Ann; she was in the hospital. He had meant to go see her after classes that afternoon, but he almost couldn't find where she was. When he finally did, after calling and asking Edwards, he was told she was still suffering severely from the shock of all that she had been through, that the doctors weren't letting anyone see her yet.

He had thought about calling her mother, but decided against it. She would have her hands full helping care for Lee Ann. There would be enough time later to talk to both of them. The main thing was that Lee Ann was now safe, and the mother who had walked sadly from his classroom had seen her fervent prayers answered.

The bell rang and he rose from his desk and walked outside. Thirty minutes later, he stopped the Maxima at the curb on Poplar, and Adrian opened the passenger door and slid onto the seat.

"What do you expect to find?" she asked.

"What did you expect to find when we went out to Dr. Anderson's?" he countered, and guided the car away from the curb. "Those kids didn't just vanish into thin air." He strangely felt amused. "Unless a spaceship picked them up."

Adrian didn't smile, and he looked back through the windshield, guided the Maxima around a car slowing in front of him, and pulled into the left lane. Ahead of them, a low line of dark clouds moved toward the city from Arkansas. Adrian looked at them for a moment, then faced across the seat toward him. "Maybe there's a planet out there we don't know about. What if there's one shielded like those aircraft you can't see?"

He looked at her.

"What are the aircraft that radar can't pick up?" she asked. "The kind the military has?"

"You mean the stealth bomber?"

"Uh huh. I know the plane's not impossible to pick up on radar, only harder. I've read about it. What if there's a planet like that out there? One a radio message could get to and come back from fast? And don't say something like that is impossible. How do you know that if some race is smart enough to visit this planet that they're not also smart enough to keep us from seeing them if they don't want us to? Maybe they even have something like a space station up there."

"Adrian, that's so far out that—"

"Don't start talking down to me. Just explain."

"Adrian, no matter what the masking technology there would still be a planet's gravitational pull, its natural radio waves, and probably a lot of other things for all I know. Nothing could be masked from the kind of careful search our radio telescopes constantly make. And even if we say there are aliens, how can they look like us? On top of everything else, how can they look exactly like us? It's a trillion to one shot, I've already told you that."

An amused expression crossed her face. She looked back across the seat. "Maybe it's like lemonade."

"What?"

"When you mix water and sugar and lemon juice, you get lemonade. You can mix it anyway you want, and it still comes out lemonade. Maybe the concentrations are different, but it's still lemonade—you can't tell any difference by looking at it. Whatever building blocks that were here—that we came from, the carbon you talked about in the restaurant—why can't carbon be other places—and oxygen and water? If they are, then when they're all mixed together, why wouldn't whatever is produced turn out to look the same? Maybe the concentration difference gives them some powers we don't have, but the looks are the same."

He couldn't help but smile. In fact the gesture felt good. "Lemonade, huh?"

"Yep," she said and crossed her arms over her chest. "Why not?"

He turned left onto Riverfront Drive and drove toward the old I-55 bridge.

"I'm going to end up fired, is what's going to happen."

"I need you along in case there's still FBI out there." And his mind was back to somber again.

"You're going to get me fired," Adrian repeated. "You just wait and see."

Jake Gaither cradled his rifle in his arms as he looked through the trees at the big, columned house. There had been quite a ruckus took place by the looks of the tire tracks cutting up the entry road. He had picked up half a dozen cartridge casings lying in the grass. The cops had damn sure got after somebody, got after them good. He assumed the blond he had seen on the roof but wasn't certain, he never read the newspaper nor watched the TV, except occasionally for weather reports, which he hadn't done today, but wished he had. The heavy, low line of black clouds nearing the place was as threatening as any he had ever seen.

He stared at them again, then back to the ruts. He decided to call his nephew on the Memphis force. He would know if there were any reward money or anything like that—if the cops did indeed catch anybody important. Dropping his rifle to his side he started forward toward the house. He had never been inside it before and now was curious.

A few minutes later he stepped up onto the porch and tried the doorknob, but it wouldn't turn. There was a window raised over to his right. He moved to it and ducked through it into the house.

It was unusually warm inside. In fact it was unusually warm outside, too, despite it being November, the Mid-South's weather as usual following its own erratic pattern. You never knew at Christmas whether you were going to need a parka or a T-shirt. It was why he always had so damn many colds in the winter, one day needing the heater on, the next day burning up. And maybe tornado weather today, from the looks of the clouds; the wind was already starting to blow. And him living in a trailer.

Shaking his head, he walked on toward a wide doorway in front of him, and stepped into a big living room.

He saw the couch back to his right. The bastards had been making a regular home of the place. He walked to his right and passed out of the living area into a hall, then on into a big dining room and spacious kitchen.

He looked at the rotted peeling wallpaper to the sides of the cabinets, their doors hanging from rusted hinges, at the cracks between the walls and the window frames, at the rain-stained ceiling. Plaster had fallen in many places, sagged in other spots. He shook his head at what the government could do when it made its mind up to help.

Still shaking his head, he walked back through the living area to the foyer and looked up the wide staircase. Glancing back over his shoulder toward the windows at the front of the house, his face tightened. Coming down the narrow road toward the house was a white car.

Damn! He didn't need no trouble with the law—and who else would it be but them back again? He looked back into the living room, then hurried toward it.

Cameron stepped from the Maxima and looked at the big house, which seemed much less threatening in the sunlight than it had been the night before. Adrian came around the front of the car.

"I can guarantee you they've searched every inch of it," she said, "a half dozen times." She looked toward the wide, wooden barn. "It, too. And the woods around here, no telling for how far—every bush."

"The blonds were here and—"

"Cain and Abel."

"Yes, Cain and Abel, and Missey and Lee Ann with them. They were only a few feet from their car, but hadn't had time to run. That means we surprised them. They only had a few minutes, maybe seconds. So what did they do with the babies before that?"

He walked around to the rear of the Maxima, opened the trunk, and lifted out an automatic shotgun. He looked toward the barn, stared at it for a moment, then walked in its direction.

Adrian came up beside him and matched him stride for stride. The clouds were there now, starting to pass over the sun, and the wind was up. A stiff gust whirling from the east passed over the barn and blew toward them. He caught a whiff of the smokehouse scent, and closed his eyes.

Stopping in the wide doorway to the structure, he looked up at the chain dangling from the rafters, then at the rotted mound of dry, yellowed straw, turned black in some places and laced with cobwebs glittering what little sunlight now streamed in through holes in the roof. He walked across the dirt floor to the mound. There was a noticeably stronger odor there, more of rot than the smokehouse scent.

He used his toe to shift the damp, heavy clumps of straw, matted together—and saw the dried, blackened strip of skin. Adrian stared at it for a moment, then turned and walked back out of the barn.

His lips tight, he stared a moment longer, then turned and followed her from the barn, and they moved to the house through the darkening of the sky and the ever increasing wind.

They went inside through the back door and stopped in the living room. He surveyed all there was to see, stopped his gaze for a moment on the TV set, now covered with black fingerprint powder, then moved into the foyer to the foot of the staircase.

As they went up the stairs, the boards creaked, something he didn't remember happening the night before. He needed to remember everything and more, what he hadn't noticed the night before. What nobody noticed. If there was anything.

At the top of the staircase, he looked down the hall. Adrian looked at the wooden steps leading up into the attic, still pulled down.

"You remember the transmitter up there, Cameron? Can somebody tell how powerful it is by looking?"

"I couldn't. I don't know anything about electronics. But I'm sure to someone in the field it wouldn't be all that hard. Why?"

"They were in contact with somebody. Wouldn't that tell how far the message was sent by seeing how strong the transmitter is? Maybe even if it's strong enough to send a message to . . . you know, somewhere up there."

There was no doubt she was serious in her question. But there was also no doubt that she was embarrassed by it too, her pausing in the midst of asking. Who in the hell did know what might be possible and wasn't? "No, the strength of the transmitter wouldn't necessarily mean anything. The radio sending the message isn't as important as the receiver."

"I thought you just said you didn't know anything about electronics."

"I don't. But I'm a scientist. Or at least I thought I was before all this started. Power isn't important. The Pioneer satellite is over five hundred billion miles out from earth now and still sending back messages to NASA or whoever it sends them back to. I'm not certain of all the details, but I remember reading that the transmitter it's using is around a half watt. That wouldn't be much stronger than a Christmas tree light, if that strong."

"I'd like to see the transmitter again, anyway," she said, and started down the hall.

Jake Gaither threw open the back door and sprinted out of the house toward the barn. Halfway to the big, sagging structure, he angled to his left and ran toward the weaving, wind-swept tree line surrounding the property.

Cameron moved ahead of Adrian up the steps into the attic. She bit her lip in thought. "There aren't any symbols in the house. I wonder what those at Dr. Anderson's were for?"

"I don't know. Maybe they left them to throw the police off, make them think a cult had been there."

"Uh huh, or maybe that's the kind of sign they leave when they kill someone. Maybe it's where the Indians got the idea to mark holy places with emblems and skulls and things like that. Maybe they were saying you better not come around here—or see what you get.''

The radio was no longer on the table at the center of the attic. Only the main wire that had run to it was left, the black cable snaking across the floor from the wall.

Adrian picked up the cable's loose end. ''Look at this.''

He walked to her side. She wasn't looking at the cable, but at the burned spot across the top of the table.

''They used so much power it left a mark,'' she said.

''Yes, or maybe they had a bad connection.''

She frowned at him. ''They did use a lot of power, Cameron. So what does that mean, if power doesn't make any difference as far as the signal goes?''

''I didn't say that it didn't make any difference. Of course a stronger signal makes a difference. I said that a weak signal *could* still be picked up.''

She stared at him. ''You don't make yourself very clear sometimes.''

He heard her, but really wasn't paying any attention. Instead he kept moving his gaze around the attic, focusing on the dark corners, looking for something—anything.

Once they were back down the attic steps into the upper hallway, Cameron looked at the doors to each side, all of them open and all of the rooms obviously carefully searched by the agents the night before.

''Cain and Abel didn't carry the babies a mile off in the woods, then come back to the house to get caught themselves,'' he said, as much thinking aloud as stating an obvious fact.

''They could have, Cameron, coming back for Missey and Lee Ann.''

''No. If they were going to take them in the car, then the babies would have been in it, too—if they were going to take them along in the first place.'' He looked back at the open doorways along the hall.

''They left them here.''

CHAPTER 37

Cameron, the butt of his shotgun resting on the floor by his feet, stood at the landing on the second floor. He had glanced into each room, not searching, but trying to see something that might cause an idea to click in his mind. But there had been no sudden revelation, not even a hint. Where were they? In the house when the FBI arrived the night before—then ran on their own? They couldn't, no matter how fast they might later grow. Missey had given birth to them only minutes before the caravan of law enforcement vehicles arrived. He looked down the hallway again.

Then his eyes narrowed as he looked at the set of steps leading up into the attic.

Adrian noticed his expression. "What?"

He walked toward the steps.

Adrian hurried up to his side. "What?"

"I'm not sure." But his pulse was beginning to surge.

He hurried up the steps and stopped with his head just above the attic floor. He looked back to the left wall. Then he lowered his head and looked down the hallway in the same direction. He felt his pulse increase.

"What, Cameron?"

"It doesn't go far enough."

"What doesn't go—"

"The hallway is longer than the attic in that direction, several feet longer."

Adrian looked back toward the landing. A cool gust of wind passed over her, coming from an opening somewhere.

He came down the steps and walked toward the bedroom door across from the landing.

He stepped inside the room and looked up at the ceiling. "The attic doesn't go over the top of this room, at least not the same attic where the radio was. It doesn't run this far."

Adrian looked at the ceiling.

"But something has to," he added. He walked toward a set of closets on the back wall, opened one of the doors and stared up at its overhead.

Adrian stepped beside him, and looked up at a trap door he was eyeing.

"The agents would have seen that, Cameron."

He raised the shotgun and used the end of its barrel to bump up on the door. It moved freely.

He looked around him for something to climb on, but saw nothing.

"You don't have a flashlight, Cameron."

"I'm just going to peek inside it."

"Uh huh, and get your head whacked off if they are up there."

"By babies?"

"By whatever might be up there."

"You don't have any matches?"

"Certainly, I carry them around with me all of the time, in case the power goes off." Rain began to fall against the roof.

"I'm going to look anyway." He held out the shotgun. "Hold this."

She caught her purse under her arm and took the gun into her hands. He got a grip on the closet door facing with one hand, hesitated a moment.

"Uh huh, what next?"

Crap! He let go of the facing, walked from the room and hurried down the stairs. A few moments later he carried an old lamp table back up to the floor. He jammed it inside the closet and grabbed the facing again.

"Don't put too much weight on it."

He raised his foot to the table's edge, put pressure on it to test its stability, then pulled on the top of the door facing and lifted himself up.

He quickly pushed the trapdoor back out of the way, caught the tops of the two-by-sixes forming the opening's edge, and pulled his head up into the space.

Cracks in the roof allowed enough dim light inside the area for him to see that nothing was there, just dusty walls and a million cobwebs. Then he noticed something. He hung at the opening a moment more, then let his foot back down to the table, rocked it, nearly losing his grip, and dropped clumsily to the floor.

Adrian had a knowing expression on her face. "You know the agents already looked up there."

"What I'm wondering now is, did they look at the room under it?"

Adrian looked at the back of the closet wall, a sheet of tightly nailed paneling.

He stepped forward and pushed against the paneling. "The flooring up there goes another eight or ten feet farther back." Moving his hands farther down the paneling to the left, he pushed again.

He moved them back to the right, and pushed once more. He pushed again at that spot, then put an effort into his next shove, and then frowned. "There are two-by-fours behind here, just like there's supposed to be. But there's something back here. There has to be." He shoved against several spots in the same area.

"Give me a minute." He walked from the room. This time Adrian didn't hold the shotgun casually, but raised it and held it toward the rear of the closet.

Down at his car, hunched against the now steady rain, he lifted a tire tool from the trunk, then hurried back toward the house.

Adrian glanced over her shoulder at him as he stepped into the room. He walked immediately to the

closet, studied the rear wall for a moment, then raised
the tire tool and jammed it hard into the wood.

Its end penetrated the paneling, and he pulled the
tool back and jammed it hard again. This time it slipped
through into an open area.

Adrian lifted the shotgun again.

He pried down on the tool. The paneling resisted,
hung, then tore. He caught an edge of it and pulled hard
on it, then used the tire tool again.

In a moment he had opened an area wide enough to
stick his head through. He leaned toward it.

"Cameron."

He leaned closer, smelled a bittersweet odor, ran his
gaze back and forth over the area behind the paneling.
But it was so dark he couldn't differentiate anything.

"It's not like in the attic, no sunlight can get into it."
He lifted the tire tool and slammed its point into a section of paneling a foot away from the hole. He worked
furiously.

In a minute, he had broken a several-inch strip of
paneling loose from the wall. He started working on the
wall below the hole.

In another minute he had created an opening most of
the way to the closet floor. It was maybe ten inches
wide, up against a two-by-four on one side.

He moved his head close again and peered into the
area. In the dim light now filtering into the area from
the bedroom behind him, he could make out several tall
bottles setting on the floor.

At the very back of the space, maybe seven or eight
feet away, there were some kind of shelves, each filled
with something too dark to make out.

"Bottles. Some shelves."

"I want to go inside it."

"No. I think I have enough room to go inside myself." He turned sideway and lifted his foot over the
bottom of the opening, stuck his leg inside, and then
brought his head back to the slit.

For a second, he didn't go any farther—because his

body now completely cut off the light. He stared into a coal black void.

Come on, dammit. If they are here they're just kids.

And besides, the agents probably noticed the room; they just had the sense to come in through the door— wherever in hell it was.

He forced his way forward and became stuck. He tried to force his chest on through, ripped his shirt, pressed harder. The paneling gave a little, a little more, with an almost human groan let him slip inside the space.

Light poured across his back onto the dusty bottles on the floor—whiskey bottles they looked like, round and tall. Six or seven feet in front of him, dozens more bottles on the cobweb-covered shelves, rack after rack of them. The area suddenly darkened, startling him.

He turned. Adrian's dark shape pressed against the opening.

"You're blocking the light, Adrian."

She stuck her leg inside and came through the opening much easier than he had, barely brushing against its sides.

The room lightened as she moved up beside him. She held the shotgun across her chest, ready, but lowered it at what she saw.

He lifted a bottle from the floor. It was full of a clear liquid. He reached to the bottle's top, struggled with it a moment, and turned the cap. He smelled the liquid.

"It *is* whiskey." A bittersweet odor.

"Bootleg," Adrian said, "no label. A little extra income made farming easier, I guess."

A bottle tinkled against another.

Adrian raised the shotgun behind him.

His eyes locked on the shadowy area near the foot of the shelves.

Another tinkle.

A large rat darted from behind the shelves and ran at an angle to their right.

Adrian jerked the shotgun barrel after it. He thought she was going to shoot.

The rat disappeared in the darkness in the corner to their right.

The room darkened again.

Cameron jerked his head toward the opening, now gone in the pitch dark blackness.

Wind whipped against the top of the house.

He heard Adrian move. "Wind shut the door," she said.

She was only a couple feet away from him, but he might as well have been listening to someone invisible.

She bumped into the wall, cursed under her breath.

He heard the paneling creak as she caught the outside edge of the opening. Her body scraped against the sides of the hole. He moved back closer to her and reached out a hand to touch her shoulder.

She suddenly jerked through the opening—was jerked. She screamed. His heart stopped and he grabbed wildly for the opening.

"Cameron!"

Behind him, the shelves suddenly slid.

He spun around, bottles toppled crashing to the floor.

And they were on him.

He struck out blindly. His fist connected. Against something small.

In the bedroom, figures slammed into a wall then crashed to the floor. Adrian's voice—a gurgling sound.

He spun back around to the wall, and his neck was gripped from behind—small hands.

Them.

In the bedroom, Adrian yelled her anger. He broke the grip at his throat, pushed the hands back away, felt them grab him again as he fought for the opening.

The shotgun roared, the noise deafening. His ears ringing.

In the bedroom, a body hit the floor.

"Adrian!"

"Oh God!"

It was her voice.

"Adrian!"

The light came back.

The hands were gone. He looked through the opening.

Adrian, one hand at her mouth, her other holding the shotgun down at her side, stood at the bedroom doorway staring at the crumpled form of a small child lying on the floor.

Cameron whirled around.

Three small children, none over four feet tall, blonds, stared back at him from the twilight in front of the shelves.

He stepped back, squeezing sideways into the opening and through it into the bedroom.

The child on the floor wiggled. His abdomen gushed blood. His left leg was nearly severed from his body.

"Oh my God," Adrian said in a low voice. "Oh my God."

The wounded child stared up at her, convulsed, then lay still.

"Oh, my God in Heaven," she said.

Cameron glanced back at the opening, then stepped to her.

Tears welling from her eyes, she shook her head. "He grabbed me. I was trying to get free. The shotgun fired."

A low guttural sound came from behind Cameron.

Dark eyes, three pair, topped by blond hair, stared from the opening.

Jake had stopped at the muffled sound of a shotgun blast coming from within the old house. He turned and, standing in the now light rain, stared in its direction. He looked at his rifle, stared back toward the house, and started toward it.

* * *

They all looked alike to Cameron, every one of them, but in two pairs a little different in age, three feet tall and four feet tall, a couple of inches difference in the ones in each pair.

The one on the floor was one of the older ones, and the slightly smaller of that pair, with the larger one staring at Cameron, while the younger pair were expressionless, not looking directly at him.

"Who are you?" he asked.

Adrian looked at him.

The smallest child in the young pair did too—the first time he had raised his face. Cameron stared directly at him.

"Who are you?"

A low, guttural sound came from the larger of the two older blonds.

The youngest child dropped his eyes from Cameron and looked at the floor.

Cameron looked at Adrian. "I want you to keep them here." He stepped forward toward the younger pair. "I want you to come with me," he said to the smaller one.

The largest child gave a quick guttural sound.

Cameron caught the smaller child's hand. There was a resistance at first, then the boy moved forward. The largest child stared, his dark eyes seeming to become even darker.

Cameron led the boy outside the room and down the hall. Adrian glanced over her shoulder at him, and then back at the other two children. Her eyes slowly went to the one on the floor, and her lip trembled. She looked up at the other two and kept her eyes there.

At the other end of the hall, Cameron stopped and looked down at the child.

"Who are you?"

The boy looked up the hall.

"Who are you?" Cameron repeated, louder this time. "Where are you from?"

The boy looked up at him.

"Do you know where you're from?"

"˜˜ˆ||/ˆ˜˜`," the boy said in a soft voice.

Cameron's heart beat in his ears. He had to make an effort to keep his voice level.

"Can you say where you're from in English—my language?"

"Stop!" Adrian shouted.

The taller boy dashed out of the room and ran toward them. He stopped in front of the young child and stared at him with threatening dark eyes. The young one dropped his gaze to the floor.

Adrian appeared in the doorway. She held the other child by his hand.

Cameron looked at the eyes of the larger child staring at the smaller one, at the smaller one with his eyes averted to the floor—and didn't try to ask any more.

Jake pulled back a branch and looked through the light rain at the house. He heard the noise—behind him.

The sound of a twig snapping.

Deer don't trail people, he thought, and turned around to face the sound. He raised his rifle in front of his chest.

Another sound. A second twig snapping.

He raised his rifle to his shoulder and looked down its sights.

Cameron looked around the room for something with which to wrap the leg to keep the blood off him as he carried the dead boy to the car. But there wasn't anything.

He leaned to lift the child from the floor. As he hoisted the small, limp form across his shoulder he couldn't help but feel a pang of sympathy, though he knew that was crazy. He turned, waited for Adrian to go in front of him with the other children, then followed along behind her.

At the open window at the front of the house he had to shrug the boy off his shoulder and hand him through the opening to Adrian on the porch. She handled him easily as the other children stared at her. He wouldn't weight over forty pounds.

Cameron saw the other children's eyes come back to him. They had kept doing that, looking at her occasionally, but their eyes always coming back to him.

He ducked through the window, stepped out onto the porch and took the limp form from her, lifting him back onto his shoulder.

It was on the way to the car, through the light rain, a drop hitting him on the forehead—a cool drop—that he suddenly realized how warm the boy was, almost hot.

A chill suddenly flashed up his spine. He had a terrible urge to heave the dead weight off to the side. He quickly got the body off of his shoulder and laid it on the ground.

"What are you doing?" Adrian asked.

"I'm not sure he's dead." He wasn't certain at all.

Adrian glanced at the other children then stared back at him.

He knelt beside the body, slowly leaned forward and placed his ear to the boy's chest. After a moment, he straightened and felt for a pulse.

He tried the other wrist.

Nothing.

He reached out his finger and lifted the child's eyelid.

The pupils were dilated noticeably. Rain drops splattered against the child's face.

He looked at Adrian, still staring down at him, then slipped his hands under the body and lifted it again. This time he carried the boy out in front of him, not across his shoulder.

Adrian opened a door to the rear seat and motioned the children inside the Maxima. He moved around to the trunk, slipped the boy off his shoulder, balanced him against his leg as he reached into his pocket for his keys.

"No, Cameron."

He looked at her, looked at the child, then caught him with both hands and lifted him up in front of him again. He moved around to the side of the car and slipped the child inside through the open door, left him lying on his back, his fixated eyes staring up at the car's overhead.

Adrian opened the passenger door to the front seat and, looking back at the other children in the rear seat, climbed inside the car. She leaned the shotgun on the seat, its butt on the floorboard.

Cameron looked into the rearview mirror, and saw the children staring back in it at him.

His attention was so riveted on their looks that he didn't notice the figures moving from the bushes toward the side of the car.

Adrian did. She grabbed for the shotgun. Too late. Two Uzi barrels stuck inside Cameron's window. He saw the black suits—and dark hair—and relaxed despite the weapons.

One of the men said, "Move your hand, lady."

Adrian's hand came away from the shotgun and back to her lap. The man gestured with the end of his Uzi, and she moved her hands on to the dashboard.

Then the man stared at the three blonds and the young body.

Cameron looked at the other man, noticed the tiny mike attached to the collar of his shirt. The wire ran up to his ear. He was talking softly.

They came from both sides of Jake at the same time, so fast he only swung the barrel halfway around before one of them grabbed it. The other leveled an Uzi at him. In a moment they had stepped out of the bushes and were walking toward the Maxima and the two men standing at its side.

The man Cameron watched kept talking softly into his mike.

The children kept staring at Cameron.

CHAPTER 38

It had quit raining now. Cameron pushed off the side of the Maxima and stared up the narrow entry road at a car bouncing rapidly in their direction.

It slid to a stop, and Edwards and Golby piled out of it. Golby stared hard. "Doctor, how in the hell do you do these things?" He stared at the children in the rear seat. "They're too old," he said. "The babies would only be . . . what in hell is going on here! Are these supposed to be the ones from Anderson's house or the ones just born?"

"Both of them," Adrian said, "and all of them. They're all the same."

"What are you talking about, woman?"

"They're all aliens. Like I said they were. You know that too, don't you? *Who are you?*"

Golby stared at her for a moment, then looked over at Jake, listening intently. Golby nodded toward the four men in dark suits, and they turned Jake around and walked him toward the bushes.

Golby waited until they were far enough away he couldn't be overheard. Then he looked back at Adrian. "No, I don't know that. My job is to prove they're not aliens. I've proved that a hundred times, sightings, nuts swearing they see things, normal people fooled by their own eyes. Why are you saying they are?"

"We got a word out of one of them. It wasn't anything I've ever heard before. Not even a tone like anything I've heard before."

"A word?"

Cameron nodded. "Not like a language so much as . . . it was almost like a humming sound—high-pitched." He had another thought, glanced at Adrian before he asked it. "That radio in the attic, did they send a message on it?"

Golby was silent, clearly thinking before he answered.

Adrian didn't wait. "What are you going to keep from us that can make any difference now?"

Golby nodded. "They sent one. Some place. The language—and the tone—is the same as you said. One of our satellites picked it up. I was informed of it last night."

"Sent to outer space," she said.

"Washington doesn't know that, or even suggest it, for that matter. It's my job to investigate. They informed me. That's all."

Golby's normally commanding voice had dropped low as he spoke. Cameron recalled the older woman at the hospital desk speaking in the same kind of low monotone after she had looked down at the list of patients and saw she was instructed to say the night watchman was not registered at the hospital. Golby had no doubt lied a million times in the past, and done it perfectly. But now . . . something so strange had been relayed to him that he had been thrown off base. "There is more, isn't there?"

When Golby didn't respond, Cameron added, "You've asked us to keep silent. We know enough now to start a panic if we wanted to."

Golby's eyes tightened, but Cameron didn't stop.

"How much can anything else hurt? You're not the only one who knows whatever it is you know. There has to be those in Washington. The Army, Air Force, or whoever it was who reported the satellite picking up the radio transmission, and politicians, and your people.

I'm in this deep. I'm feeling responsible, too. I'm *going* to know what you do. One way or the other, whatever it takes. If I have to threaten someone in Washington that I'm going to disclose what I already know, I'm going to find out what you're holding back.''

Golby took a moment more but, surprisingly, only a moment. He nodded slowly. ''The transmission was funnelled in some concentrated manner—like a laser beam. It passed through the satellite and nearly burned it out.''

Golby answered Adrian's next question before she even asked it. ''It was beamed straight up. But it could have been meant to bounce off of the stratosphere and come back to a point on earth. We simply don't know where it went.''

Cameron glanced into the backseat more than once on their way back to Memphis; Golby had wanted the dead child left where he lay. The other three had been walked off into the woods by the men in dark suits. Golby's car disappeared when they turned onto interstate 55.

It had pulled into a service station. A moment later Golby spoke on a pay telephone.

Seconds after he replaced the receiver, the dark-suited men in the headquarters taking up the entire top floor of the Wilson World Hotel on Cherry Street in east Memphis, a location not so noticeable as one in the downtown area, sent still another message out through the antennas now bristling from the top of that building —the children had been found.

Those receiving the messages included those members of a group with their hair cut so short their scalps showed on the sides of their heads. A unit so elite it was not even named.

A second group that received the messages also had short haircuts, but not so short you could see their scalps. Another outfit so secret they had no known name.

The third group receiving the messages was made up of men older than the personnel in the first two groups. They sported all kinds of coifs, from short hair to locks hanging past their shoulders.

And while all the members of each group were strongly built, with cleaved faces, this last group featured men who tended to have broader faces, stronger jaws, and, in many cases, scars; they easily could have been pulled from penitentiaries or army stockades, had debts to pay for escaping the death penalty, or been brought from mountain caves in Afghanistan in a arrangement for modern arms sent to their countrymen in the past.

Dressed in suits, they patrolled the streets of Memphis and West Memphis; dressed in jeans and overalls, they drove pickup trucks over the back roads of the area; dressed in camouflage hunting gear, they tread the thickets, marshes, and weed-strewn fields of the lowlands of the river; dressed in a variety of civilian uniforms, they drove milk and bread and meat delivery trucks on every blacktop and gravel road throughout the area.

A single-engine crop duster, strangely out of place for the time of year, swept down over the lowlands, passing over the brown stubble of a soybean field cut a month before. The pilot, a veteran of a hundred secret missions over places as far-flung as North Korea and Colombia, reached for his mike and reported no sign of anyone resembling a stocky blond between twenty and thirty of even a similarly built person of that age who might have dyed his hair a different color but still sported a telltale protruding chin—the one they still must find, the one who must have come to the morgue and carried off his brother's body. The two men who had accosted Adrian and Cameron heard every bit of the message as they sat in their car silently, staring at the old, columned house.

Then the last part of the message forwarded from Golby, the same message he had sent before: *Don't dis-*

regard the possibility of there still being two of the older ones.

The medical examiner waited at the morgue, courtesy of Edwards' radioing ahead. He started examining the young boy's body after one of Golby's men carried him through the door.

He *was* dead—no heartbeat or brain waves of any kind.

They all received a surprise when Golby, staring at the boy the entire time the examiner worked over him, turned his head to the dark-suited man standing next to him and said, "I want him carried to a cell, too." He already had ordered the other three to be taken to the jail, put in a cellblock that he had taken over, courtesy of a special order from the Justice Department.

The man stepped forward to the table and lifted the small body.

"I want the cell locked," Golby added, "and I want it kept locked at all times." He looked over at Edwards and added, "And I want you to have your men keep looking for the blonds, the older ones—*both* of them."

Edwards stared.

"Just act like the one's not dead," Golby said. "Tell your people we received a report somebody saw him. I don't want lackadaisical efforts."

Edwards stared a moment longer, then finally nodded.

When Golby stepped away from the agent, Cameron moved to intercept him. "Mr. Golby."

Golby stopped and looked back.

Cameron stepped up close to him. "I've been thinking. It might be way out of line—I can imagine the brain power in Washington that's working on this—but I have an idea. I thought you might call and talk to whoever in Washington is working on this. Maybe the message should be sent again."

"Sent again?"

"Send it in the same direction, at the exact same time

it was sent originally, from the same place. I would even want to use the same equipment—duplicate the last time to a T.''

Golby actually smiled. ''She has you believing.''

''Wondering.''

''Okay, even if there was someone out there listening, why in hell send it again? In case they didn't get it right the first time?''

''What I've been thinking is that—assuming there is somebody out there—we could show them some intelligence from us by our being able to beam a message back to them—maybe add something to its end.''

Golby's brow wrinkled in confusion.

Cameron went on. ''Look at it this way. If they are out there, then they already know *we're* here. So sending a message is not going to tell them any more about where we are than what they already know. But if it has been five hundred thousand years since they were last here, we could let them know we're a lot more advanced now.''

''For what purpose?''

Cameron thought of the veal—the baby cow. Adrian had said—*if cattle's intelligence was close to ours we wouldn't think of eating them*. It was crazy, but what was there to lose?

''If they found out we were smart enough to communicate with them, then it might follow in their thinking that we were smart enough to be better prepared if they came again.''

''You mean a 'no trespassing' sign?''

''It's only a thought. I knew you could pass it along to the right people if you wanted to. Let them think about it.''

That night they stayed at his apartment, but they didn't sleep very well, a problem he imagined affected a lot of other people that night. He looked over at Adrian.

''No trouble out of the chief?''

She shook her head. ''Some remark he made to the

lieutenant about a nutty female sergeant and her crazy paleontologist friend, but nothing said to me directly. What's he going to do, fire me for working overtime?"

The next morning she took her car to work, and he took his to the university.

After his last lecture he held a tutor session in a separate, empty classroom, his not available because of another scheduled class. It was almost dark by the time he stopped by a store, bought a sack of dog food for Napoleon, and made it back to Adrian's apartment.

She shook her head when he walked through the doorway. "You're not going to believe this. I don't."

Her telephone had rung as soon as she arrived home, a bit early. It was a call from Washington, looking for him. The caller had already telephoned the university and been told his last lecture had ended an hour before. The caller had telephoned his apartment and received no answer, then been given her number by the police department.

Of course she hadn't known where he was; in fact had expected him there already and told the caller that. At that same moment there was a knock on her door and she told the caller that it must be him.

She had laid the receiver down and opened the door to a young man who had been positive that a Shannon Langston lived there, but who finally decided it must be the same apartment number but in a different block at the complex.

She went back to the telephone to tell the caller she had been mistaken. A different voice had responded, a deep voice, but one with a pleasantness about it. After she told him it hadn't been Cameron at the door, the man asked her to leave a message the president had called—and indicated that that was in fact with whom she presently was speaking—she was so stunned she didn't even get the number he gave her and had to ask for it to be repeated.

Realizing what the call had to be about, she had asked him if it was in regard to the message the blonds sent, then quickly explained to the flabbergasted president she knew everything and why.

She had then gone on to say that if the call was in regard to Cameron's idea of sending a message, she completely agreed with the idea.

The president didn't take her unsolicited suggestion at all lightly, instead asking her why. She had stammered for a moment, told the president what she could of Cameron's thoughts and ended her explanation with the idea—they should send a message so that whoever it was would know they weren't dealing with cattle, and that Americans didn't take being eaten lying down.

There had been a brief silence on the other end. Then the president had informed her that was a damn good reason to send the message, better than any he had heard yet.

"Those were his exact words, Cameron. A damn good reason, better than any he had heard yet."

Even before dawn the next day a flurry of activity took place at the big, columned house in Crittenden County. By the precise hour the satellite had earlier picked up the message sent from the house, the two-way radio was hooked back to the cable running across the attic floor, and everything was ready.

"We won't be in the same line with regard to the rest of the galaxy the day the message was sent," one of the scientists said. "But everything else is as exact as possible."

The message was one of beeps and squeals that had been separated from the first message and rearranged in a random selection. If anybody received it, they would be able to discern it had been taken apart and reassembled by other beings—denoting at least a measure of intelligence.

A second message was also to be sent, a group of mathematical equations that some brain with NASA had come up with. Surely that would show intelligence.

Mathematical symbols would have to be universal, the brain said.

The scientist in charge, an older, pale, spectacled man in a rumpled suit, looked at his watch, counted silently as the second hand moved slowly to the exact time, then nodded.

A gray-haired man in a white lab coat depressed the switch to the recorder spliced to the radio. The single attic bulb hanging from an exposed cord at the center of the attic dimmed as the message sped quickly up the antenna and radiated out into the bright, cloudless sky.

The scientist in charge waited a few seconds, mentally counting, then nodded again. The man at the recorder again depressed the switch.

A wisp of light smoke rose from the back of the radio as the bulb dimmed once more, then went out, leaving the attic lit only by the dim light coming from the hole in the roof as the message again sped up the antenna and flashed through the air with a vast surge of power.

Then the wait started.

And so did the sarcastic comments.

"I would suggest we add a psychiatrist to the president's medical team," one scientist said, only half jokingly.

Another one said, "It won't be him, but his great grandchildren—several generations—by the time any message could come back."

One younger man in the group of mostly older men around the table said, "As far as a message being able to travel much farther in a shorter period of time than is thought—there has been a possible precedent. Dubious, but possible."

Six sets of spectacled eyes turned toward him.

"As you are all aware," he continued, "the object 3C273 was one of the initial radio sources to be linked with a quasar. It has been highly researched and we have excellent resolution studies. In only a four-year period some faint spots within it have moved away from the core by over thirty-three light years—obviously superluminal motion, over eight times faster than the theory of relativity would allow.''

"Yes, yes,'' one of the scientists said, surprised that the younger man had even taken time to bring that well-known fact to their attention. "But that is thought likely to be only an illusion, based on the fact the spots are moving toward us at barely under the speed of light, therefore creating a Doppler effect.''

"Yes,'' one of the other scientists, the oldest one at the meeting, said, and proceeded to explain as if he were talking to a group of students, which he did daily.

"A Doppler effect—like when the horn blasts from an oncoming train seem to get closer and closer together. It's that the train is catching up to the first blasts at the same time as it emits the later blasts, therefore you hear them at shorter and shorter intervals. I believe the consensus is that these spots from 3C273 are coming toward us at nearly the speed of light themselves, so they're always emitting light waves, then almost catching up to them, making the later rays seem closer to the first than they are, giving the appearance that the spots are moving faster than they are.''

The younger scientist had sat patiently as the two older men had spoken. He'd been glad he wasn't a student having to make sense out of such a convoluted explanation as the latter man had given. Now, he nodded his agreement, but said, "That is the accepted hypothesis. But I believe it is accepted only because it is assumed that nothing can move faster than the speed of light. If the theory of relativity wasn't already in vogue, the movement would be looked upon in quite another perspective, quite possibly the spots indeed *are* moving toward us at over eight times the speed of light. It has not been proven they are not.''

The first scientist reentered the conversation, his tone formal, even a little condescending. "So you are saying these people who sent the message have learned how to overcome natural law?''

The young scientist nodded. "If these spots are moving at eight times the speed of light, then it follows there is no universal speed limit, no natural law in that respect, only one we assume because we have accepted the theory for so long."

"Assuming that is a possibility," the older scientist came back, "then this meeting is a waste of time. The answer to what is the shortest time a message could reach a planet with any possibility of life on it is anytime. We might as well go home."

The younger scientist didn't hold back. "Yes, sir, I would say that is correct."

CHAPTER 39

The *Whole Truth* hit the grocery stores the next day.

ALIEN CANNIBALS HAVE ARRIVED—IN MEMPHIS
CULT NO LONGER SUSPECT IN ANDERSON MURDER
DR. MALONE NOT POSITIVE BLONDS DEAD.

Everybody was stunned.

Cameron looked at the photograph of him and Adrian, taken as they exited the morgue. The reporter had to have followed them to the restaurant, the only place he could have heard all he had written in the article under the photo.

Chief Young was concerned about a panic. There could even be an accidental killing of someone doing nothing more foolish than walking across a neighbor's yard after dark. Having been kept mostly in the dark by Golby, not even knowing the blonds had sent a message, and thinking they were dead, even if one of the bodies had been stolen, and the children were in custody, he wanted to issue a statement that the matter was now closed.

"For God's sake, why not?" he asked. "It's bad enough some crazed bastards have been brought back from the past—this character had to label them aliens on top of that?"

FBI Agent Edwards was still in shock from all the

things he knew. He didn't do much of anything at the meeting other than sit and stare, occasionally mopping his forehead with a grayed handkerchief.

Golby waited until after Chief Young had left the meeting, still angry that Golby wouldn't go along with him on allowing a statement to be issued. "Nobody is going to believe it. This is the same rag that printed the story about a woman giving birth to a kitten after sleeping with her cats, and only a few months ago did a piece on having documentary evidence from NASA of there being a real man on the moon."

He looked around the table and added, "My wife leaves it laying around the house; I've glanced through it a couple of times."

That taken care of he added, "All we have to do is make sure there are no follow-up stories. No more *The Whole Truth*, if it comes down to that."

He looked down the table. "Dr. Malone, since your name is in the article, you're probably going to be getting a lot of phone calls. Kooks, mostly, but maybe curious reporters, too."

"I can handle it."

"Just laugh a lot, that would be best."

"What about the children?"

"Noticeably older today than when we brought them in. You can almost see it hour to hour."

"What is going to happen to them?"

"Washington hasn't said."

"Have you tried to talk to them?"

"The children?"

"Yes."

"Even the one who spoke to you won't say a word now. I think the bigger one's dominant."

"The dead one, is—"

"Still dead, at least medically. But there's been no rigor mortis, no pooling of the blood, nothing you would expect in a corpse."

"When I carried him from that house, his body was

not only warm but hot, like it was vibrant. And I, uh, I had this sensation just before I noticed it."

Golby seemed to become more attentive. "What kind of sensation?"

"A feeling of some sort. Almost like you'd get walking down a dark alley."

Golby nodded. "You sensed something. Did you sense anything when you were in the house with them, or in the car while you were waiting for me?"

"No."

"I did when I got there; I had a feeling like they were scared of something. I could almost smell it. You didn't notice it at all when you were in there, you felt nothing?"

"Hell, they might have been scared of Adrian, maybe; she killed one of them. But for me to really say I sensed it—no. The only time I sensed anything, if you want to call it that, was when I had him on my shoulder and started feeling funny."

"You didn't notice them keep staring at you? Not Adrian, but you? It's almost like they were scared of you in particular."

He did remember that. Golby then seemed to go into deep thought, his eyes still looking, but seeming to stare past everything.

"They *are* scared of you!" he suddenly said loudly.

When they reached the receiving area outside the sealed-off cellblock, a middle-aged man in a dark suit and tie rose from his chair and picked up a set of keys off his desktop.

A similarly dressed, tall, heavy, wide-shouldered man with thick black eyebrows and a shaved head sat in a straight-backed chair next to the metal door leading into the cellblock. He seemed not even to notice them, staring silently ahead at the wall. A carrying case more than twice the size of an attaché case sat on the concrete floor next to his chair.

After the heavy door was unlocked, Golby pushed it back and they stepped into the cellblock.

Before they moved any farther, Golby looked over at Cameron and said, "I need you to think angry. I mean to do it every minute we're around the children."

Cameron started to smile. "How do you think angry?"

"For one, you can think of that male nurse and the orderly they killed at the morgue, not to mention Dr. Anderson. But you have to do it, you have to keep thinking angry every minute. Force yourself. Be bitter. Whether you're able to pull it off or not might make the difference in whether we can get anything out of them. You have to try. And, another thing. If I say anything, no matter how it catches you by surprise, I want you to immediately think, I do, I know that, or that's right."

The small, dead body of the child was in the first cell to the right, its door shut like all the rest. Three men, all in dark suits, buttoned and with dark ties, were in the hallway, two of them near the far end and one, a short, broad-shouldered man, sat halfway down the block.

The other three children sat on a bunk at the rear of a cell at the end of the block.

They looked at Golby as he stepped to their door. Then Cameron watched all three sets of eyes come around to his and remain there.

He tried to think angry and couldn't, then thought of Lee Ann and her mother and all the pain they suffered. It began to work.

"I can feel it as sure as I'm standing here," Golby said. "They're as scared of you as death. I can smell it."

The three kept staring.

Golby stepped back from the cell and caught the attention of the squat, broad-shouldered man. He immediately came forward and unlocked the door. Cameron noticed the other two men now paying close attention to what was taking place, then refocused his anger on the children. Lee Ann's mother, Lee Ann, herself, and the dead men at the morgue, their necks broken.

"That one," Golby said, indicating the smallest child with a nod of his head. The squat man walked to the bed.

Before he reached out, the child stood and started forward toward the door. The larger one his age and the older one looked at each other but made no sound.

Outside the cell, Cameron stared closely at the boy. He did look older than the day before. Or was that only imagination? Cameron realized his anger was slipping, and he renewed it.

Golby nodded the boy down the hall. In a few seconds they were outside the cell block. The blond stared at the large, bald-headed man sitting in the chair to the side of the door, and the man stared back expressionlessly.

"Down there," Golby said and pointed to a door at the end of the waiting area.

It was a small conference room, its only illumination furnished by a bare overhead bulb and what light came through a wire mesh covered glass plate filling the top half of the door.

There was a small table. Golby pulled back a chair and directed the child to it. Then he moved around to sit at the end of the table. Cameron moved to the chair directly across the table from the child.

As he lowered himself into the seat, he glared directly at the young face. The child lowered his eyes.

God, it was hard—no matter what they represented, what they would become, now they were only kids, and to be glaring at one . . . the child's eyes started back up again, and Cameron forced himself to think— you damn bastard cannibal killer. *Damn you all to hell for eternity.*

The eyes immediately dropped.

"Dr. Malone knows all about you," Golby said. "He told us the one in the other cell isn't dead."

It took Cameron a moment. *Uh, I do know that. Not dead, dammit, he's not. I know that.*

"The one in the other cell," Golby said, *"and* the one

stolen from the morgue, the older one—neither one of them are dead, are they?''

Neither one of them, Cameron thought. *Neither one of them are dead, are they?*

"If you don't answer my questions," Golby said, "Dr. Malone is going to kill you, all of you. He knows how to do that, and how to find the others, too. Do you hear me?''

Damn right, Cameron mimicked mentally. *I do know how. How to find you and how to kill you—all of you. I did find you, didn't I? Came right out there and found you.*

"Who are you?" Golby asked. "Why did you leave, or did you leave? Are you from here?''

You did, dammit. Which? Cameron thought. *You better say. We killed the Ancient Man, didn't we? We killed him, didn't we? We killed him. Speak!*

"~^`~|`~|/^~~`"

Cameron's thoughts froze despite having heard the same melodic tone before. *In our language,* he finally forced out of his mind. *In our language, dammit!*

"The one you call the Ancient Man developed a sickness." The boy spoke slowly. "All of us developed a sickness that ate at our vitality. The others went back, leaving us."

Leaving us? As if he were actually one of them from back then.

"If we developed an immunity and were able to keep living, we were to make contact."

The radio message.

"Yes," the boy answered.

"Make contact where?" Golby asked.

Make contact where? Cameron thought.

The boy's lips started to move. He looked across his shoulder toward the wall.

And through the wall, Cameron thought. *He's looking back at—or hearing—the dominant one.*

The boy's eyes came back to his. *Dammit! Answer us!* But the boy spoke no more, no matter what Golby roared or Cameron thought, no matter that he thought things so angry and evil and repulsive he would never repeat them to anyone.

That night Adrian stayed at his apartment, her idea, showing how nervous she was, it was the second night in a row. She lay in bed next to him, her tight body clothed to mid-thigh with one of his T-shirts, her hands back on the pillow and her head resting in them as she stared up at the ceiling.

"I wonder why they were afraid of you?" she asked.

"If anybody else had been thinking the things I was, maybe the kid would have answered him, too."

"You don't believe Golby sensed it earlier—like he said he did?"

"Hell, I don't know. I'm not sure I know anything anymore. I don't know anything anymore."

Adrian scooted toward him and lay her head against his shoulder. "In any case, he was right about the child speaking to you if you confronted him—at least until whatever it was he saw. Or heard. Or thought. Damn, it is crazy, isn't it?"

Her voice suddenly became lower. "Cameron, I thought about what happened to Gerald. It could have been them. His photo was in the tabloid; your name was under it—the name of the man the article said was going to find them. I pushed it out of my mind as being too far out, then I thought what if they are scared of you in particular—for some reason."

"You keep that kind of talk up and you're going to make my day."

"Really, Cameron."

"I thought about it myself when we were out at the house to pick up the boy's body. You can't keep something like that from going through your mind—especially damn cannibals. Christ. But what do I do—lock myself inside? Lightning could strike me too—but that doesn't mean I'm going to stop going outside."

"Cameron, I think there's a little more possibility to

this than lightning striking you." She sat up off his shoulder and looked straight at him. "And I don't want something happening to you especially now."

"Especially?"

"When we were at that house, you jumped ahead of me everywhere we went, you were obviously protecting me, and me the cop—that, for one. And, just overall, I think I finally found the right one."

He smiled a little, feeling better now. "So if I'd walked behind you, you wouldn't care if something happened to me, huh?"

"You know what I mean. You have any wine left from last night?"

"I bought two more bottles." He looked at the shape of her pert breasts under her T-shirt. Despite himself he was starting to feel a lot better. "But wine is not exactly what I have on my mind right now."

"Damn, Cameron, I thought you were depressed. I am. And wine's cheaper than sleeping pills. That's one thing I've learned out of all this."

He threw the sheet back and sat to the side of the bed. "I might eat a sandwich, too. It's gotten where I try to eat as much as I can on a day when I haven't seen blood."

"Blood," she said as she came off the bed on its other side. "I've been seriously thinking about becoming a vegetarian."

They slipped on bathrobes and walked toward the kitchen, passing Napoleon asleep in his closet.

They settled on cheese and crackers with the wine, and sat together on the couch as they ate. The only illumination came from a night light on a far wall and the light that came through the curtained windows to each side of the door.

He was the one who first saw the shadow pass by, but she caught it, too, smiled at his stare. She nodded toward the window on the far side of the door as the shadow went on past it.

"You have two windows, Cameron. So long as it goes by the second window after the first, we're okay. It hasn't stopped at the door." She chuckled lightly. "So you're a little more nervous than you sounded in the bedroom."

At that moment another shadow passed the nearest window. He looked at his watch. "Damn, it's two in the morning, late for a lot of traffic."

He leaned forward to the coffee table for another cracker.

"Cameron," Adrian whispered. "It didn't go past the next window."

He looked at her face. She was serious.

There was a slight sound at the door, barely perceptible, metal on metal.

Adrian came instantly up off the couch and hurried toward the dining room table and her purse. He came to his feet. The door slowly opened.

Adrian raised her automatic.

"Jesus, God Almighty!" Dr. Baringer yelled and threw his arm up across his face.

"What in hell?" Cameron said.

Dr. Baringer still held his arm up, but it was at the level of his bow tie now.

Adrian lowered the automatic.

"Jesus, Cameron, what in the hell is she?"

Cameron shook his head in amusement. "My bodyguard. What are you doing breaking into my apartment like that? And what are you doing in Memphis, anyway?"

Baringer looked back at Adrian. "Is she going to shoot if I come on in?"

"Depends on what you're breaking in here for."

"I'm breaking in because I assumed your butt was asleep and didn't want to wake you." He stepped inside the apartment and shut the door behind him. He looked around. "You didn't pay your light bill?"

"The switch is by the door. I wondered where my spare key had gone when you left."

Baringer flipped on the light switch, then watched Adrian as she slipped her gun back into her purse. "Damn good-looking, Cameron, I'll give you that. But dangerous." He pitched the door key to Cameron and walked to Adrian. He held out his hand. "Friends?" he questioned.

She shook his hand. "Adrian Cummings."

"Ron Baringer."

Cameron was wondering. "What are you doing in town?"

Baringer looked at the glasses on the coffee table. "That's wine, isn't it?"

"Uh huh."

"I was afraid of that. Do you have any real stuff?"

Adrian shook her head. "Only wine. It's good for you."

"I wasn't really looking for a health potion. I guess that'll have to do, though." He walked to the couch. "Now tell me what's this garbage I read in *The Whole Truth*."

Cameron began to explain what had happened since he had last called, ending it with, "A telephone call would have been a lot cheaper than a plane ticket."

Baringer, still thinking about all he had just heard, was at a loss for words for the first time Cameron could ever remember.

"Damn," Dr. Baringer finally said. "We're all going to be dinner for some extinct link from the past—or space cadets who landed here five hundred thousand years ago. Is that what you're saying? Damn, Damn, Damn."

He quit his damns long enough to finish the glass of wine Adrian had handed him as he had listened to all that had happened in the last few days.

"Do you want some more?" she asked.

"I think I'll take the bottle to bed with me if you two are finished with it."

"Bed's a good idea," Adrian said. "Even with not having to go in until the afternoon shift, I have to get *some* sleep."

Baringer pushed down on the couch. "This still fold out?"

"Just like it did when you were here last time."

"I'm still damaged from some damn metal thing that sticks up."

Cameron rose.

Adrian picked up her purse and turned to head down the hall. "Goodnight, Dr. Baringer," she said over her shoulder.

"You, too. Did you leave the bottle of wine on the counter?"

"Uh huh."

Cameron followed her down the hall.

When they entered his room, she said, "He's sorta cute."

"Him?"

"Sorta. And he doesn't say everything's impossible. He didn't say it one time."

CHAPTER 40

When at first he couldn't fall asleep, Dr. Baringer turned off the night light in the living room, hoping the darkness would help. But there *was* a section of the frame that didn't unfold properly in the couch. He kept feeling a hard, blunt point against his back. Finally, he sat up. "Crap!"

He slipped his feet to the floor and stood. The damn air conditioner was on, too, and way too damn cold.

He fumbled his way through the dark to the kitchen. The wine bottle, half empty, was on the counter.

"Damned if that's going to be enough."

He raised the bottle and drank directly from it. "Ugh, tastes like crap." Though it wasn't bad for wine, it wasn't good either.

Still holding the bottle, he turned to start back toward the couch.

He felt a slight whiff of wind against his back.

He turned and looked deeper into the narrow, dark kitchen. The light outside the window plainly showed the window was halfway up. With the air conditioner running? He started to think, *how stupid.* But the words never fully formed in his mind before he noticed a form off to the right of the window.

The form stepped out of the dark toward him.

He yelled and pushed the wine bottle hard toward it.

* * *

Cameron sat up in bed at the sound of a yell and a bottle smashing to the floor.

"What in hell?"

Adrian was instantly out of bed and toward her purse on the dresser.

Cameron dashed into the hall.

A shape started down it from the far end.

"Dr. Baringer?"

The figure stopped.

Napoleon growled loudly from the closet.

Cameron started to scold Napoleon. Then he realized the shoulders were too wide to be Baringer's.

Adrian was suddenly beside him. She raised her automatic down the hall. "Stop!"

Two eyes suddenly glowed darker than the rest of the hall. It was like two black holes in a shadow. The form started forward.

"Shoot!" he yelled.

The eyes *did* glow black. Another step forward, a slight limp.

"Shoot!"

Another step forward, then the next one was another limp.

A limp?

The blond falling at the riverbank and the bullet holes in the thigh of his pants.

The child Adrian had shot, nearly severing the leg from the body—at the thigh.

The ancient man and the two gaping wounds in his thighs, where flesh had been removed.

He stared at the thick thighs as Abel drew closer.

"Shoot him in the thigh!"

But Adrian didn't. Her eyes wide, she stared back at the dark eyes glaring into hers. Her eyes weren't only wide, they were fixed—*held.*

Abel reached out his thick hands for her. Cameron roared and lunged forward into him.

It was like slamming into a gorilla. Abel hardly

moved, then grabbed quickly. Cameron ducked only a hair quicker.

Napoleon growled loudly and rushed out of the closet biting. Cameron drove his balled fist hard up under Abel's chin, and it was like hitting a section of hard clay. Abel grabbed Cameron and lifted him from the floor. The blond's hands felt like a vise. Cameron jabbed his finger's wildly into the blond's eyes. Abel threw him backward. Cameron slammed hard into Adrian, and they crashed to the floor, the automatic knocked out of her hand and spinning to the side of the hall as the blond stepped toward them.

Napoleon bit harder. Abel reached down, caught him and lifted him squirming into the air. The sausage-shaped animal lunged through Abel's hands, biting his face, and the blond threw him swirling down the hall— and Cameron dove for the automatic.

He clasped it, felt himself grabbed by the back of his neck and yanked upward. Abel's other hand slapped the weapon away. Cameron went higher. Abel grabbed his throat in a crushing grip and raised his arms high out in front of him. Cameron's head twisted painfully to the side, his neck about to break, he saw through his blurring vision the other bulky shape coming down the hall. Adrian dove for the pistol, rolled to her back, held it toward Abel's thigh—and fired, and fired, and fired.

Abel grunted hoarsely, grabbed his thigh and fell.

Cameron slammed hard to the floor.

Adrian fired at the other shape, and fired again.

Cain sprinted back toward the entrance to the hall and disappeared around the corner.

Abel squirmed on the floor. Napoleon bit at his face.

Adrian stepped over Abel and fired twice into each thigh.

Abel convulsed and lay still. Napoleon stepped back.

Cameron sprung to his feet.

They heard the apartment door slam back against the wall.

When they reached the living room the door was still

standing open. Dr. Baringer groaned on the kitchen floor.

They rushed to him.

Slowly shaking his head, he tried to rise.

"No, lie still," Adrian said.

Cameron looked back over his shoulder toward the hallway.

Golby was the first to reach the apartment. The door still stood open, and he rushed through it holding his automatic in front of him.

"Where is he?" Golby asked.

"In the hall," Cameron said. "It's in their thighs. Their Achilles heel is in their thighs. Tell everyone that's where to shoot."

Golby rushed into the hall. Sounds of cars screeching to a halt in front of the apartment came through the open door.

Golby stepped back out of the hall. "Is he okay?" he asked, looking at Baringer lying on the couch.

"I think all he has is a concussion."

Baringer looked at them. "And a hole in my back," he said painfully.

"What?" Adrian said and stepped to the couch.

"It's the damn bed frame," Baringer complained. "May I sit up?"

Irritated at being frightened into worrying for him, Adrian spoke sharply. "No, you can't."

Baringer looked at her pistol and said nothing more.

Golby stood in the door. A man in a dark suit and dark tie stopped on the walkway in front of him. A shorter, dark-skinned man dressed the same way stood on the grass a few feet away from the door. They both carried Uzis.

"Get our people all around the place," Golby ordered, speaking to the taller man. "Use the local cops for traffic control, but keep them out of the main search. I doubt the son of a bitch still being around, but he might be. Tell our people to shoot for his thighs.

Everybody. Shoot for the thighs. You can't hurt them any other way."

The man didn't question the strange order. He turned and sprinted down the walkway.

Golby spoke to the other man. "I want you to come in and stay with the body in the hall. Make sure it doesn't get up."

The man stepped through the doorway past Golby, then walked on into the hall without looking at them.

Golby walked to the telephone on the coffee table and lifted the receiver to his ear.

In a few seconds he said to whoever answered his call, "You kill them by shooting them in the thighs. You remember the photographs we saw of the Ancient Man, the big gaps he had in his thighs? That's why they're there. Somebody got smart five hundred thousand years ago and pulled out whatever's in there that keeps them alive. And brings them back to life."

Golby replaced the receiver and turned back to them. "That's why they were afraid of you. They knew you had discovered the Ancient Man and they thought you might know how he had been killed because you knew about the places in his legs. That's why they came here tonight. You told the boy at the jail you knew how to kill them. He believed you."

"I didn't tell him that, you did; I only thought it."

"We both told him, then."

After the man at the jail had finished the telephone conversation with Golby, he walked toward the entrance of the sealed off cell block.

Just outside the steel door to the cell block, a tall, heavy, wide-shouldered man with a shaved head sat in a straight-backed chair. He had his arms folded across his buttoned suit coat and was so still he looked to be almost in a trance.

The man who had spoken with Golby simply said, "It's something in their thighs. Whatever it is, it's where they have to be killed—and what brings them back to life.''

The bald-headed man unfolded his arms and stood.

In a moment he had lifted the oversized attaché case from the floor next to him, opened the steel door and stepped inside the cell block.

The other man peered through the small window in the door, then turned and, tightening his tie and smoothing it, walked back to the desk where the row of phones had been installed.

He lifted the receiver of a red phone and pressed a button on it.

A second later he said, "It's being done. I wanted to make certain one more time—the orders are still the same?''

The deep voice on the other end of the line said, "What if one should escape? Maybe some stupid bleeding heart son-of-a-bitch would try to get them released, claim they only did what came naturally to them, scream about what we could learn from them. The orders stand.''

Cameron lifted his shotgun out of the closet. Napoleon sat in his bed and looked up at him. Cameron leaned and patted his head, then turned and walked past Abel's body and the dark-skinned man standing over it.

Adrian, her automatic in one hand and a flashlight in the other, waited at the open apartment door.

CHAPTER 41

Cameron and Adrian met Golby at the edge of the woods directly behind the apartment block. A score of flashlights moved back and forth through the trees.

"If only he has stayed close," Golby said. "But I'm afraid I might as well be praying for snow in August." As he paused, he glanced into the woods. There were so many lights now, it looked like a laser show.

Golby shook his head. "Son of a bitch. The last one. But even if he is gone, we'll get him. We have to. The three kids and the dead body in the cell, he and the one in your apartment—we're going to get every one of them, once and for all."

His eyes suddenly narrowed with his thought, and he looked back toward the apartments. "I'll see you two later," he said, and turned and walked back toward the parking area in front of the apartments.

They stepped into the woods.

"He's strange," Adrian said.

"Strange?"

"Oh, I like him. But he's strange."

In a few minutes they were well into the thick oaks. The trees ran for nearly two hundred yards back to an old creek and were spread out to each side for a distance the length of three football fields, maybe a little more, but not enough for Cain to elude at least fifty men with flashlights if he were still there, something Cameron was sure wouldn't be true by now.

The last one, Golby had said. But for how long? There could be another pair in weeks, several other pairs if enough women were procured.

"Somebody back then—five hundred thousand years ago—was smart enough to learn how to kill them," Adrian said. "But how could they have? If you hadn't had that example to go by—the Ancient Man having those places in his thighs—we might never have known."

Cameron nodded. "Whether they're from somewhere else or were an advanced race here back then, someone, no matter how lesser, could have found out about their weakness, maybe by coincidence, maybe by being around when one of them was injured or killed accidentally. When DeSoto first came to South America, the Indians thought he and his men were the gods their legends spoke of—the white-skinned men who had supposedly ruled them once and left, promising to return one day. Then one of the Spaniards got sick and died, and the Indians, who had up until then put up with terrible mistreatment, saw the white men weren't gods and started fighting.

"That could have happened five hundred thousand years ago. One of the blonds could have been killed by a tree falling on him, or in a rock slide—something. Maybe one was injured so badly he never did recover, or died for all intents and purposes, then came back to life. But by then our ancestors were aware of their weakness."

He ducked under a low oak limb and waited for Adrian to come under it before he spoke again.

"The boy I talked to left the impression that only a few of them stayed here when the others left. Maybe there was a hell of a fight and the ones left were overwhelmed by sheer numbers. Whatever the case, after they were killed, something was cut out of their thighs —whatever it is."

Adrian nodded. "Uh huh, like sticking a stake in a vampire's heart keeps them from coming back to life."

He nodded. "But even dead they're a lot different than us. Their bodies, even with the wounds in the thighs, don't deteriorate the way ours do. I know now why we found a body in near perfect shape. Any human from that time would have been at the very most only bones by now."

Adrian smiled a little. "Not if they were in permafrost." Then she spoke seriously. "Cameron, you said maybe there were only a few of them left from what the boy said. Why only a few of them?"

Cameron knew what she was thinking. He had wondered the same thing. "Why didn't they produce others? If they had, there could have been thousands in no time with their short gestation rate. Who knows? Maybe they did try and were too sick to produce young. As I said, even dead they were a lot different than us, something in their thighs. Maybe they're different sexually, too—the ones five hundred thousand years ago were, anyway. Maybe they couldn't mate with our direct ancestors with any result. Maybe their sperm couldn't fertilize our eggs. Maybe when Dr. Anderson artificially transferred the ancient man's DNA from his sperm to a human egg, that created a hybrid of some sort, a being that *could* mate successfully. The ones Dr. Anderson produced quickly realized that and started mating. One guess is as good as another."

Adrian grinned. "Maybe they didn't mate with humans back then because they found it repugnant—like mating with cattle. You said only a few of them were left, so where did the others go, if they weren't aliens?"

He shook his head. "Died out. A catastrophe happening where they lived." An amusing thought passed through his head. "Maybe Atlantis."

A pair of men in dark suits and ties passed them on their way to the far side of the woods. Almost all of the men had moved in that direction now.

* * *

The large, bald-headed man ordered the other men out of the cellblock with a gesture of his head. Now he moved to the cell with the three blonds sitting on a bunk.

They stared at him as he laid his large case down just outside the bars and opened it. Inside one side of the case, each in a sunken area molded to their particular shape, were a choice of two automatics, one of them with a small laser aiming device clipped to its top, a long-barreled revolver, and a rifle, disassembled into four sections.

He choose the automatic with the aiming device and lifted it from the case.

On the side of the case opposite the weapons were four kinds of ammunition, all the same caliber, but each with a different nose and a different purpose.

He chose a straight, expanding lead variety, already in a clip. He jammed it up into the handle of the automatic and pulled the weapon's slide back, then released it.

He propped his left forearm parallel across a cross bar of the cell, and rested the wrist of his other hand across his forearm, steadying the weapon. He hesitated for a moment, not because of their youth, but at their staring back at him, the only expression he noticed, a slight tightening of their lips.

The first shot sounded like the loud crack of a whip within the cellblock but could barely be heard outside it.

Cain grunted a loud guttural sound, stared up at the heavens, and dropped back down within the clump of bushes.

Cameron stopped at the sound coming to them from somewhere on the other side of the small creek. It had been like the hoarse, quick growl of a dog, then faded.

He continued to stare across the creek. There was a clump of heavy bushes about fifty feet beyond it, then an open space, then another wide clump of bushes and small trees running a hundred feet up to the rear of an apartment complex fronting the next road over.

He looked to his right. The other men were out of sight now, their flashlights shining back and forth at the far edge of the woods.

He looked at Adrian, then started down the near bank of the creek toward the shallow, running water, only a few feet wide.

Cain contained his voice, but shivered violently two more times. His eyes closed. His always expressionless face almost changed.

He looked down at his thigh, bleeding from Adrian's shot in the apartment. He could feel his vitality slowly draining from him. He raised his eyes and stared back at Cameron Malone and the woman moving toward him.

The bald-headed man opened the door and walked inside the cell. The three blonds, each with neat round holes in his thighs, lay silent in the positions into which they had fallen, two of them backwards onto the bunk, one on his face on the concrete floor.

The man reached inside his coat and pulled out the black, plastic garbage sack he had retrieved from a waste basket in the hall, then moved to the body on the floor and turned it over. A large knife flashed in the man's hand as he leaned down toward a thin thigh; the overhead light in the cell glinted off his shaved head.

Cain shuddered with the cut, felt a momentary flash of pain in his thigh.

Cameron and Adrian came up the bank toward the clump of bushes.

Cain looked at the apartment complex behind him, most of the windows darkened. The tenants who had come out when the lights were first flashing through the trees were now off their balconies. He edged backward.

* * *

Cameron used the muzzle of the shotgun to part the bushes in front of him. Adrian, ten feet to his right side, held her pistol carefully in front of her as she pushed a clump of branches back out of the way with her flashlight and shined it deeper into the growth.

Cameron had a strange feeling. "Adrian."

"What?"

"Don't go any farther."

"What?"

"Don't step in there. We need some of the men back here first."

"We've both got guns."

Cameron stared into the middle of the bushes. They were so thick they completely blocked her flashlight's beam.

"Well?" Adrian asked.

He nodded, and she stepped into the bushes. He went in from his side, hurrying to make sure that he was ahead of her, but her flashlight beam did as much harm as good, the light reflecting back off the thick bushes and blinding him from seeing any deeper into the thicket.

Cain dropped lower at the beam of light. He glanced over his shoulder at the twenty feet of open space between him and the next bushes. He shut his eyes. His other thigh felt a sharp pain. He shuddered again.

Then there was a gouging sensation; the sensation of life being taken from a vitality, the children's vitality.

He felt another pain, and his eyes looked in the direction of Cameron's apartment. A vitality was being drained there, too. His mind flashed back to that other time long ago—when vitalities were being drained all around him by the blocky, hunched savages. Hordes of them attacking in overwhelming numbers now that they had learned the secret of the vitality's being the key to the life of their enslavers.

Hundreds of the savages ripped and torn apart, lying dead everywhere on the desolate landscape, but the others still kept coming, grunting their cries of anger, jabbing with pointed sticks and sharpened stones at the thighs, then diving on a fallen enslaver the moment he collapsed, ripping into his thighs with jagged fingernails.

Cain could bear the thought of it happening again no longer. For the first time in over five hundred thousand years heavy tears formed in his eyes.

He stood, roared loudly, and lunged forward.

Cameron jumped back, pulled the shotgun's trigger, and the weapon exploded its mass of shot and jumped in his hands.

The blast spun Cain halfway around. He stumbled, regained his footing, came out of the bushes, and Adrian fired from the side. Cain shuddered and turned toward her flashlight.

Cameron fired again. Cain was jolted sideway. Adrian stepped nearer him, held her automatic out toward his thighs, and fired.

Cain went to his knees; his hands reached out to grasp empty air.

Adrian fired again.

Cain roared and shuddered.

Cameron stepped forward, held the shotgun toward Cain's thigh, and fired again, and Adrian fired once more. Cain quivered, but remained erect on his knees, his dark eyes widening, glowing shiny black in the flashlight beam, then seeming to fade.

A guttural sound rumbled from deep within him, trailed off into a faint, almost plaintive grunt, and he toppled forward onto his face, his hands outstretched and touching Cameron's shoes.

The wooded area behind them flashed with lights. Men poured down the creek bank and up its side, weapons at the ready.

The men stopped at the sight of the body on the ground.

Golby was suddenly beside Cameron and Adrian. He glanced at them and they him. He looked down at Cain lying on his face, then dropped to his knees and turned the body over.

He stared at the blank face for a moment, then ran his gaze down to Cain's lower body, a mass of blood.

Golby looked back up at them. "You better go on now," he said.

Two other of the men dropped down to their knees next to the body.

Cameron caught Adrian by the elbow and turned her back toward the apartments. Neither of them looked back.

The bald-headed man, hands streaked with blood, his garbage bag weighted with a mass that hung heavy at its bottom, stepped from the cell in the sealed cell block. He didn't shut the door behind him.

CHAPTER 42

"Cameron, the boy said the others went back to wherever they came from. They have to be aliens or we would know about them, wouldn't we?"

"Not necessarily. I told you about the Indians. Whole tribes perished even after the first white men left their villages and went back to Europe. Maybe when the healthy blonds left and went back to whatever continent they lived on, maybe they weren't as healthy as they thought and carried the disease back with them. They died, and the centuries took care of the rest, erasing all trace of them. Tens of thousands of years at a time passed, glaciers formed and melted, the bodies froze and rotted in the heat. Mountains eroded and buried them, oceans rose and fell and washed them away. Who knows?"

"Cameron, maybe they're not all dead. Maybe they're still there and understand now that we're not like cattle."

"Still there?" He theatrically glanced up into the sky. She gave no notice of his smile.

The Whole Truth was enjoined by a federal judge from mentioning another word regarding the alien cannibal story.

The Supreme Court, acting with record speed, agreed with the judge's injunction. There *is* free speech, and it *is* almost inviolate under the United States Constitution, all the members of the Court agreed unanimously, but as the great jurist Oliver Wendell Holmes once said, the right of free speech does not give an individual the right to falsely yell fire in a crowded theater, nor does it give a newspaper the right to publish a false story that creates a world wide panic.

Ben Utterback was privately sought out by a tall, wide-shouldered, bald-headed man in a dark suit, and given a choice. He decided on the one million dollars tax free for his notes and swore mightily to never mention them again.

Cassandra and Missey received private settlements of two million dollars for the damages they suffered due to the genetic experiment gone bad.

Cassandra's father and mother were jointly awarded another one million, all of this contingent on the four of them never mentioning the details of the case again.

Lee Ann got the best deal of all, to her manner of thinking. "Money is not as important to me as my right to do and say as I wish and when I wish, unhindered in any way," she had said, then explained that what she really wished was to be able to help abused children from all walks of life.

She received a special presidential appointment as head of a foundation, its mission to provide care and assistance to abused children. It was funded immediately by Congress—though only the most senior party leaders ever knew why.

In addition, Lee Ann, as head of the program, was awarded a hundred thousand dollars a year in salary, adjusted each year for inflation, and an eventual lifetime pension based on one hundred percent of what she made in her two highest years of work. Her mother *had said* she always got her way.

The only negative thing: it turned out she was infertile, and there was nothing medical science could do about it. But, shortly after marrying, she and her husband adopted three children.

Cameron and Adrian, a year after they were married, stood close together on the balcony of their new home and stared up through a bright, clear sky at the full moon.

Adrian looked past the moon for a moment. "At least we didn't eat them."

"Huh?"

"I said, at least we didn't eat them." The bodies, minus the large mass of nerve concentrations found in their thighs, had been cremated, the resulting ashes buried in titanium containers welded shut and sealed in concrete at a location known to only a very few senior officials in the government.

The nerve concentrations had been handled separately, not only cremated, but the ashes then dissolved in acid and the slurry disposed of at a location again known only to a very few people.

Two other items had also been removed from the bodies and handled in the same separate manner, their testes and their brains, but only the testes from the two original blonds born of Dr. Anderson's experiment. Quickly performed tests had shown the later blonds were effectively sterile, their sperm incompatible with a *Homo sapiens* egg, with only the hybrids created during the direct transfer of DNA able to propagate with humans. The destruction of the brains was just an extra safeguard. Since the Ancient Man's brain had been removed, they had decided to take no chances, even though all believed that his brain removal had been done only as an afterthought by whoever had killed him originally. There certainly seemed to be nothing unusual about the blond's brains. And, of course, the Ancient Man disappeared from his glass case, stolen—at least that was what the Italian government was told by

the State Department. And his body met the same fate
as the others.

Cameron smiled. "I don't think of them anymore."
Though he *had* just focused on three small dark spots
to the side of the moon, watched them until he was
certain they were high, drifting clouds.

When a moment later, across the several acre lake
behind their house there came a growl loud enough for
them to hear, Adrian shuddered.

"What?" he asked.

"That sound was so much like the one the larger
blonds made."

"That was a dog."

"Uh huh, I know."

He chuckled, slipped an arm around her shoulders
and pulled her close against his side.

"Adrian, Adrian, for all I love you, sometimes you are
a little bit . . . "

"Impossible?" she said.

"No, you're not going to get me to say that again.
Maybe incorrigible."

"I am that."

"Yeah," he said, and pulled her tighter against him.

Napoleon continued to stare across the lake.

The Dollmaker was a serial killer who stalked Los Angeles and left a grisly calling card on the faces of his female victims. With a single faultless shot, Detective Harry Bosch thought he had ended the city's nightmare.

Now, the dead man's widow is suing Harry and the LAPD for killing the wrong man—an accusation that rings terrifyingly true when a new victim is discovered with the Dollmaker's macabre signature.

Now, for the second time, Harry must hunt down a death-dealer who is very much alive, before he strikes again. It's a blood-tracked quest that will take Harry from the hard edges of the L.A. night to the last place he ever wanted to go—the darkness of his own heart.

THE CONCRETE BLONDE

"Exceptional...A stylish blend of grit and elegance."
—Nelson DeMille

THE CONCRETE BLONDE
Michael Connelly
_____ 95500-6 $5.99 U.S./$6.99 Can.

SHATTERED

*...by a mindless act of violence that changed his life forever,
James Dewitt decided to become a cop.*

SHACKLED

*...by a web of red tape and corruption, Dewitt now fights
desperately to solve a string of murders cleverly
staged to look like suicides.*

SUBMERGED

*...in the deranged world of the psychopathic mind, Dewitt
struggles to outwit the killer—before it's too late...*

Pr•bable CAUSE

RIDLEY PEARSON

"FASCINATING...BREATHLESS!"—*Chicago Tribune*

Ellen Francis thinks that the hospital patients around her are disappearing. But then, Ellen herself is a schizophrenic—and her daughter, Dr. Sharon Francis, thinks it's just another passing delusion.

Then strange "accidents" start to happen. One of Sharon's patients vanishes—and suddenly Sharon's not so sure what's real and what's illusion anymore....

PAINKILLER

A NOVEL OF MEDICAL TERROR

STEVEN SPRUILL

"Thriller lovers rejoice—add this to your 'must read' list."
—Bestselling author TONY HILLERMAN

Head coach Vance White's brutal regimen encourages a viciousness on the field that shocks even the most hardened NFL veterans. But when the mysterious ingredient fueling the Ruffians' aggressive fury leads to tragedy on his own team, tackle Clay Blackwell rebels. Now, trapped between his conscience and his desire to join his teammates on their steamroller ride to the top, Clay faces the most agonizing choice of his life.

RUFFIANS

TIM GREEN

**"Like *NORTH DALLAS FORTY* crossed with *THE FIRM*."
—*USA Today***

RUFFIANS
Tim Green
_____ 95388-7 $4.99 U.S./$5.99 CAN.